HIT-GIRL
IN INDIA

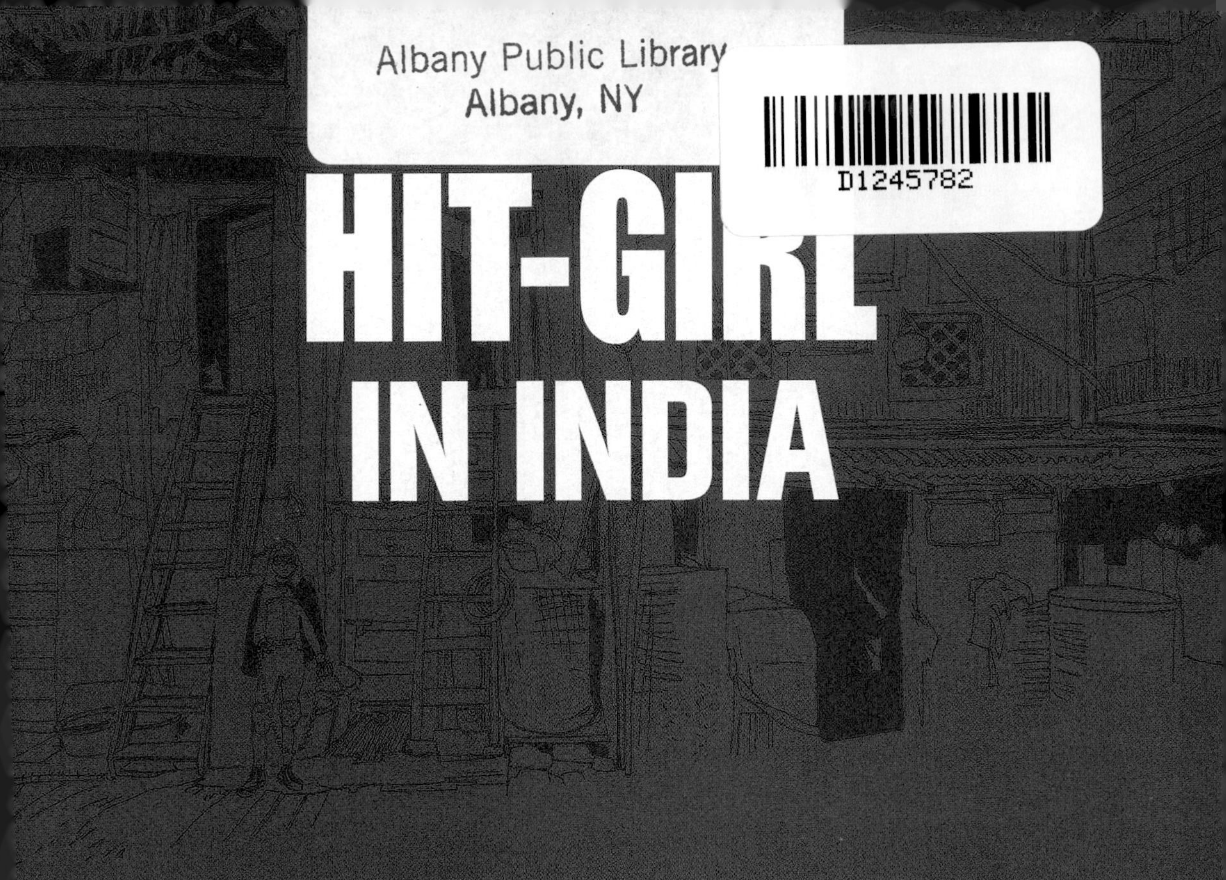

PETER MILLIGAN WRITER
ALISON SAMPSON ARTIST
TRÍONA FARRELL COLORIST
CLEM ROBINS LETTERER

MELINA MIKULIC DESIGN AND PRODUCTION
RACHAEL FULTON EDITOR

FRONT COVER **DECLAN SHALVEY**
BACK COVER **SANFORD GREENE**

Dedicated to Kiron,
who features in this book

The names of some historical figures
and locations have been changed.

HIT-GIRL and KICK-ASS created by **MARK MILLAR** and **JOHN ROMITA JR.**

IMAGE COMICS, INC.
Robert Kirkman — Chief Operating Officer
Erik Larsen — Chief Financial Officer
Todd McFarlane — President
Marc Silvestri — Chief Executive Officer
Jim Valentino — Vice President

Eric Stephenson — Publisher / Chief Creative Officer
Jeff Boison — Director of Publishing Planning
    & Book Trade Sales
Chris Ross — Director of Digital Services
Jeff Stang — Director of Direct Market Sales
Kat Salazar — Director of PR & Marketing
Drew Gill — Cover Editor
Heather Doornink — Production Director
Nicole Lapalme — Controller
IMAGECOMICS.COM

ONE

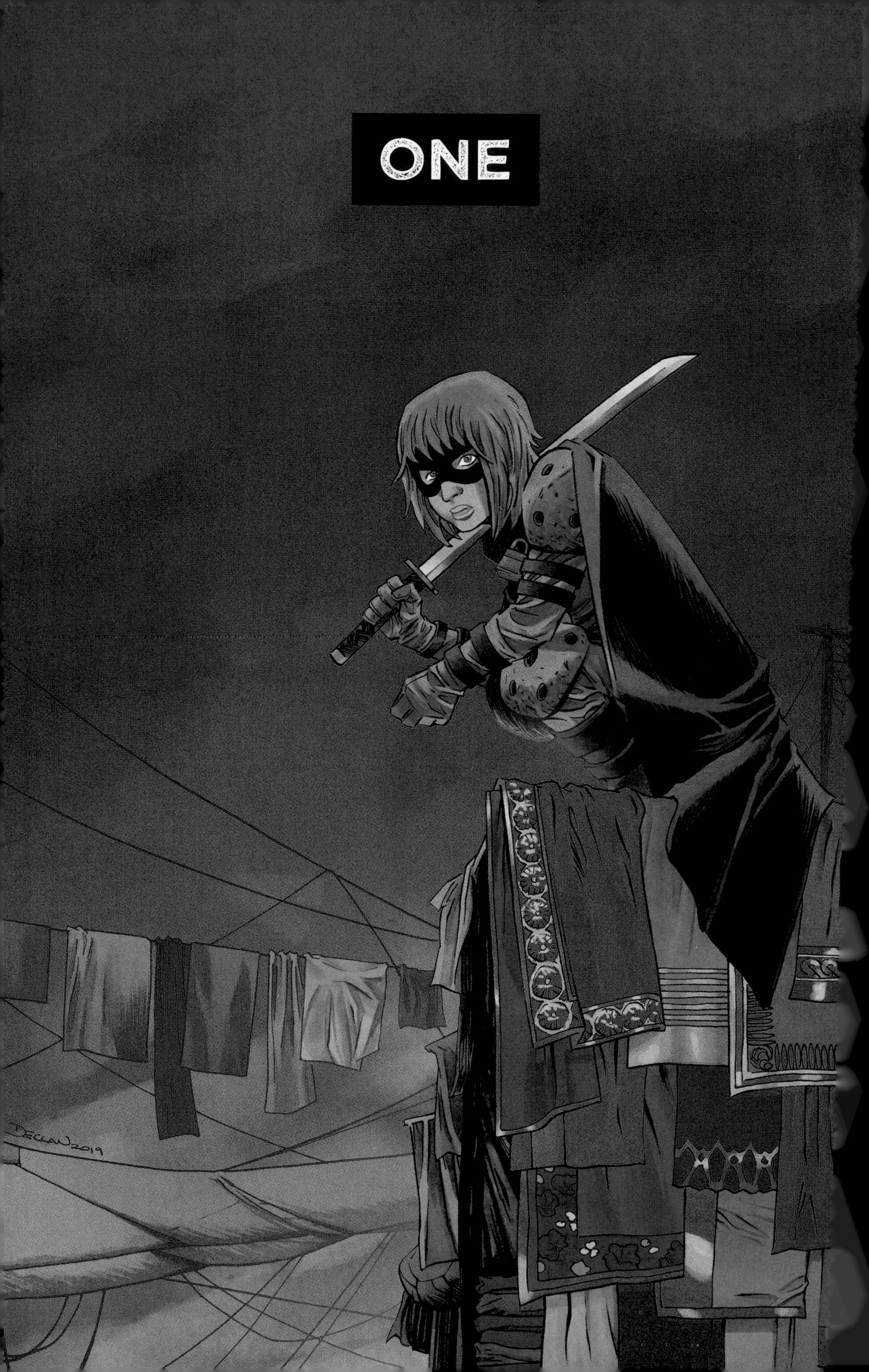
DECLAN 2019

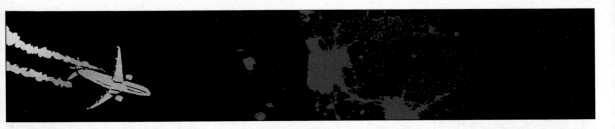

MISS McCREADY? WE'LL BE LANDING IN AN HOUR.

WE DO A KIDS' BREAKFAST, WITH PEANUT BUTTER AND CHOCOLATE PUFFS AND SUGAR COOKIES. ALL WASHED DOWN WITH A YUMMY STRAWBERRY SHAKE.

JUST A BLACK COFFEE, PLEASE. AND A COPY OF THE MUMBAI TIMES.

MUMBAI.

I'VE NO CLEAR IDEA WHAT I'LL BE DOING DOWN THERE YET.

BUT WITH A POPULATION OF ALMOST NINETEEN MILLION, THIS IS INDIA'S LARGEST CITY...

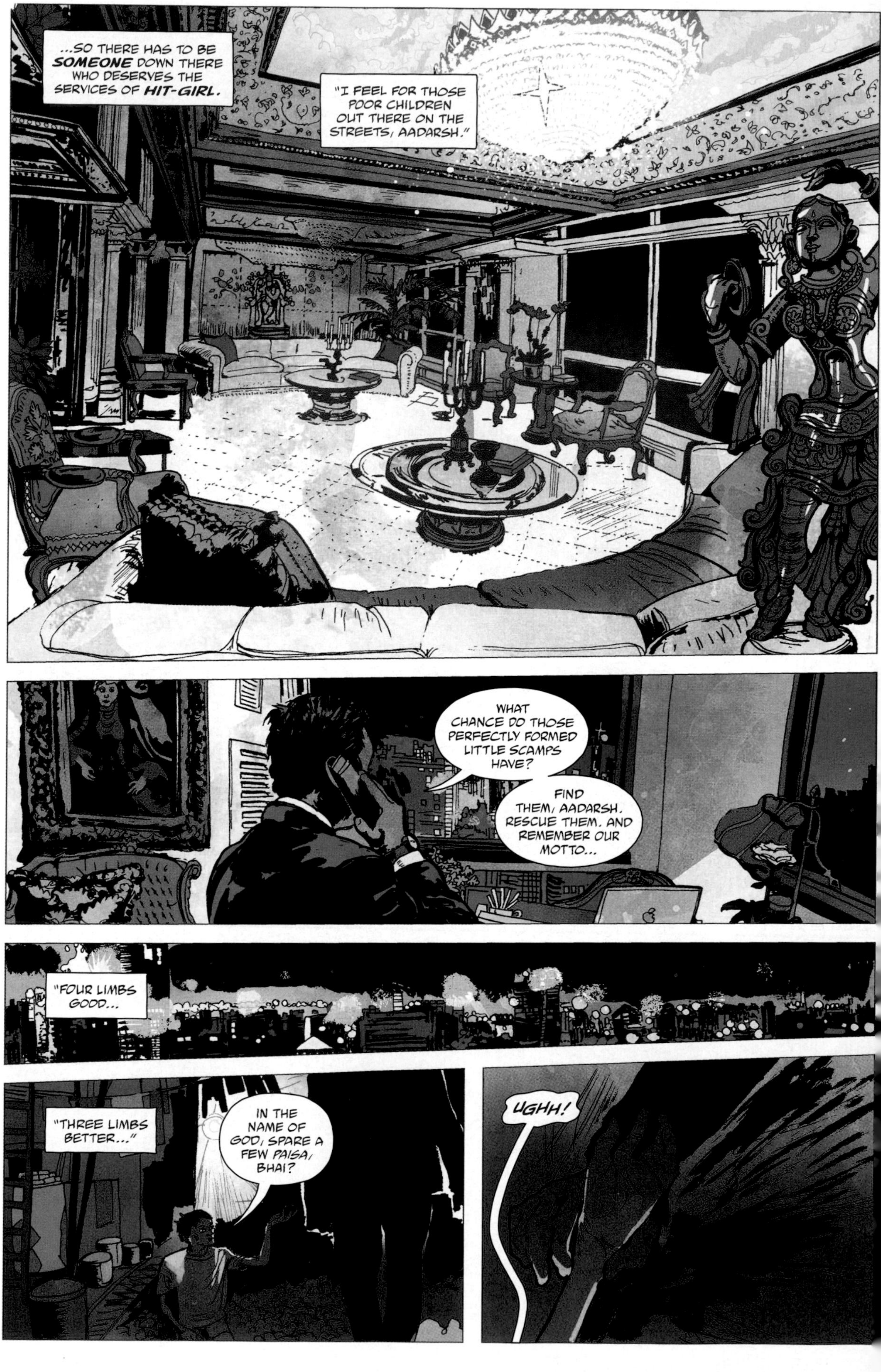
...SO THERE HAS TO BE SOMEONE DOWN THERE WHO DESERVES THE SERVICES OF HIT-GIRL.
"I FEEL FOR THOSE POOR CHILDREN OUT THERE ON THE STREETS, AADARSH."
WHAT CHANCE DO THOSE PERFECTLY FORMED LITTLE SCAMPS HAVE?
FIND THEM, AADARSH. RESCUE THEM. AND REMEMBER OUR MOTTO...
"FOUR LIMBS GOOD...
"THREE LIMBS BETTER..."
IN THE NAME OF GOD, SPARE A FEW PAISA, BHAI?
UGHH!

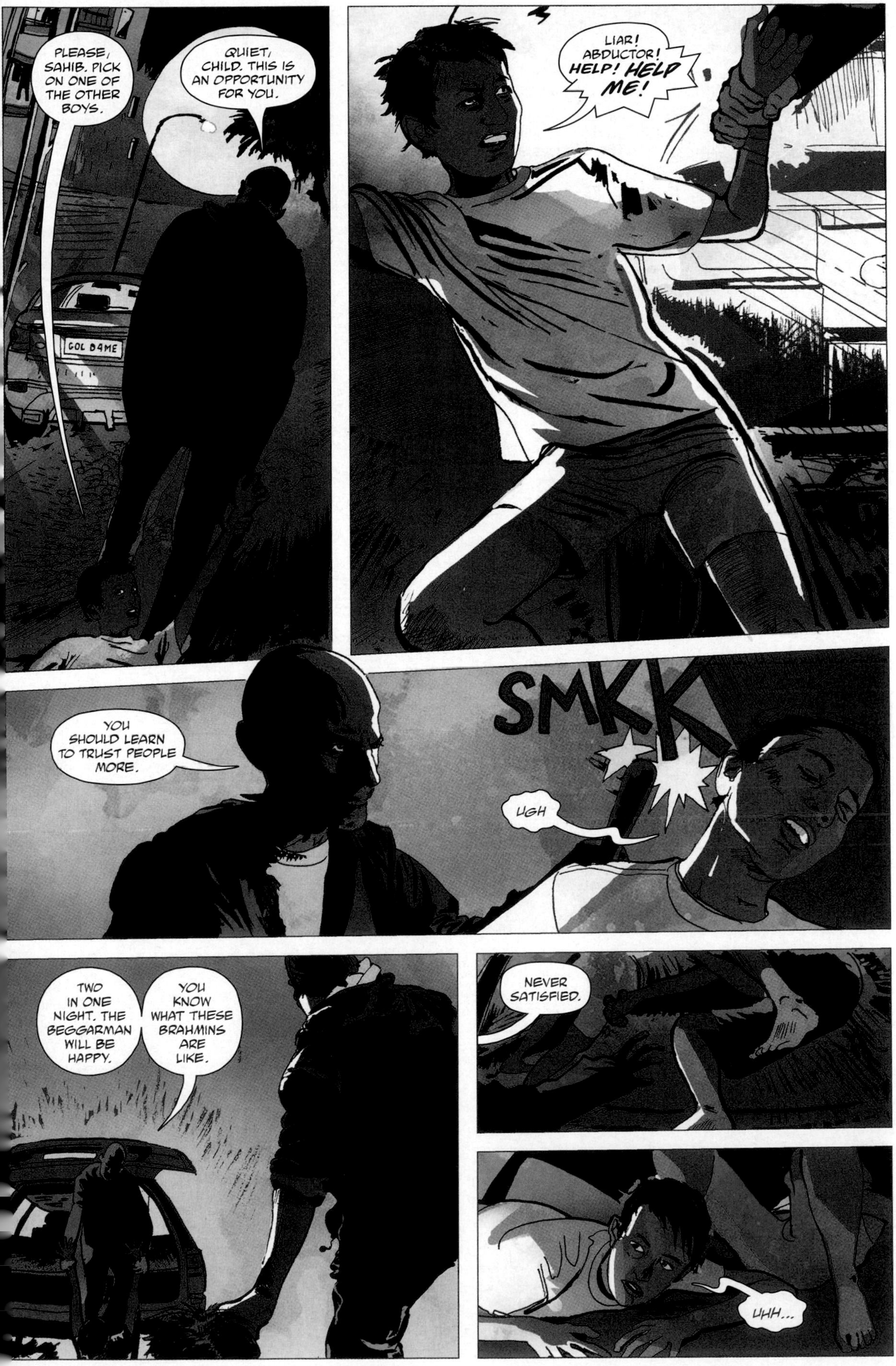
PLEASE, SAHIB. PICK ON ONE OF THE OTHER BOYS.
QUIET, CHILD. THIS IS AN OPPORTUNITY FOR YOU.
GOL B4ME
LIAR! ABDUCTOR! HELP! HELP ME!
YOU SHOULD LEARN TO TRUST PEOPLE MORE.
SMKK
UGH
TWO IN ONE NIGHT. THE BEGGARMAN WILL BE HAPPY.
YOU KNOW WHAT THESE BRAHMINS ARE LIKE.
NEVER SATISFIED.
UHH...

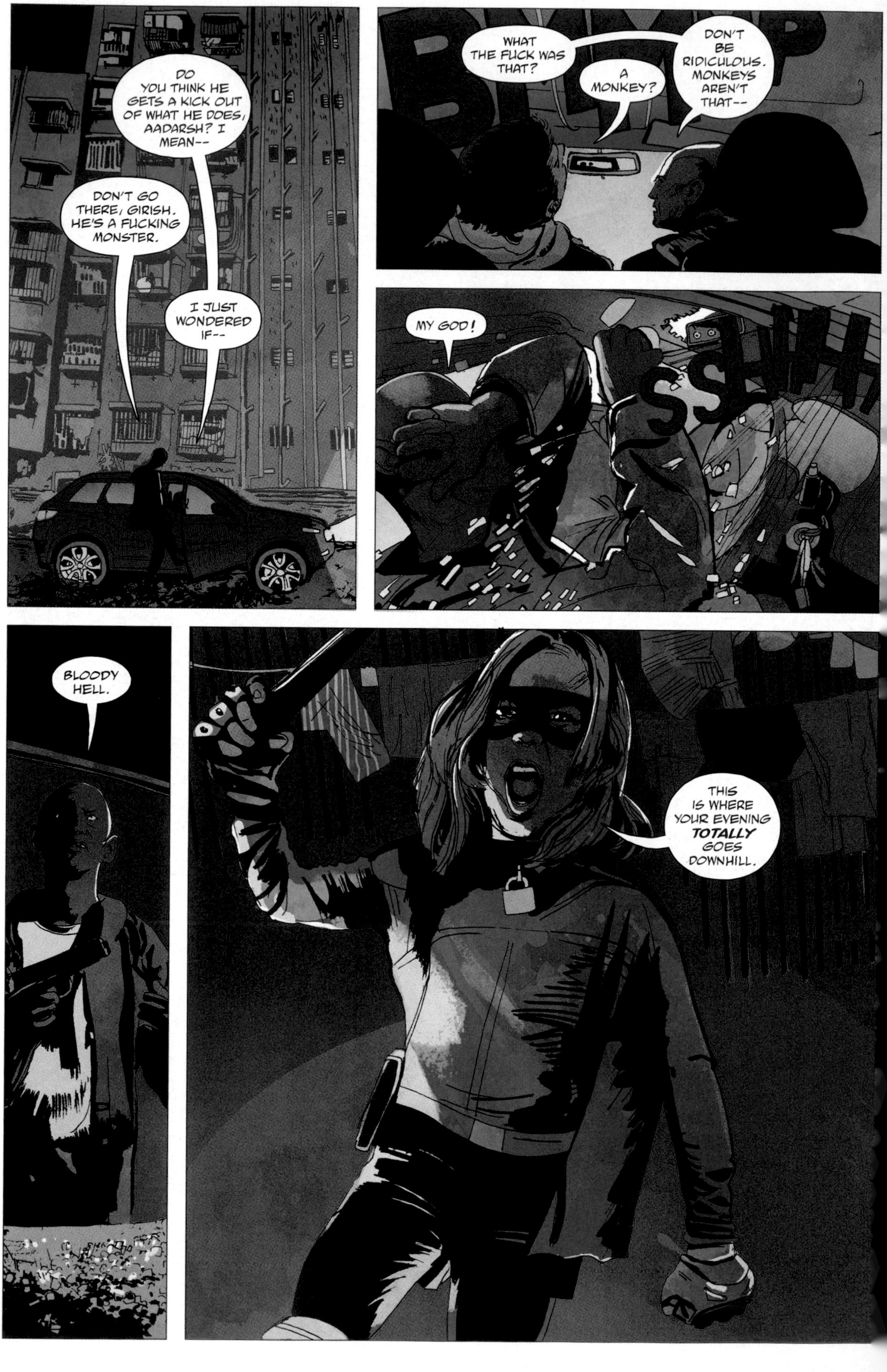
DO YOU THINK HE GETS A KICK OUT OF WHAT HE DOES, AADARSH? I MEAN--
DON'T GO THERE, GIRISH. HE'S A FUCKING MONSTER.
I JUST WONDERED IF--
WHAT THE FUCK WAS THAT?
A MONKEY?
DON'T BE RIDICULOUS. MONKEYS AREN'T THAT--
MY GOD!
SSHH
BLOODY HELL.
THIS IS WHERE YOUR EVENING TOTALLY GOES DOWNHILL.

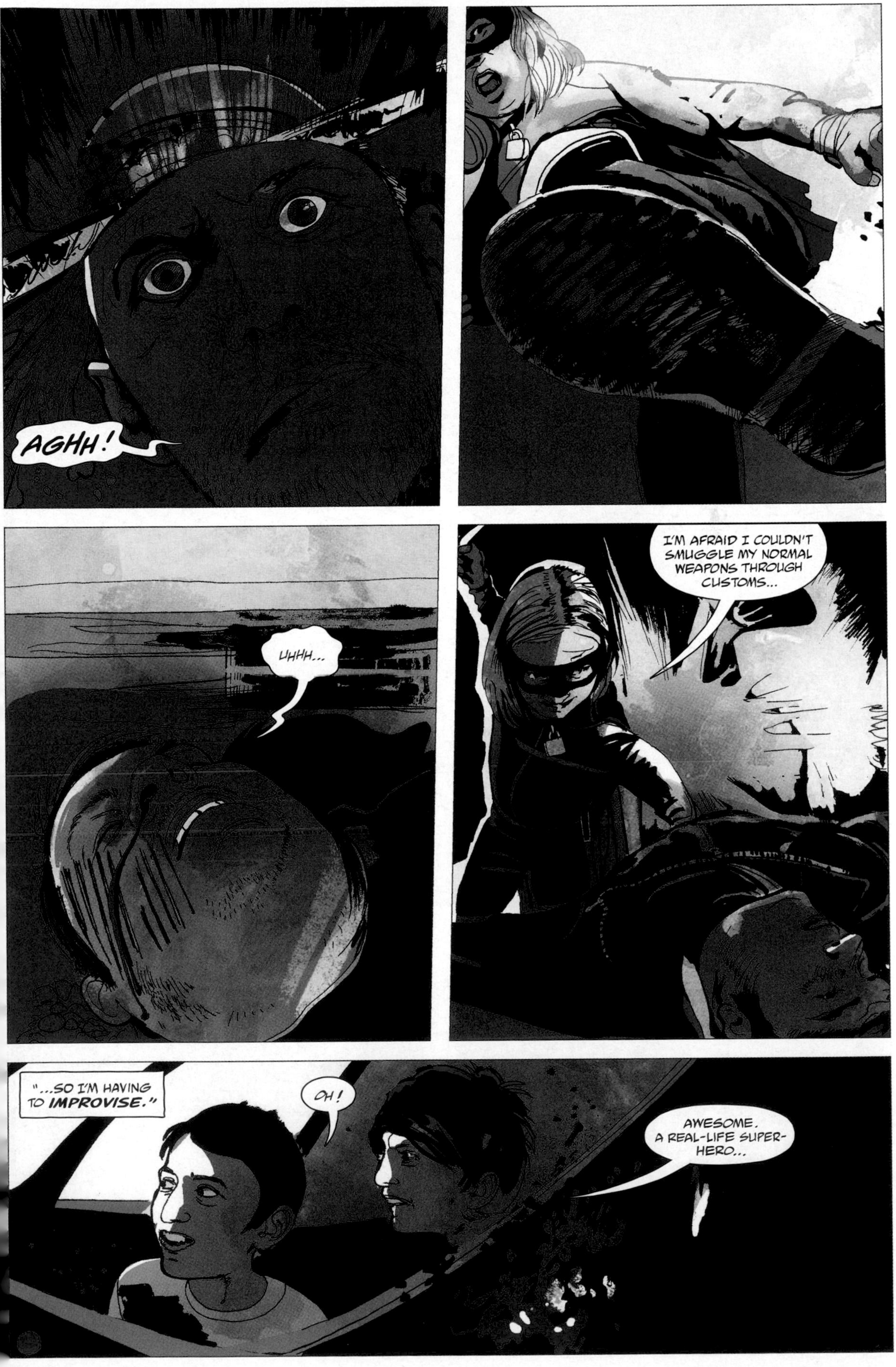
AGHH!
UHHH...
I'M AFRAID I COULDN'T SMUGGLE MY NORMAL WEAPONS THROUGH CUSTOMS...
"...SO I'M HAVING TO IMPROVISE."
OH!
AWESOME. A REAL-LIFE SUPER-HERO...

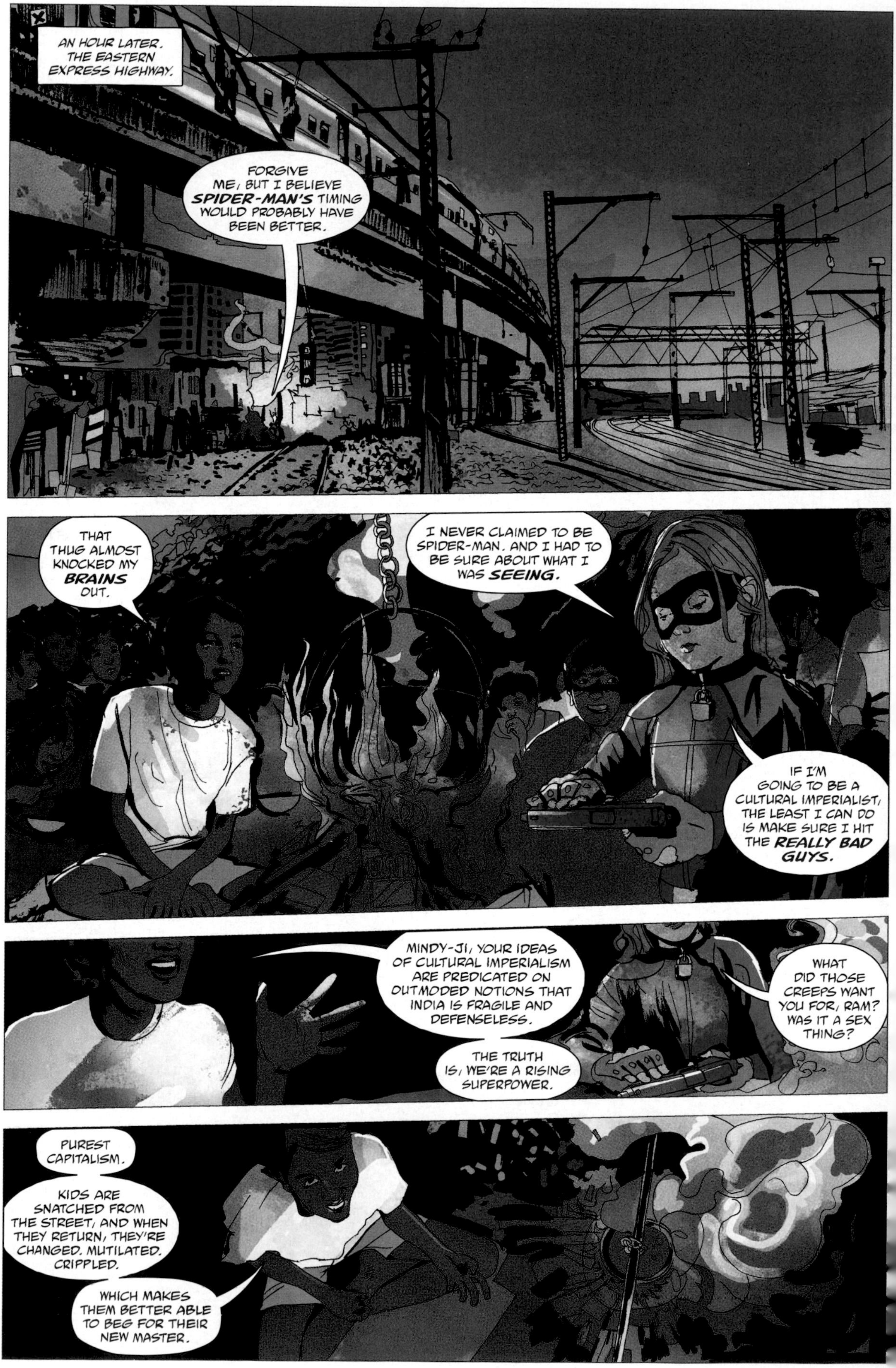
AN HOUR LATER. THE EASTERN EXPRESS HIGHWAY.
FORGIVE ME, BUT I BELIEVE SPIDER-MAN'S TIMING WOULD PROBABLY HAVE BEEN BETTER.
THAT THUG ALMOST KNOCKED MY BRAINS OUT.
I NEVER CLAIMED TO BE SPIDER-MAN. AND I HAD TO BE SURE ABOUT WHAT I WAS SEEING.
IF I'M GOING TO BE A CULTURAL IMPERIALIST, THE LEAST I CAN DO IS MAKE SURE I HIT THE REALLY BAD GUYS.
MINDY-JI, YOUR IDEAS OF CULTURAL IMPERIALISM ARE PREDICATED ON OUTMODED NOTIONS THAT INDIA IS FRAGILE AND DEFENSELESS.
THE TRUTH IS, WE'RE A RISING SUPERPOWER.
WHAT DID THOSE CREEPS WANT YOU FOR, RAM? WAS IT A SEX THING?
PUREST CAPITALISM.
KIDS ARE SNATCHED FROM THE STREET, AND WHEN THEY RETURN, THEY'RE CHANGED. MUTILATED. CRIPPLED.
WHICH MAKES THEM BETTER ABLE TO BEG FOR THEIR NEW MASTER.

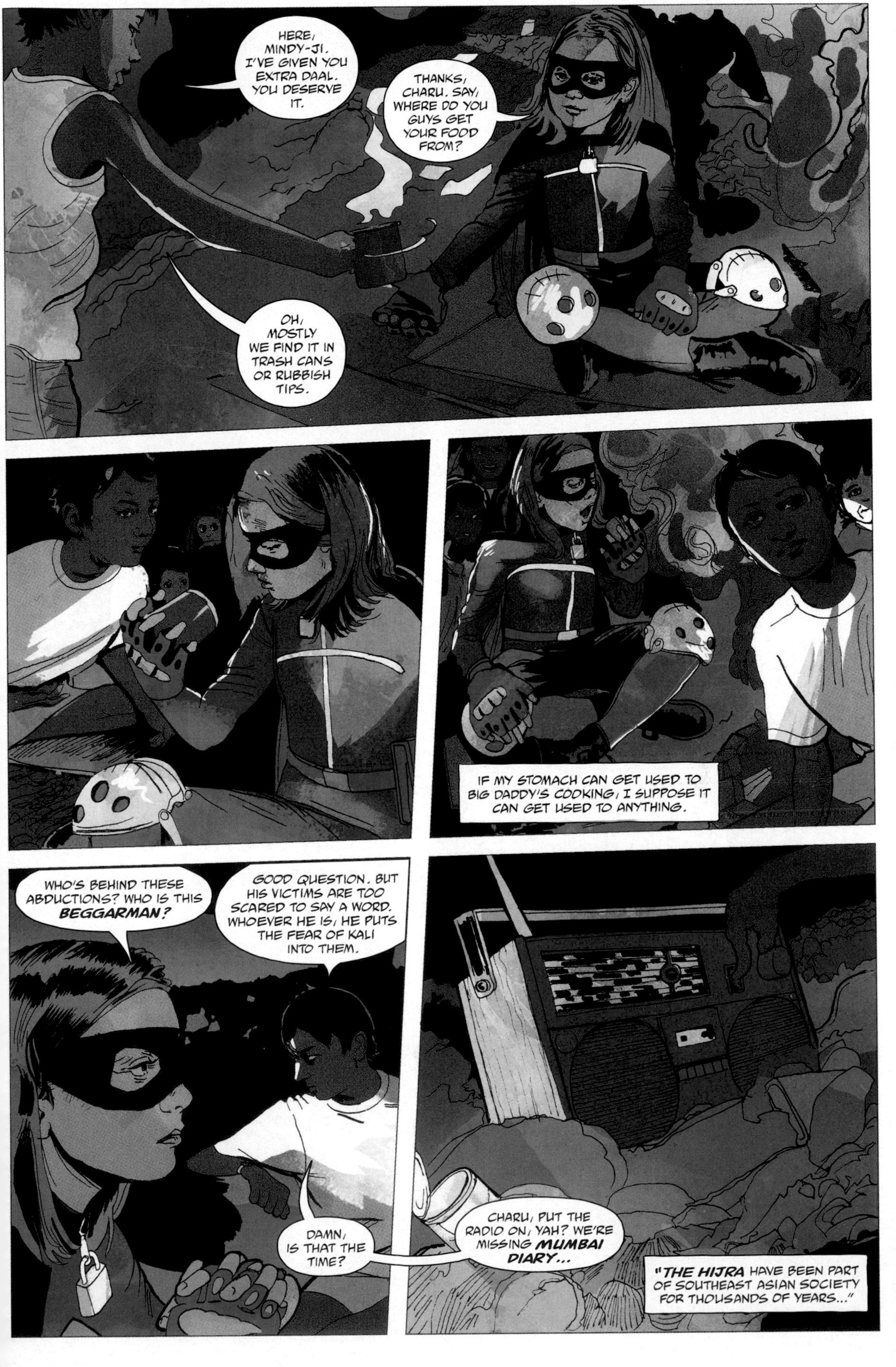
HERE, MINDY-JI. I'VE GIVEN YOU EXTRA DAAL. YOU DESERVE IT.
THANKS, CHARU. SAY, WHERE DO YOU GUYS GET YOUR FOOD FROM?
OH, MOSTLY WE FIND IT IN TRASH CANS OR RUBBISH TIPS.
IF MY STOMACH CAN GET USED TO BIG DADDY'S COOKING, I SUPPOSE IT CAN GET USED TO ANYTHING.
WHO'S BEHIND THESE ABDUCTIONS? WHO IS THIS **BEGGARMAN?**
GOOD QUESTION. BUT HIS VICTIMS ARE TOO SCARED TO SAY A WORD. WHOEVER HE IS, HE PUTS THE FEAR OF KALI INTO THEM.
DAMN, IS THAT THE TIME?
CHARU, PUT THE RADIO ON, YAH? WE'RE MISSING **MUMBAI DIARY...**
"**THE HIJRA** HAVE BEEN PART OF SOUTHEAST ASIAN SOCIETY FOR THOUSANDS OF YEARS..."

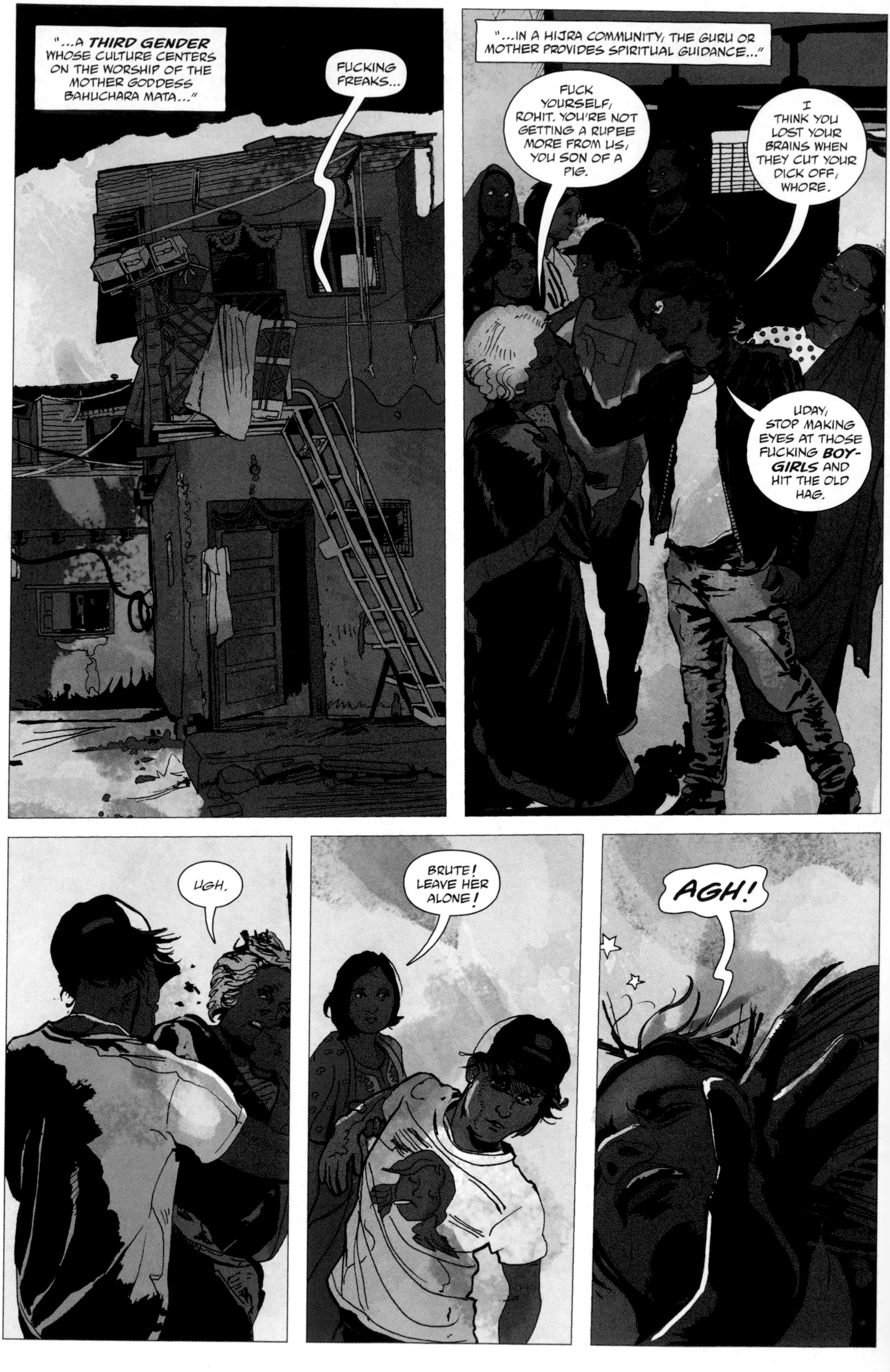
"...A THIRD GENDER WHOSE CULTURE CENTERS ON THE WORSHIP OF THE MOTHER GODDESS BAHUCHARA MATA..."
FUCKING FREAKS...
"...IN A HIJRA COMMUNITY, THE GURU OR MOTHER PROVIDES SPIRITUAL GUIDANCE..."
FUCK YOURSELF, ROHIT. YOU'RE NOT GETTING A RUPEE MORE FROM US, YOU SON OF A PIG.
I THINK YOU LOST YOUR BRAINS WHEN THEY CUT YOUR DICK OFF, WHORE.
UDAY, STOP MAKING EYES AT THOSE FUCKING BOY-GIRLS AND HIT THE OLD HAG.
UGH.
BRUTE! LEAVE HER ALONE!
AGH!

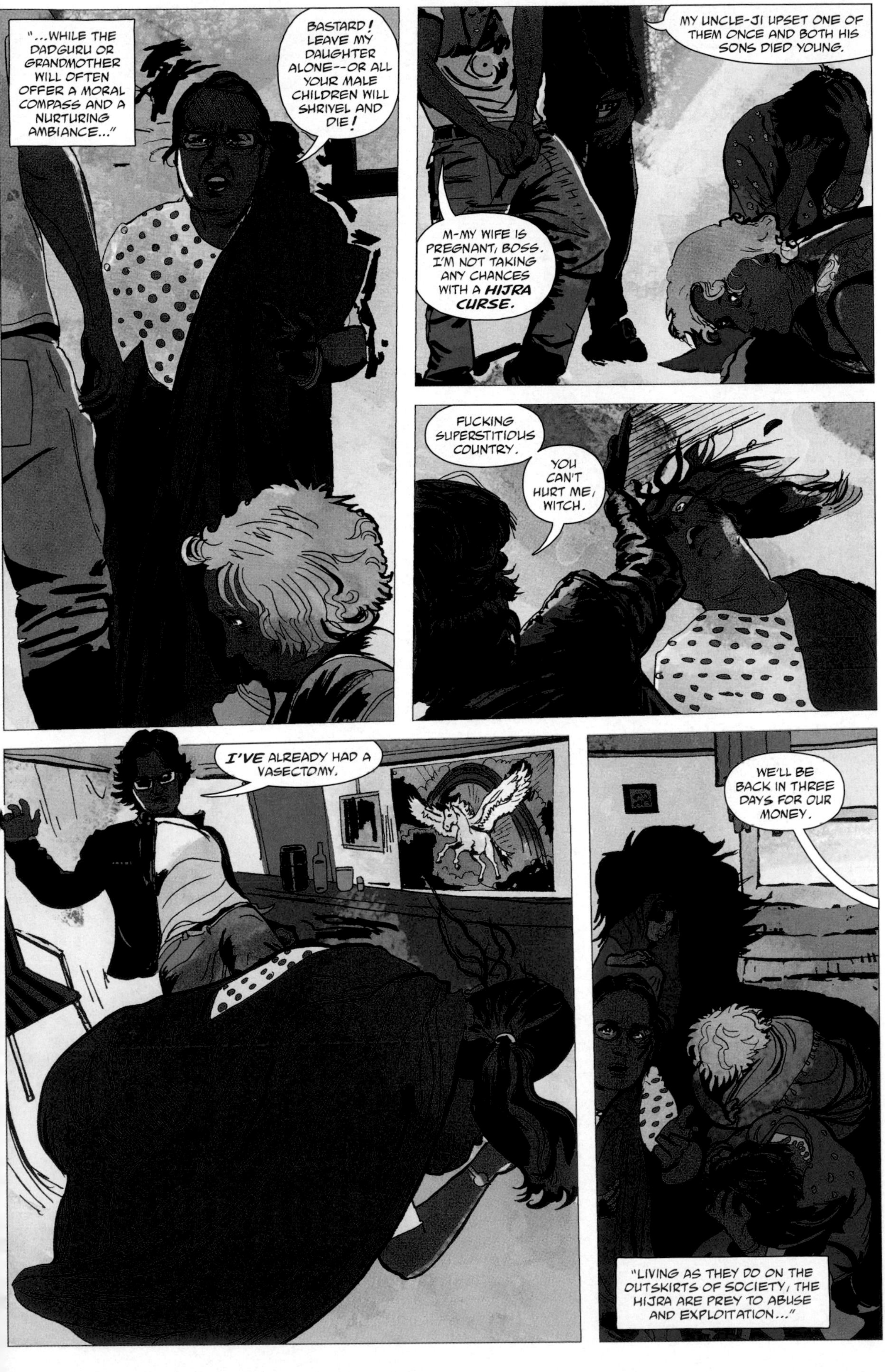
"...WHILE THE DADGURU OR GRANDMOTHER WILL OFTEN OFFER A MORAL COMPASS AND A NURTURING AMBIANCE..."
BASTARD! LEAVE MY DAUGHTER ALONE--OR ALL YOUR MALE CHILDREN WILL SHRIVEL AND DIE!
MY UNCLE-JI UPSET ONE OF THEM ONCE AND BOTH HIS SONS DIED YOUNG.
M-MY WIFE IS PREGNANT, BOSS. I'M NOT TAKING ANY CHANCES WITH A HIJRA CURSE.
FUCKING SUPERSTITIOUS COUNTRY.
YOU CAN'T HURT ME, WITCH.
I'VE ALREADY HAD A VASECTOMY.
WE'LL BE BACK IN THREE DAYS FOR OUR MONEY.
"LIVING AS THEY DO ON THE OUTSKIRTS OF SOCIETY, THE HIJRA ARE PREY TO ABUSE AND EXPLOITATION..."

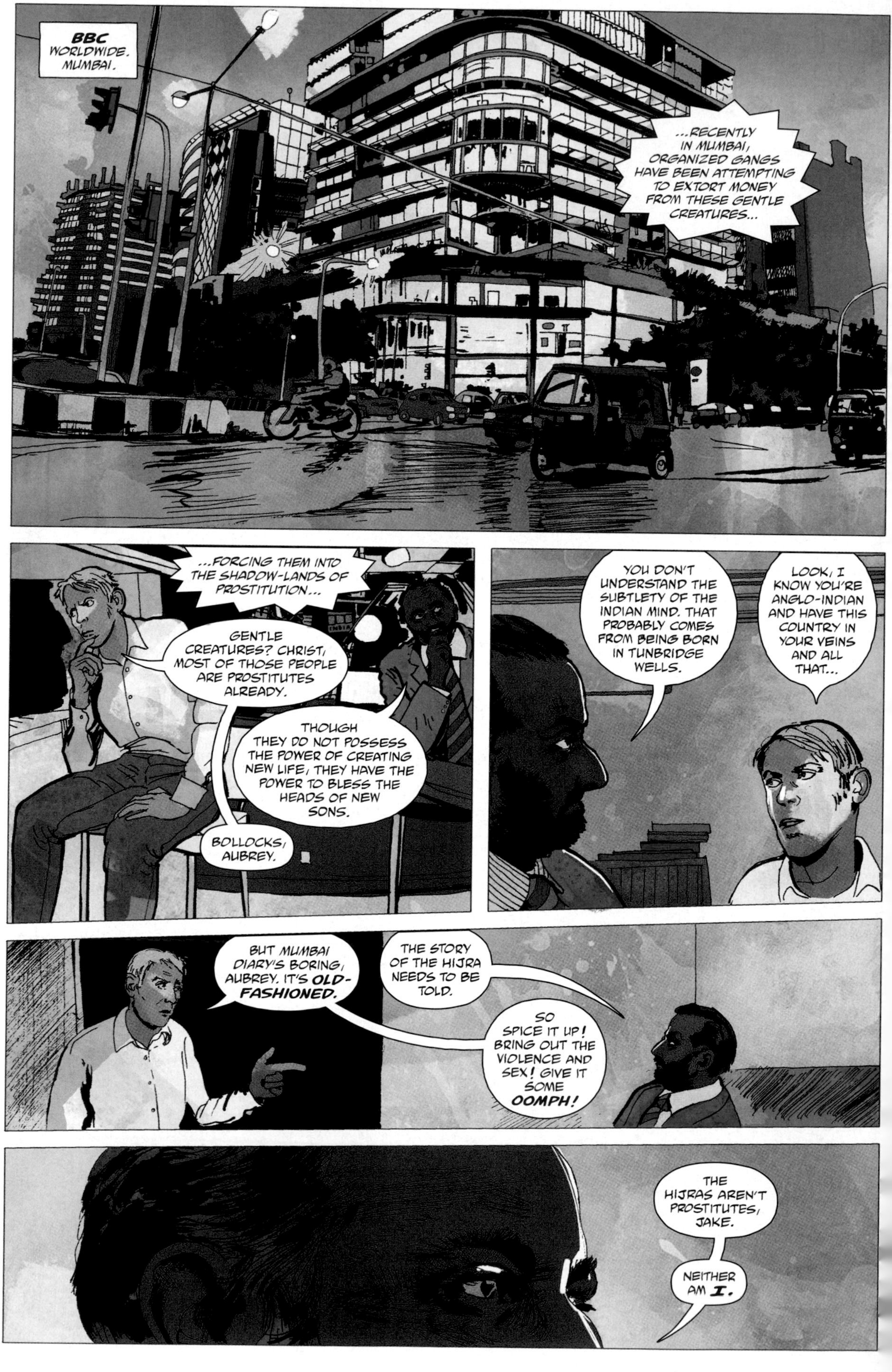
BBC WORLDWIDE. MUMBAI.
...RECENTLY IN MUMBAI, ORGANIZED GANGS HAVE BEEN ATTEMPTING TO EXTORT MONEY FROM THESE GENTLE CREATURES...
...FORCING THEM INTO THE SHADOW-LANDS OF PROSTITUTION...
GENTLE CREATURES? CHRIST, MOST OF THOSE PEOPLE ARE PROSTITUTES ALREADY.
THOUGH THEY DO NOT POSSESS THE POWER OF CREATING NEW LIFE, THEY HAVE THE POWER TO BLESS THE HEADS OF NEW SONS.
BOLLOCKS, AUBREY.
YOU DON'T UNDERSTAND THE SUBTLETY OF THE INDIAN MIND. THAT PROBABLY COMES FROM BEING BORN IN TUNBRIDGE WELLS.
LOOK, I KNOW YOU'RE ANGLO-INDIAN AND HAVE THIS COUNTRY IN YOUR VEINS AND ALL THAT...
BUT MUMBAI DIARY'S BORING, AUBREY. IT'S OLD-FASHIONED.
THE STORY OF THE HIJRA NEEDS TO BE TOLD.
SO SPICE IT UP! BRING OUT THE VIOLENCE AND SEX! GIVE IT SOME OOMPH!
THE HIJRAS AREN'T PROSTITUTES, JAKE.
NEITHER AM I.

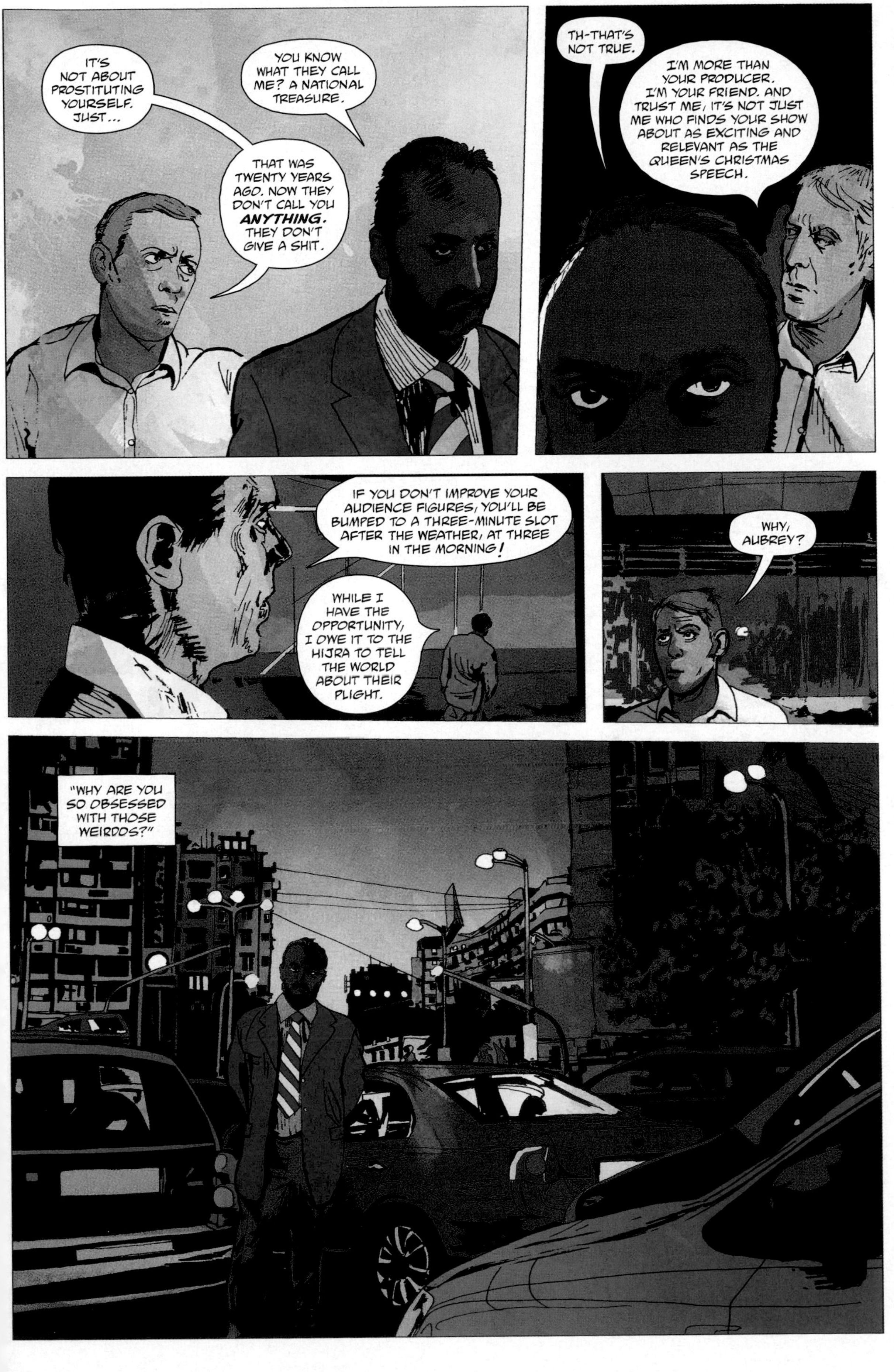
YOU KNOW WHAT THEY CALL ME? A NATIONAL TREASURE.
IT'S NOT ABOUT PROSTITUTING YOURSELF. JUST...
THAT WAS TWENTY YEARS AGO. NOW THEY DON'T CALL YOU ANYTHING. THEY DON'T GIVE A SHIT.
TH-THAT'S NOT TRUE.
I'M MORE THAN YOUR PRODUCER. I'M YOUR FRIEND. AND TRUST ME, IT'S NOT JUST ME WHO FINDS YOUR SHOW ABOUT AS EXCITING AND RELEVANT AS THE QUEEN'S CHRISTMAS SPEECH.
IF YOU DON'T IMPROVE YOUR AUDIENCE FIGURES, YOU'LL BE BUMPED TO A THREE-MINUTE SLOT AFTER THE WEATHER, AT THREE IN THE MORNING!
WHILE I HAVE THE OPPORTUNITY, I OWE IT TO THE HIJRA TO TELL THE WORLD ABOUT THEIR PLIGHT.
WHY, AUBREY?
"WHY ARE YOU SO OBSESSED WITH THOSE WEIRDOS?"

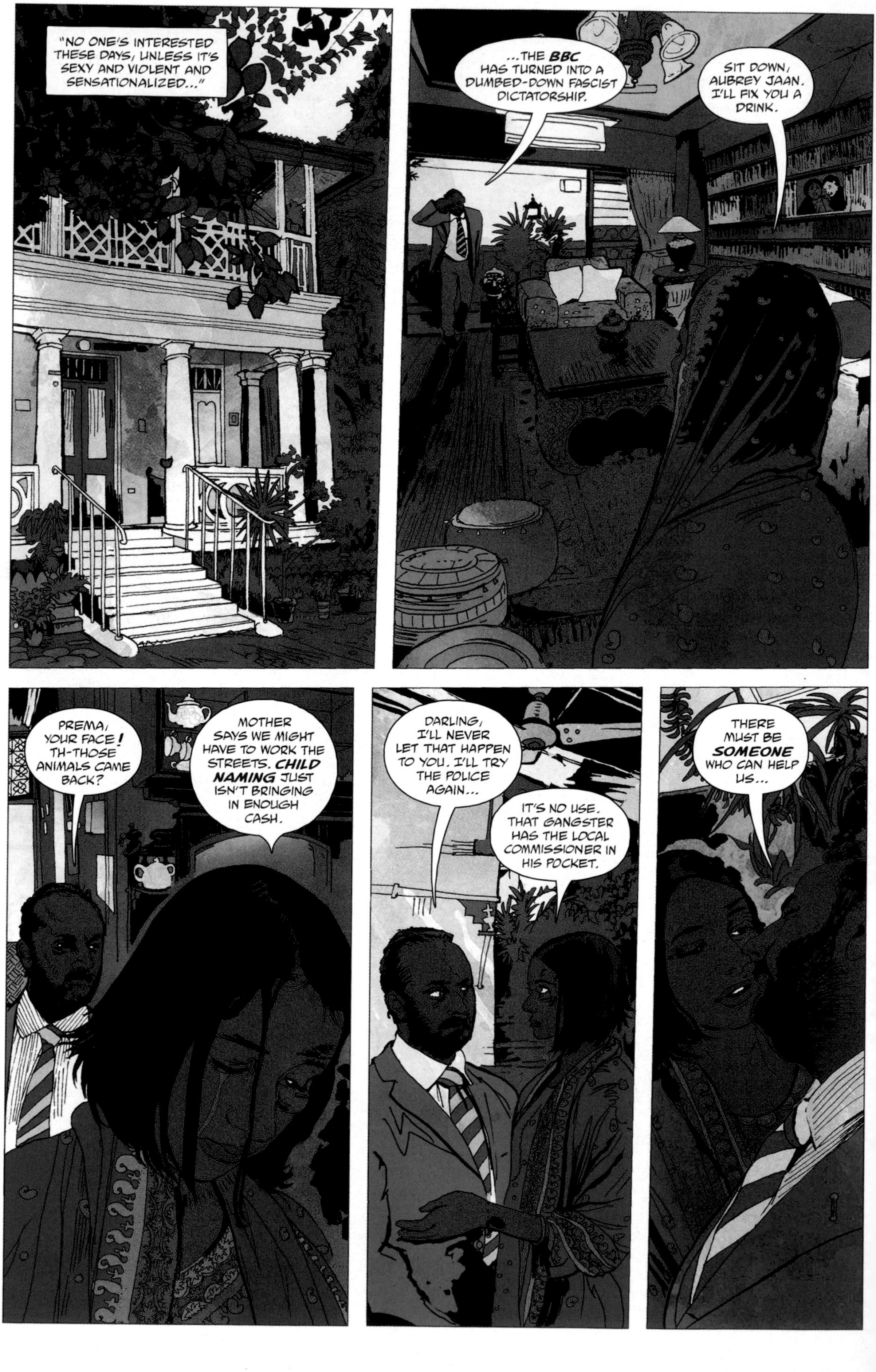
"NO ONE'S INTERESTED THESE DAYS, UNLESS IT'S SEXY AND VIOLENT AND SENSATIONALIZED..."
...THE BBC HAS TURNED INTO A DUMBED-DOWN FASCIST DICTATORSHIP.
SIT DOWN, AUBREY JAAN. I'LL FIX YOU A DRINK.
PREMA, YOUR FACE! TH-THOSE ANIMALS CAME BACK?
MOTHER SAYS WE MIGHT HAVE TO WORK THE STREETS. CHILD NAMING JUST ISN'T BRINGING IN ENOUGH CASH.
DARLING, I'LL NEVER LET THAT HAPPEN TO YOU. I'LL TRY THE POLICE AGAIN...
IT'S NO USE. THAT GANGSTER HAS THE LOCAL COMMISSIONER IN HIS POCKET.
THERE MUST BE SOMEONE WHO CAN HELP US...

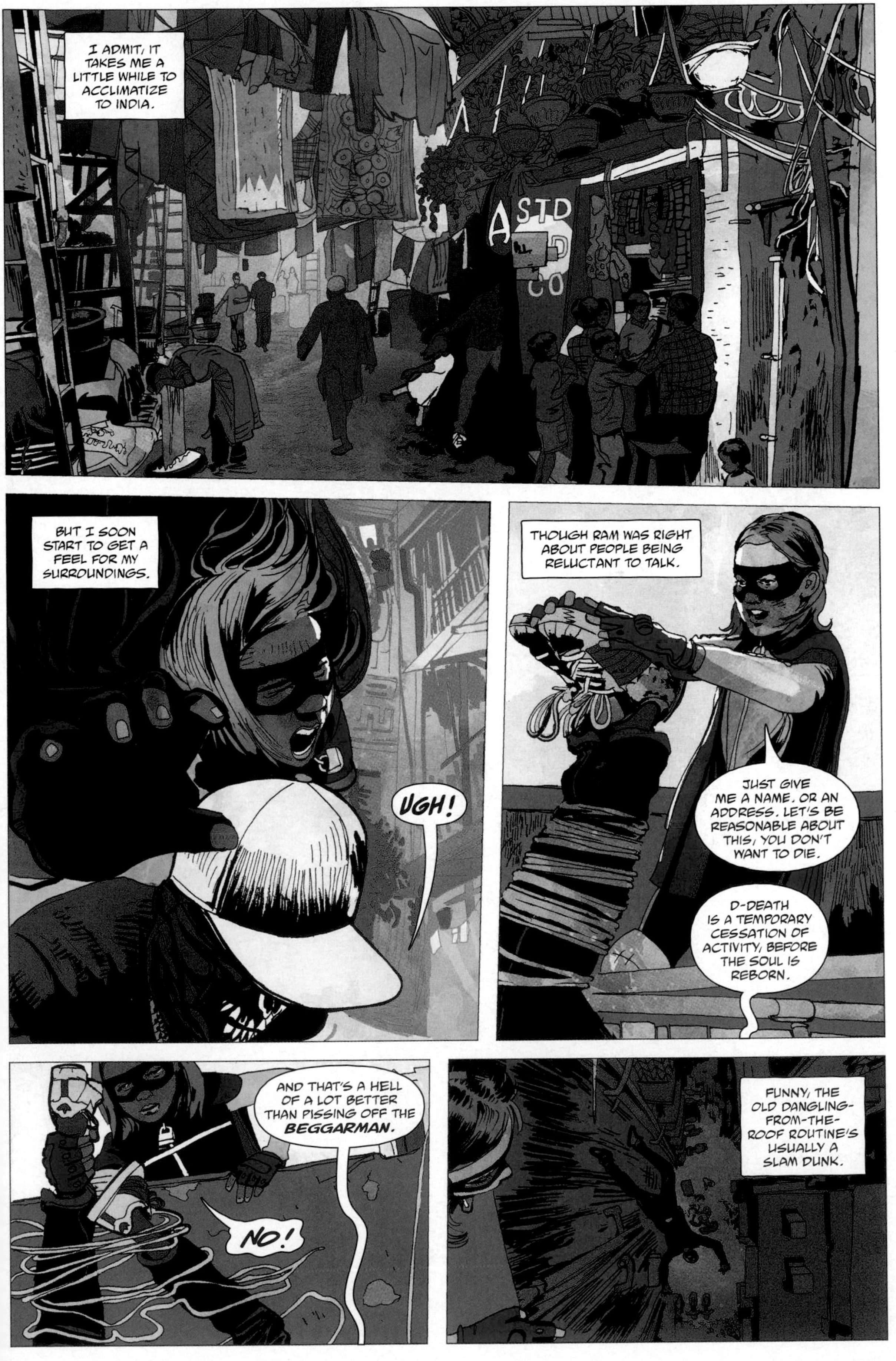
I ADMIT, IT TAKES ME A LITTLE WHILE TO ACCLIMATIZE TO INDIA.
STD
CO
BUT I SOON START TO GET A FEEL FOR MY SURROUNDINGS.
UGH!
THOUGH RAM WAS RIGHT ABOUT PEOPLE BEING RELUCTANT TO TALK.
JUST GIVE ME A NAME. OR AN ADDRESS. LET'S BE REASONABLE ABOUT THIS, YOU DON'T WANT TO DIE.
D-DEATH IS A TEMPORARY CESSATION OF ACTIVITY, BEFORE THE SOUL IS REBORN.
AND THAT'S A HELL OF A LOT BETTER THAN PISSING OFF THE **BEGGARMAN**.
NO!
FUNNY, THE OLD DANGLING-FROM-THE-ROOF ROUTINE'S USUALLY A SLAM DUNK.

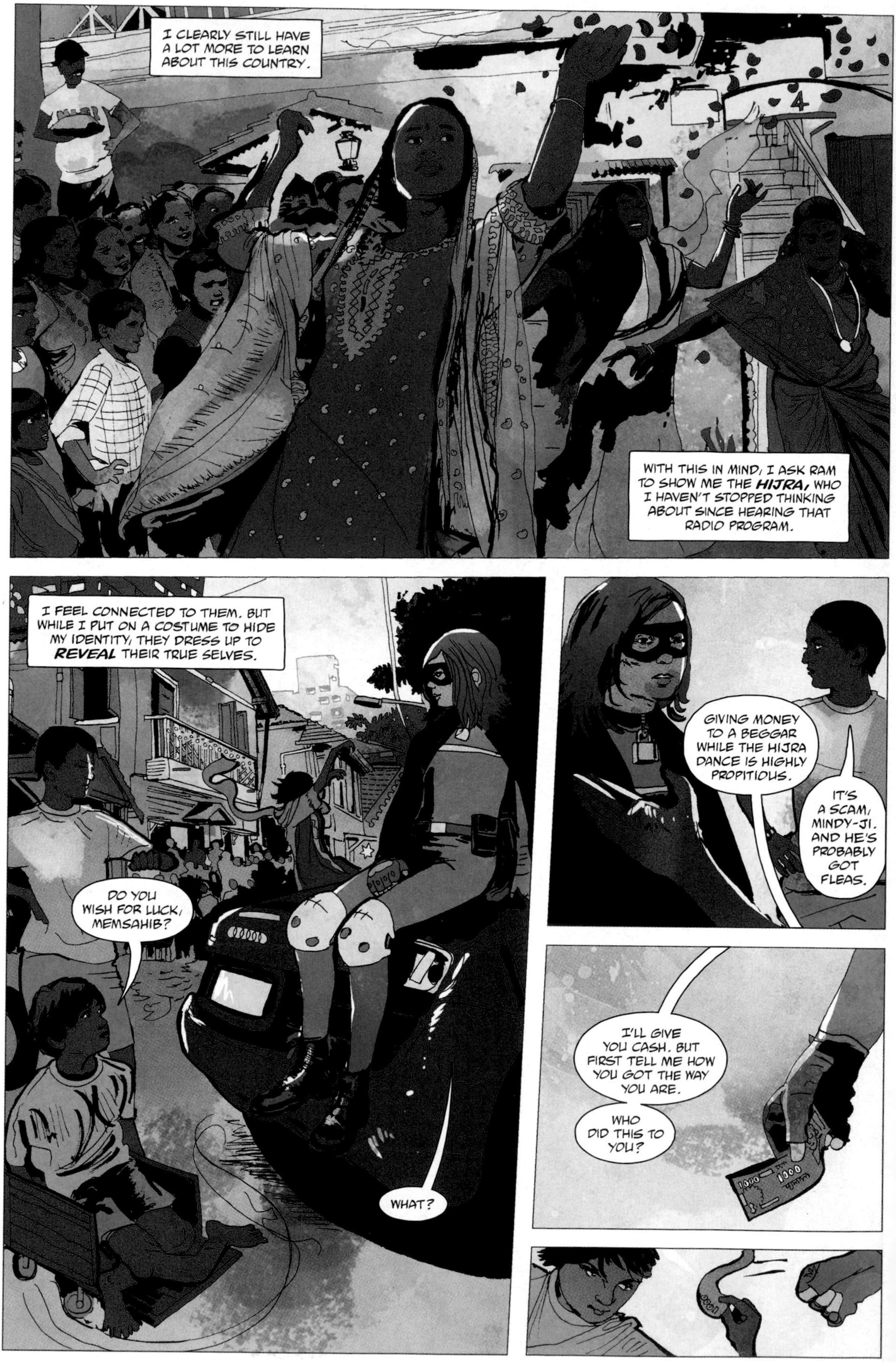
I CLEARLY STILL HAVE A LOT MORE TO LEARN ABOUT THIS COUNTRY.
WITH THIS IN MIND, I ASK RAM TO SHOW ME THE HIJRA, WHO I HAVEN'T STOPPED THINKING ABOUT SINCE HEARING THAT RADIO PROGRAM.
I FEEL CONNECTED TO THEM. BUT WHILE I PUT ON A COSTUME TO HIDE MY IDENTITY, THEY DRESS UP TO REVEAL THEIR TRUE SELVES.
DO YOU WISH FOR LUCK, MEMSAHIB?
WHAT?
GIVING MONEY TO A BEGGAR WHILE THE HIJRA DANCE IS HIGHLY PROPITIOUS.
IT'S A SCAM, MINDY-JI. AND HE'S PROBABLY GOT FLEAS.
I'LL GIVE YOU CASH. BUT FIRST TELL ME HOW YOU GOT THE WAY YOU ARE.
WHO DID THIS TO YOU?

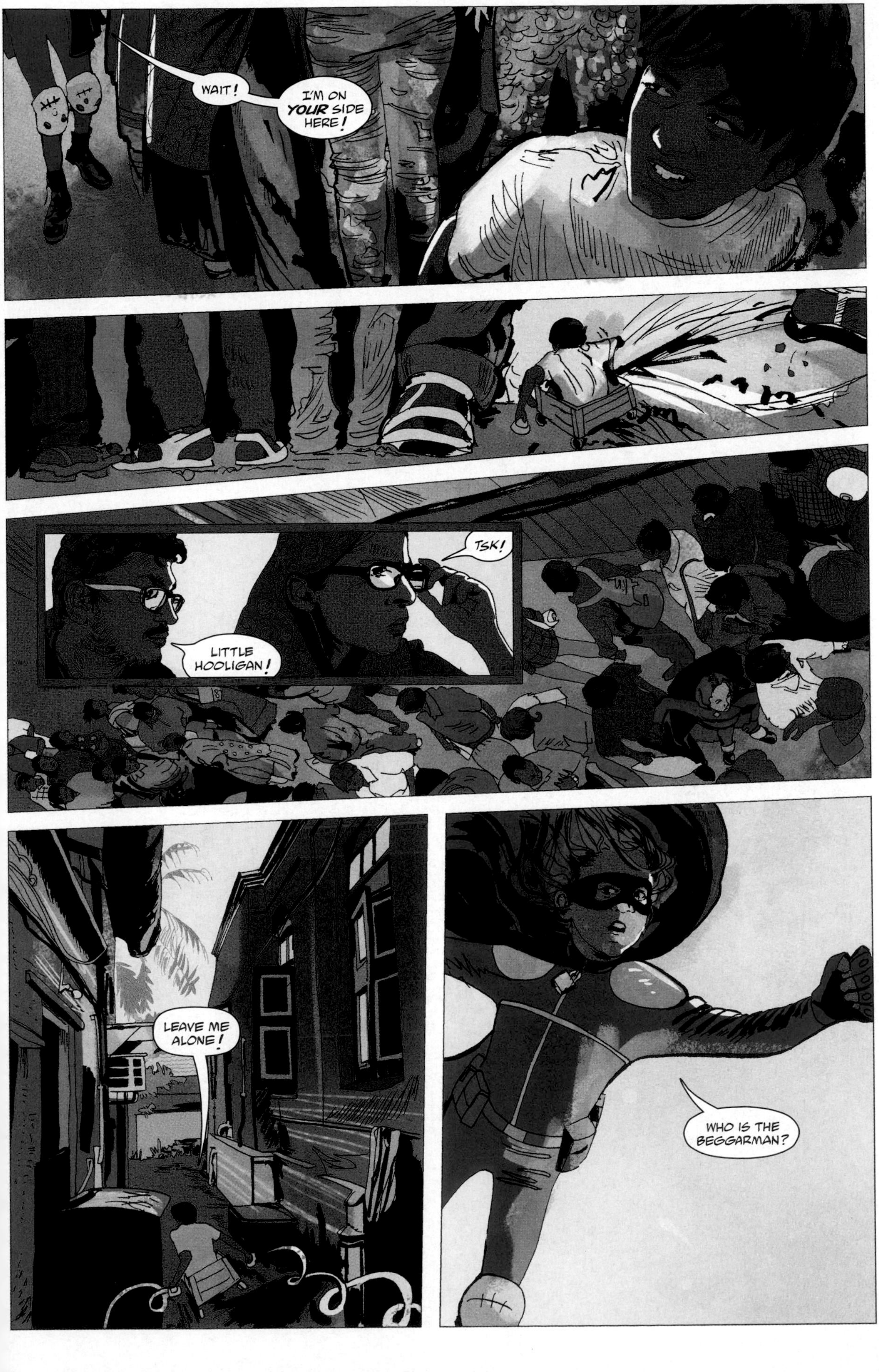
WAIT!
I'M ON YOUR SIDE HERE!
TSK!
LITTLE HOOLIGAN!
LEAVE ME ALONE!
WHO IS THE BEGGARMAN?

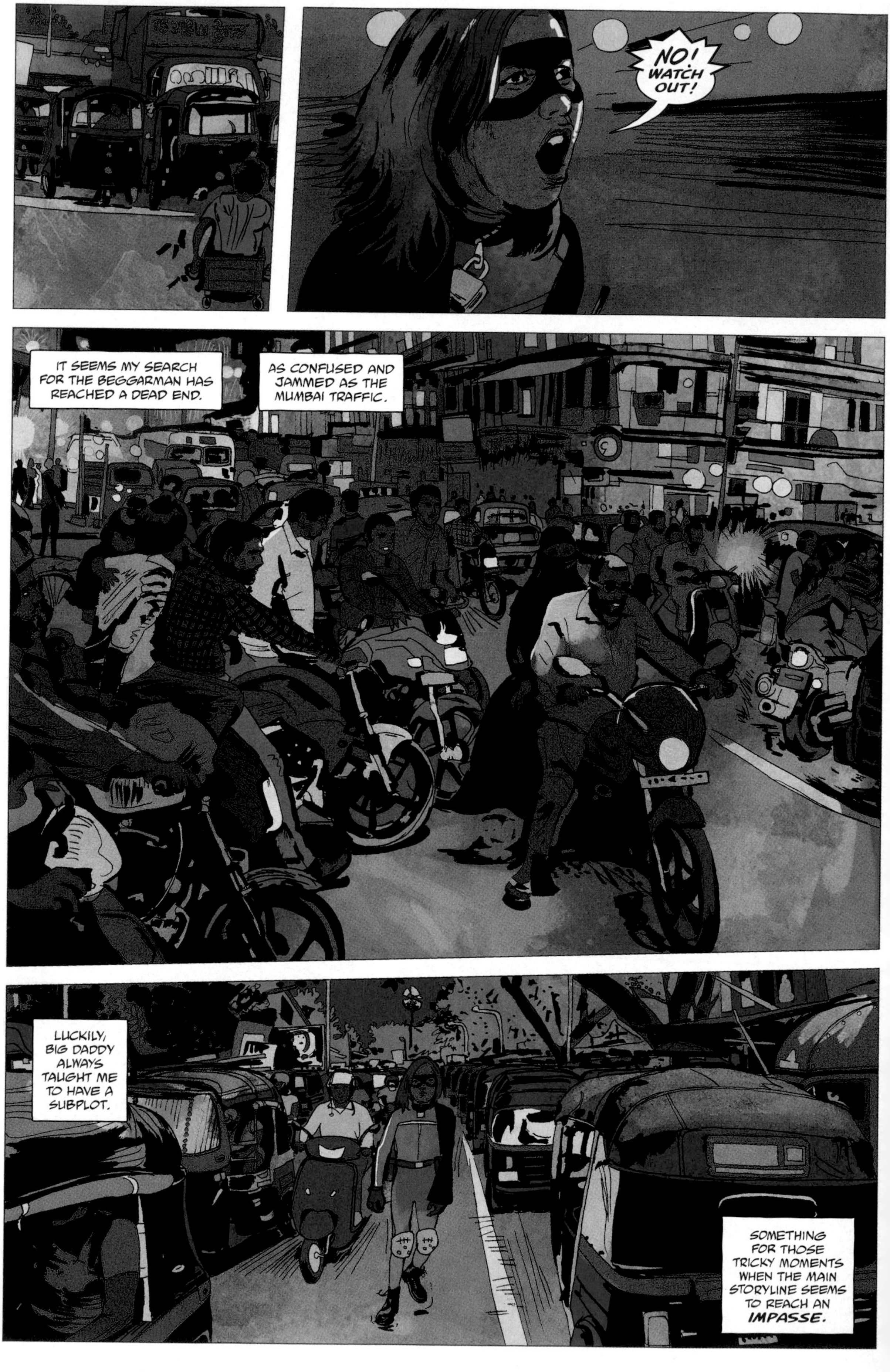
NO! WATCH OUT!
IT SEEMS MY SEARCH FOR THE BEGGARMAN HAS REACHED A DEAD END.
AS CONFUSED AND JAMMED AS THE MUMBAI TRAFFIC.
LUCKILY, BIG DADDY ALWAYS TAUGHT ME TO HAVE A SUBPLOT.
SOMETHING FOR THOSE TRICKY MOMENTS WHEN THE MAIN STORYLINE SEEMS TO REACH AN IMPASSE.

DAUGHTERS, YOU ARE GOING TO HAVE TO DO THE WORK THAT I KNOW OFFENDS YOUR SENSIBILITIES.

BUT WE ARE NOT PROSTITUTES, MOTHER.

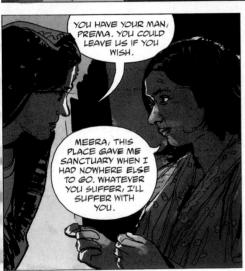

YOU HAVE YOUR MAN, PREMA. YOU COULD LEAVE US IF YOU WISH.

MEERA, THIS PLACE GAVE ME SANCTUARY WHEN I HAD NOWHERE ELSE TO GO. WHATEVER YOU SUFFER, I'LL SUFFER WITH YOU.

IT WON'T BE FOR LONG. WE'LL PRETEND TO DO WHAT THEY WANT US TO DO.

IN THE MEANTIME, I'VE MADE CONTACT WITH THE HOUSEMAID OF THE GANGSTER WHO CONTROLS ROHIT AND HIS RUFFIANS. SHE IS ALSO A DAUGHTER OF BAHUCHARA MATA...

SHE WILL HELP US?

ENOUGH, CHILDREN. THE EVIL ONES COME...

MY BOSS IS GIVING ME A HARD TIME BECAUSE OF YOU BITCHES.

SO NO MORE BULL-SHIT. NO MORE HIJRA FUCKING CURSES. YOU ARE GOING TO START *EARNING*.

P-PLEASE, ROHIT-JI. IF YOU'LL KINDLY LET ME...TALK.

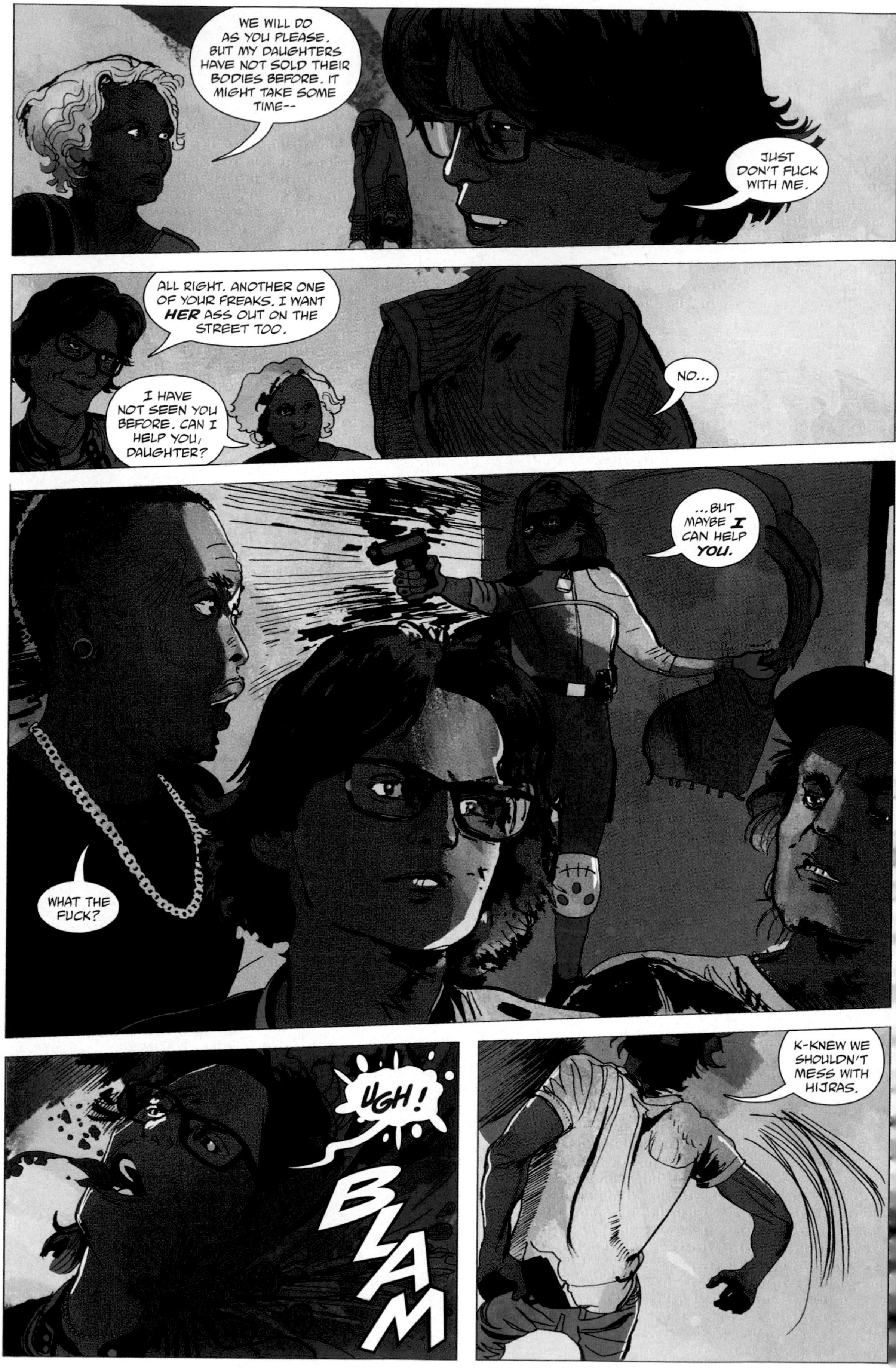
WE WILL DO AS YOU PLEASE. BUT MY DAUGHTERS HAVE NOT SOLD THEIR BODIES BEFORE. IT MIGHT TAKE SOME TIME--
JUST DON'T FUCK WITH ME.
ALL RIGHT. ANOTHER ONE OF YOUR FREAKS. I WANT HER ASS OUT ON THE STREET TOO.
I HAVE NOT SEEN YOU BEFORE. CAN I HELP YOU, DAUGHTER?
NO...
...BUT MAYBE I CAN HELP YOU.
WHAT THE FUCK?
UGH!
BLAM
K-KNEW WE SHOULDN'T MESS WITH HIJRAS.

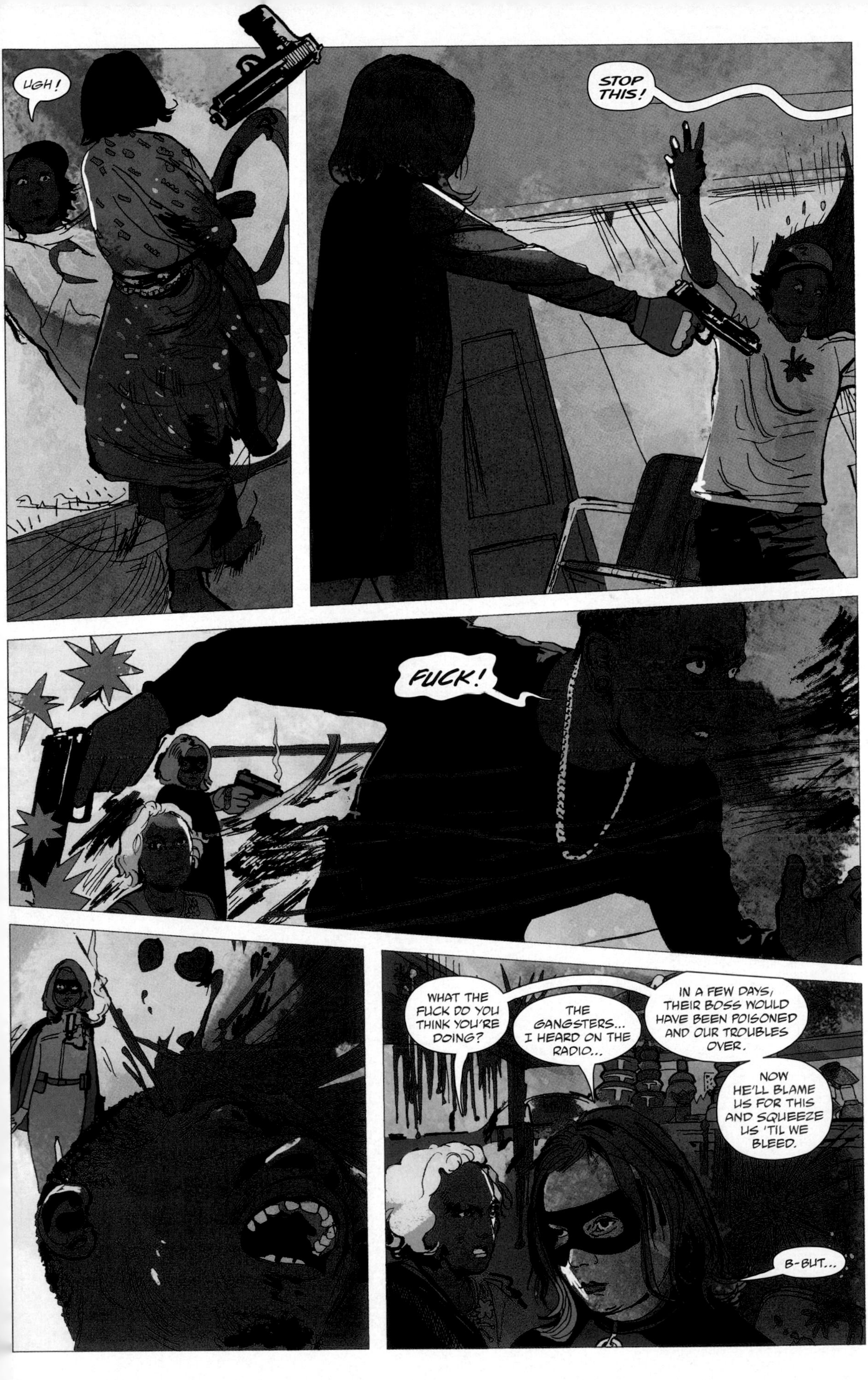
UGH!
STOP THIS!
FUCK!
WHAT THE FUCK DO YOU THINK YOU'RE DOING?
THE GANGSTERS... I HEARD ON THE RADIO...
IN A FEW DAYS, THEIR BOSS WOULD HAVE BEEN POISONED AND OUR TROUBLES OVER.
NOW HE'LL BLAME US FOR THIS AND SQUEEZE US 'TIL WE BLEED.
B-BUT...

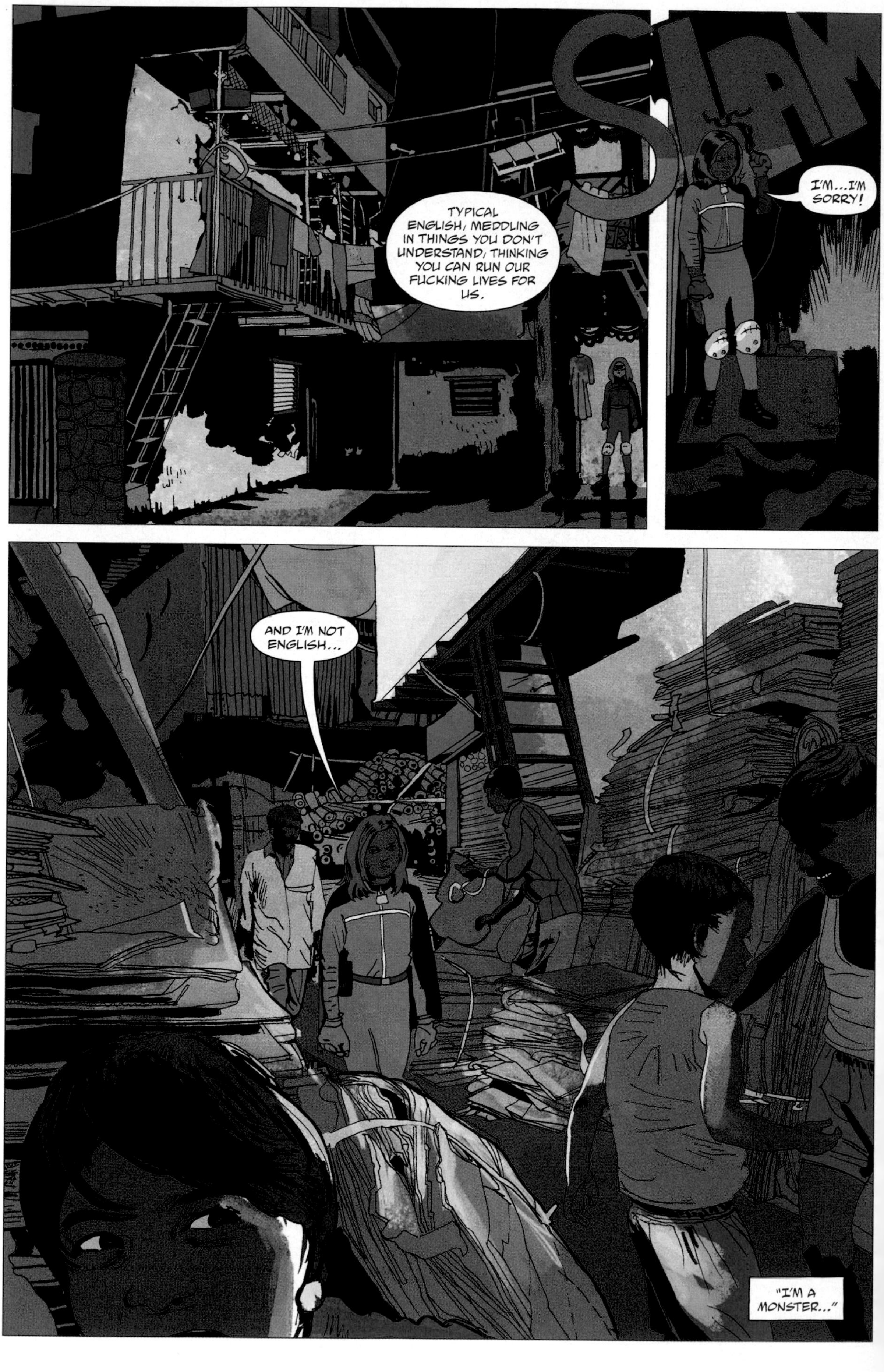
SLAM
TYPICAL ENGLISH, MEDDLING IN THINGS YOU DON'T UNDERSTAND, THINKING YOU CAN RUN OUR FUCKING LIVES FOR US.
I'M...I'M SORRY!
AND I'M NOT ENGLISH...
"I'M A MONSTER..."

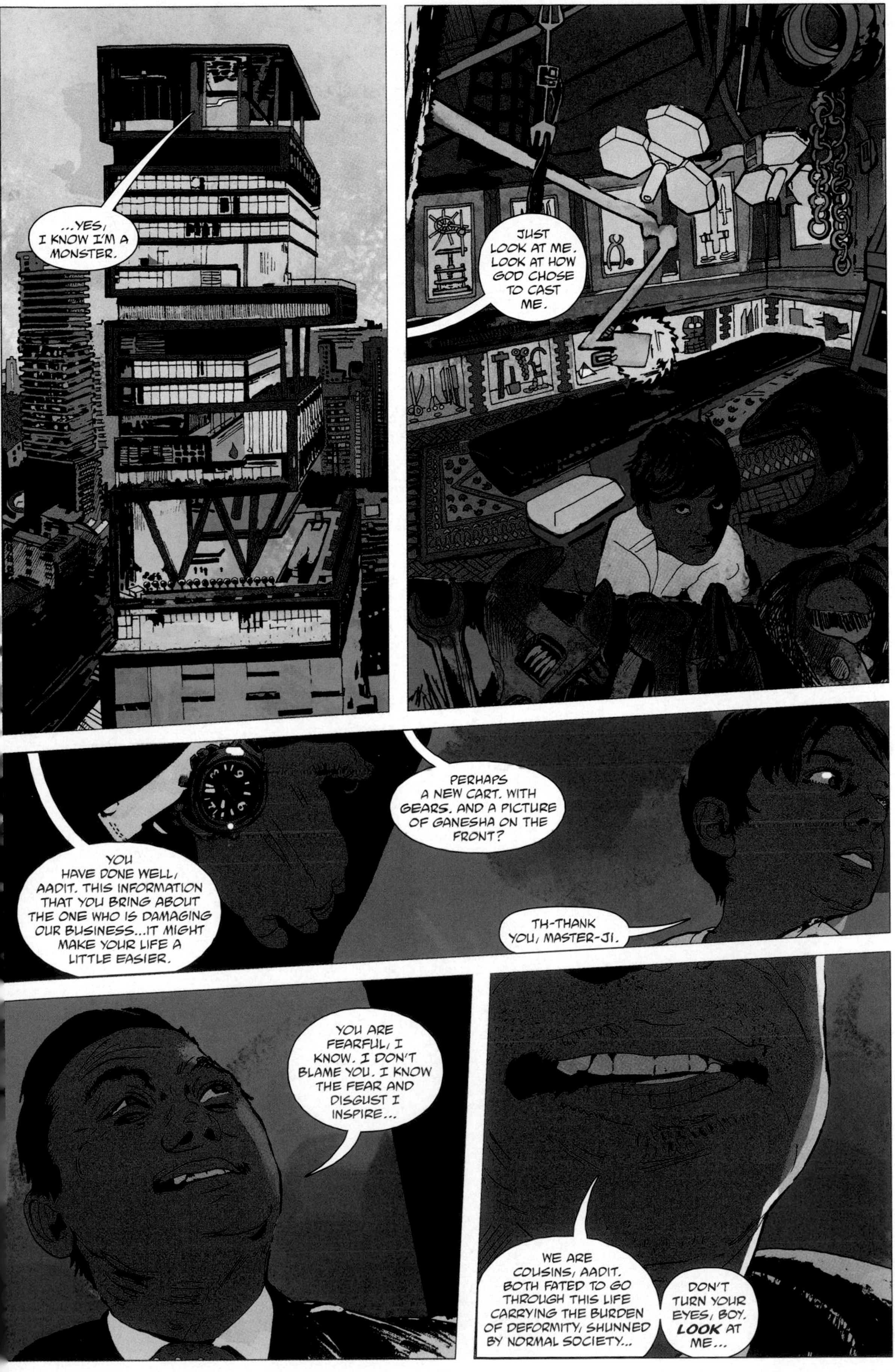
...YES, I KNOW I'M A MONSTER.
JUST LOOK AT ME. LOOK AT HOW GOD CHOSE TO CAST ME.
YOU HAVE DONE WELL, AADIT. THIS INFORMATION THAT YOU BRING ABOUT THE ONE WHO IS DAMAGING OUR BUSINESS...IT MIGHT MAKE YOUR LIFE A LITTLE EASIER.
PERHAPS A NEW CART. WITH GEARS. AND A PICTURE OF GANESHA ON THE FRONT?
TH-THANK YOU, MASTER-JI.
YOU ARE FEARFUL, I KNOW. I DON'T BLAME YOU. I KNOW THE FEAR AND DISGUST I INSPIRE...
WE ARE COUSINS, AADIT. BOTH FATED TO GO THROUGH THIS LIFE CARRYING THE BURDEN OF DEFORMITY, SHUNNED BY NORMAL SOCIETY...
DON'T TURN YOUR EYES, BOY. **LOOK** AT ME...

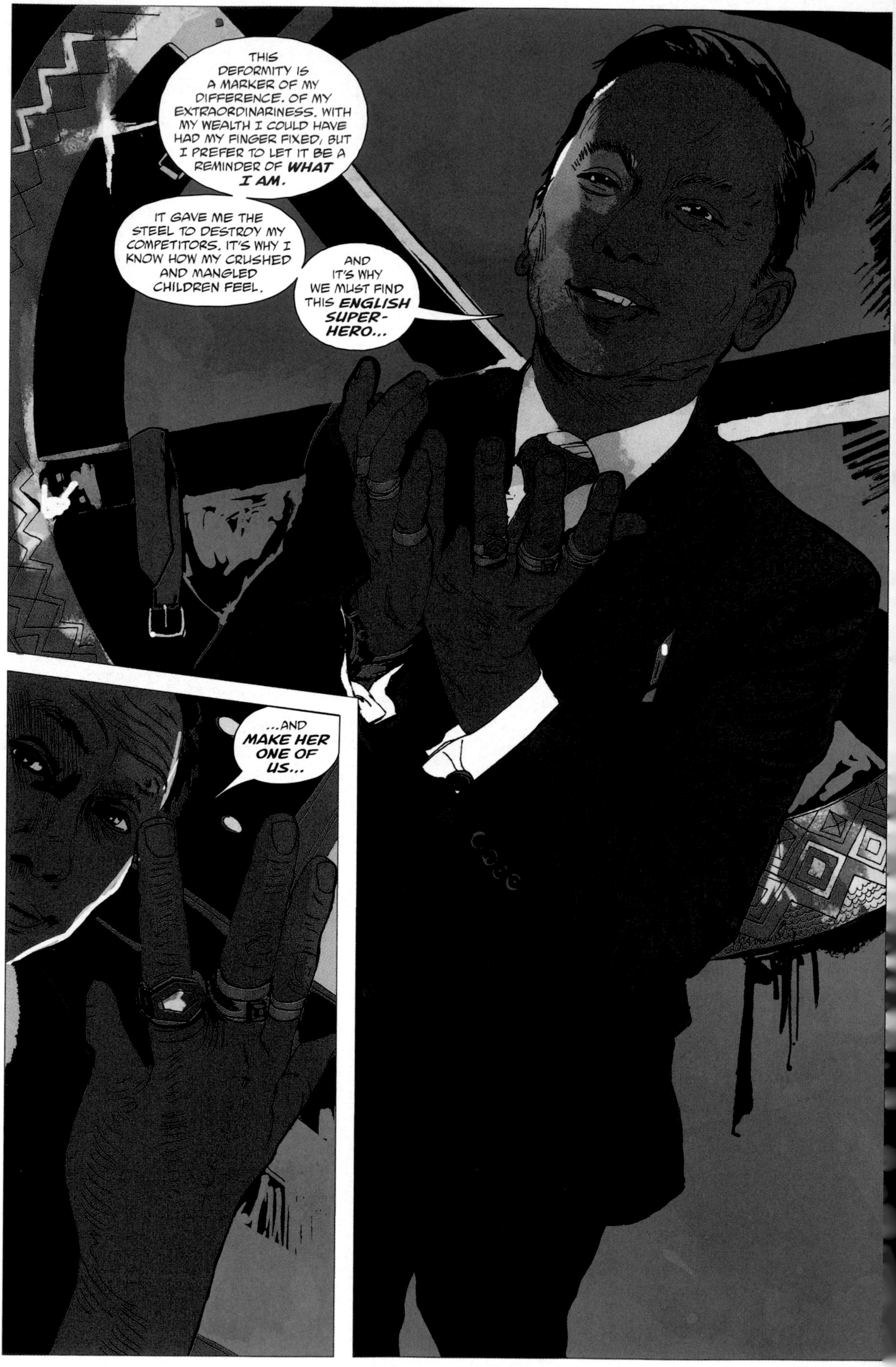
THIS DEFORMITY IS A MARKER OF MY DIFFERENCE. OF MY EXTRAORDINARINESS. WITH MY WEALTH I COULD HAVE HAD MY FINGER FIXED, BUT I PREFER TO LET IT BE A REMINDER OF WHAT I AM.
IT GAVE ME THE STEEL TO DESTROY MY COMPETITORS. IT'S WHY I KNOW HOW MY CRUSHED AND MANGLED CHILDREN FEEL.
AND IT'S WHY WE MUST FIND THIS ENGLISH SUPER-HERO...
...AND MAKE HER ONE OF US...

TWO

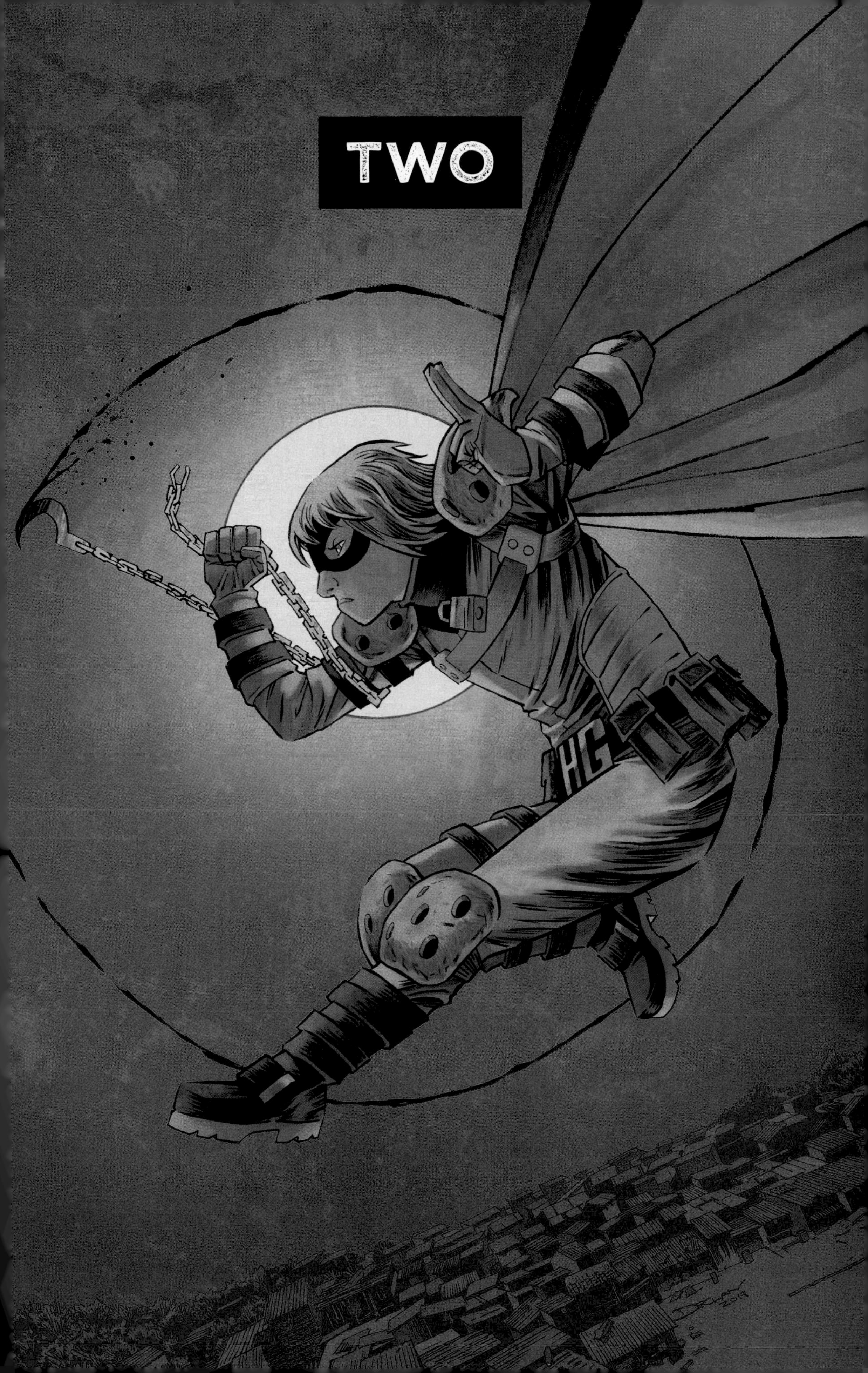

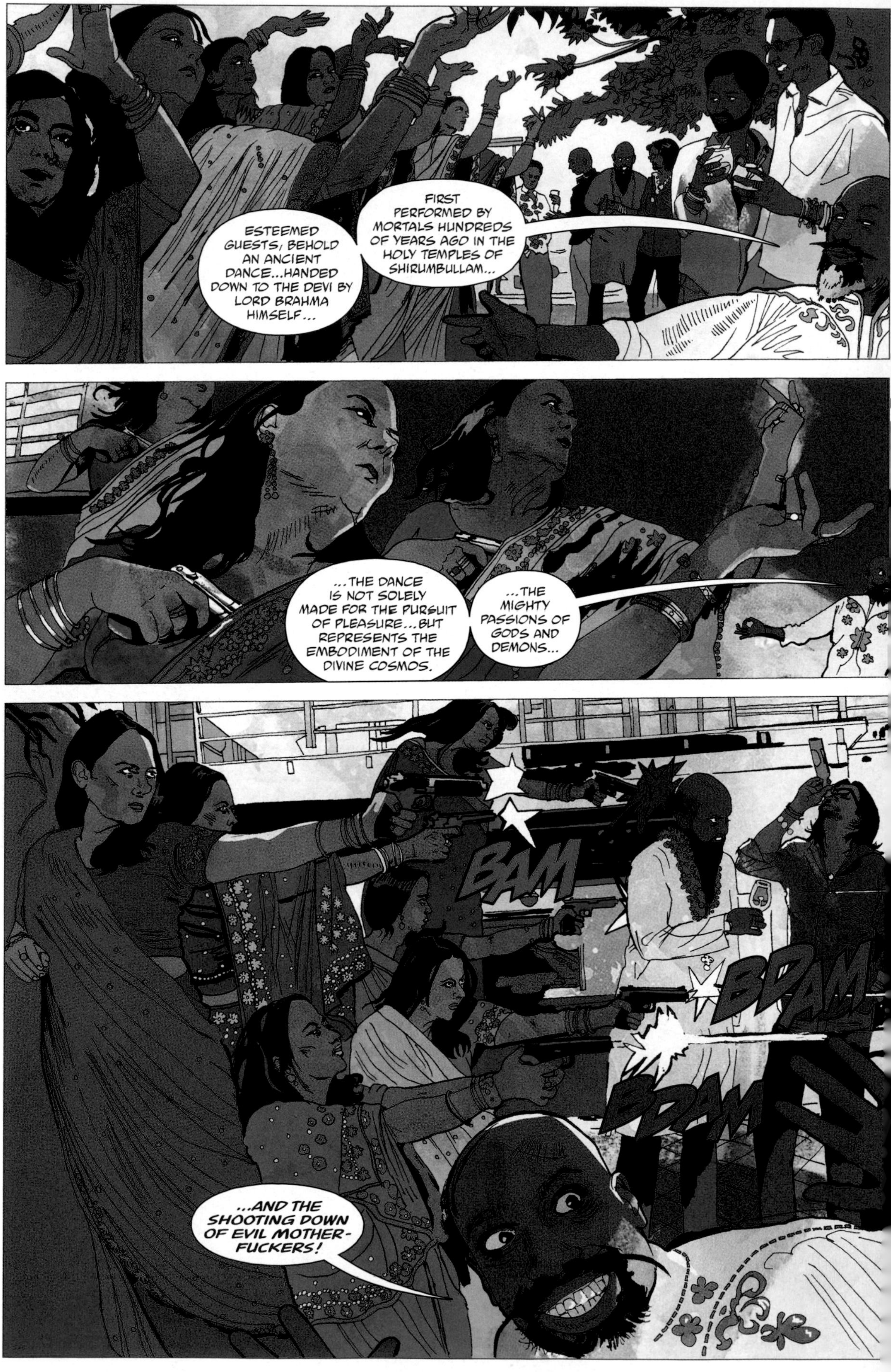
ESTEEMED GUESTS, BEHOLD AN ANCIENT DANCE...HANDED DOWN TO THE DEVI BY LORD BRAHMA HIMSELF...
FIRST PERFORMED BY MORTALS HUNDREDS OF YEARS AGO IN THE HOLY TEMPLES OF SHIRUMBULLAM...
...THE DANCE IS NOT SOLELY MADE FOR THE PURSUIT OF PLEASURE...BUT REPRESENTS THE EMBODIMENT OF THE DIVINE COSMOS.
...THE MIGHTY PASSIONS OF GODS AND DEMONS...
BAM
BDAM
BDAM
...AND THE SHOOTING DOWN OF EVIL MOTHER-FUCKERS!

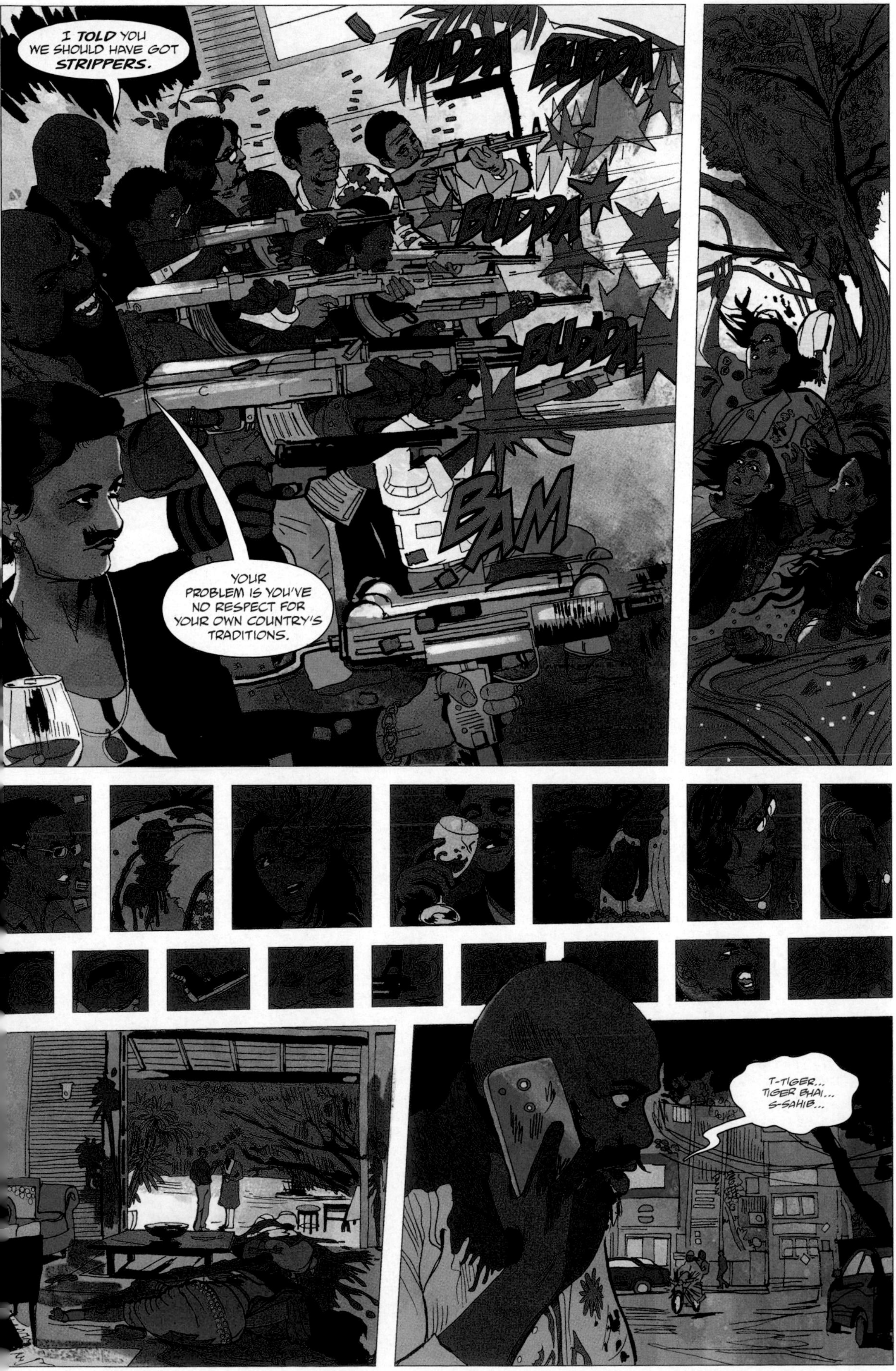
I TOLD YOU WE SHOULD HAVE GOT STRIPPERS.
BUDDA BUDDA
BUDDA
BUDDA
BAM
YOUR PROBLEM IS YOU'VE NO RESPECT FOR YOUR OWN COUNTRY'S TRADITIONS.
T-TIGER... TIGER BHAI... S-SAHIB...

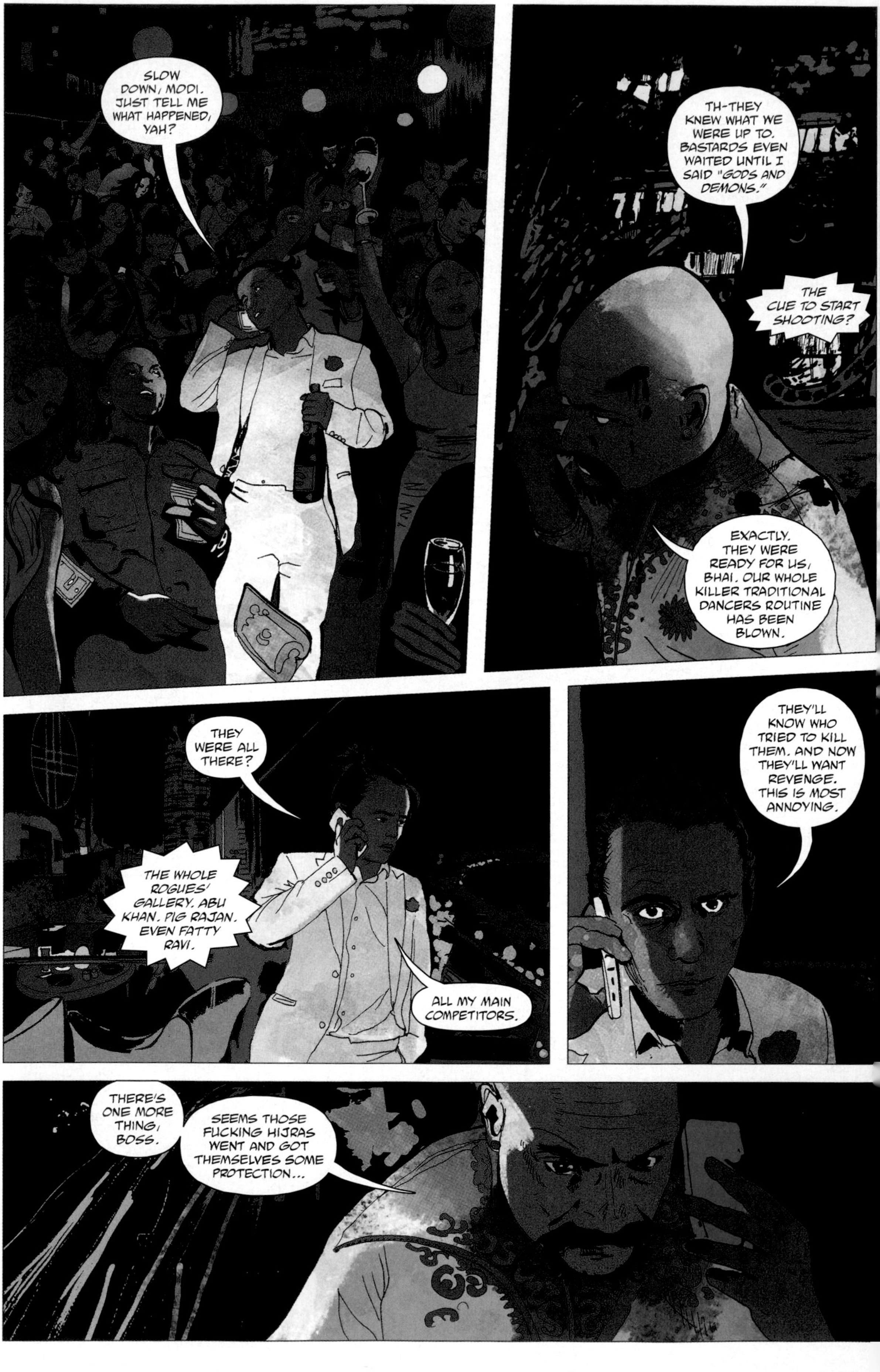
SLOW DOWN, MODI. JUST TELL ME WHAT HAPPENED, YAH?
TH-THEY KNEW WHAT WE WERE UP TO. BASTARDS EVEN WAITED UNTIL I SAID "GODS AND DEMONS."
THE CUE TO START SHOOTING?
EXACTLY. THEY WERE READY FOR US, BHAI. OUR WHOLE KILLER TRADITIONAL DANCERS ROUTINE HAS BEEN BLOWN.
THEY WERE ALL THERE?
THE WHOLE ROGUES' GALLERY. ABU KHAN. PIG RAJAN. EVEN FATTY RAVI.
ALL MY MAIN COMPETITORS.
THEY'LL KNOW WHO TRIED TO KILL THEM. AND NOW THEY'LL WANT REVENGE. THIS IS MOST ANNOYING.
THERE'S ONE MORE THING, BOSS.
SEEMS THOSE FUCKING HIJRAS WENT AND GOT THEMSELVES SOME PROTECTION...

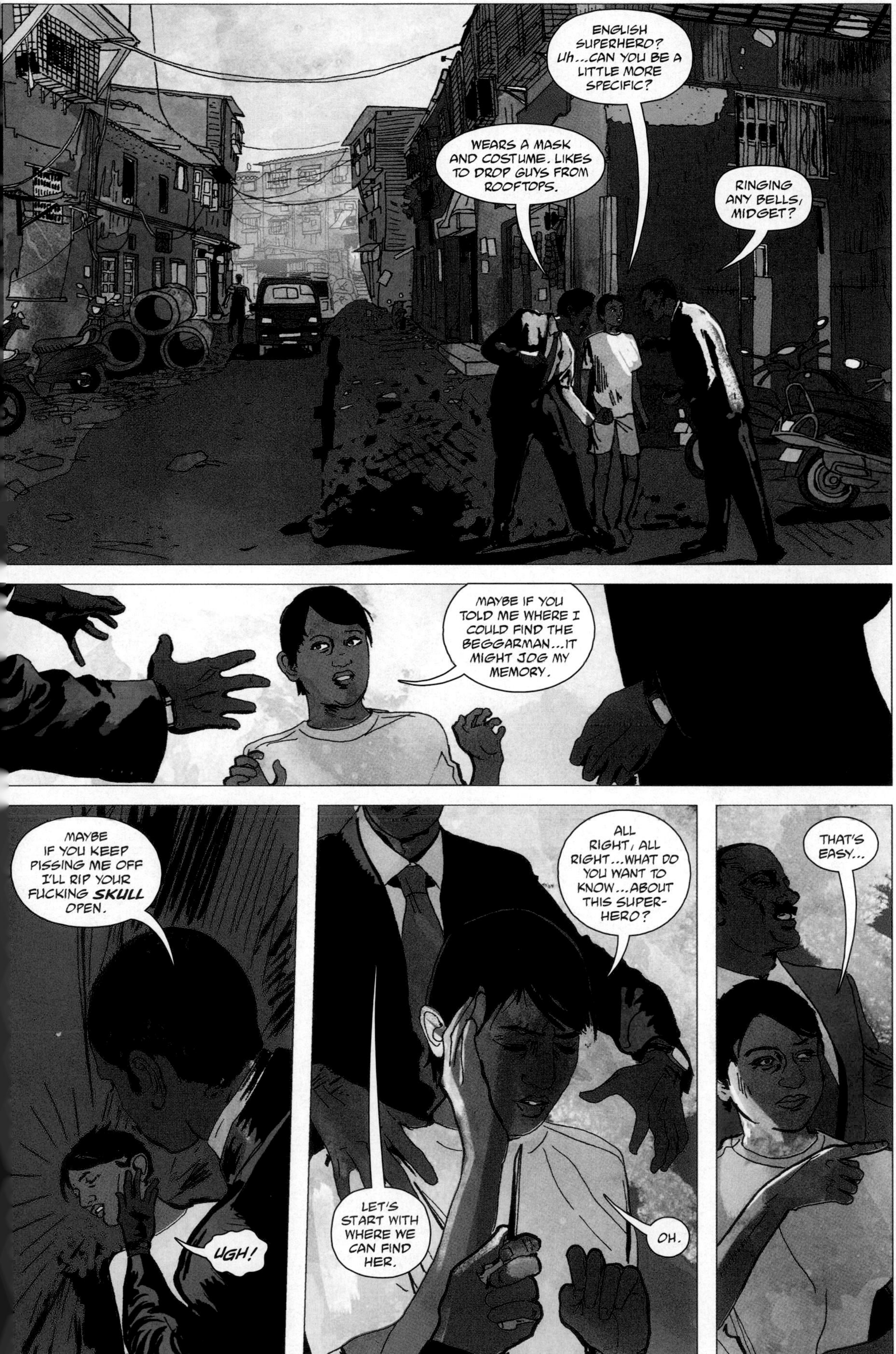
WEARS A MASK AND COSTUME. LIKES TO DROP GUYS FROM ROOFTOPS.
ENGLISH SUPERHERO? Uh...CAN YOU BE A LITTLE MORE SPECIFIC?
RINGING ANY BELLS, MIDGET?
MAYBE IF YOU TOLD ME WHERE I COULD FIND THE BEGGARMAN...IT MIGHT JOG MY MEMORY.
MAYBE IF YOU KEEP PISSING ME OFF I'LL RIP YOUR FUCKING SKULL OPEN.
UGH!
ALL RIGHT, ALL RIGHT...WHAT DO YOU WANT TO KNOW...ABOUT THIS SUPER-HERO?
LET'S START WITH WHERE WE CAN FIND HER.
OH.
THAT'S EASY...

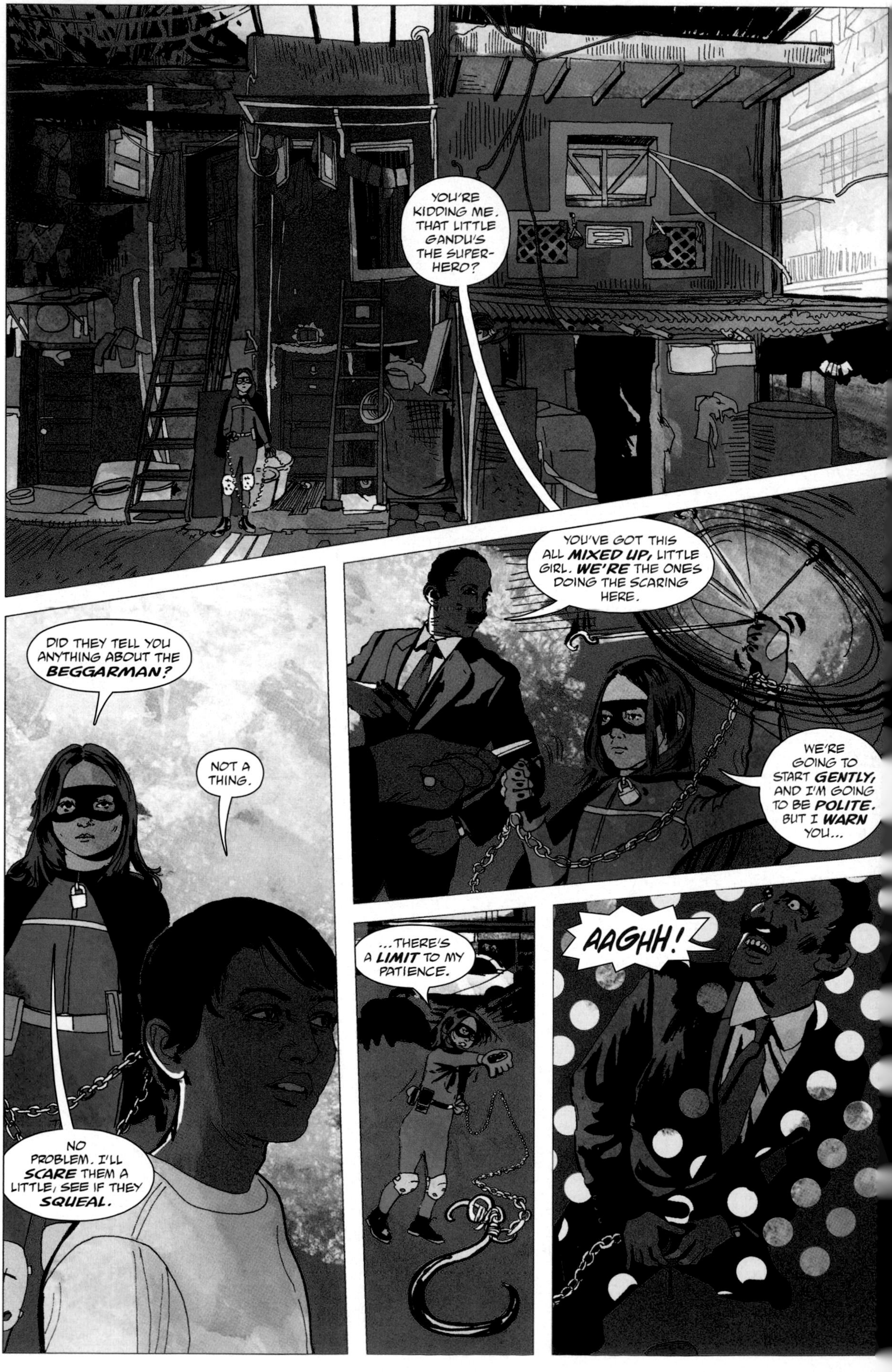
YOU'RE KIDDING ME. THAT LITTLE GANDU'S THE SUPER-HERO?
DID THEY TELL YOU ANYTHING ABOUT THE BEGGARMAN?
NOT A THING.
NO PROBLEM. I'LL SCARE THEM A LITTLE, SEE IF THEY SQUEAL.
YOU'VE GOT THIS ALL MIXED UP, LITTLE GIRL. WE'RE THE ONES DOING THE SCARING HERE.
WE'RE GOING TO START GENTLY, AND I'M GOING TO BE POLITE. BUT I WARN YOU...
...THERE'S A LIMIT TO MY PATIENCE.
AAGHH!

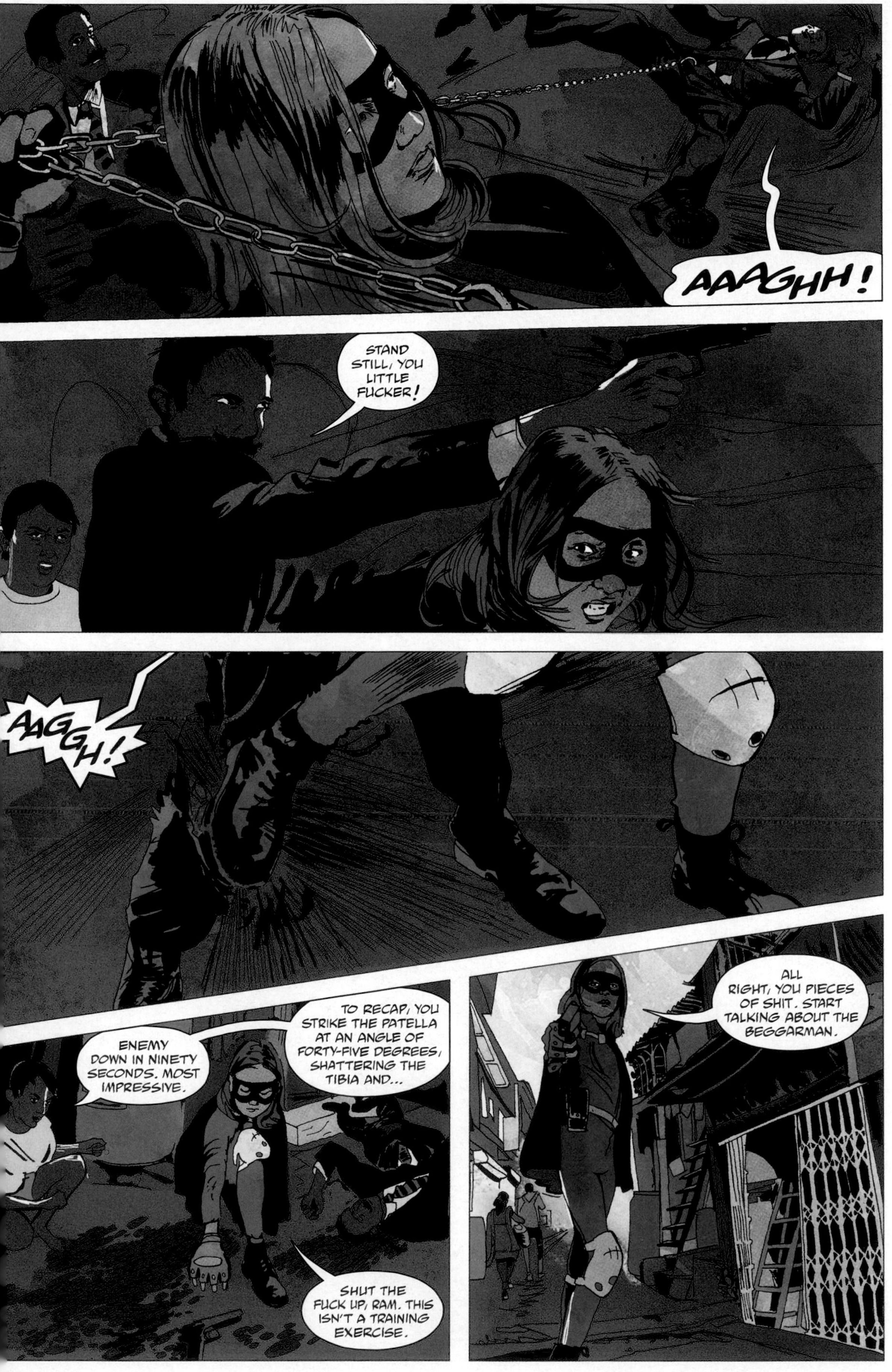
AAAGHH!
STAND STILL, YOU LITTLE FUCKER!
AAGGH!
ENEMY DOWN IN NINETY SECONDS. MOST IMPRESSIVE.
TO RECAP, YOU STRIKE THE PATELLA AT AN ANGLE OF FORTY-FIVE DEGREES, SHATTERING THE TIBIA AND...
SHUT THE FUCK UP, RAM. THIS ISN'T A TRAINING EXERCISE.
ALL RIGHT, YOU PIECES OF SHIT. START TALKING ABOUT THE BEGGARMAN.

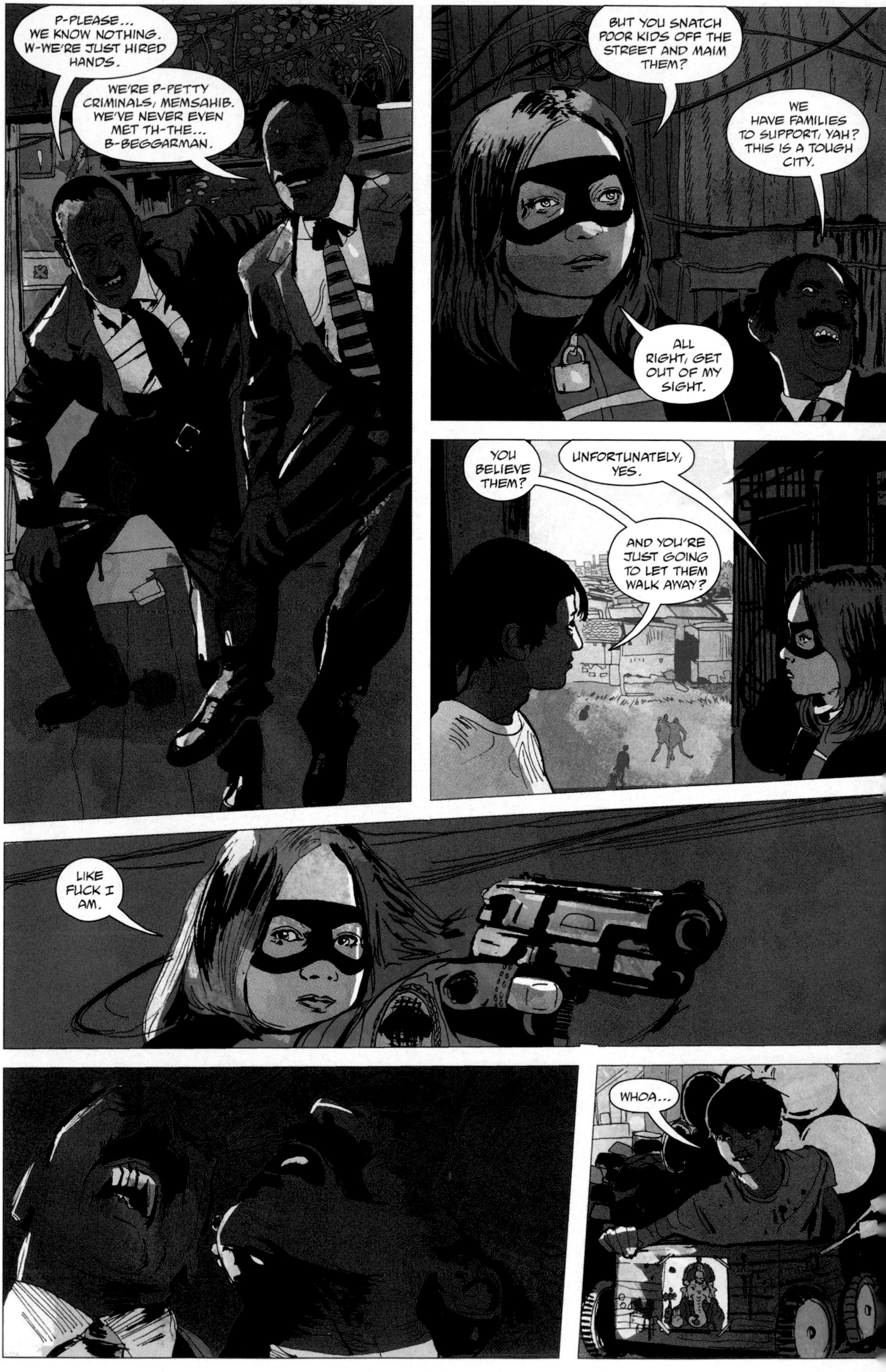
P-PLEASE... WE KNOW NOTHING. W-WE'RE JUST HIRED HANDS.
WE'RE P-PETTY CRIMINALS, MEMSAHIB. WE'VE NEVER EVEN MET TH-THE... B-BEGGARMAN.
BUT YOU SNATCH POOR KIDS OFF THE STREET AND MAIM THEM?
WE HAVE FAMILIES TO SUPPORT, YAH? THIS IS A TOUGH CITY.
ALL RIGHT, GET OUT OF MY SIGHT.
YOU BELIEVE THEM?
UNFORTUNATELY, YES.
AND YOU'RE JUST GOING TO LET THEM WALK AWAY?
LIKE FUCK I AM.
WHOA...

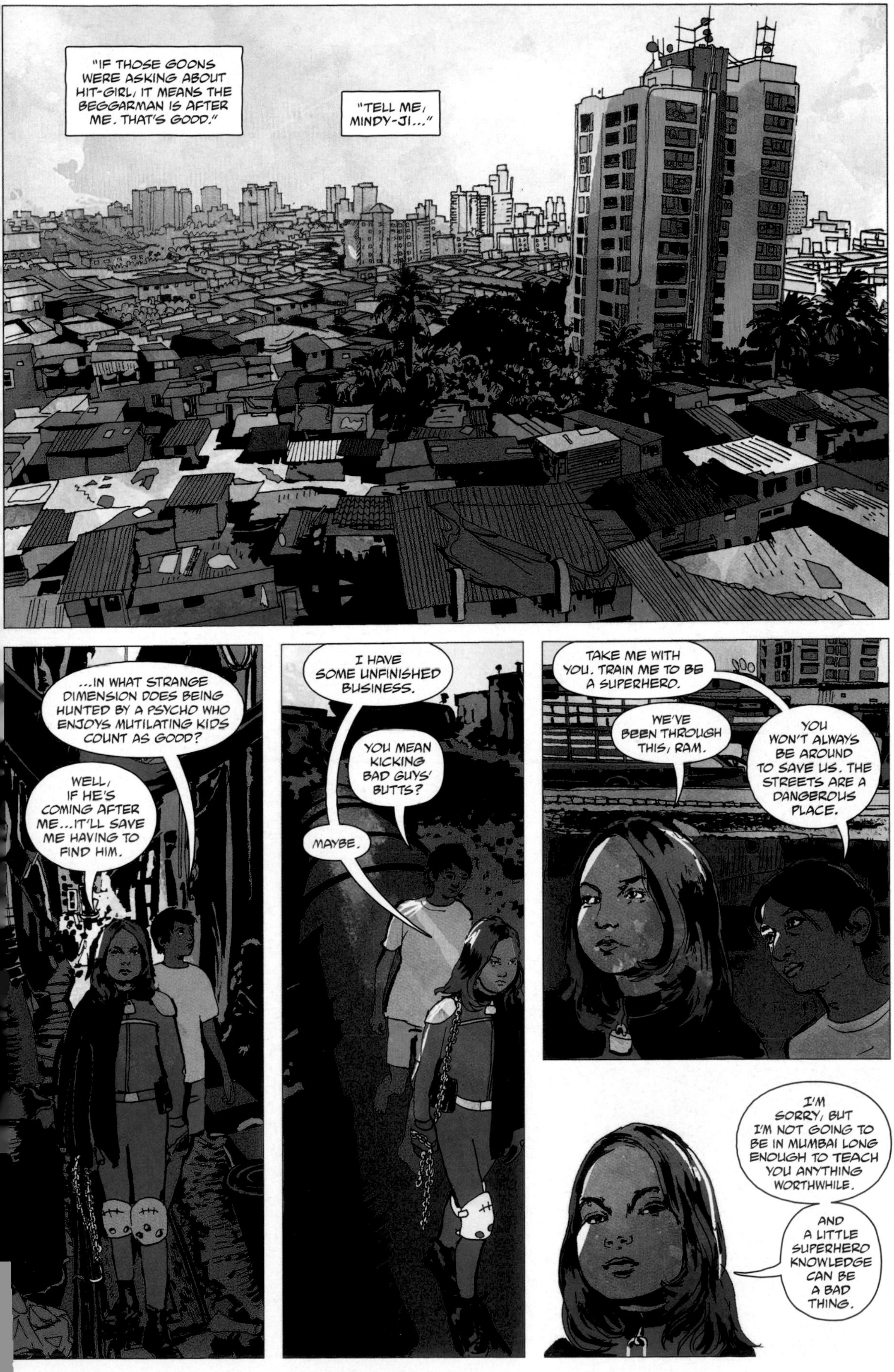
"IF THOSE GOONS WERE ASKING ABOUT HIT-GIRL, IT MEANS THE BEGGARMAN IS AFTER ME. THAT'S GOOD."
"TELL ME, MINDY-JI..."
...IN WHAT STRANGE DIMENSION DOES BEING HUNTED BY A PSYCHO WHO ENJOYS MUTILATING KIDS COUNT AS GOOD?
WELL, IF HE'S COMING AFTER ME...IT'LL SAVE ME HAVING TO FIND HIM.
I HAVE SOME UNFINISHED BUSINESS.
YOU MEAN KICKING BAD GUYS' BUTTS?
MAYBE.
TAKE ME WITH YOU. TRAIN ME TO BE A SUPERHERO.
WE'VE BEEN THROUGH THIS, RAM.
YOU WON'T ALWAYS BE AROUND TO SAVE US. THE STREETS ARE A DANGEROUS PLACE.
I'M SORRY, BUT I'M NOT GOING TO BE IN MUMBAI LONG ENOUGH TO TEACH YOU ANYTHING WORTHWHILE.
AND A LITTLE SUPERHERO KNOWLEDGE CAN BE A BAD THING.

IF I END UP BEING SNATCHED OFF THE STREET AND TURNED INTO A CIRCUS FREAK IT'LL BE YOUR FAULT.

YOU'LL PROBABLY NEVER BE ABLE TO SLEEP AT NIGHT AGAIN.

GOODBYE, MINDY!

RAM! COME BACK HERE! WE CAN STILL BE FRIENDS!

I KNOW I'M RIGHT. TRAINING A SUPERHERO TAKES TIME.

LOOK HOW LONG IT TOOK TO TURN *KICK-ASS* INTO A FORMIDABLE CRIME-FIGHTING MACHINE.

THERE'S A WHOLE WORLD OF EVIL OUT THERE.

AS SOON AS I'VE DEALT WITH THE BEGGARMAN AND THE HIJRA THING, I'LL BE LEAVING MUMBAI.

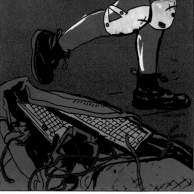

FUCK.

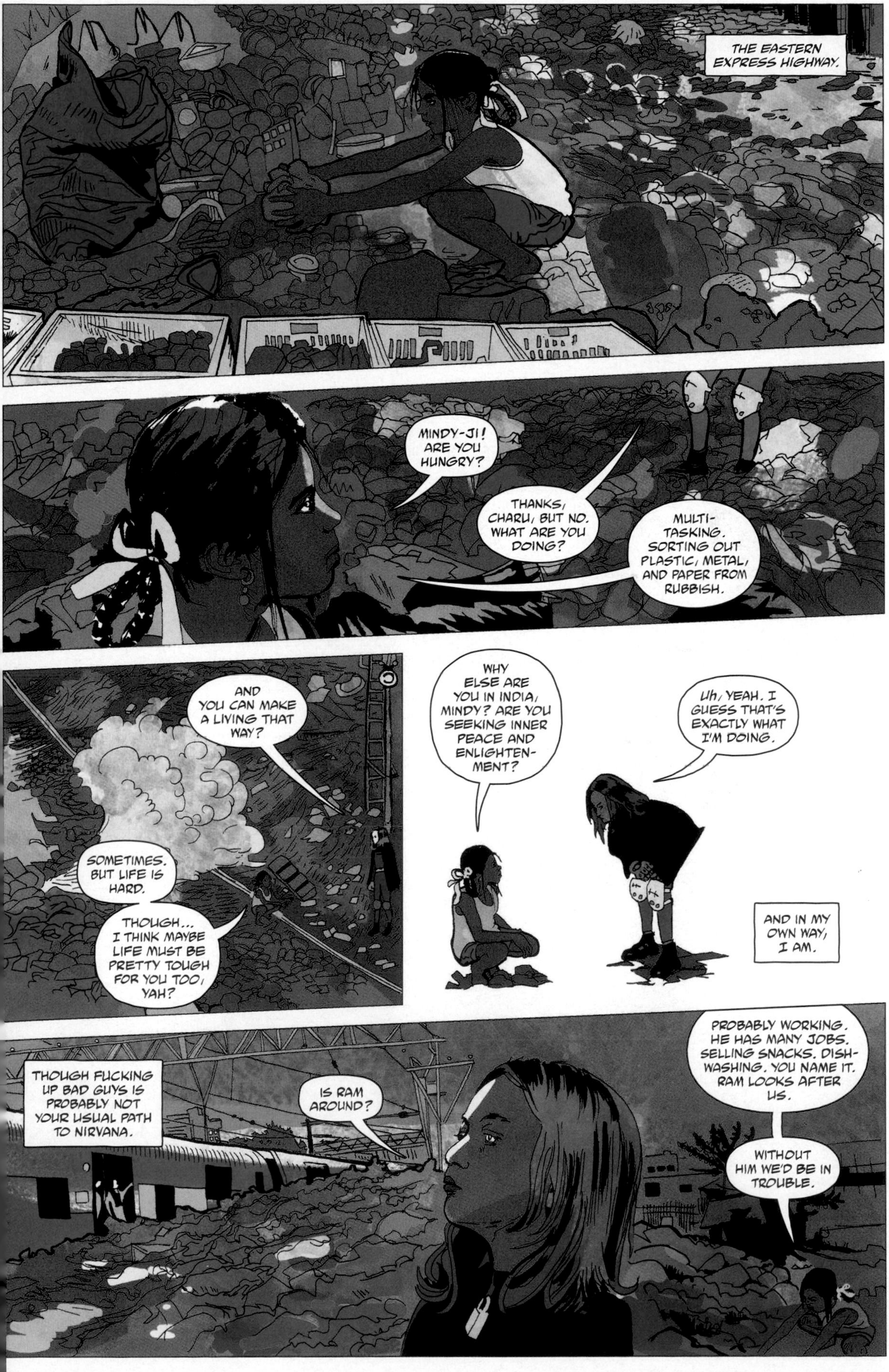
THE EASTERN EXPRESS HIGHWAY.
MINDY-JI! ARE YOU HUNGRY?
THANKS, CHARU, BUT NO. WHAT ARE YOU DOING?
MULTI-TASKING. SORTING OUT PLASTIC, METAL, AND PAPER FROM RUBBISH.
AND YOU CAN MAKE A LIVING THAT WAY?
SOMETIMES. BUT LIFE IS HARD.
THOUGH... I THINK MAYBE LIFE MUST BE PRETTY TOUGH FOR YOU TOO, YAH?
WHY ELSE ARE YOU IN INDIA, MINDY? ARE YOU SEEKING INNER PEACE AND ENLIGHTEN-MENT?
UH, YEAH. I GUESS THAT'S EXACTLY WHAT I'M DOING.
AND IN MY OWN WAY, I AM.
THOUGH FUCKING UP BAD GUYS IS PROBABLY NOT YOUR USUAL PATH TO NIRVANA.
IS RAM AROUND?
PROBABLY WORKING. HE HAS MANY JOBS. SELLING SNACKS. DISH-WASHING. YOU NAME IT. RAM LOOKS AFTER US.
WITHOUT HIM WE'D BE IN TROUBLE.

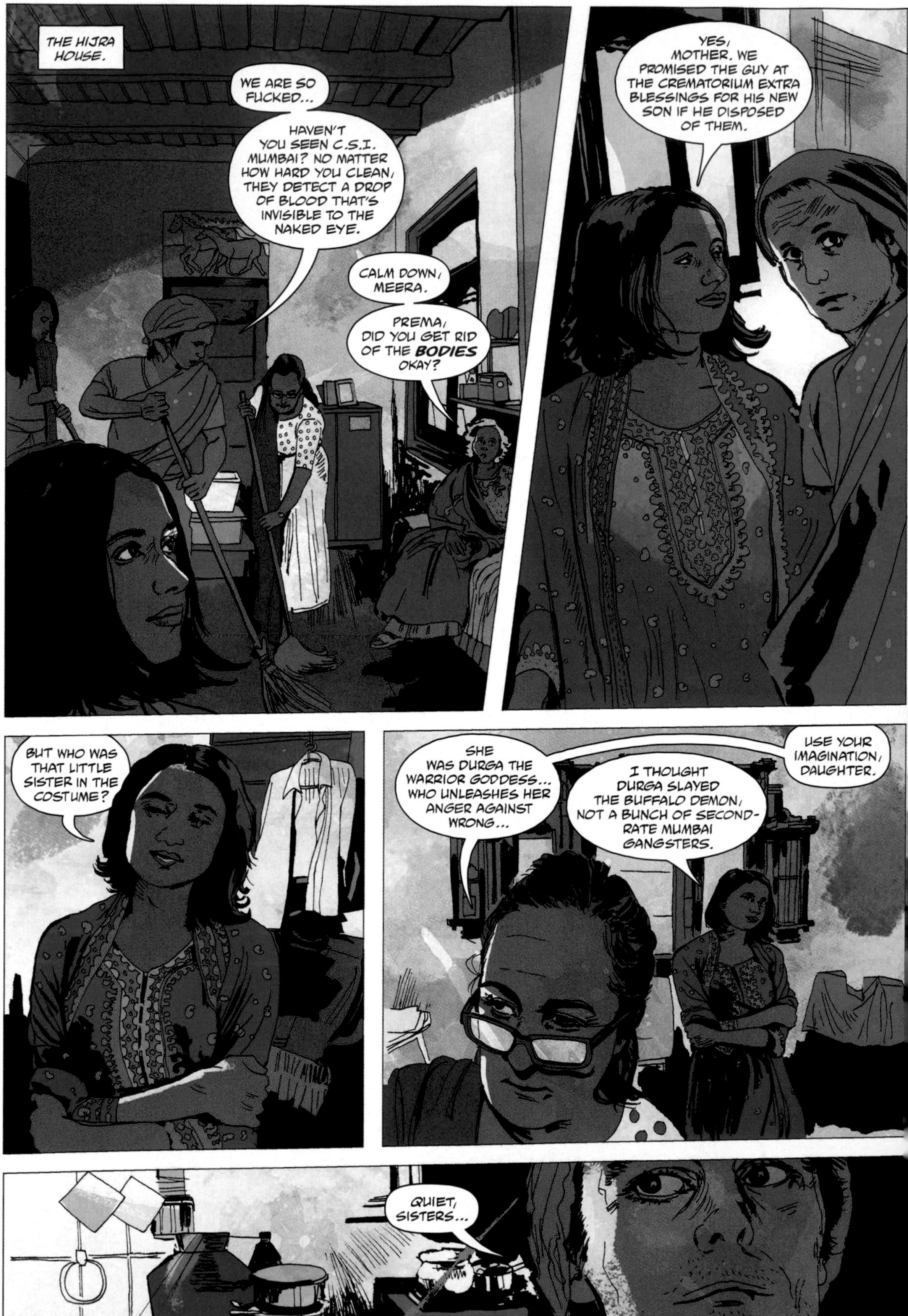
THE HIJRA HOUSE.
WE ARE SO FUCKED...
HAVEN'T YOU SEEN C.S.I. MUMBAI? NO MATTER HOW HARD YOU CLEAN, THEY DETECT A DROP OF BLOOD THAT'S INVISIBLE TO THE NAKED EYE.
CALM DOWN, MEERA.
PREMA, DID YOU GET RID OF THE BODIES OKAY?
YES, MOTHER. WE PROMISED THE GUY AT THE CREMATORIUM EXTRA BLESSINGS FOR HIS NEW SON IF HE DISPOSED OF THEM.
BUT WHO WAS THAT LITTLE SISTER IN THE COSTUME?
SHE WAS DURGA THE WARRIOR GODDESS... WHO UNLEASHES HER ANGER AGAINST WRONG...
I THOUGHT DURGA SLAYED THE BUFFALO DEMON, NOT A BUNCH OF SECOND-RATE MUMBAI GANGSTERS.
USE YOUR IMAGINATION, DAUGHTER.
QUIET, SISTERS...

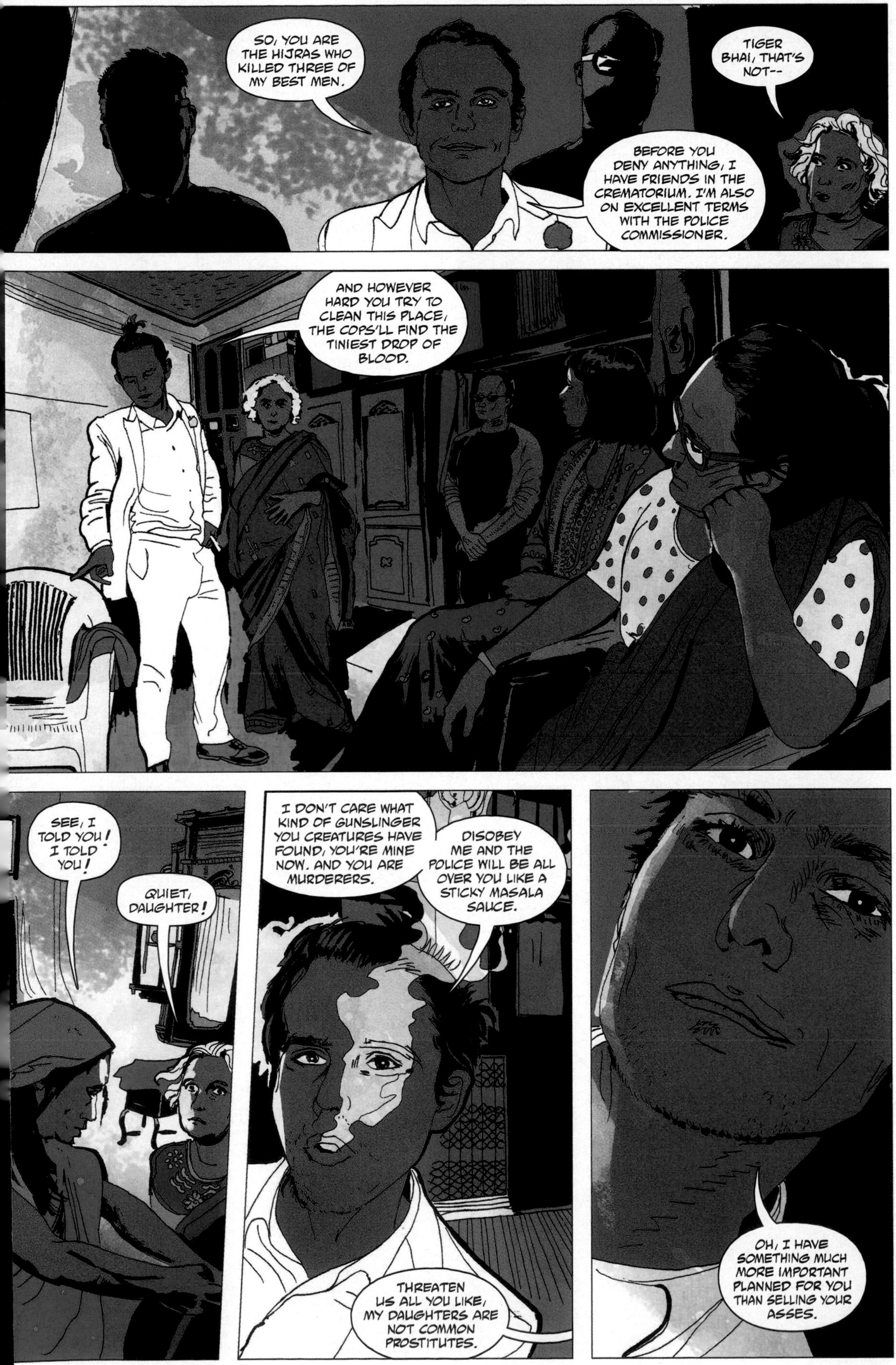
SO, YOU ARE THE HIJRAS WHO KILLED THREE OF MY BEST MEN.
TIGER BHAI, THAT'S NOT--
BEFORE YOU DENY ANYTHING, I HAVE FRIENDS IN THE CREMATORIUM. I'M ALSO ON EXCELLENT TERMS WITH THE POLICE COMMISSIONER.
AND HOWEVER HARD YOU TRY TO CLEAN THIS PLACE, THE COPS'LL FIND THE TINIEST DROP OF BLOOD.
SEE, I TOLD YOU! I TOLD YOU!
QUIET, DAUGHTER!
I DON'T CARE WHAT KIND OF GUNSLINGER YOU CREATURES HAVE FOUND, YOU'RE MINE NOW. AND YOU ARE MURDERERS.
DISOBEY ME AND THE POLICE WILL BE ALL OVER YOU LIKE A STICKY MASALA SAUCE.
THREATEN US ALL YOU LIKE, MY DAUGHTERS ARE NOT COMMON PROSTITUTES.
OH, I HAVE SOMETHING MUCH MORE IMPORTANT PLANNED FOR YOU THAN SELLING YOUR ASSES.

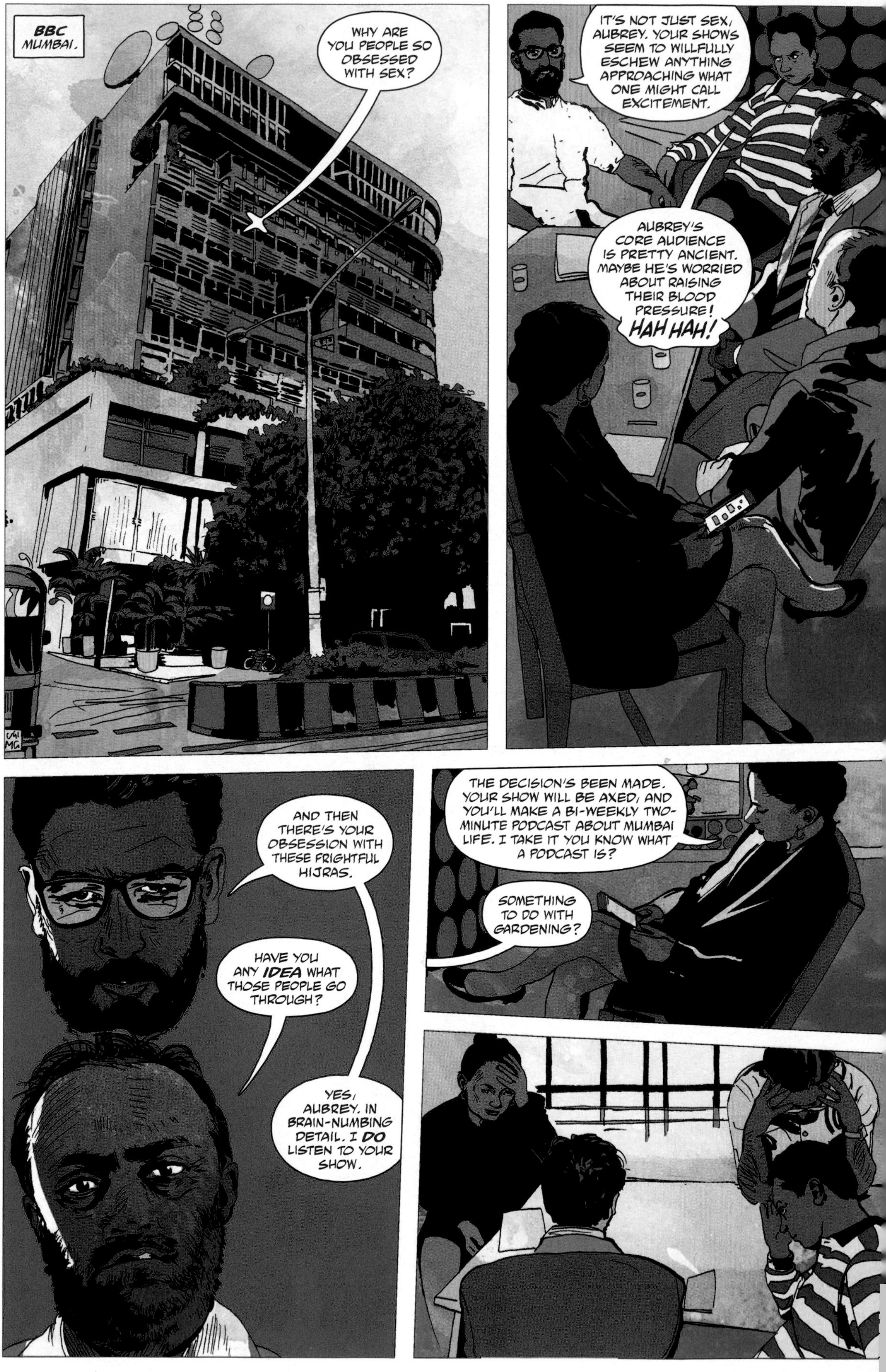
BBC MUMBAI.
WHY ARE YOU PEOPLE SO OBSESSED WITH SEX?
IT'S NOT JUST SEX, AUBREY. YOUR SHOWS SEEM TO WILLFULLY ESCHEW ANYTHING APPROACHING WHAT ONE MIGHT CALL EXCITEMENT.
AUBREY'S CORE AUDIENCE IS PRETTY ANCIENT. MAYBE HE'S WORRIED ABOUT RAISING THEIR BLOOD PRESSURE! HAH HAH!
AND THEN THERE'S YOUR OBSESSION WITH THESE FRIGHTFUL HIJRAS.
HAVE YOU ANY IDEA WHAT THOSE PEOPLE GO THROUGH?
YES, AUBREY. IN BRAIN-NUMBING DETAIL. I DO LISTEN TO YOUR SHOW.
THE DECISION'S BEEN MADE. YOUR SHOW WILL BE AXED, AND YOU'LL MAKE A BI-WEEKLY TWO-MINUTE PODCAST ABOUT MUMBAI LIFE. I TAKE IT YOU KNOW WHAT A PODCAST IS?
SOMETHING TO DO WITH GARDENING?

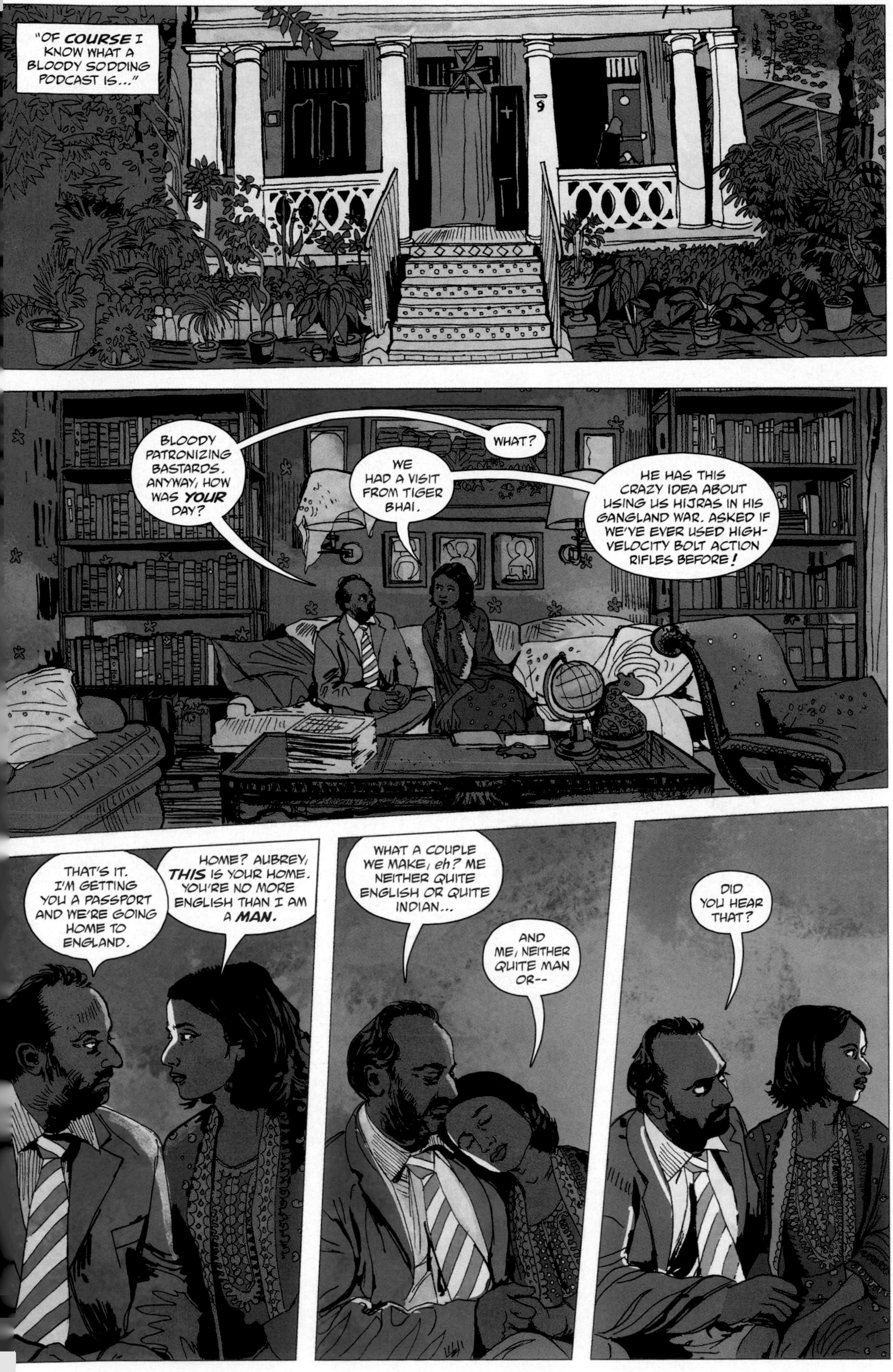
"OF COURSE I KNOW WHAT A BLOODY SODDING PODCAST IS..."
BLOODY PATRONIZING BASTARDS. ANYWAY, HOW WAS YOUR DAY?
WHAT?
WE HAD A VISIT FROM TIGER BHAI.
HE HAS THIS CRAZY IDEA ABOUT USING US HIJRAS IN HIS GANGLAND WAR. ASKED IF WE'VE EVER USED HIGH-VELOCITY BOLT ACTION RIFLES BEFORE!
THAT'S IT. I'M GETTING YOU A PASSPORT AND WE'RE GOING HOME TO ENGLAND.
HOME? AUBREY, THIS IS YOUR HOME. YOU'RE NO MORE ENGLISH THAN I AM A MAN.
WHAT A COUPLE WE MAKE, eh? ME NEITHER QUITE ENGLISH OR QUITE INDIAN...
AND ME, NEITHER QUITE MAN OR--
DID YOU HEAR THAT?

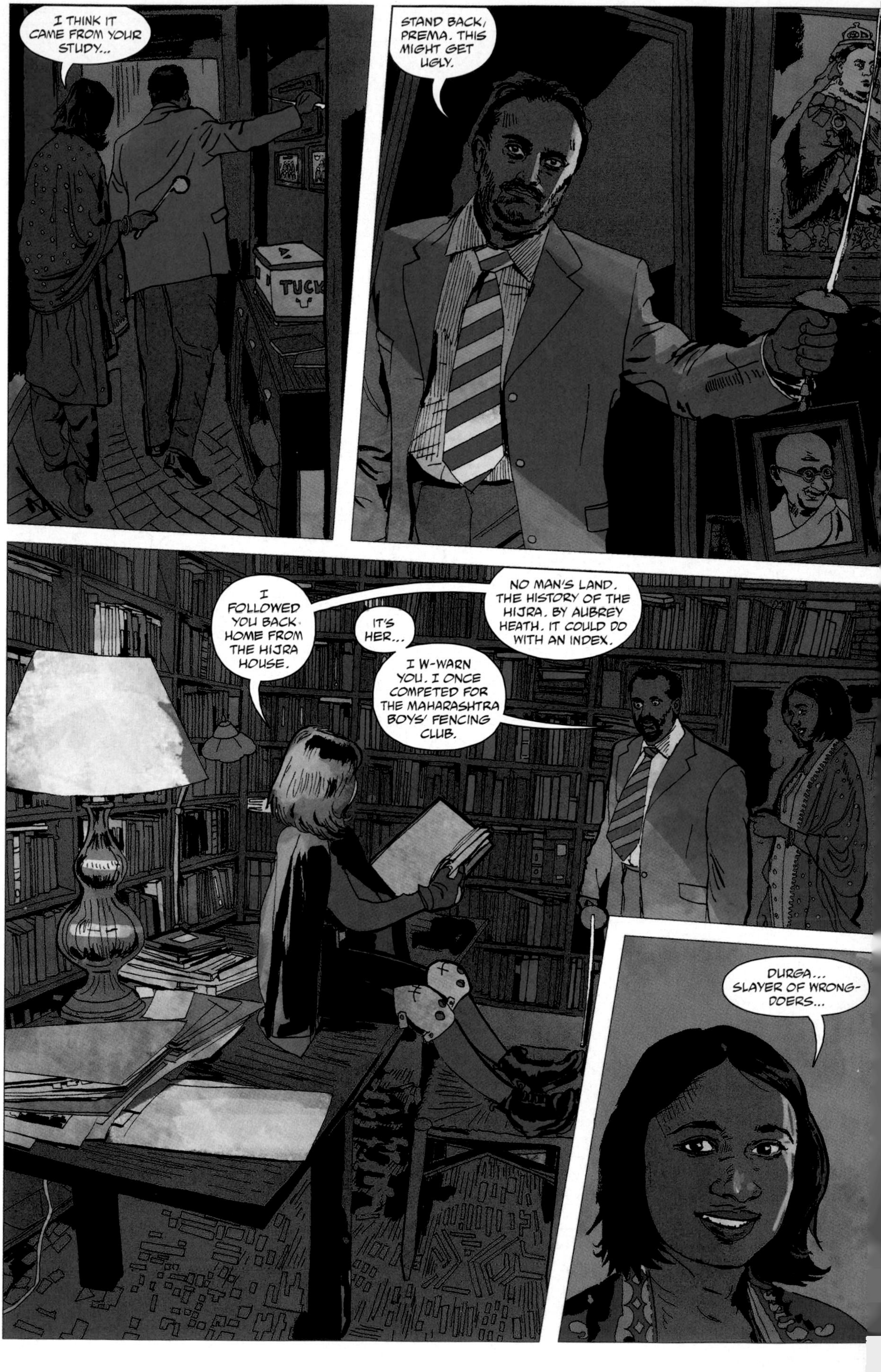
I THINK IT CAME FROM YOUR STUDY...
STAND BACK, PREMA. THIS MIGHT GET UGLY.
TUCK
I FOLLOWED YOU BACK HOME FROM THE HIJRA HOUSE.
NO MAN'S LAND. THE HISTORY OF THE HIJRA. BY AUBREY HEATH. IT COULD DO WITH AN INDEX.
IT'S HER...
I W-WARN YOU. I ONCE COMPETED FOR THE MAHARASHTRA BOYS' FENCING CLUB.
DURGA... SLAYER OF WRONG-DOERS...

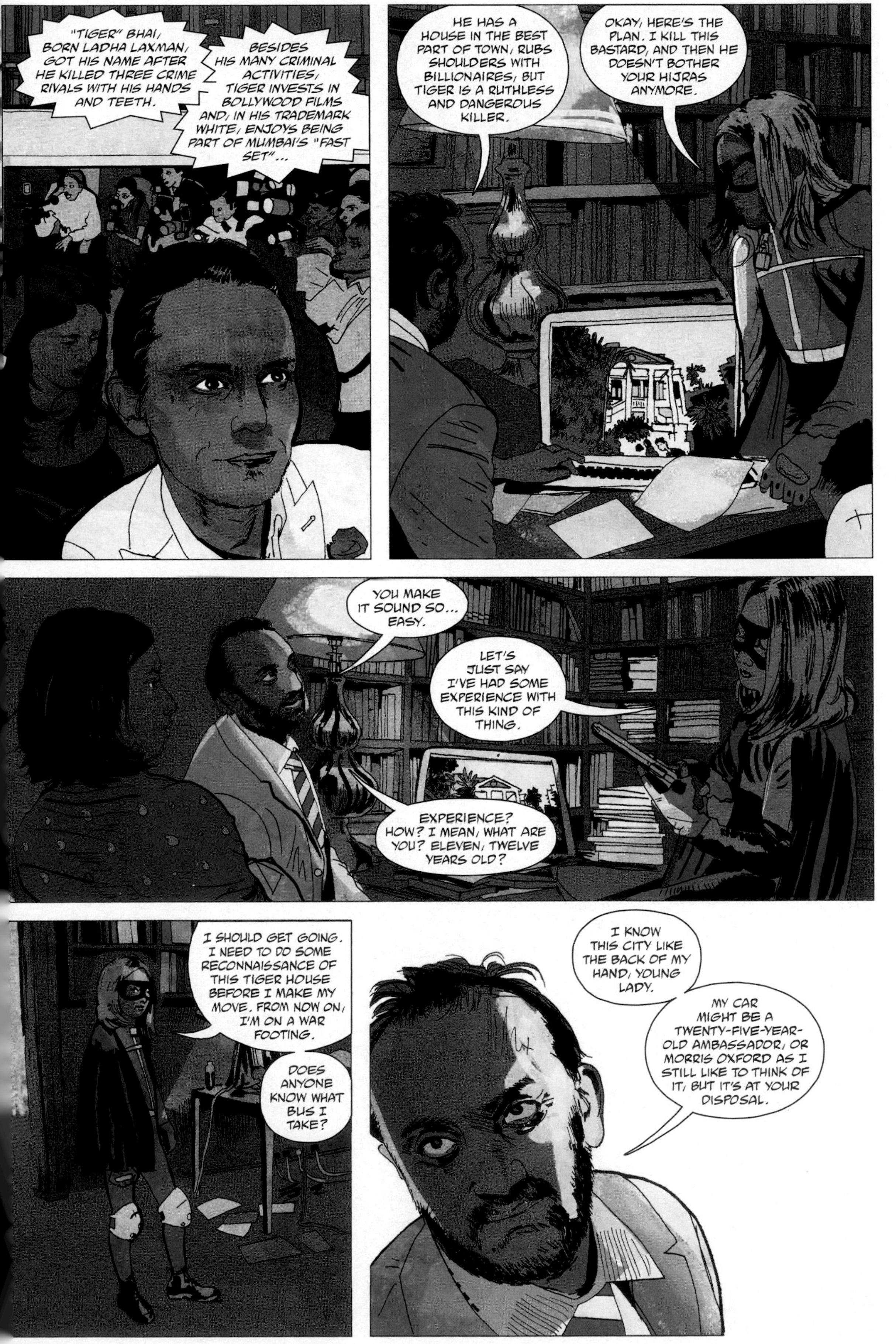
"TIGER" BHAI, BORN LADHA LAXMAN, GOT HIS NAME AFTER HE KILLED THREE CRIME RIVALS WITH HIS HANDS AND TEETH.
BESIDES HIS MANY CRIMINAL ACTIVITIES, TIGER INVESTS IN BOLLYWOOD FILMS AND, IN HIS TRADEMARK WHITE, ENJOYS BEING PART OF MUMBAI'S "FAST SET"...
HE HAS A HOUSE IN THE BEST PART OF TOWN, RUBS SHOULDERS WITH BILLIONAIRES, BUT TIGER IS A RUTHLESS AND DANGEROUS KILLER.
OKAY, HERE'S THE PLAN. I KILL THIS BASTARD, AND THEN HE DOESN'T BOTHER YOUR HIJRAS ANYMORE.
YOU MAKE IT SOUND SO... EASY.
LET'S JUST SAY I'VE HAD SOME EXPERIENCE WITH THIS KIND OF THING.
EXPERIENCE? HOW? I MEAN, WHAT ARE YOU? ELEVEN, TWELVE YEARS OLD?
I SHOULD GET GOING. I NEED TO DO SOME RECONNAISSANCE OF THIS TIGER HOUSE BEFORE I MAKE MY MOVE. FROM NOW ON, I'M ON A WAR FOOTING.
DOES ANYONE KNOW WHAT BUS I TAKE?
I KNOW THIS CITY LIKE THE BACK OF MY HAND, YOUNG LADY.
MY CAR MIGHT BE A TWENTY-FIVE-YEAR-OLD AMBASSADOR, OR MORRIS OXFORD AS I STILL LIKE TO THINK OF IT, BUT IT'S AT YOUR DISPOSAL.

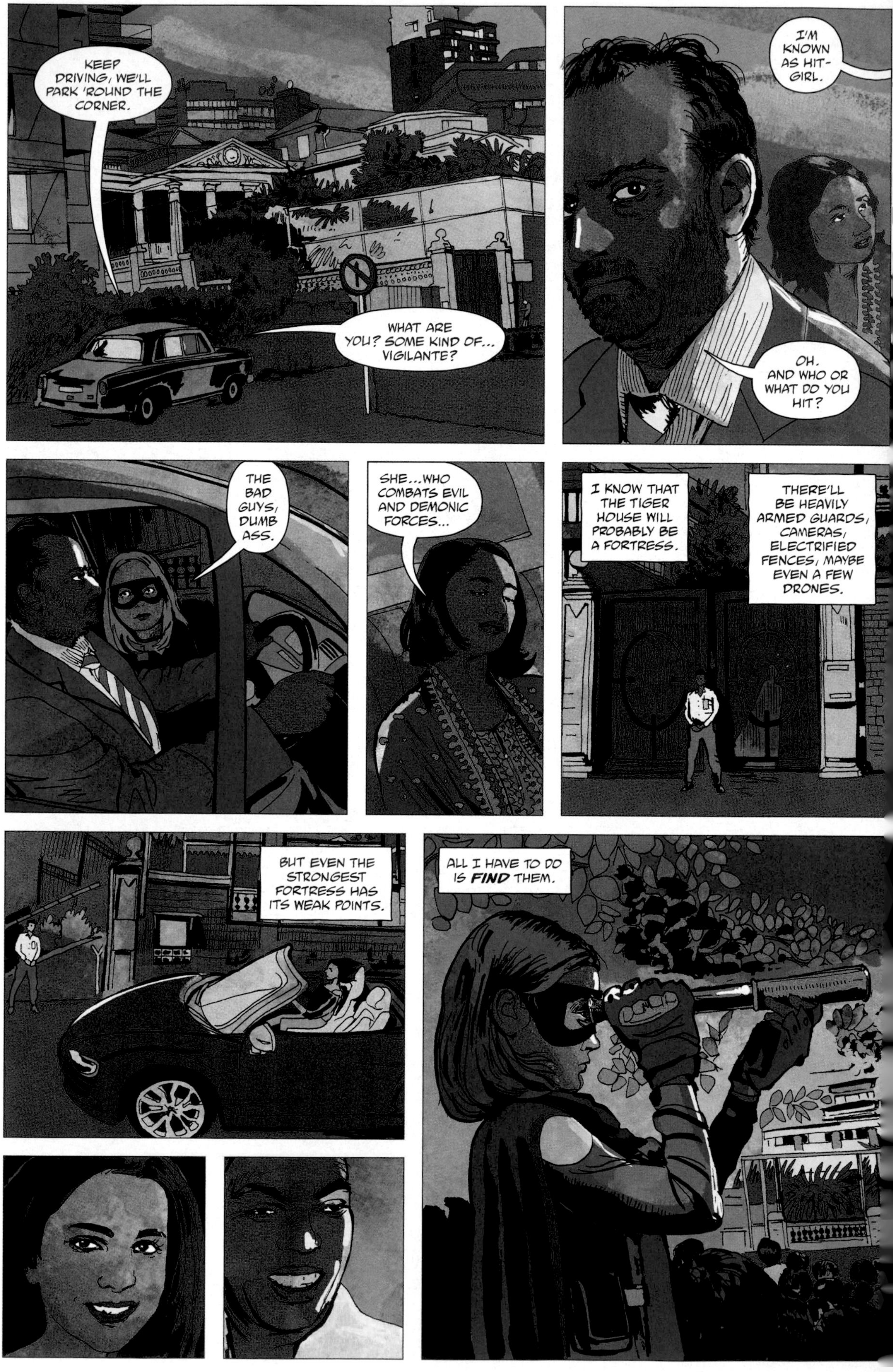
KEEP DRIVING, WE'LL PARK 'ROUND THE CORNER.
WHAT ARE YOU? SOME KIND OF... VIGILANTE?
I'M KNOWN AS HIT-GIRL.
OH. AND WHO OR WHAT DO YOU HIT?
THE BAD GUYS, DUMB ASS.
SHE...WHO COMBATS EVIL AND DEMONIC FORCES...
I KNOW THAT THE TIGER HOUSE WILL PROBABLY BE A FORTRESS.
THERE'LL BE HEAVILY ARMED GUARDS, CAMERAS, ELECTRIFIED FENCES, MAYBE EVEN A FEW DRONES.
BUT EVEN THE STRONGEST FORTRESS HAS ITS WEAK POINTS.
ALL I HAVE TO DO IS FIND THEM.

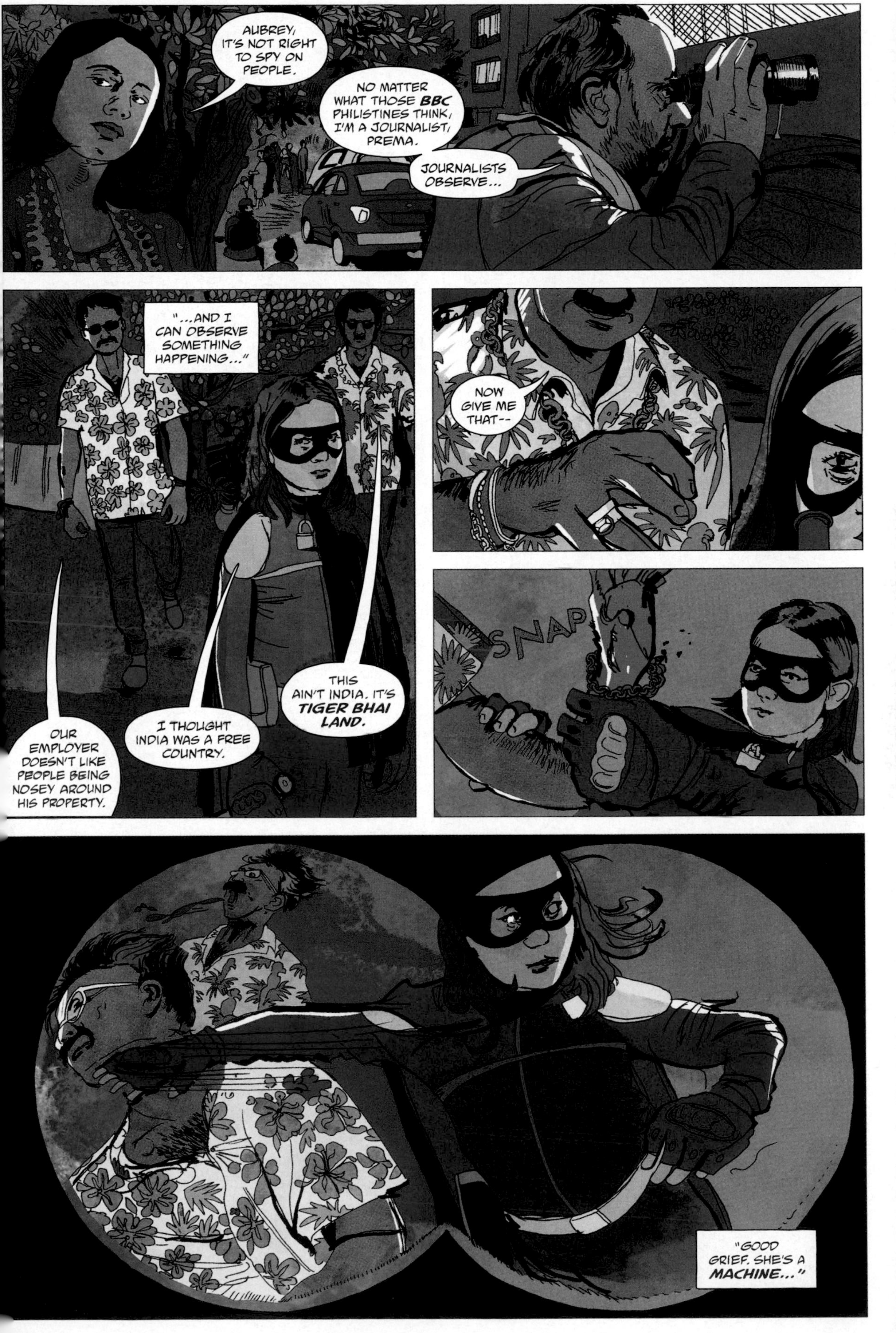
AUBREY, IT'S NOT RIGHT TO SPY ON PEOPLE.
NO MATTER WHAT THOSE BBC PHILISTINES THINK, I'M A JOURNALIST, PREMA.
JOURNALISTS OBSERVE...
"...AND I CAN OBSERVE SOMETHING HAPPENING..."
OUR EMPLOYER DOESN'T LIKE PEOPLE BEING NOSEY AROUND HIS PROPERTY.
I THOUGHT INDIA WAS A FREE COUNTRY.
THIS AIN'T INDIA. IT'S TIGER BHAI LAND.
NOW GIVE ME THAT--
SNAP
"GOOD GRIEF. SHE'S A MACHINE..."

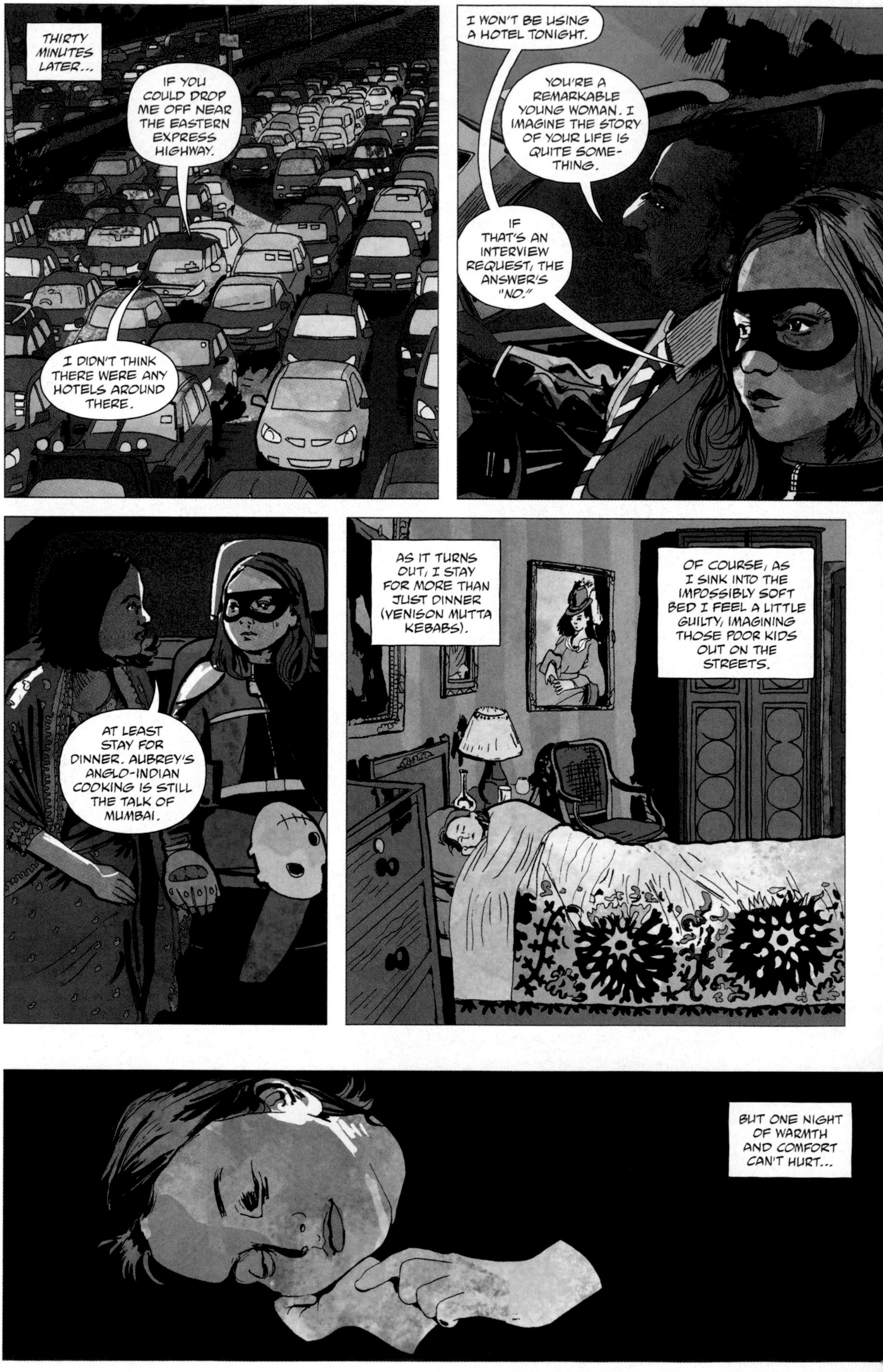
THIRTY MINUTES LATER...
IF YOU COULD DROP ME OFF NEAR THE EASTERN EXPRESS HIGHWAY.
I DIDN'T THINK THERE WERE ANY HOTELS AROUND THERE.
I WON'T BE USING A HOTEL TONIGHT.
YOU'RE A REMARKABLE YOUNG WOMAN. I IMAGINE THE STORY OF YOUR LIFE IS QUITE SOME-THING.
IF THAT'S AN INTERVIEW REQUEST, THE ANSWER'S "NO."
AT LEAST STAY FOR DINNER. AUBREY'S ANGLO-INDIAN COOKING IS STILL THE TALK OF MUMBAI.
AS IT TURNS OUT, I STAY FOR MORE THAN JUST DINNER (VENISON MUTTA KEBABS).
OF COURSE, AS I SINK INTO THE IMPOSSIBLY SOFT BED I FEEL A LITTLE GUILTY, IMAGINING THOSE POOR KIDS OUT ON THE STREETS.
BUT ONE NIGHT OF WARMTH AND COMFORT CAN'T HURT...

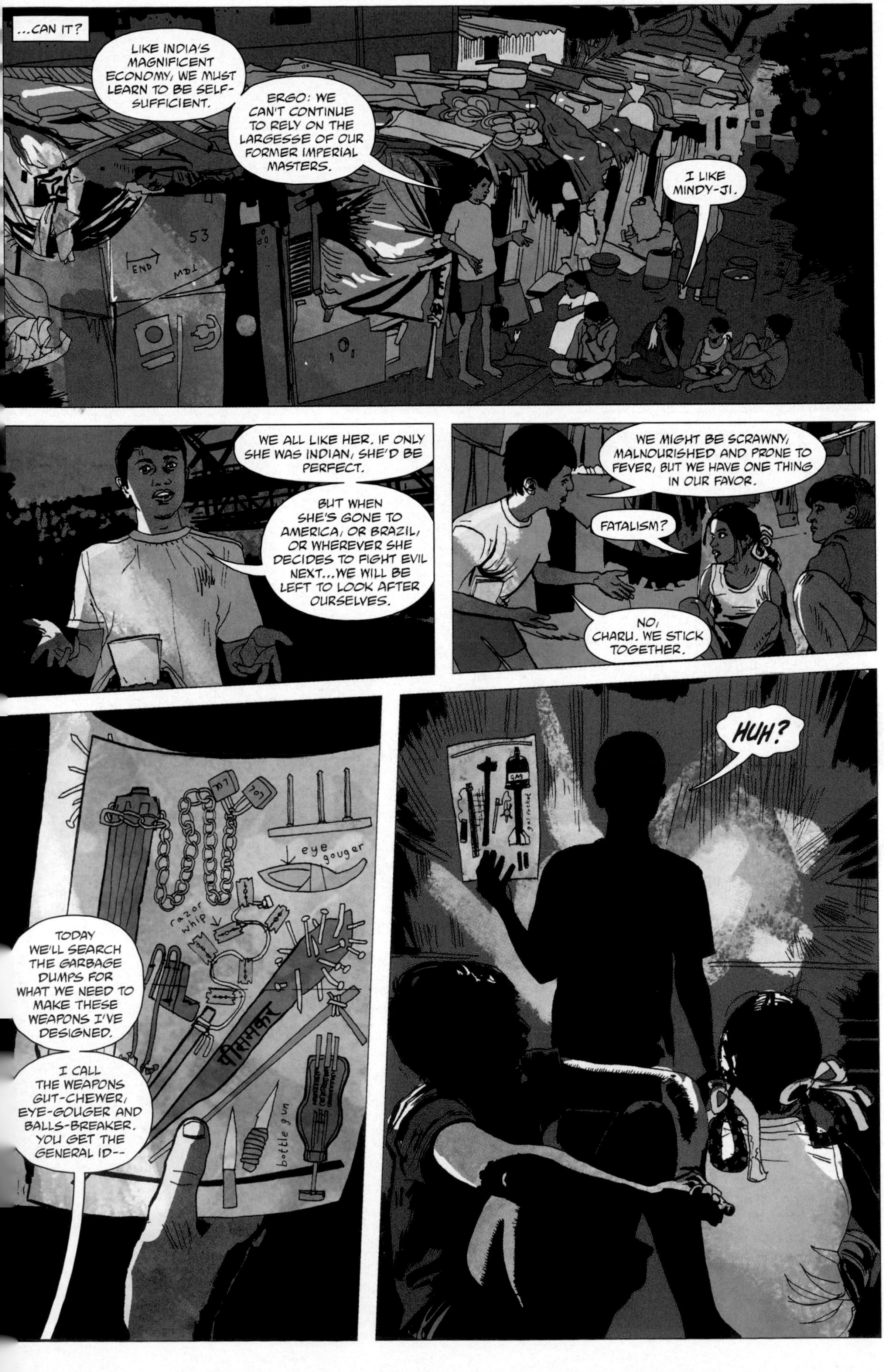
...CAN IT?
LIKE INDIA'S MAGNIFICENT ECONOMY, WE MUST LEARN TO BE SELF-SUFFICIENT.
ERGO: WE CAN'T CONTINUE TO RELY ON THE LARGESSE OF OUR FORMER IMPERIAL MASTERS.
I LIKE MINDY-JI.
WE ALL LIKE HER. IF ONLY SHE WAS INDIAN, SHE'D BE PERFECT.
BUT WHEN SHE'S GONE TO AMERICA, OR BRAZIL, OR WHEREVER SHE DECIDES TO FIGHT EVIL NEXT...WE WILL BE LEFT TO LOOK AFTER OURSELVES.
WE MIGHT BE SCRAWNY, MALNOURISHED AND PRONE TO FEVER, BUT WE HAVE ONE THING IN OUR FAVOR.
FATALISM?
NO, CHARU. WE STICK TOGETHER.
eye gouger
razor whip
bottle gun
TODAY WE'LL SEARCH THE GARBAGE DUMPS FOR WHAT WE NEED TO MAKE THESE WEAPONS I'VE DESIGNED.
I CALL THE WEAPONS GUT-CHEWER, EYE-GOUGER AND BALLS-BREAKER. YOU GET THE GENERAL ID--
HUH?

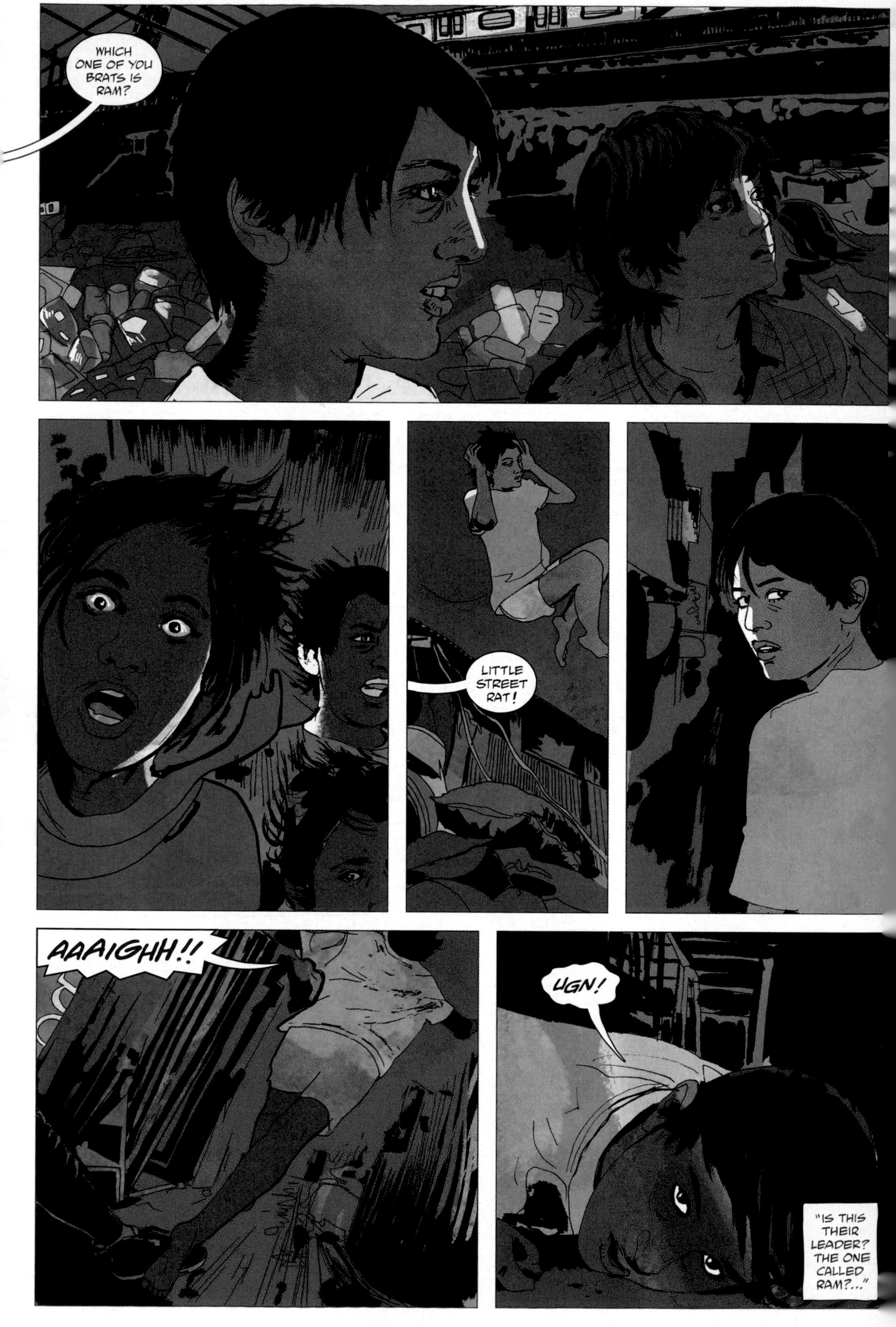

WHICH ONE OF YOU BRATS IS RAM?
LITTLE STREET RAT!
AAAIGHH!!
UGN!
"IS THIS THEIR LEADER? THE ONE CALLED RAM?..."

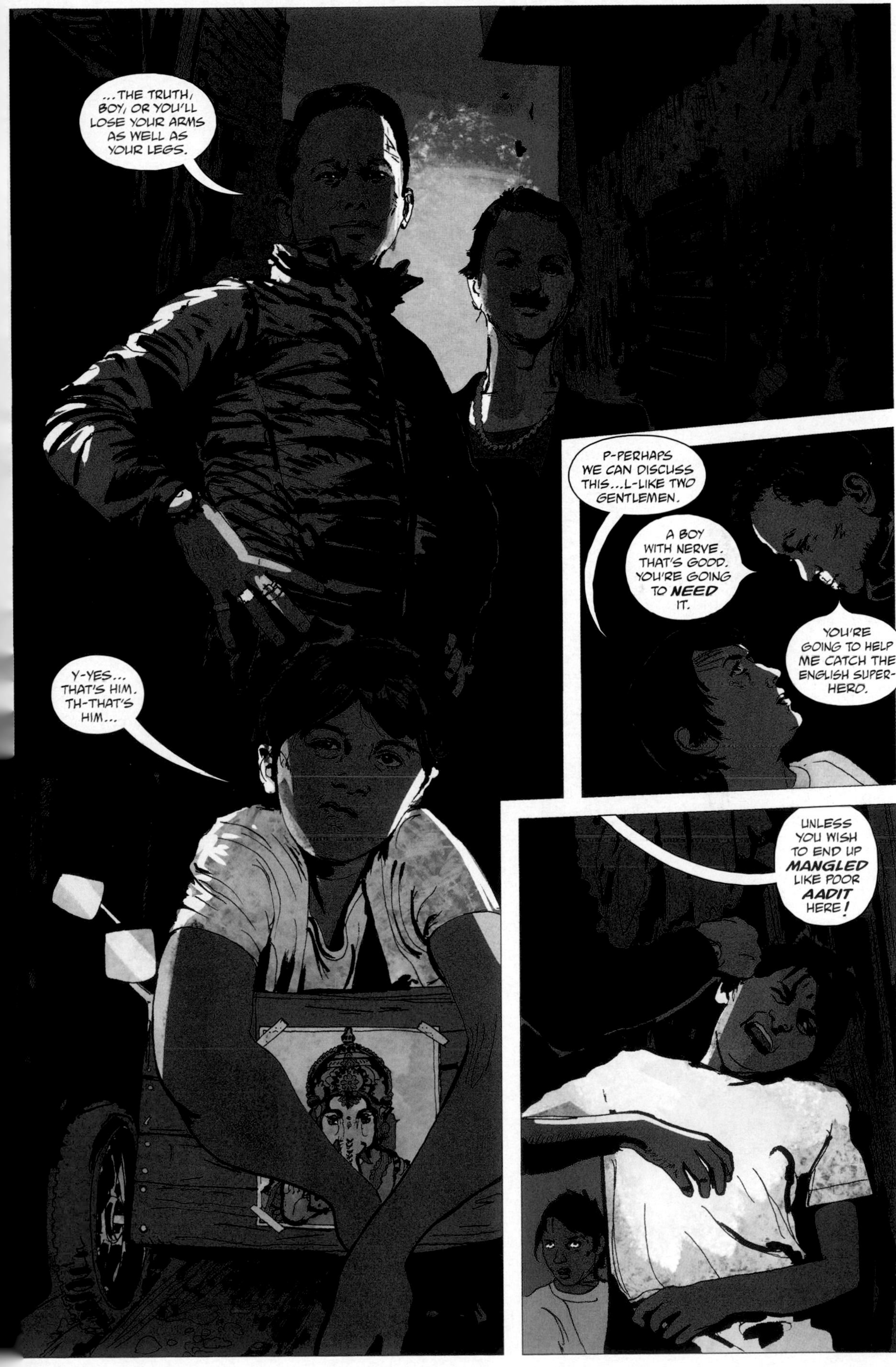
...THE TRUTH, BOY, OR YOU'LL LOSE YOUR ARMS AS WELL AS YOUR LEGS.
Y-YES... THAT'S HIM. TH-THAT'S HIM...
P-PERHAPS WE CAN DISCUSS THIS...L-LIKE TWO GENTLEMEN.
A BOY WITH NERVE. THAT'S GOOD. YOU'RE GOING TO **NEED** IT.
YOU'RE GOING TO HELP ME CATCH THE ENGLISH SUPER-HERO.
UNLESS YOU WISH TO END UP **MANGLED** LIKE POOR **AADIT** HERE!

THREE

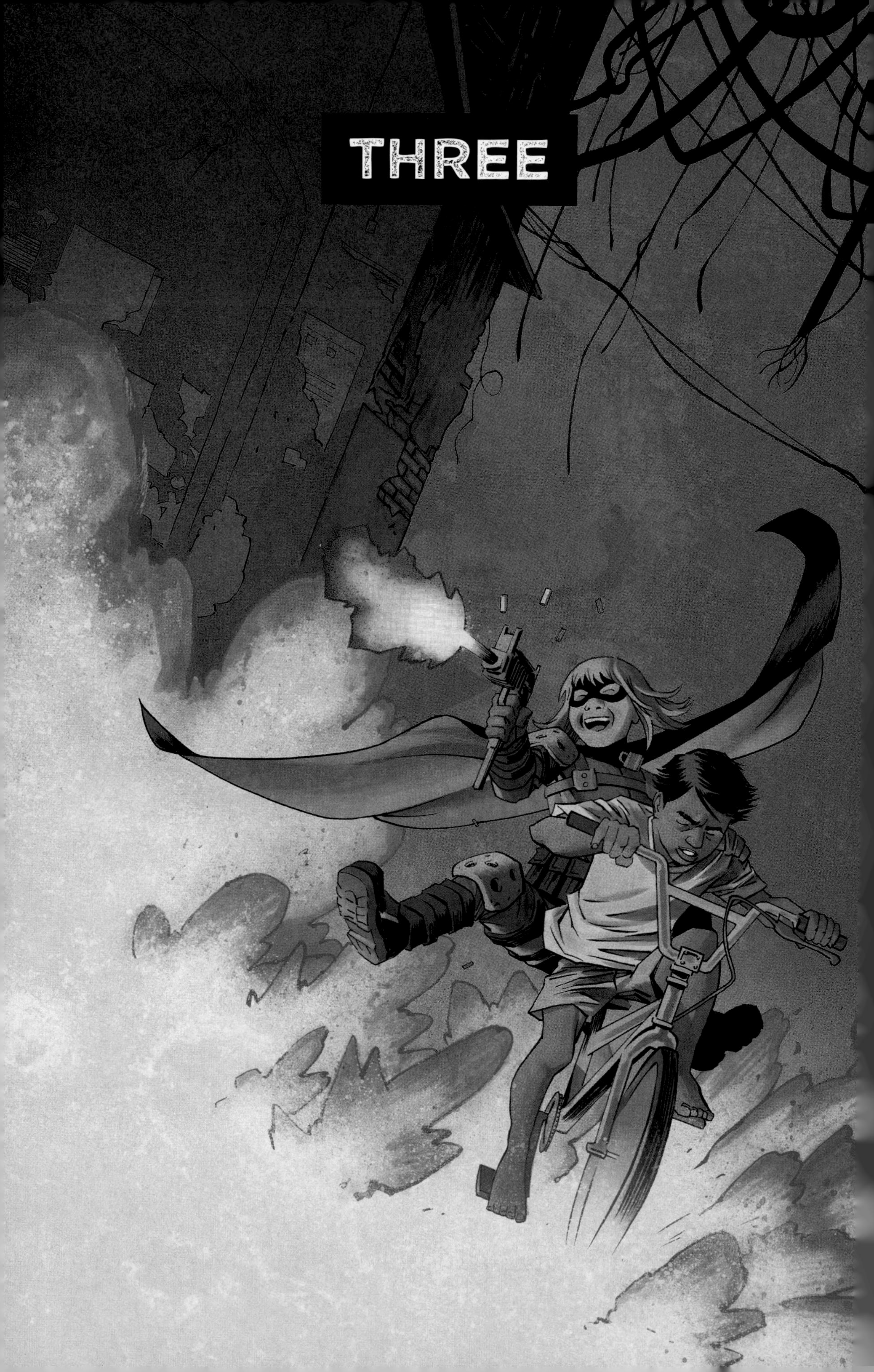

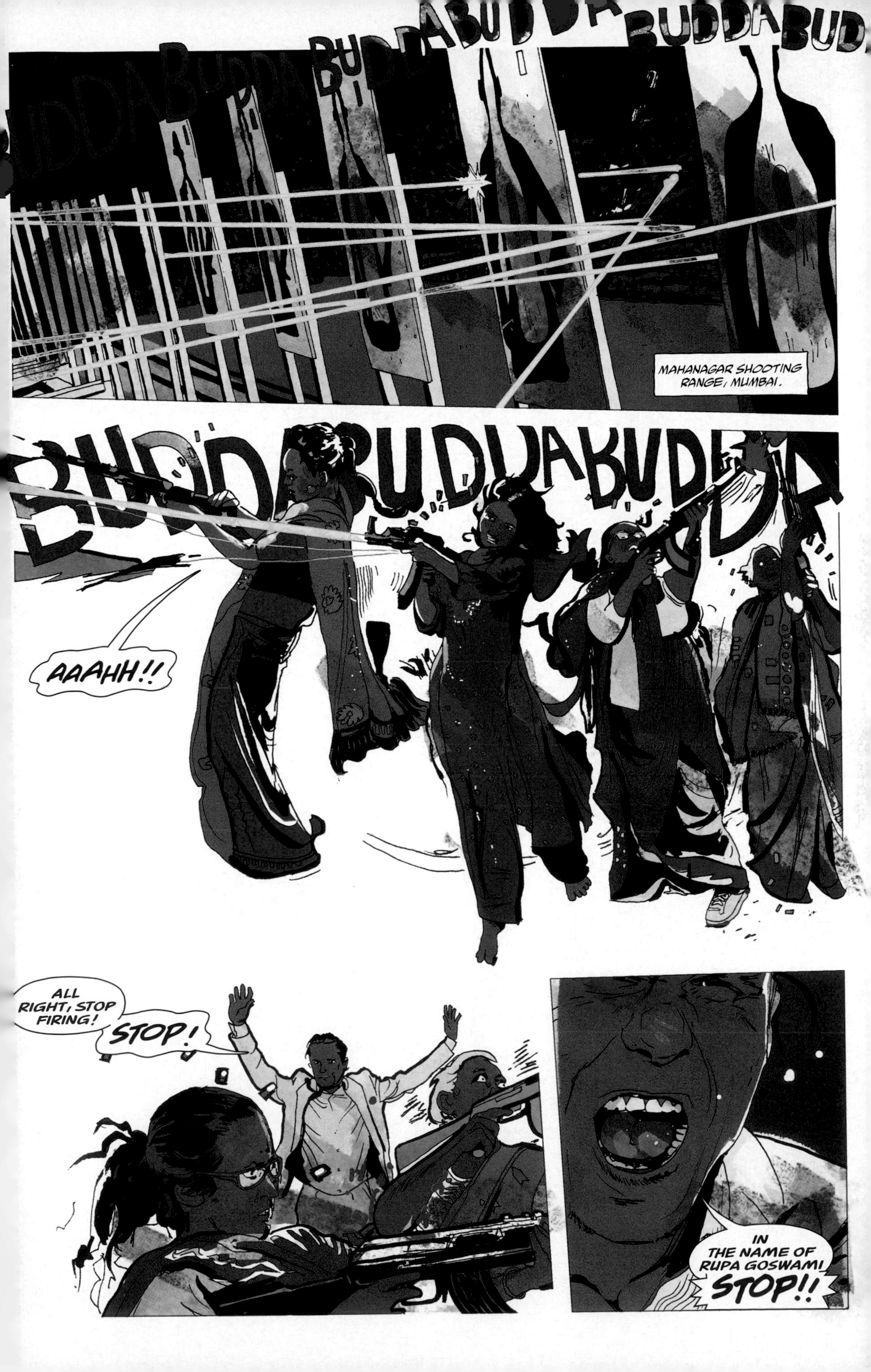
BUDDABUDDABUDDABUDDABUDDABUD
MAHANAGAR SHOOTING RANGE, MUMBAI.
BUDDABUDDABUDDABUDDA
AAAHH!!
ALL RIGHT, STOP FIRING!
STOP!
IN THE NAME OF RUPA GOSWAMI
STOP!!

UGH...OH... TH-THAT WAS LIKE A D-DANCE OF DEATH WITH KALI HERSELF...

Y-YOU ARE RIGHT, MOTHER. WE HIJRA ARE SPIRITUAL BEINGS UNSUITED FOR SUCH VIOLENT ACTION...

M-MY FUCKING SHOULDER'S POPPED RIGHT OUT OF ITS SOCKET.

YOU EACH GOT THROUGH A MAGAZINE. THAT'S THIRTY ROUNDS EACH. IN ALL, THAT'S ONE HUNDRED AND TWENTY ROUNDS OF SEMI-AUTOMATIC GUNFIRE.

AND IF THIS WAS A REAL-LIFE SCENARIO, YOU WOULD HAVE GRAZED THE RIGHT EAR OF **ONE** OF YOUR TARGETS. WELL DONE.

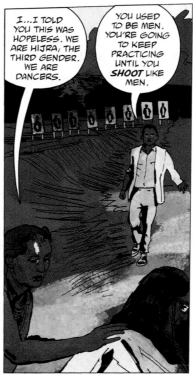

I...I TOLD YOU THIS WAS HOPELESS. WE ARE HIJRA, THE THIRD GENDER. WE ARE DANCERS.

YOU USED TO BE MEN. YOU'RE GOING TO KEEP PRACTICING UNTIL YOU **SHOOT** LIKE MEN.

THERE'S A WEDDING IN TWO DAYS THAT MOST OF MY ENEMIES WILL BE ATTENDING.

HALFWAY THROUGH YOUR DANCE TO BLESS THE GROOM'S VIRILITY, YOU'LL PROVE YOUR **OWN** VIRILITY BY WHIPPING OUT YOUR WEAPONS AND SHOOTING.

TAKE COURAGE, MEERA. ALL IS NOT LOST.

ISN'T IT? WE'LL BE SHOT TO PIECES, YOU KNOW THAT. ONLY GOD CAN SAVE US.

GOD. OR PERHAPS...SOME-ONE **SENT** BY GOD...

BEFORE I DO ANYTHING, I'M GONNA NEED TO TOOL UP.

I DON'T HAVE ANY CONTACTS IN MUMBAI, BUT THERE ARE SOME PLACES WHERE YOU CAN ALWAYS FIND HARDWARE.

A GOOD START.

BUT FOR WHAT I'VE GOT PLANNED, I'M GOING TO NEED A *HIGHER GRADE* OF HARDWARE.

AND FOR THAT, I'M GOING TO NEED A HIGHER GRADE OF *SCUMBAG.*

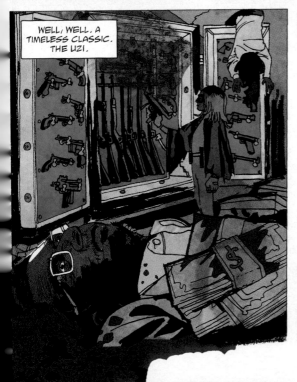

WELL, WELL. A TIMELESS CLASSIC. THE UZI.

LIMITED RANGE AND ACCURACY, AND REALLY ONLY GOOD FOR FULL AUTO-FIRE.

BUT I'LL MAKE DO.

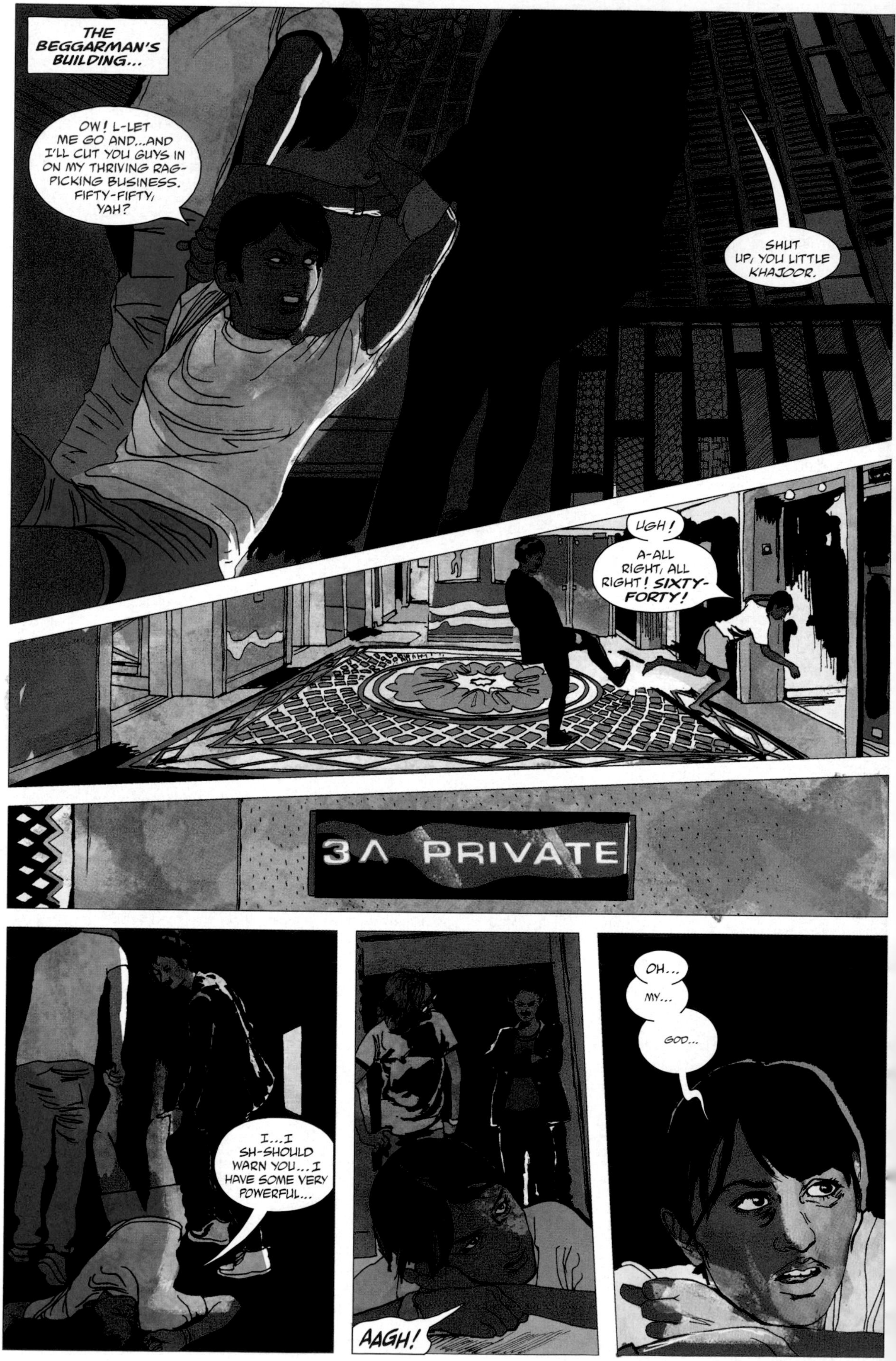
THE BEGGARMAN'S BUILDING...
OW! L-LET ME GO AND...AND I'LL CUT YOU GUYS IN ON MY THRIVING RAG-PICKING BUSINESS. FIFTY-FIFTY, YAH?
SHUT UP, YOU LITTLE KHAJOOR.
UGH!
A-ALL RIGHT, ALL RIGHT! SIXTY-FORTY!
3A PRIVATE
I...I SH-SHOULD WARN YOU...I HAVE SOME VERY POWERFUL...
AAGH!
OH...
MY...
GOD...

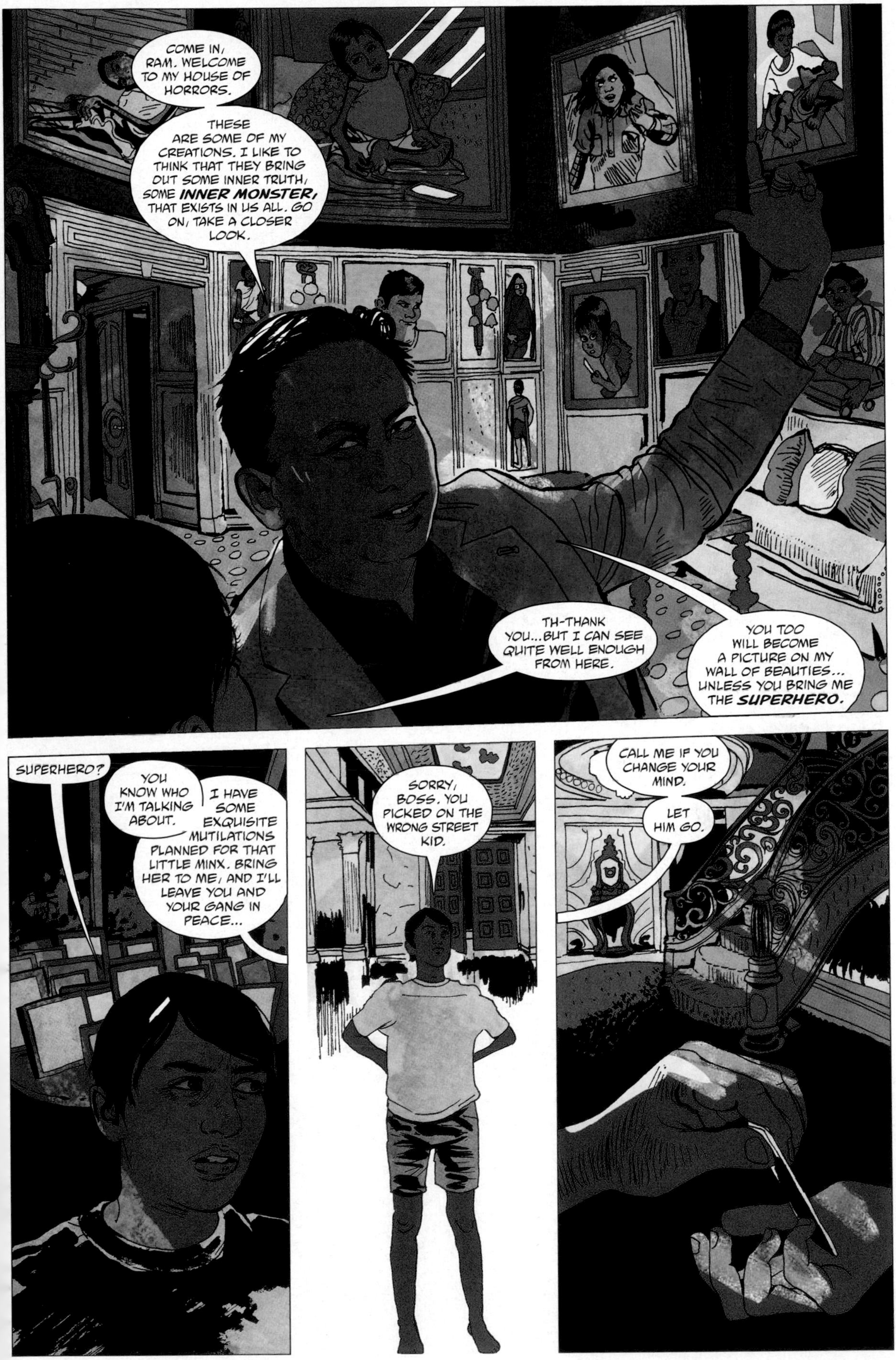
COME IN, RAM. WELCOME TO MY HOUSE OF HORRORS.
THESE ARE SOME OF MY CREATIONS. I LIKE TO THINK THAT THEY BRING OUT SOME INNER TRUTH, SOME INNER MONSTER, THAT EXISTS IN US ALL. GO ON, TAKE A CLOSER LOOK.
TH-THANK YOU...BUT I CAN SEE QUITE WELL ENOUGH FROM HERE.
YOU TOO WILL BECOME A PICTURE ON MY WALL OF BEAUTIES... UNLESS YOU BRING ME THE SUPERHERO.
SUPERHERO?
YOU KNOW WHO I'M TALKING ABOUT.
I HAVE SOME EXQUISITE MUTILATIONS PLANNED FOR THAT LITTLE MINX. BRING HER TO ME, AND I'LL LEAVE YOU AND YOUR GANG IN PEACE...
SORRY, BOSS. YOU PICKED ON THE WRONG STREET KID.
CALL ME IF YOU CHANGE YOUR MIND.
LET HIM GO.

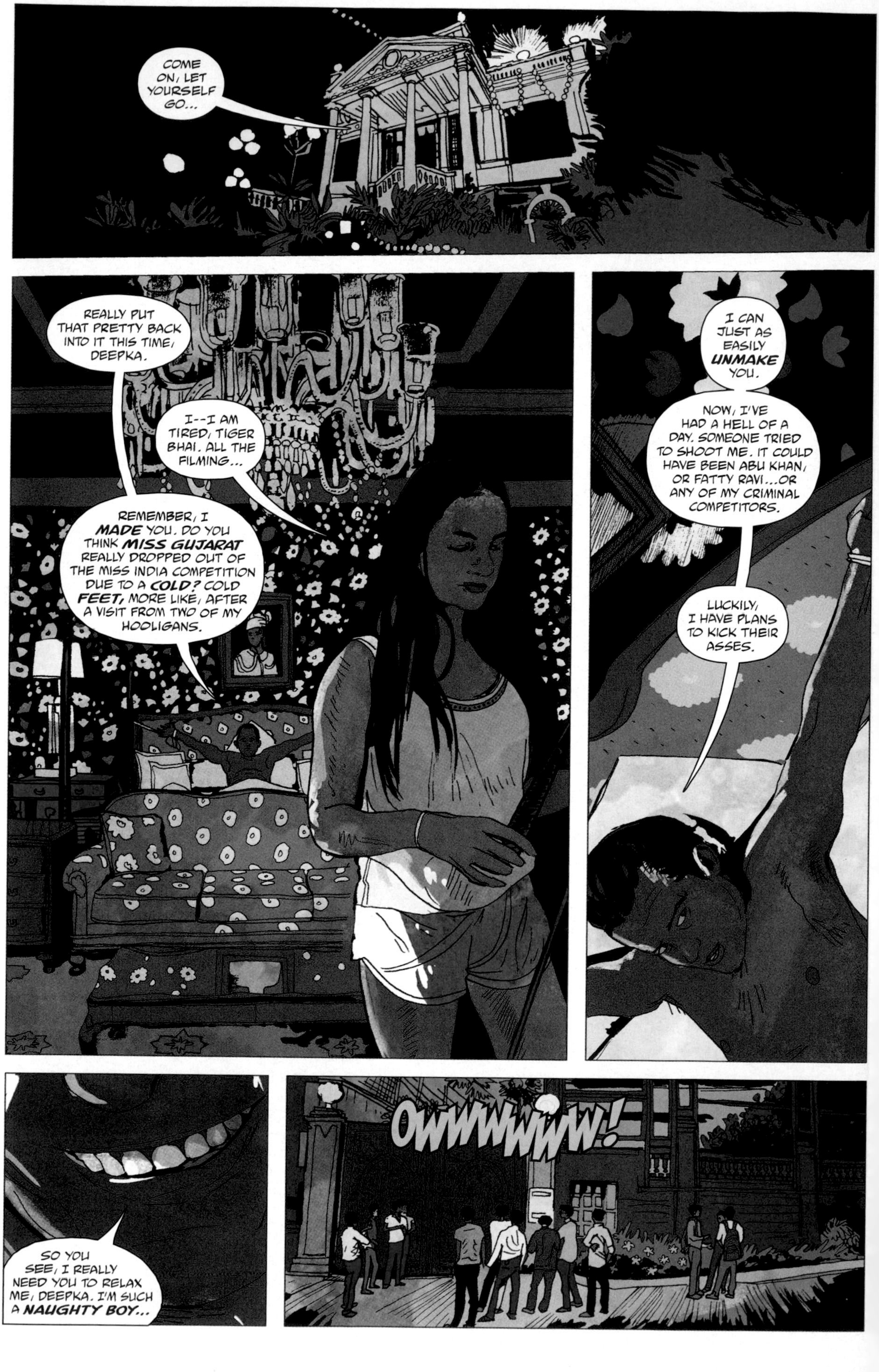
COME ON, LET YOURSELF GO...
REALLY PUT THAT PRETTY BACK INTO IT THIS TIME, DEEPKA.
I--I AM TIRED, TIGER BHAI. ALL THE FILMING...
REMEMBER, I MADE YOU. DO YOU THINK MISS GUJARAT REALLY DROPPED OUT OF THE MISS INDIA COMPETITION DUE TO A COLD? COLD FEET, MORE LIKE, AFTER A VISIT FROM TWO OF MY HOOLIGANS.
I CAN JUST AS EASILY UNMAKE YOU.
NOW, I'VE HAD A HELL OF A DAY. SOMEONE TRIED TO SHOOT ME. IT COULD HAVE BEEN ABU KHAN, OR FATTY RAVI...OR ANY OF MY CRIMINAL COMPETITORS.
LUCKILY, I HAVE PLANS TO KICK THEIR ASSES.
SO YOU SEE, I REALLY NEED YOU TO RELAX ME, DEEPKA. I'M SUCH A NAUGHTY BOY...
OWWWWWW!

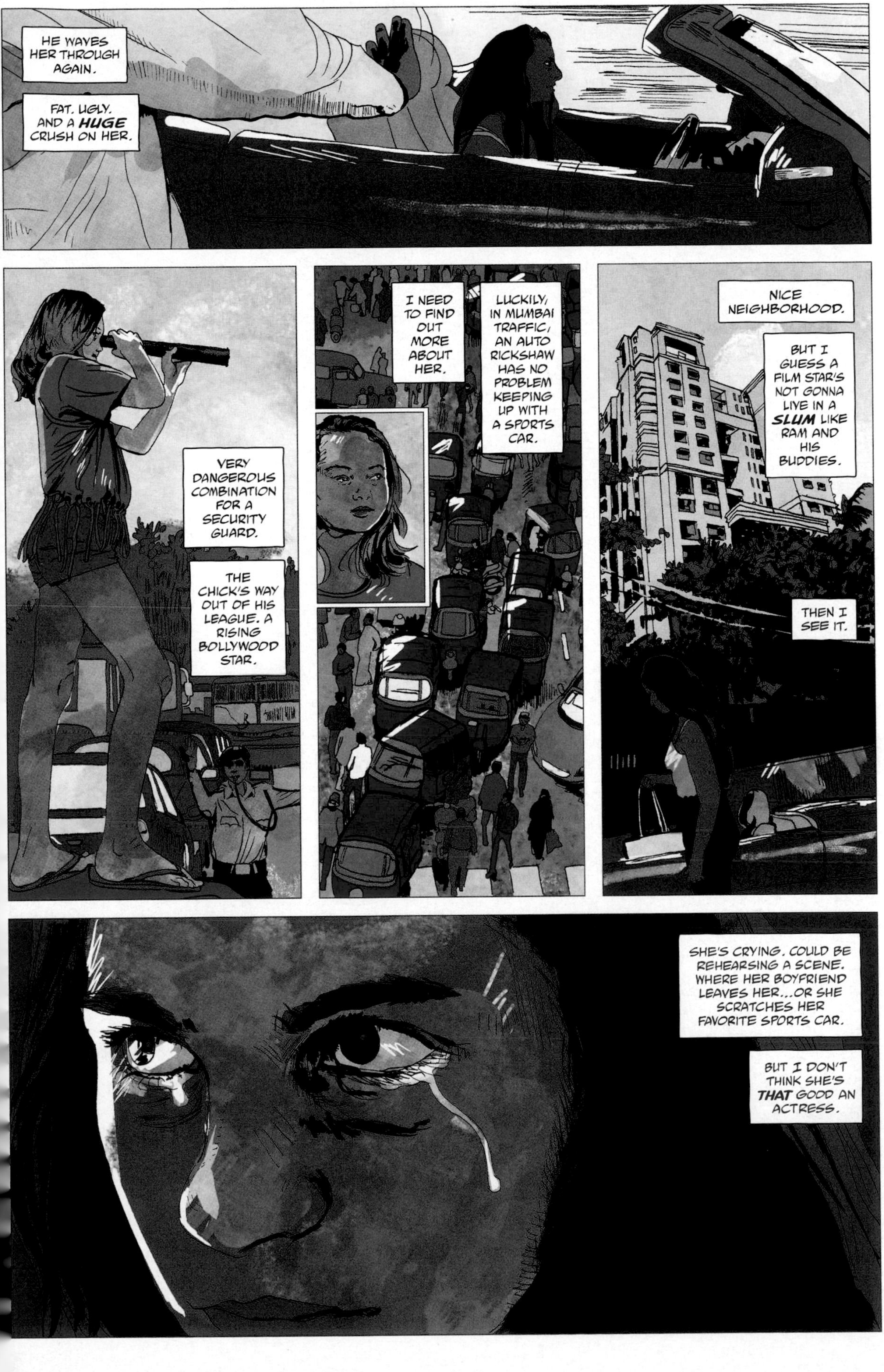
HE WAVES HER THROUGH AGAIN.
FAT. UGLY. AND A **HUGE** CRUSH ON HER.
VERY DANGEROUS COMBINATION FOR A SECURITY GUARD.
THE CHICK'S WAY OUT OF HIS LEAGUE. A RISING BOLLYWOOD STAR.
I NEED TO FIND OUT MORE ABOUT HER.
LUCKILY, IN MUMBAI TRAFFIC, AN AUTO RICKSHAW HAS NO PROBLEM KEEPING UP WITH A SPORTS CAR.
NICE NEIGHBORHOOD.
BUT I GUESS A FILM STAR'S NOT GONNA LIVE IN A **SLUM** LIKE RAM AND HIS BUDDIES.
THEN I SEE IT.
SHE'S CRYING. COULD BE REHEARSING A SCENE. WHERE HER BOYFRIEND LEAVES HER...OR SHE SCRATCHES HER FAVORITE SPORTS CAR.
BUT I DON'T THINK SHE'S **THAT** GOOD AN ACTRESS.

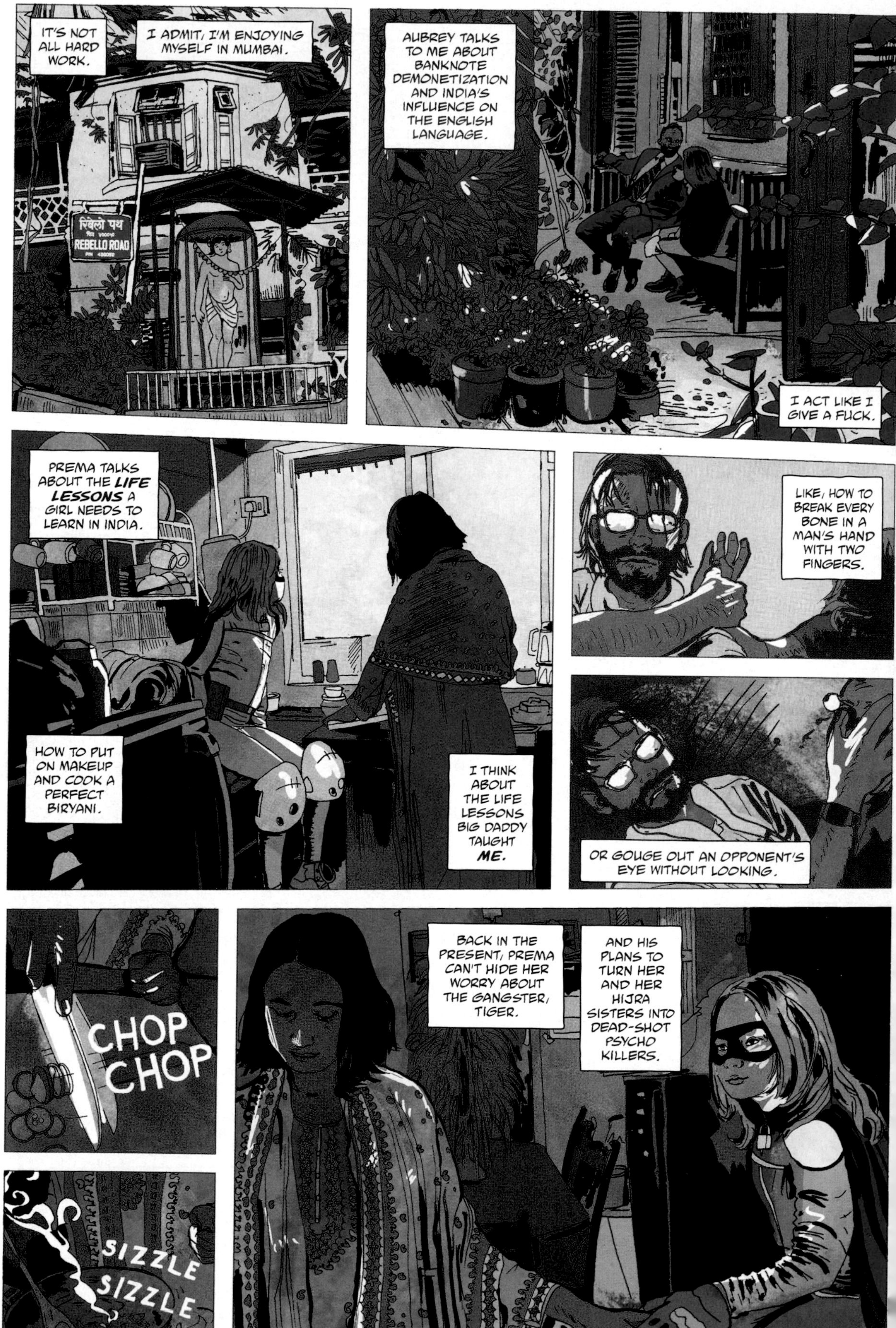
IT'S NOT ALL HARD WORK.
I ADMIT, I'M ENJOYING MYSELF IN MUMBAI.
रिबेलो पथ
REBELLO ROAD
AUBREY TALKS TO ME ABOUT BANKNOTE DEMONETIZATION AND INDIA'S INFLUENCE ON THE ENGLISH LANGUAGE.
I ACT LIKE I GIVE A FUCK.
PREMA TALKS ABOUT THE LIFE LESSONS A GIRL NEEDS TO LEARN IN INDIA.
HOW TO PUT ON MAKEUP AND COOK A PERFECT BIRYANI.
I THINK ABOUT THE LIFE LESSONS BIG DADDY TAUGHT ME.
LIKE, HOW TO BREAK EVERY BONE IN A MAN'S HAND WITH TWO FINGERS.
OR GOUGE OUT AN OPPONENT'S EYE WITHOUT LOOKING.
CHOP CHOP
SIZZLE SIZZLE
BACK IN THE PRESENT, PREMA CAN'T HIDE HER WORRY ABOUT THE GANGSTER, TIGER.
AND HIS PLANS TO TURN HER AND HER HIJRA SISTERS INTO DEAD-SHOT PSYCHO KILLERS.

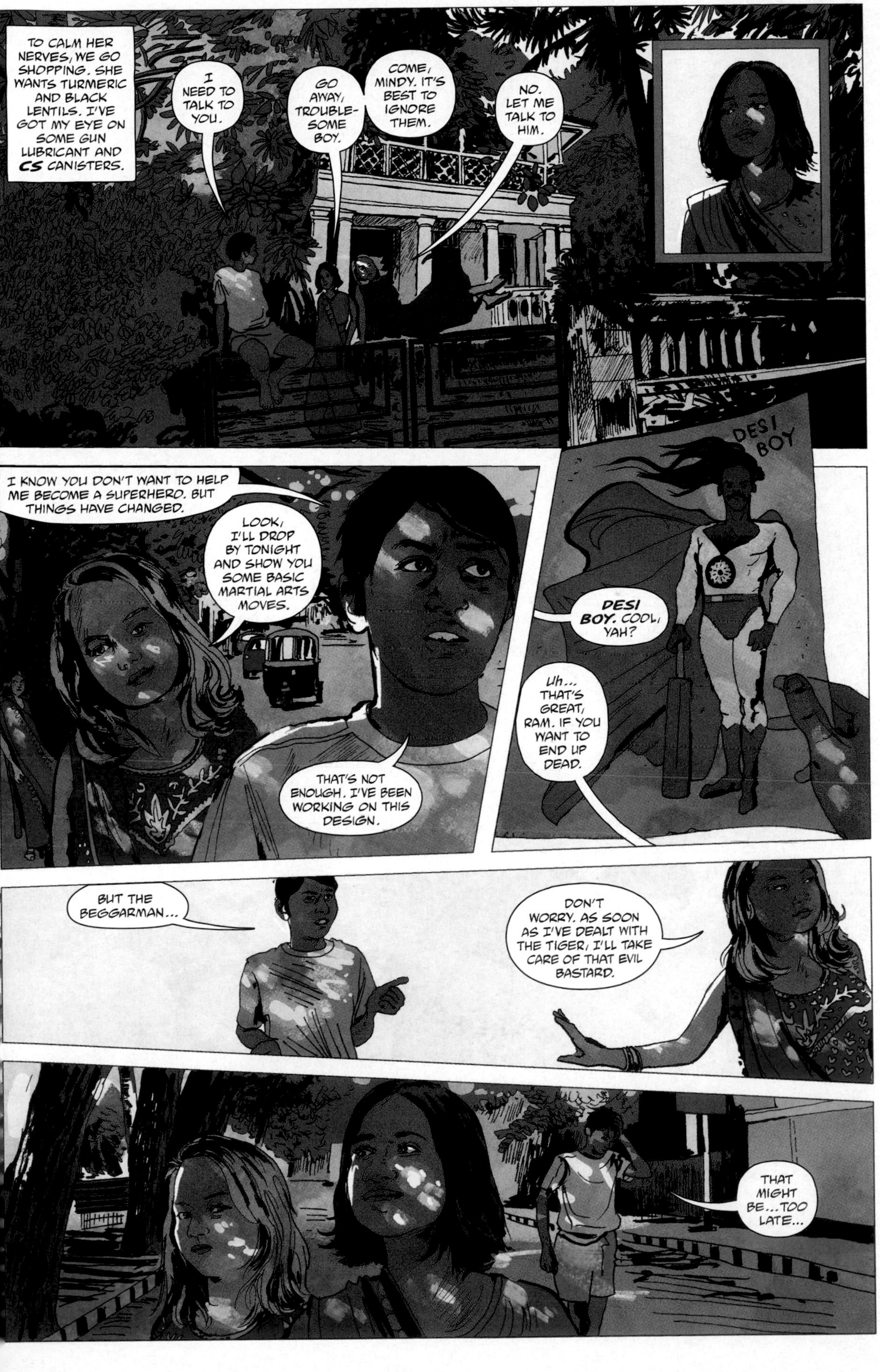

TO CALM HER NERVES, WE GO SHOPPING. SHE WANTS TURMERIC AND BLACK LENTILS. I'VE GOT MY EYE ON SOME GUN LUBRICANT AND CS CANISTERS.
I NEED TO TALK TO YOU.
GO AWAY, TROUBLE-SOME BOY.
COME, MINDY. IT'S BEST TO IGNORE THEM.
NO. LET ME TALK TO HIM.
I KNOW YOU DON'T WANT TO HELP ME BECOME A SUPERHERO. BUT THINGS HAVE CHANGED.
LOOK, I'LL DROP BY TONIGHT AND SHOW YOU SOME BASIC MARTIAL ARTS MOVES.
THAT'S NOT ENOUGH. I'VE BEEN WORKING ON THIS DESIGN.
DESI BOY
DESI BOY. COOL, YAH?
Uh... THAT'S GREAT, RAM. IF YOU WANT TO END UP DEAD.
BUT THE BEGGARMAN...
DON'T WORRY. AS SOON AS I'VE DEALT WITH THE TIGER, I'LL TAKE CARE OF THAT EVIL BASTARD.
THAT MIGHT BE...TOO LATE...

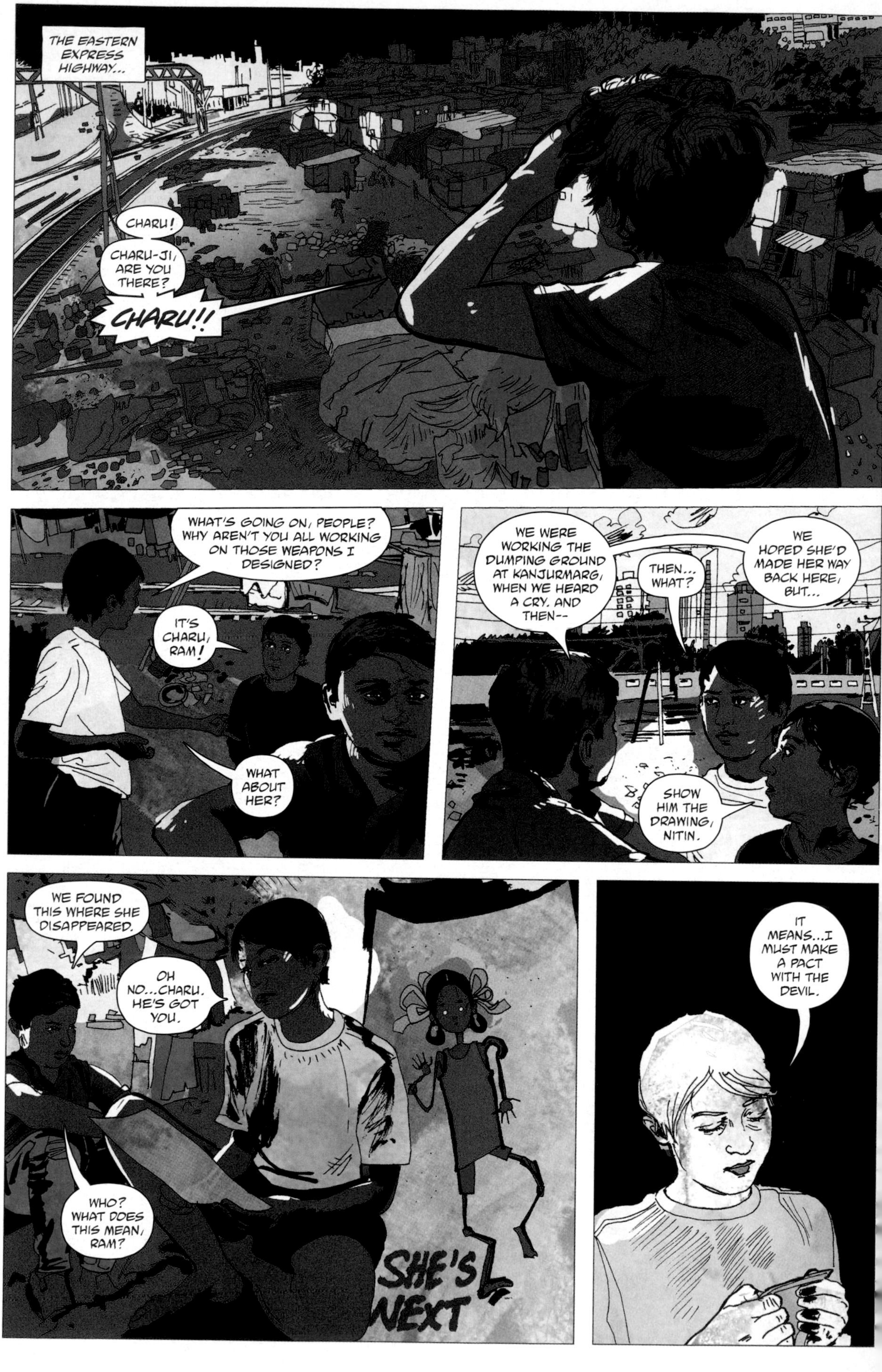
THE EASTERN EXPRESS HIGHWAY...
CHARU!
CHARU-JI, ARE YOU THERE?
CHARU!!
WHAT'S GOING ON, PEOPLE? WHY AREN'T YOU ALL WORKING ON THOSE WEAPONS I DESIGNED?
IT'S CHARU, RAM!
WHAT ABOUT HER?
WE WERE WORKING THE DUMPING GROUND AT KANJURMARG, WHEN WE HEARD A CRY. AND THEN--
THEN... WHAT?
WE HOPED SHE'D MADE HER WAY BACK HERE, BUT...
SHOW HIM THE DRAWING, NITIN.
WE FOUND THIS WHERE SHE DISAPPEARED.
OH NO...CHARU. HE'S GOT YOU.
WHO? WHAT DOES THIS MEAN, RAM?
SHE'S NEXT
IT MEANS...I MUST MAKE A PACT WITH THE DEVIL.

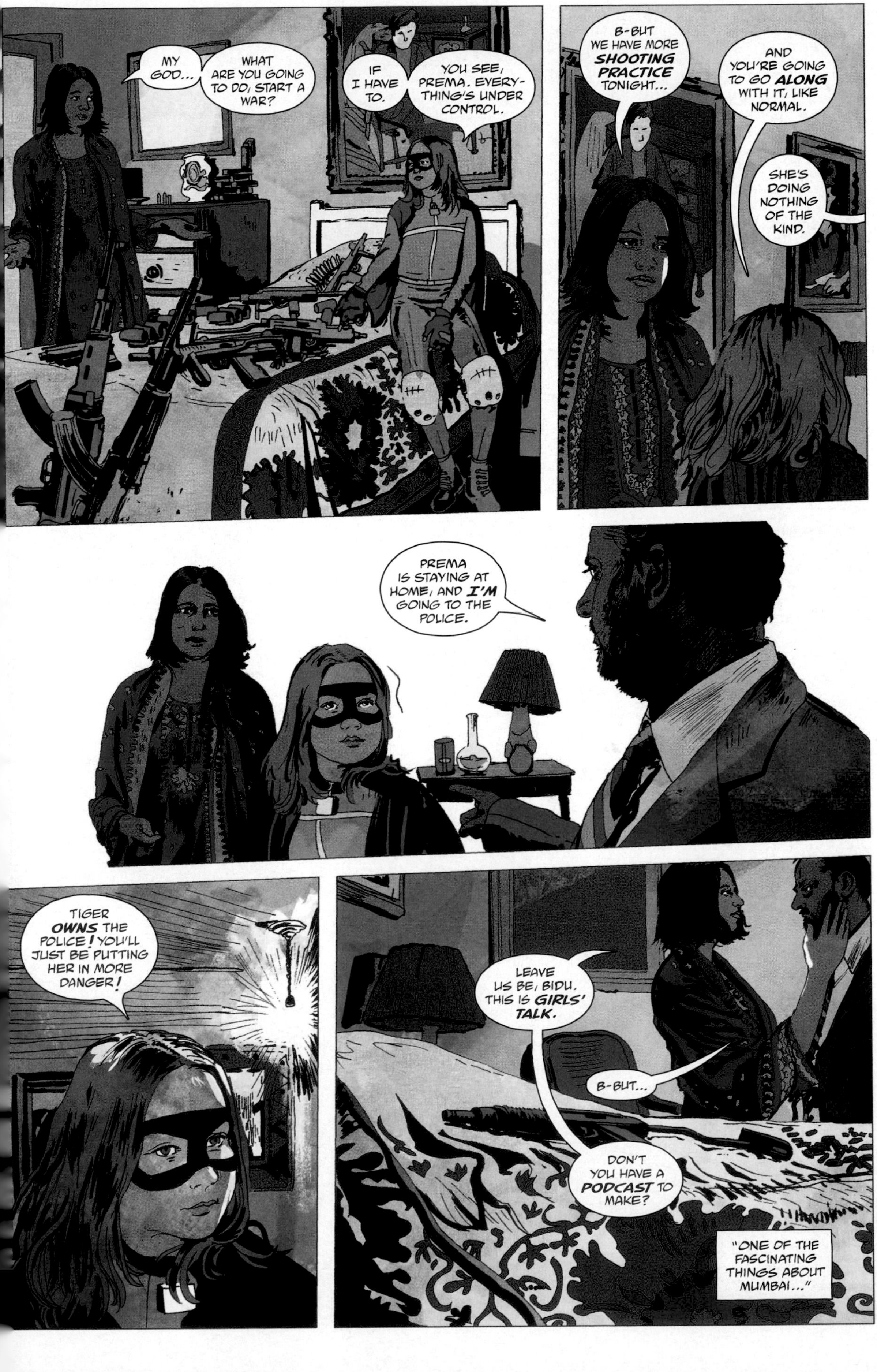
MY GOD...
WHAT ARE YOU GOING TO DO, START A WAR?
IF I HAVE TO.
YOU SEE, PREMA. EVERYTHING'S UNDER CONTROL.
B-BUT WE HAVE MORE **SHOOTING PRACTICE** TONIGHT...
AND YOU'RE GOING TO GO **ALONG** WITH IT, LIKE NORMAL.
SHE'S DOING NOTHING OF THE KIND.
PREMA IS STAYING AT HOME, AND **I'M** GOING TO THE POLICE.
TIGER **OWNS** THE POLICE! YOU'LL JUST BE PUTTING HER IN MORE DANGER!
LEAVE US BE, BIDU. THIS IS **GIRLS' TALK.**
B-BUT...
DON'T YOU HAVE A **PODCAST** TO MAKE?
"ONE OF THE FASCINATING THINGS ABOUT MUMBAI..."

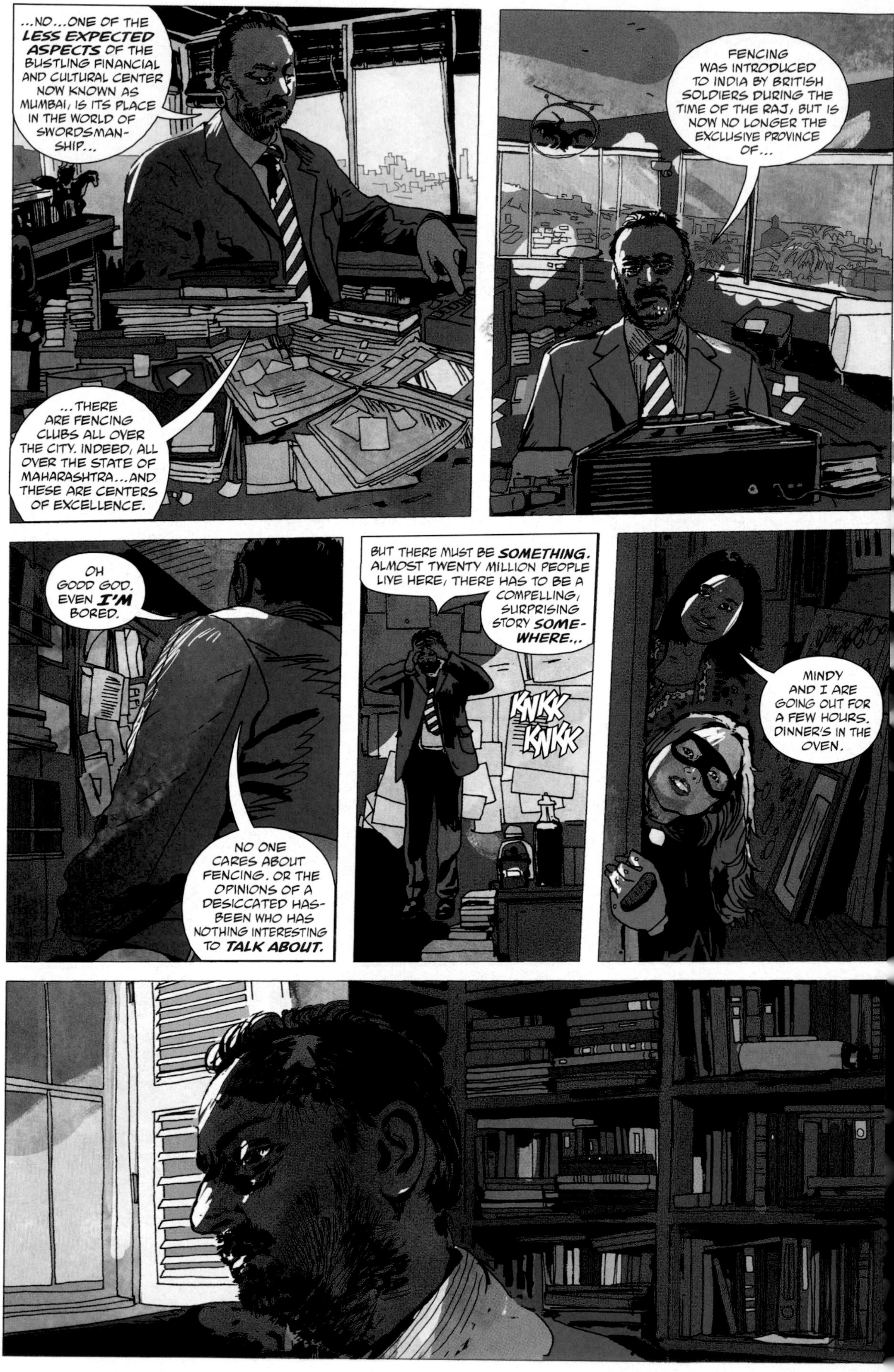
...NO...ONE OF THE LESS EXPECTED ASPECTS OF THE BUSTLING FINANCIAL AND CULTURAL CENTER NOW KNOWN AS MUMBAI, IS ITS PLACE IN THE WORLD OF SWORDSMANSHIP...
...THERE ARE FENCING CLUBS ALL OVER THE CITY. INDEED, ALL OVER THE STATE OF MAHARASHTRA...AND THESE ARE CENTERS OF EXCELLENCE.
FENCING WAS INTRODUCED TO INDIA BY BRITISH SOLDIERS DURING THE TIME OF THE RAJ, BUT IS NOW NO LONGER THE EXCLUSIVE PROVINCE OF...
OH GOOD GOD. EVEN I'M BORED.
NO ONE CARES ABOUT FENCING. OR THE OPINIONS OF A DESICCATED HAS-BEEN WHO HAS NOTHING INTERESTING TO TALK ABOUT.
BUT THERE MUST BE SOMETHING. ALMOST TWENTY MILLION PEOPLE LIVE HERE, THERE HAS TO BE A COMPELLING, SURPRISING STORY SOMEWHERE...
KNKK KNKK
MINDY AND I ARE GOING OUT FOR A FEW HOURS. DINNER'S IN THE OVEN.

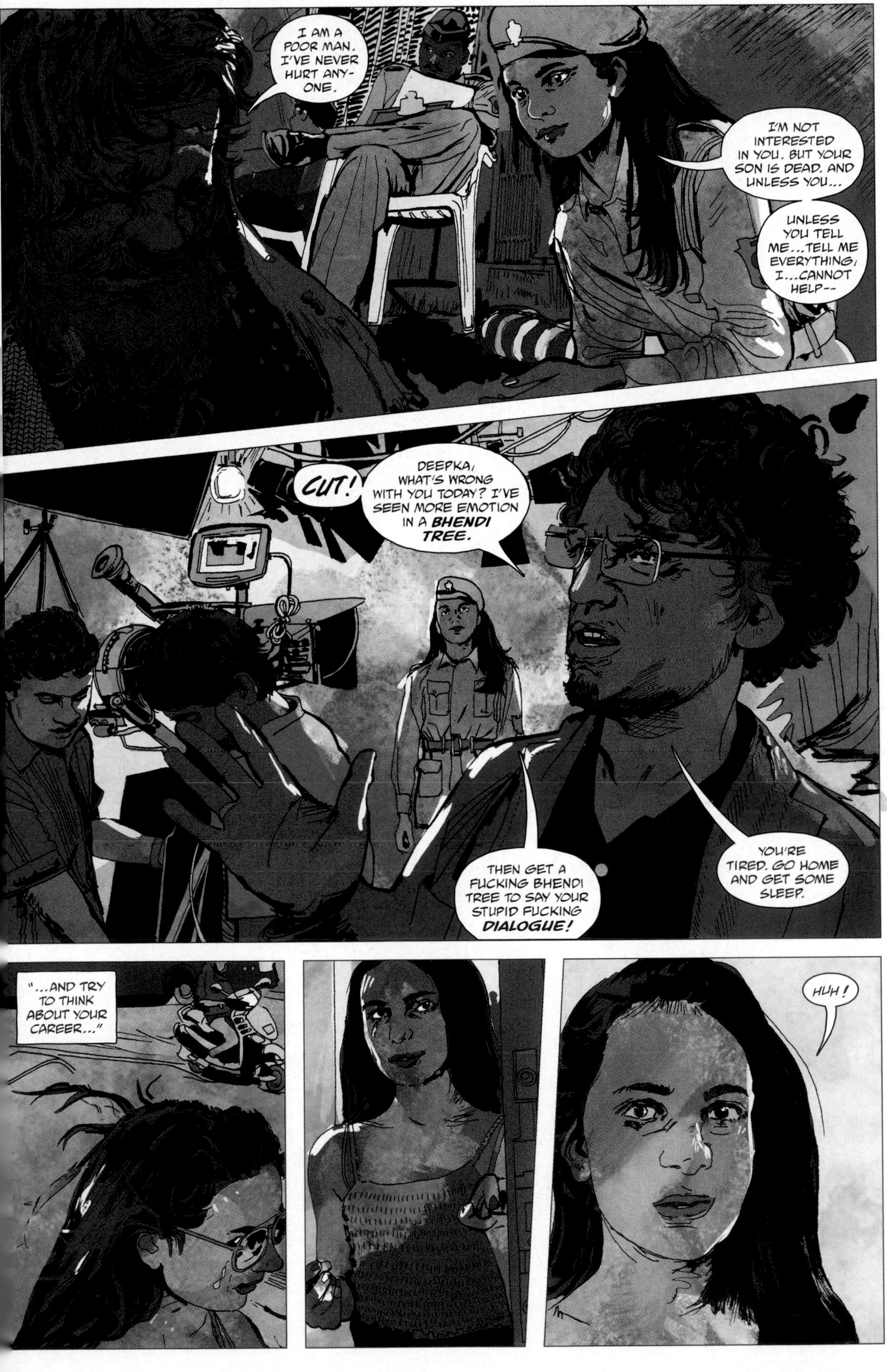
I AM A POOR MAN. I'VE NEVER HURT ANY-ONE.
I'M NOT INTERESTED IN YOU. BUT YOUR SON IS DEAD. AND UNLESS YOU...
UNLESS YOU TELL ME...TELL ME EVERYTHING, I...CANNOT HELP--
CUT!
DEEPKA, WHAT'S WRONG WITH YOU TODAY? I'VE SEEN MORE EMOTION IN A **BHENDI TREE.**
THEN GET A FUCKING BHENDI TREE TO SAY YOUR STUPID FUCKING **DIALOGUE!**
YOU'RE TIRED. GO HOME AND GET SOME SLEEP.
"...AND TRY TO THINK ABOUT YOUR CAREER..."
HUH!

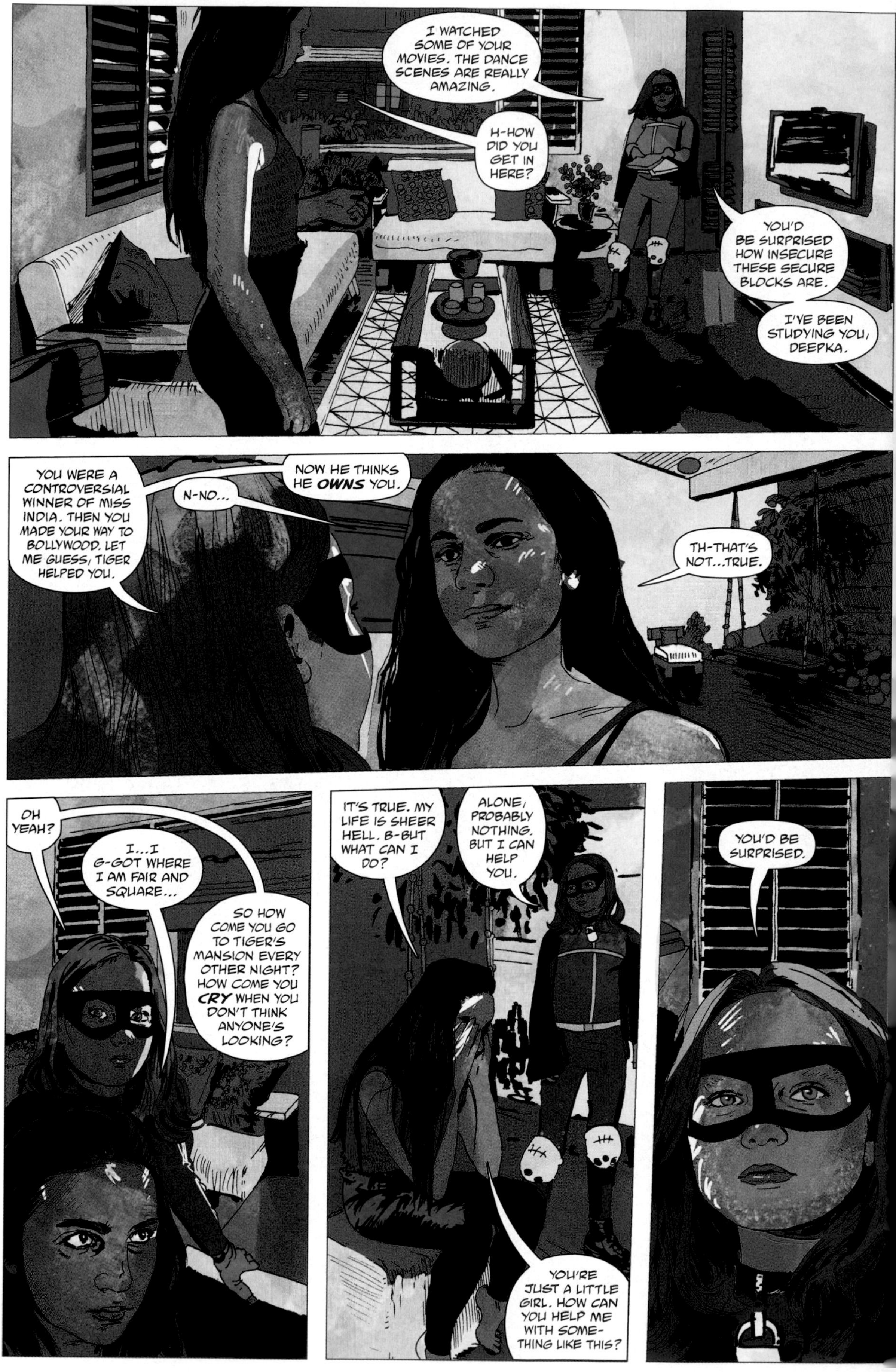
I WATCHED SOME OF YOUR MOVIES. THE DANCE SCENES ARE REALLY AMAZING.
H-HOW DID YOU GET IN HERE?
YOU'D BE SURPRISED HOW INSECURE THESE SECURE BLOCKS ARE.
I'VE BEEN STUDYING YOU, DEEPKA.
YOU WERE A CONTROVERSIAL WINNER OF MISS INDIA. THEN YOU MADE YOUR WAY TO BOLLYWOOD. LET ME GUESS, TIGER HELPED YOU.
N-NO...
NOW HE THINKS HE **OWNS** YOU.
TH-THAT'S NOT...TRUE.
OH YEAH?
I...I G-GOT WHERE I AM FAIR AND SQUARE...
SO HOW COME YOU GO TO TIGER'S MANSION EVERY OTHER NIGHT? HOW COME YOU **CRY** WHEN YOU DON'T THINK ANYONE'S LOOKING?
IT'S TRUE. MY LIFE IS SHEER HELL. B-BUT WHAT CAN I DO?
ALONE, PROBABLY NOTHING. BUT I CAN HELP YOU.
YOU'RE JUST A LITTLE GIRL. HOW CAN YOU HELP ME WITH SOME-THING LIKE THIS?
YOU'D BE SURPRISED.

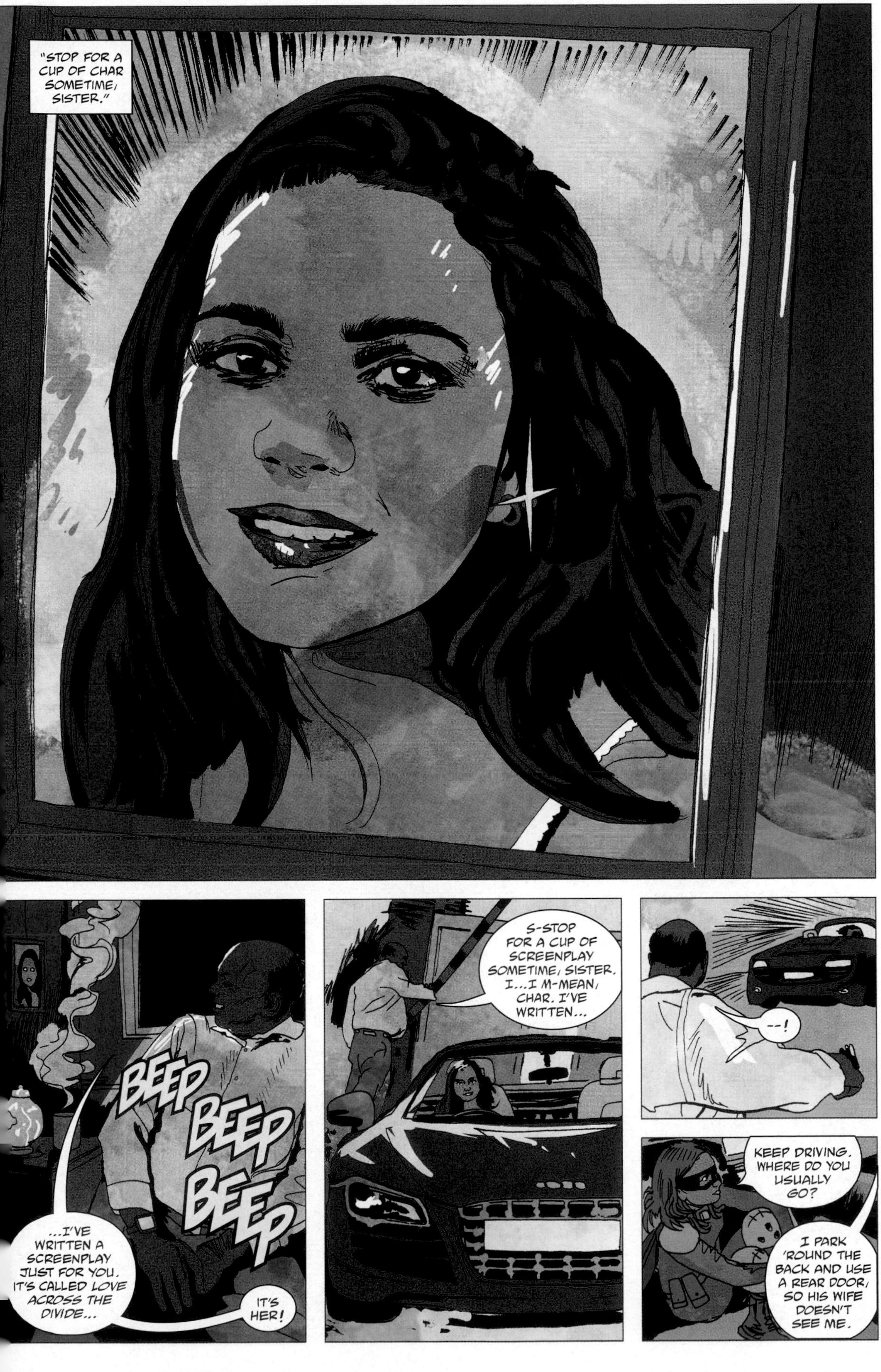
"STOP FOR A CUP OF CHAR SOMETIME, SISTER."
BEEP BEEP BEEP
...I'VE WRITTEN A SCREENPLAY JUST FOR YOU. IT'S CALLED LOVE ACROSS THE DIVIDE...
IT'S HER!
S-STOP FOR A CUP OF SCREENPLAY SOMETIME, SISTER. I...I M-MEAN, CHAR. I'VE WRITTEN...
--!
KEEP DRIVING. WHERE DO YOU USUALLY GO?
I PARK 'ROUND THE BACK AND USE A REAR DOOR, SO HIS WIFE DOESN'T SEE ME.

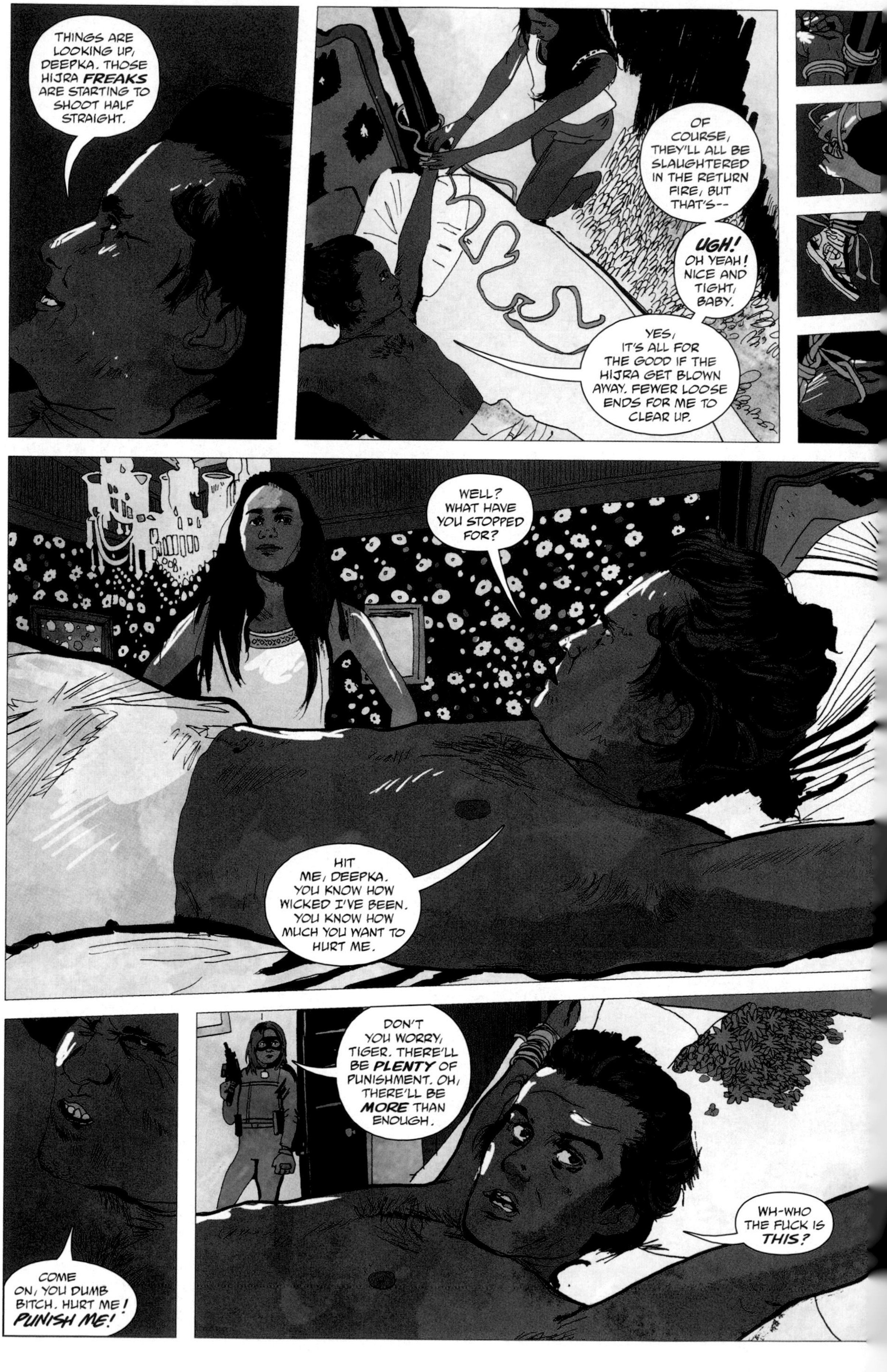
THINGS ARE LOOKING UP, DEEPKA. THOSE HIJRA FREAKS ARE STARTING TO SHOOT HALF STRAIGHT.
OF COURSE, THEY'LL ALL BE SLAUGHTERED IN THE RETURN FIRE, BUT THAT'S--
UGH! OH YEAH! NICE AND TIGHT, BABY.
YES, IT'S ALL FOR THE GOOD IF THE HIJRA GET BLOWN AWAY. FEWER LOOSE ENDS FOR ME TO CLEAR UP.
WELL? WHAT HAVE YOU STOPPED FOR?
HIT ME, DEEPKA. YOU KNOW HOW WICKED I'VE BEEN. YOU KNOW HOW MUCH YOU WANT TO HURT ME.
COME ON, YOU DUMB BITCH. HURT ME! PUNISH ME!
DON'T YOU WORRY, TIGER. THERE'LL BE PLENTY OF PUNISHMENT. OH, THERE'LL BE MORE THAN ENOUGH.
WH-WHO THE FUCK IS THIS?

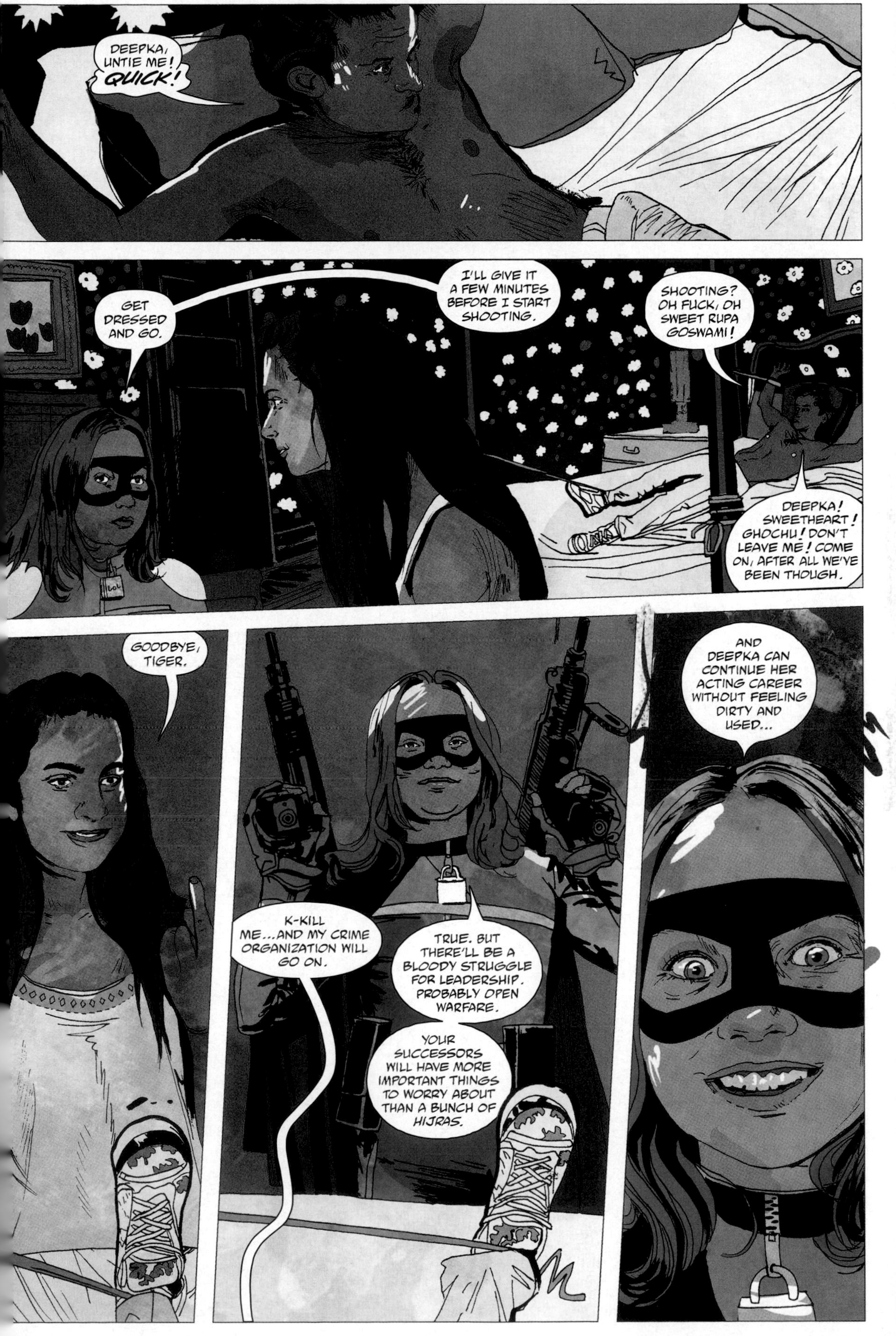
DEEPKA, UNTIE ME! QUICK!
GET DRESSED AND GO.
I'LL GIVE IT A FEW MINUTES BEFORE I START SHOOTING.
SHOOTING? OH FUCK, OH SWEET RUPA GOSWAMI!
DEEPKA! SWEETHEART! GHOCHU! DON'T LEAVE ME! COME ON, AFTER ALL WE'VE BEEN THOUGH.
GOODBYE, TIGER.
K-KILL ME...AND MY CRIME ORGANIZATION WILL GO ON.
TRUE. BUT THERE'LL BE A BLOODY STRUGGLE FOR LEADERSHIP. PROBABLY OPEN WARFARE.
YOUR SUCCESSORS WILL HAVE MORE IMPORTANT THINGS TO WORRY ABOUT THAN A BUNCH OF HIJRAS.
AND DEEPKA CAN CONTINUE HER ACTING CAREER WITHOUT FEELING DIRTY AND USED...

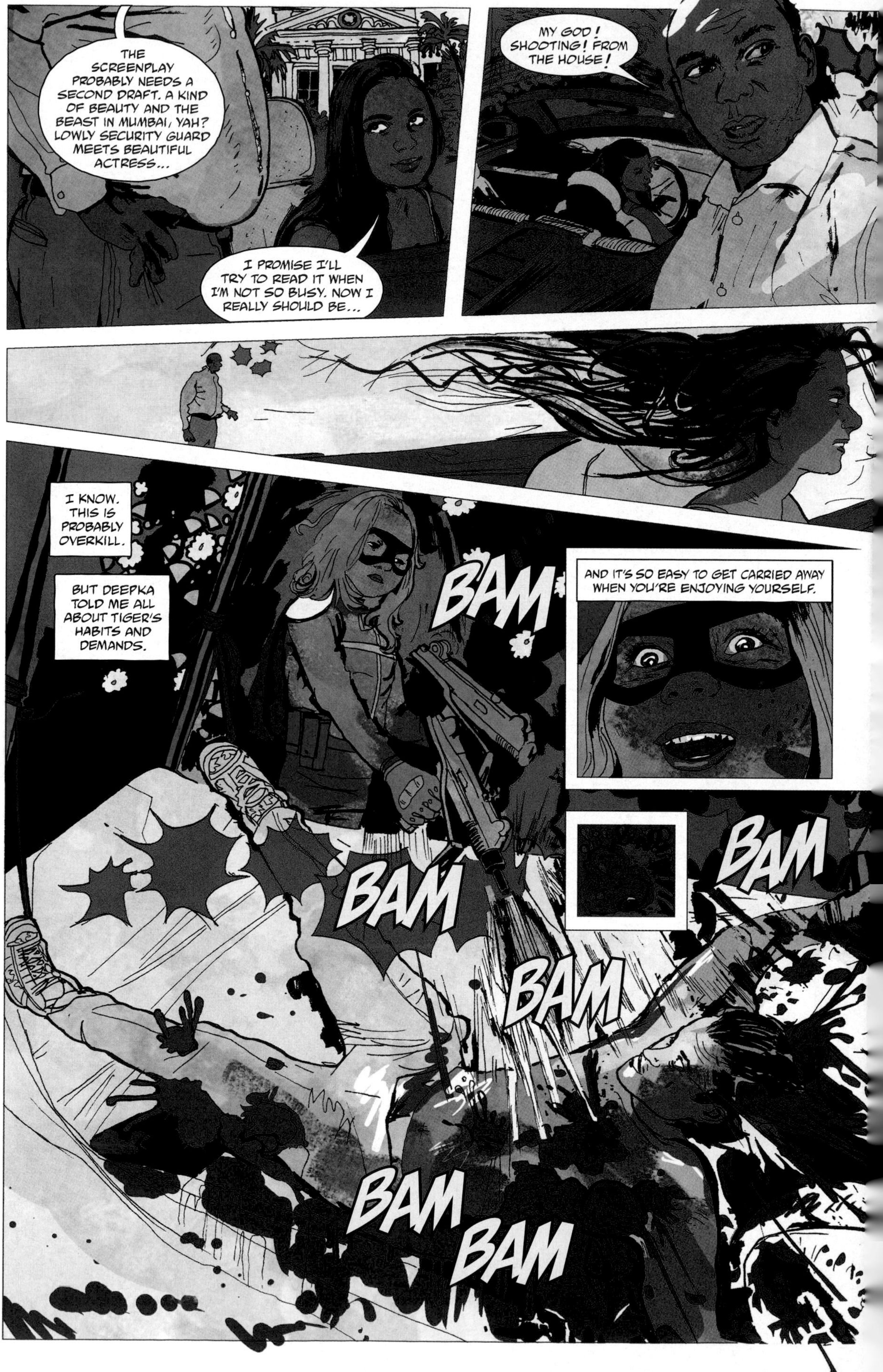
THE SCREENPLAY PROBABLY NEEDS A SECOND DRAFT. A KIND OF BEAUTY AND THE BEAST IN MUMBAI, YAH? LOWLY SECURITY GUARD MEETS BEAUTIFUL ACTRESS...
I PROMISE I'LL TRY TO READ IT WHEN I'M NOT SO BUSY. NOW I REALLY SHOULD BE...
MY GOD! SHOOTING! FROM THE HOUSE!
I KNOW. THIS IS PROBABLY OVERKILL.
BUT DEEPKA TOLD ME ALL ABOUT TIGER'S HABITS AND DEMANDS.
BAM
AND IT'S SO EASY TO GET CARRIED AWAY WHEN YOU'RE ENJOYING YOURSELF.
BAM
BAM
BAM
BAM
BAM

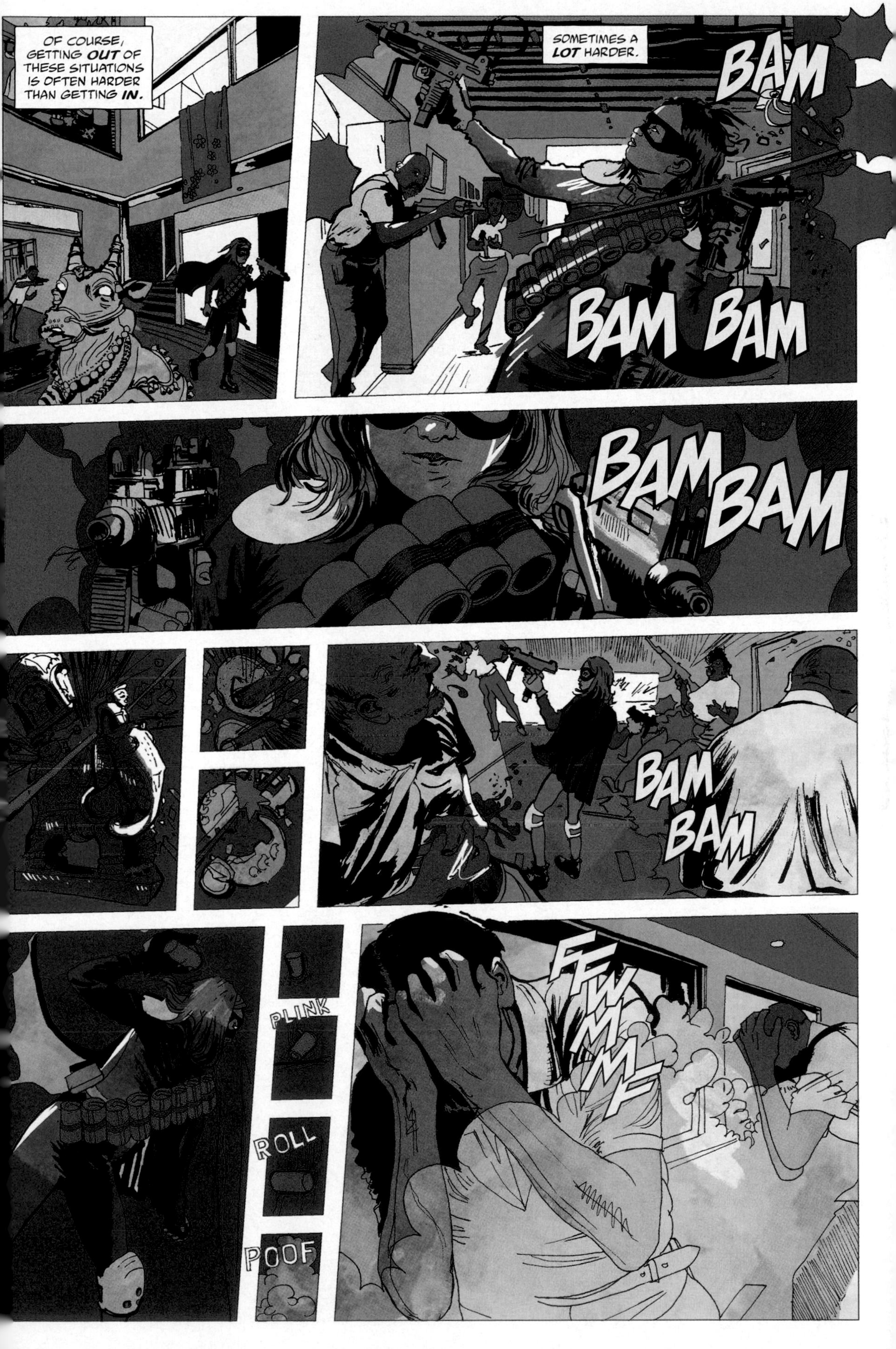
OF COURSE, GETTING OUT OF THESE SITUATIONS IS OFTEN HARDER THAN GETTING IN.
SOMETIMES A LOT HARDER.
BAM
BAM BAM
BAM BAM
BAM BAM
PLINK
ROLL
POOF
FFWMMMF

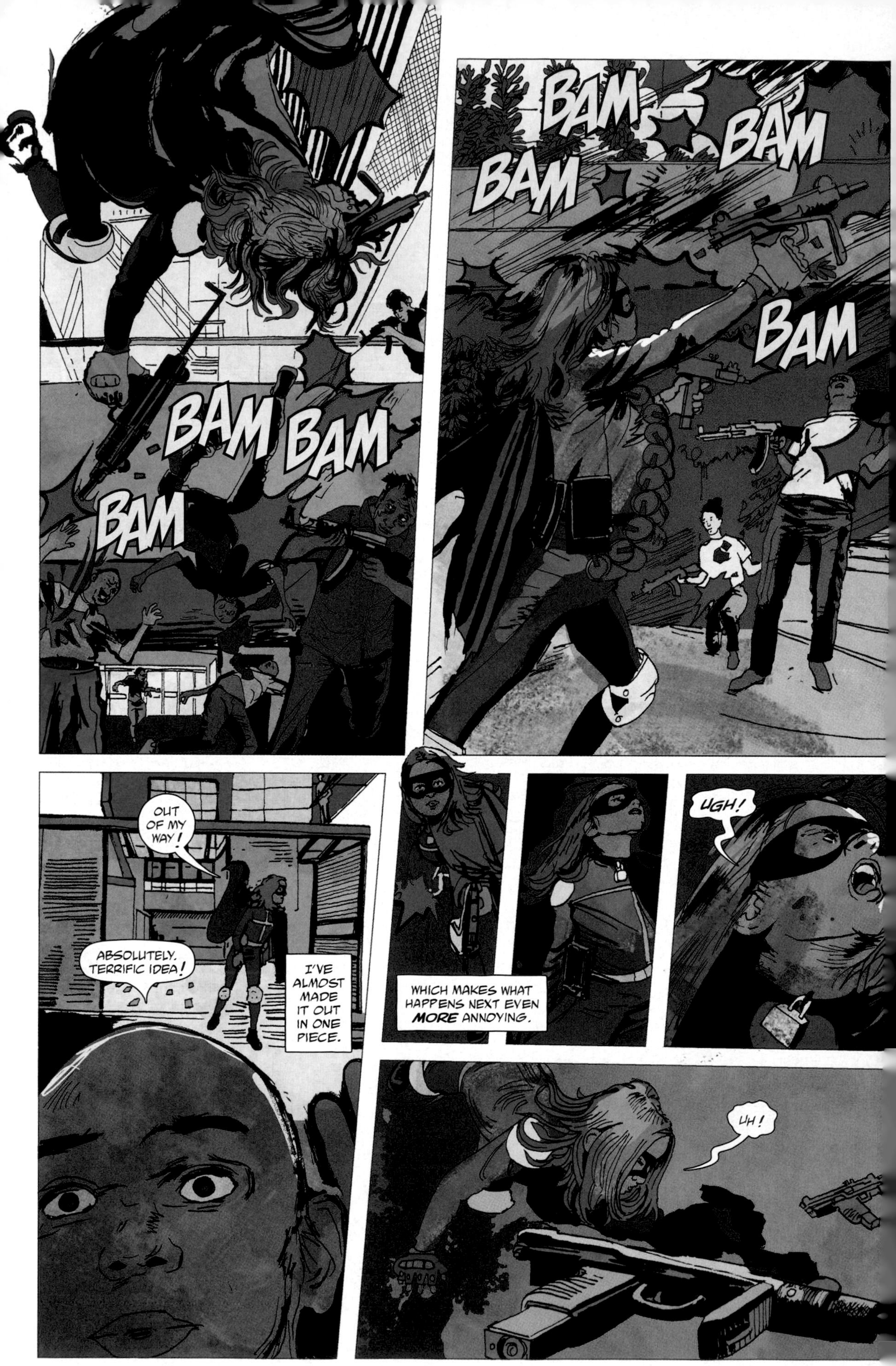
BAM
BAM
BAM
BAM
BAM
BAM
BAM
OUT OF MY WAY!
ABSOLUTELY. TERRIFIC IDEA!
I'VE ALMOST MADE IT OUT IN ONE PIECE.
WHICH MAKES WHAT HAPPENS NEXT EVEN MORE ANNOYING.
UGH!
UH!

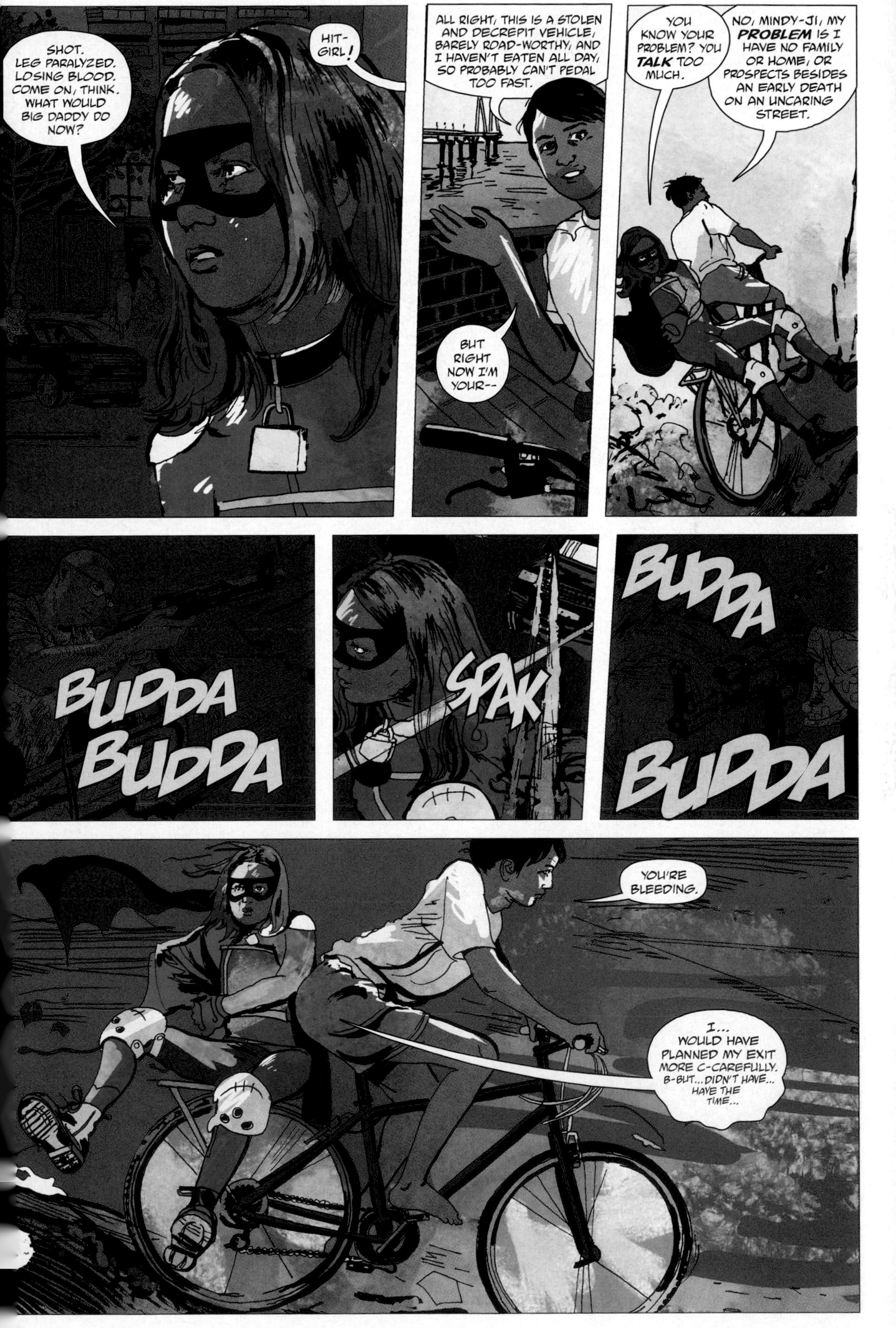
SHOT. LEG PARALYZED. LOSING BLOOD. COME ON, THINK. WHAT WOULD BIG DADDY DO NOW?
HIT-GIRL!
ALL RIGHT, THIS IS A STOLEN AND DECREPIT VEHICLE, BARELY ROAD-WORTHY, AND I HAVEN'T EATEN ALL DAY, SO PROBABLY CAN'T PEDAL TOO FAST.
BUT RIGHT NOW I'M YOUR--
YOU KNOW YOUR PROBLEM? YOU TALK TOO MUCH.
NO, MINDY-JI, MY PROBLEM IS I HAVE NO FAMILY OR HOME, OR PROSPECTS BESIDES AN EARLY DEATH ON AN UNCARING STREET.
BUDDA BUDDA
SPAK
BUDDA BUDDA
YOU'RE BLEEDING.
I... WOULD HAVE PLANNED MY EXIT MORE C-CAREFULLY. B-BUT... DIDN'T HAVE... HAVE THE TIME...

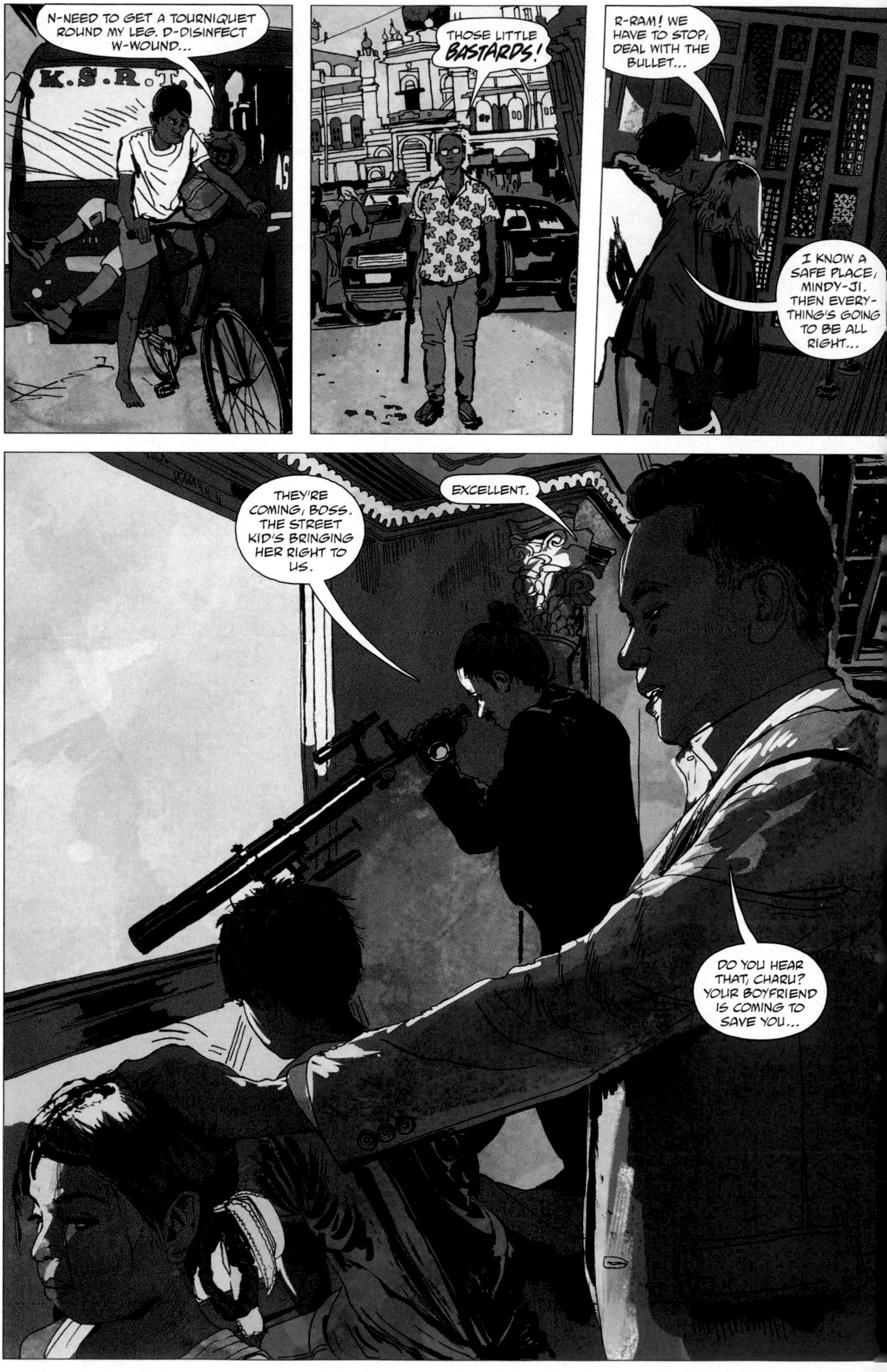

K.S.R.T.
N-NEED TO GET A TOURNIQUET ROUND MY LEG. D-DISINFECT W-WOUND...
THOSE LITTLE BASTARDS!
R-RAM! WE HAVE TO STOP, DEAL WITH THE BULLET...
I KNOW A SAFE PLACE, MINDY-JI. THEN EVERYTHING'S GOING TO BE ALL RIGHT...
THEY'RE COMING, BOSS. THE STREET KID'S BRINGING HER RIGHT TO US.
EXCELLENT.
DO YOU HEAR THAT, CHARU? YOUR BOYFRIEND IS COMING TO SAVE YOU...

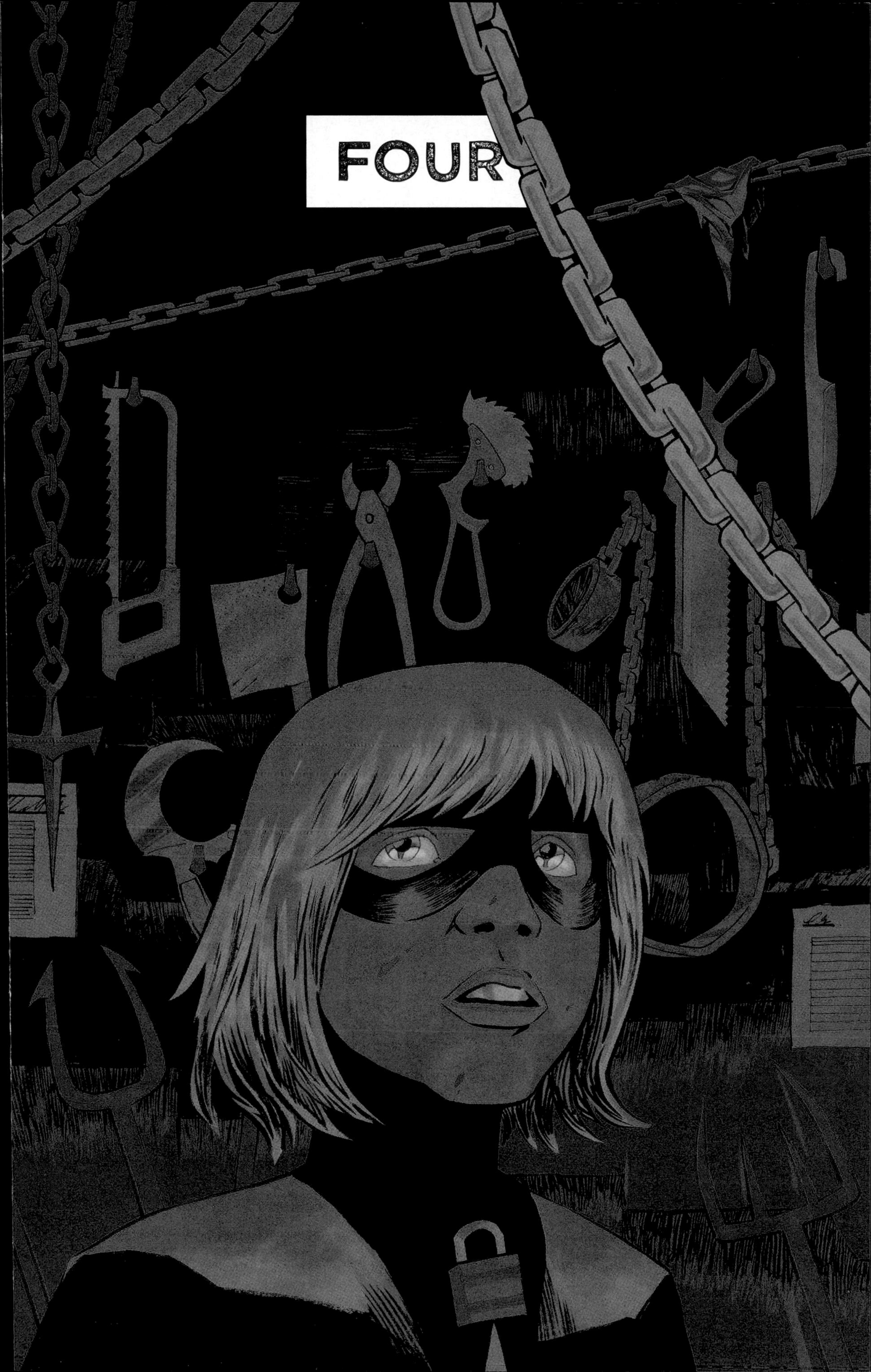
FOUR

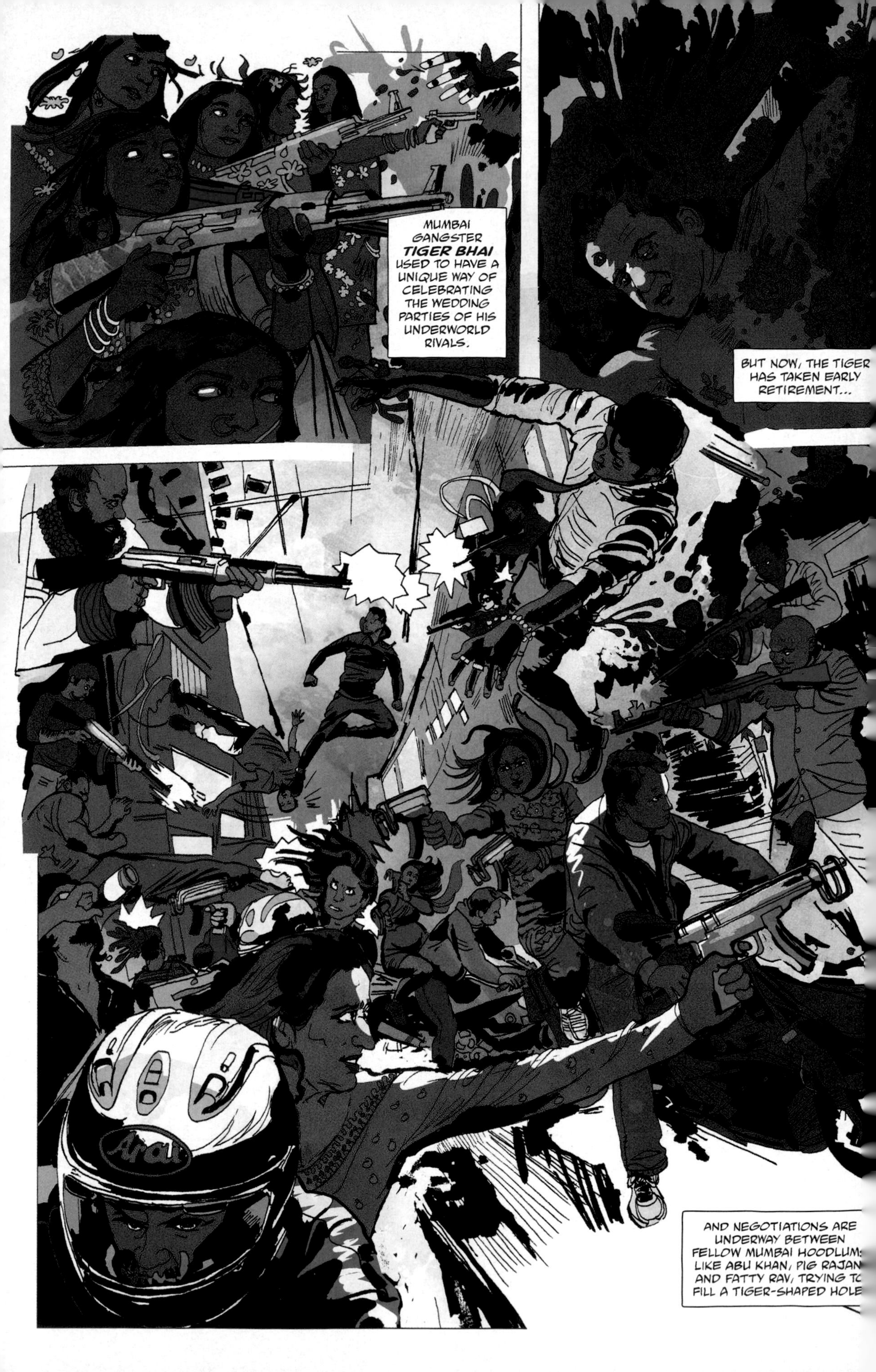
MUMBAI GANGSTER **TIGER BHAI** USED TO HAVE A UNIQUE WAY OF CELEBRATING THE WEDDING PARTIES OF HIS UNDERWORLD RIVALS.
BUT NOW, THE TIGER HAS TAKEN EARLY RETIREMENT...
AND NEGOTIATIONS ARE UNDERWAY BETWEEN FELLOW MUMBAI HOODLUMS LIKE ABU KHAN, PIG RAJAN AND FATTY RAV, TRYING TO FILL A TIGER-SHAPED HOLE

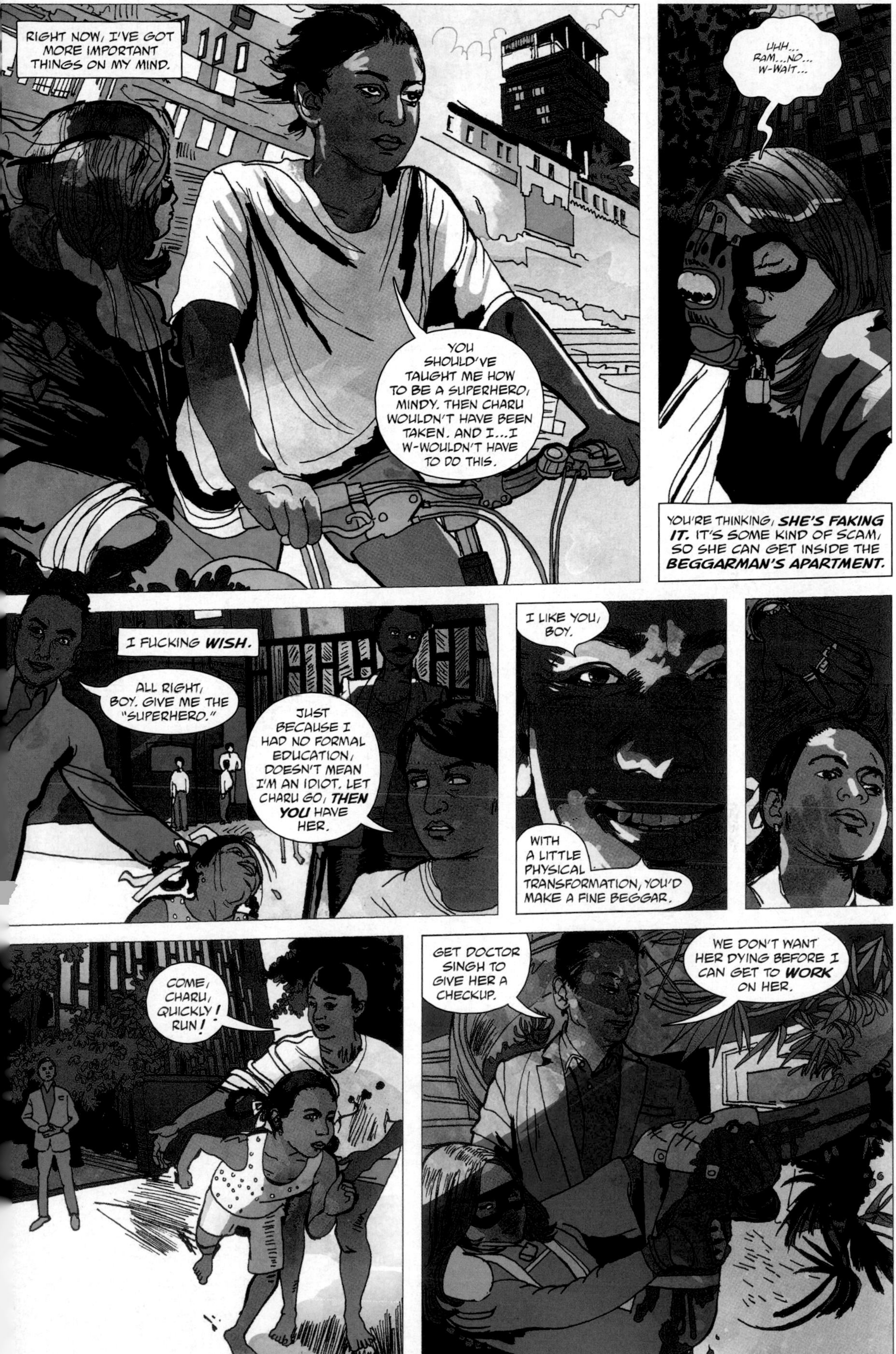
RIGHT NOW, I'VE GOT MORE IMPORTANT THINGS ON MY MIND.
YOU SHOULD'VE TAUGHT ME HOW TO BE A SUPERHERO, MINDY. THEN CHARU WOULDN'T HAVE BEEN TAKEN. AND I...I W-WOULDN'T HAVE TO DO THIS.
UHH... RAM...NO... W-WAIT...
YOU'RE THINKING, SHE'S FAKING IT. IT'S SOME KIND OF SCAM, SO SHE CAN GET INSIDE THE BEGGARMAN'S APARTMENT.
I FUCKING WISH.
ALL RIGHT, BOY. GIVE ME THE "SUPERHERO."
JUST BECAUSE I HAD NO FORMAL EDUCATION, DOESN'T MEAN I'M AN IDIOT. LET CHARU GO, THEN YOU HAVE HER.
I LIKE YOU, BOY.
WITH A LITTLE PHYSICAL TRANSFORMATION, YOU'D MAKE A FINE BEGGAR.
COME, CHARU, QUICKLY! RUN!
GET DOCTOR SINGH TO GIVE HER A CHECKUP.
WE DON'T WANT HER DYING BEFORE I CAN GET TO WORK ON HER.

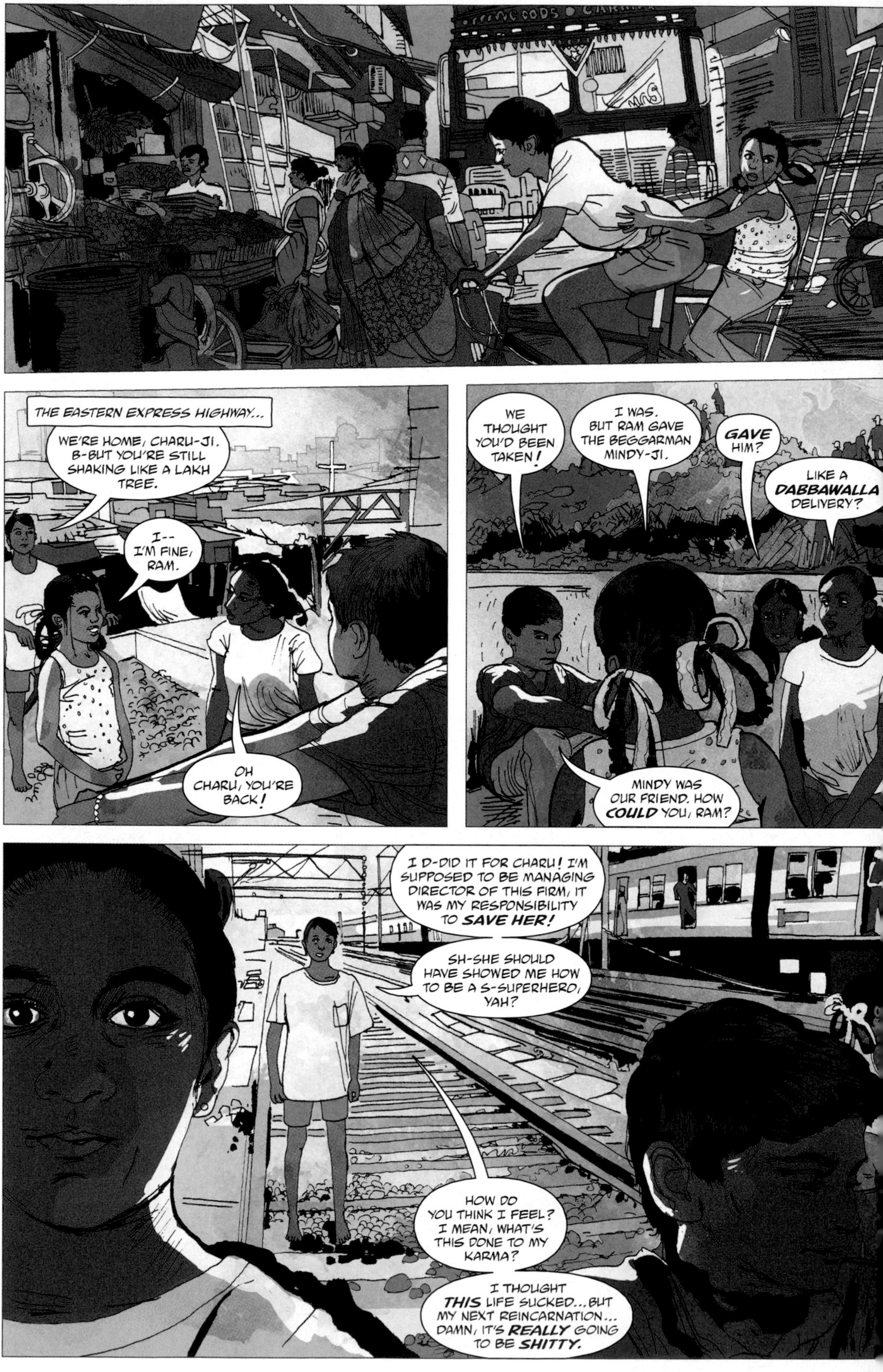
THE EASTERN EXPRESS HIGHWAY...
WE'RE HOME, CHARU-JI. B-BUT YOU'RE STILL SHAKING LIKE A LAKH TREE.
I-- I'M FINE, RAM.
OH CHARU, YOU'RE BACK!
WE THOUGHT YOU'D BEEN TAKEN!
I WAS. BUT RAM GAVE THE BEGGARMAN MINDY-JI.
GAVE HIM?
LIKE A DABBAWALLA DELIVERY?
MINDY WAS OUR FRIEND. HOW COULD YOU, RAM?
I D-DID IT FOR CHARU! I'M SUPPOSED TO BE MANAGING DIRECTOR OF THIS FIRM, IT WAS MY RESPONSIBILITY TO SAVE HER!
SH-SHE SHOULD HAVE SHOWED ME HOW TO BE A S-SUPERHERO, YAH?
HOW DO YOU THINK I FEEL? I MEAN, WHAT'S THIS DONE TO MY KARMA?
I THOUGHT THIS LIFE SUCKED... BUT MY NEXT REINCARNATION... DAMN, IT'S REALLY GOING TO BE SHITTY.

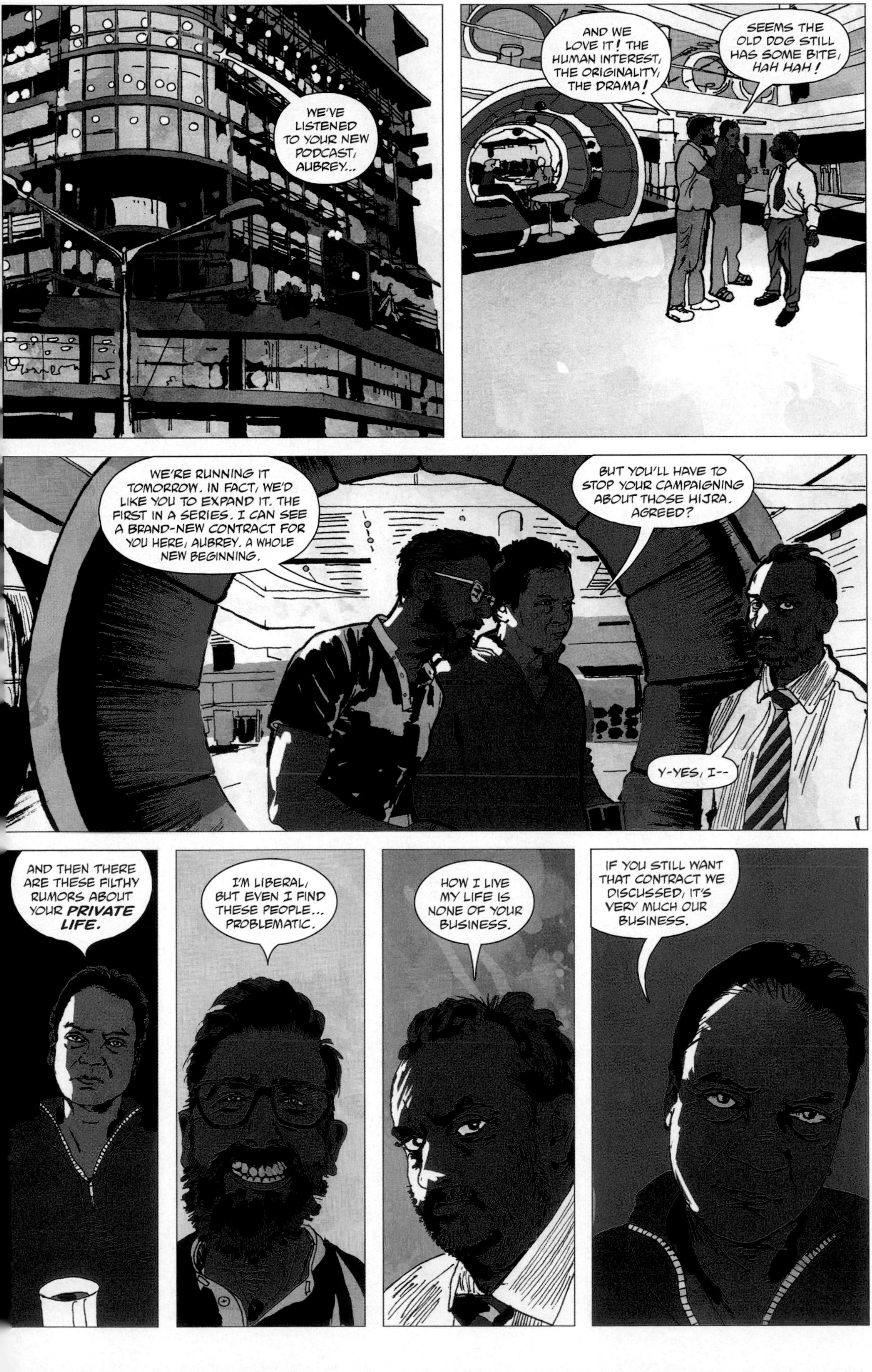
WE'VE LISTENED TO YOUR NEW PODCAST, AUBREY...
AND WE LOVE IT! THE HUMAN INTEREST, THE ORIGINALITY, THE DRAMA!
SEEMS THE OLD DOG STILL HAS SOME BITE, HAH HAH!
WE'RE RUNNING IT TOMORROW. IN FACT, WE'D LIKE YOU TO EXPAND IT. THE FIRST IN A SERIES. I CAN SEE A BRAND-NEW CONTRACT FOR YOU HERE, AUBREY. A WHOLE NEW BEGINNING.
BUT YOU'LL HAVE TO STOP YOUR CAMPAIGNING ABOUT THOSE HIJRA. AGREED?
Y-YES, I--
AND THEN THERE ARE THESE FILTHY RUMORS ABOUT YOUR *PRIVATE LIFE.*
I'M LIBERAL, BUT EVEN I FIND THESE PEOPLE... PROBLEMATIC.
HOW I LIVE MY LIFE IS NONE OF YOUR BUSINESS.
IF YOU STILL WANT THAT CONTRACT WE DISCUSSED, IT'S VERY MUCH OUR BUSINESS.

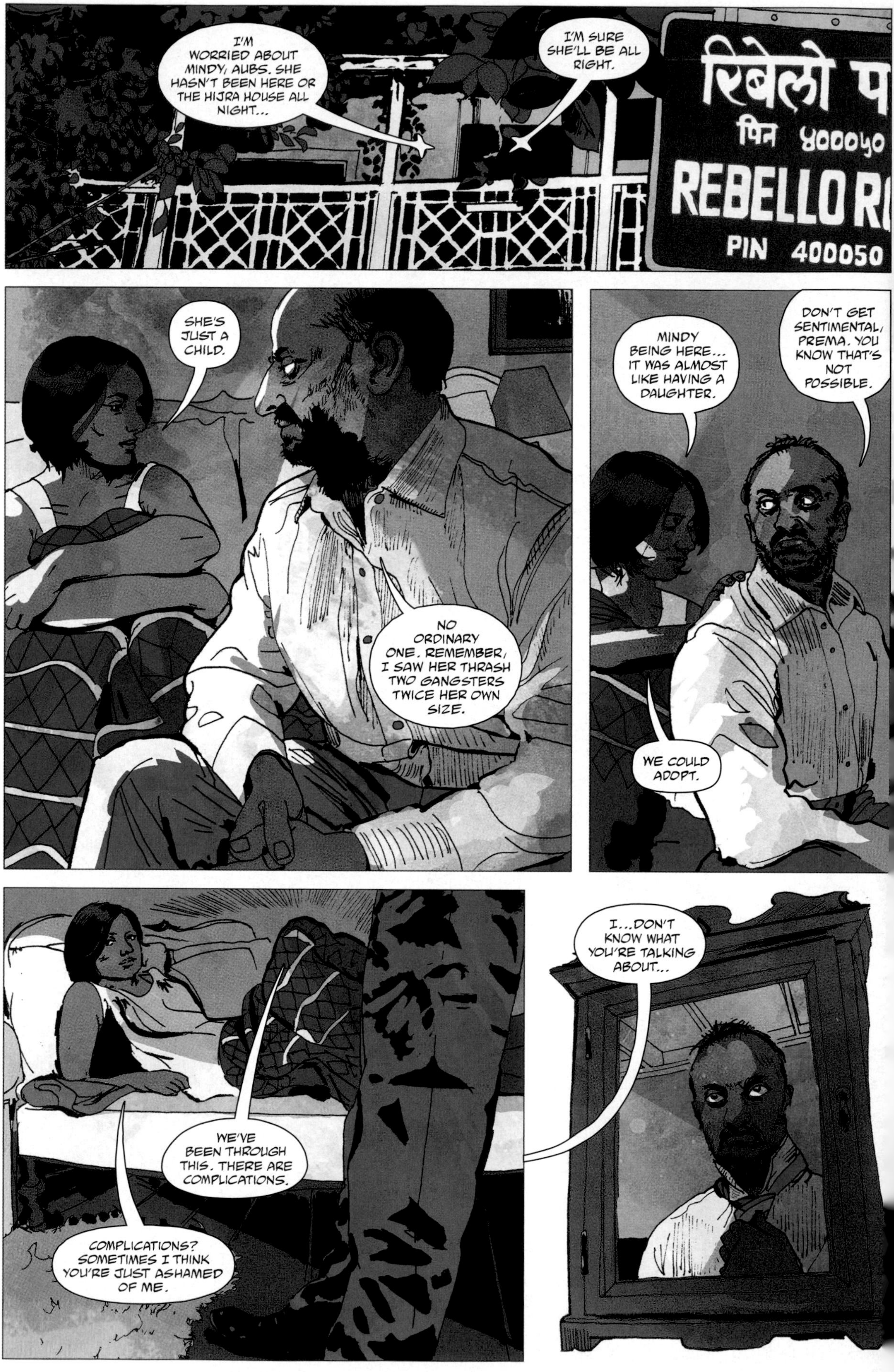
I'M WORRIED ABOUT MINDY, AUBS. SHE HASN'T BEEN HERE OR THE HIJRA HOUSE ALL NIGHT...
I'M SURE SHE'LL BE ALL RIGHT.
रिबेलो प
पिन ४०००५०
REBELLO R
PIN 400050
SHE'S JUST A CHILD.
NO ORDINARY ONE. REMEMBER, I SAW HER THRASH TWO GANGSTERS TWICE HER OWN SIZE.
MINDY BEING HERE... IT WAS ALMOST LIKE HAVING A DAUGHTER.
DON'T GET SENTIMENTAL, PREMA. YOU KNOW THAT'S NOT POSSIBLE.
WE COULD ADOPT.
WE'VE BEEN THROUGH THIS. THERE ARE COMPLICATIONS.
COMPLICATIONS? SOMETIMES I THINK YOU'RE JUST ASHAMED OF ME.
I...DON'T KNOW WHAT YOU'RE TALKING ABOUT...

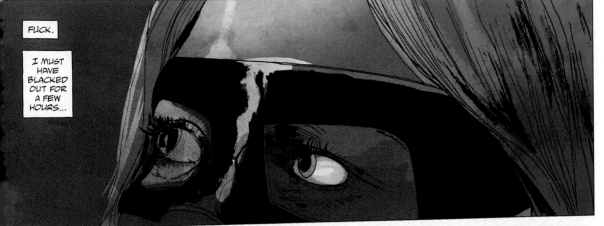

FUCK.

I MUST HAVE BLACKED OUT FOR A FEW HOURS...

THEY GAVE YOU A FEW SHOTS TO HELP YOU SLEEP.

BUT THE BEGGARMAN LIKES HIS VICTIMS TO BE AWAKE WHEN HE WORKS ON THEM. THAT'S WHY YOU'VE STILL GOT FOUR WORKING LIMBS.

UGH... I FEEL LIKE... SHIT.

HEY... I REMEMBER YOU. WHAT HAPPENED, CART GOT A FLAT?

THE NAME'S AADIT. MY CART IS FOR STREET WORK. MY CRUTCH ALLOWS ME TO SNEAK AROUND INSIDE. SO I CAN COLLECT THINGS...LIKE THE KEY TO THIS ROOM.

IF YOU WANT, I CAN ALSO SHOW YOU A WAY OUT.

YOU'RE ALL RIGHT, AADIT.

AND WHAT HAPPENED TO ME WAS ALL *WRONG*, BUT I'M MORE PROFITABLE TO THE BEGGARMAN THIS WAY.

I WARNED HIM...

I *WARNED* THE BEGGAR BHAI NOT TO LET YOU GO SNEAKING AROUND THE PLACE. SHIFTY LITTLE FREAK.

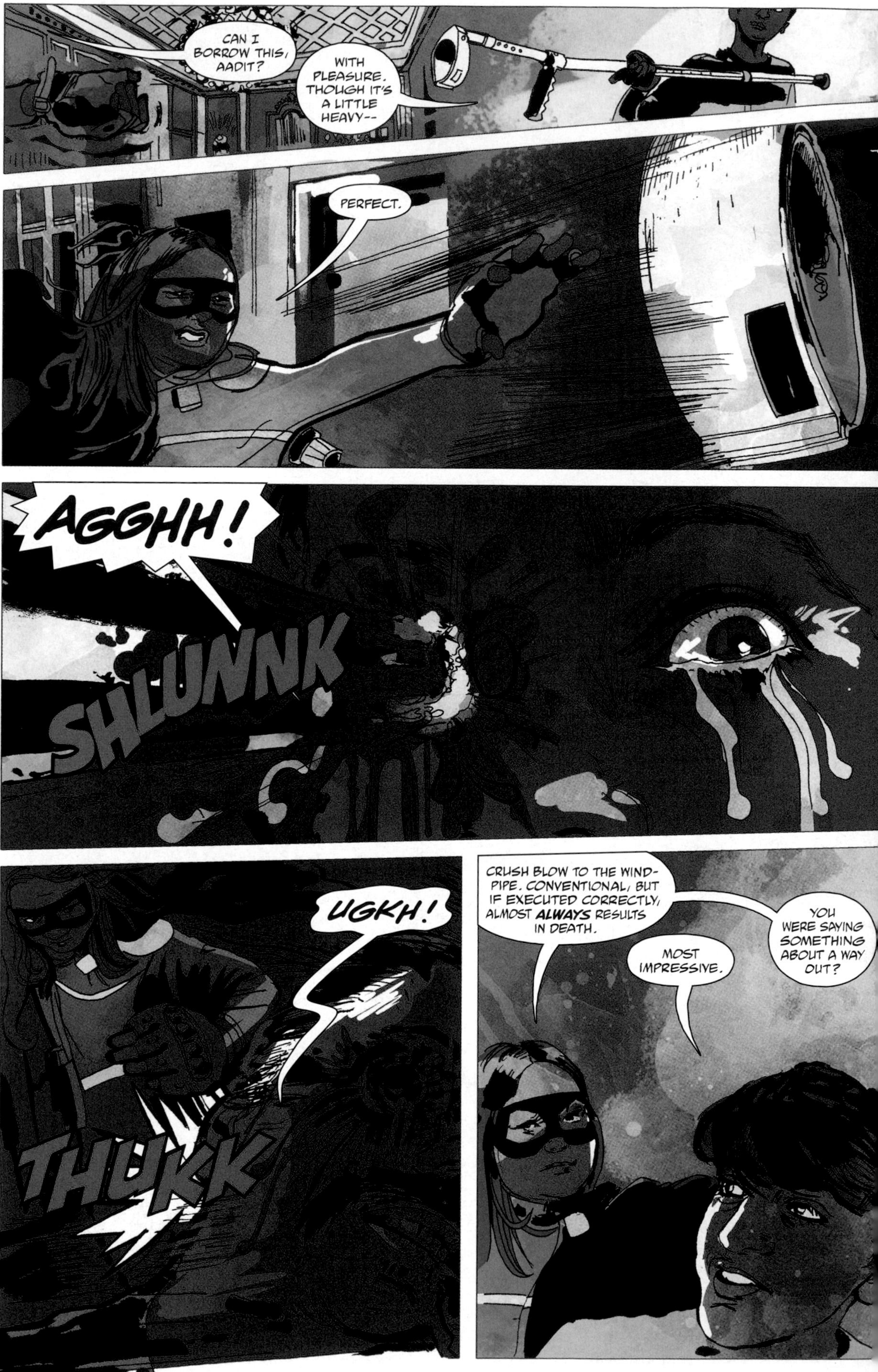
CAN I BORROW THIS, AADIT?
WITH PLEASURE. THOUGH IT'S A LITTLE HEAVY--
PERFECT.
AGGHH!
SHLUNNK
UGKH!
THUKK
CRUSH BLOW TO THE WIND-PIPE. CONVENTIONAL, BUT IF EXECUTED CORRECTLY, ALMOST ALWAYS RESULTS IN DEATH.
MOST IMPRESSIVE.
YOU WERE SAYING SOMETHING ABOUT A WAY OUT?

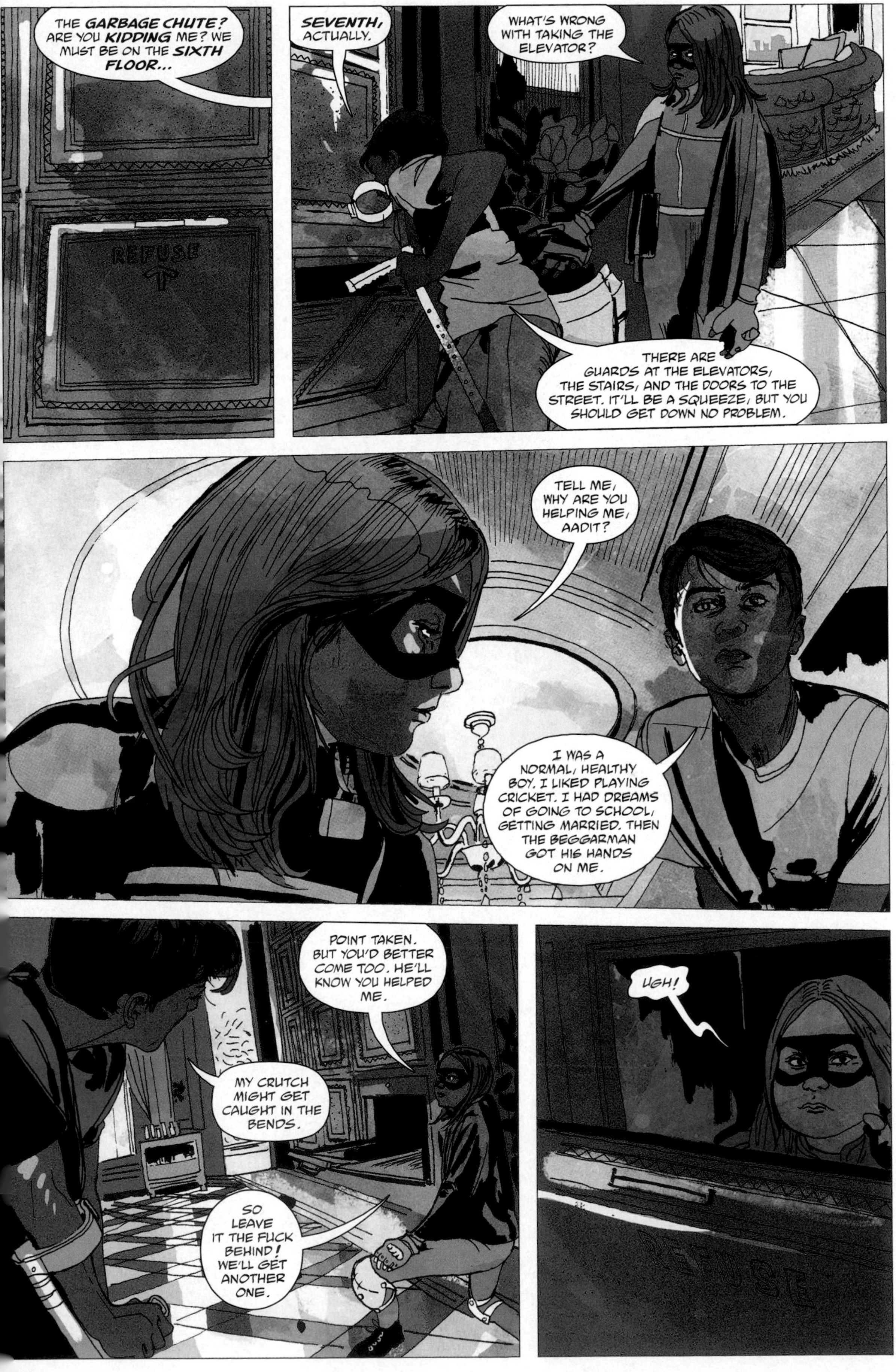
THE GARBAGE CHUTE? ARE YOU KIDDING ME? WE MUST BE ON THE SIXTH FLOOR...
REFUSE
SEVENTH, ACTUALLY.
WHAT'S WRONG WITH TAKING THE ELEVATOR?
THERE ARE GUARDS AT THE ELEVATORS, THE STAIRS, AND THE DOORS TO THE STREET. IT'LL BE A SQUEEZE, BUT YOU SHOULD GET DOWN NO PROBLEM.
TELL ME, WHY ARE YOU HELPING ME, AADIT?
I WAS A NORMAL, HEALTHY BOY. I LIKED PLAYING CRICKET. I HAD DREAMS OF GOING TO SCHOOL, GETTING MARRIED. THEN THE BEGGARMAN GOT HIS HANDS ON ME.
POINT TAKEN. BUT YOU'D BETTER COME TOO. HE'LL KNOW YOU HELPED ME.
MY CRUTCH MIGHT GET CAUGHT IN THE BENDS.
SO LEAVE IT THE FUCK BEHIND! WE'LL GET ANOTHER ONE.
UGH!

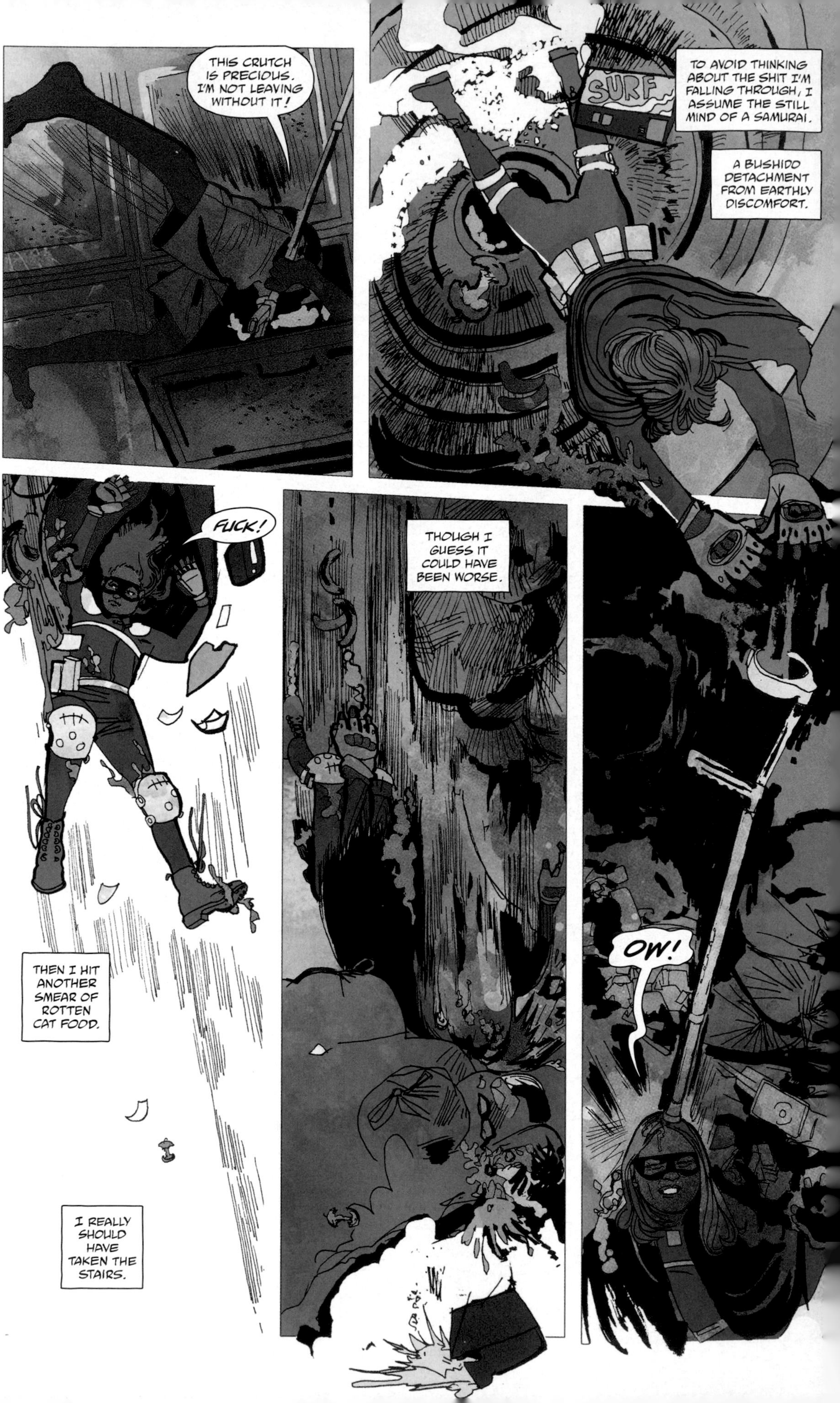
THIS CRUTCH IS PRECIOUS. I'M NOT LEAVING WITHOUT IT!
TO AVOID THINKING ABOUT THE SHIT I'M FALLING THROUGH, I ASSUME THE STILL MIND OF A SAMURAI.
A BUSHIDO DETACHMENT FROM EARTHLY DISCOMFORT.
SURF
FUCK!
THEN I HIT ANOTHER SMEAR OF ROTTEN CAT FOOD.
I REALLY SHOULD HAVE TAKEN THE STAIRS.
THOUGH I GUESS IT COULD HAVE BEEN WORSE.
OW!

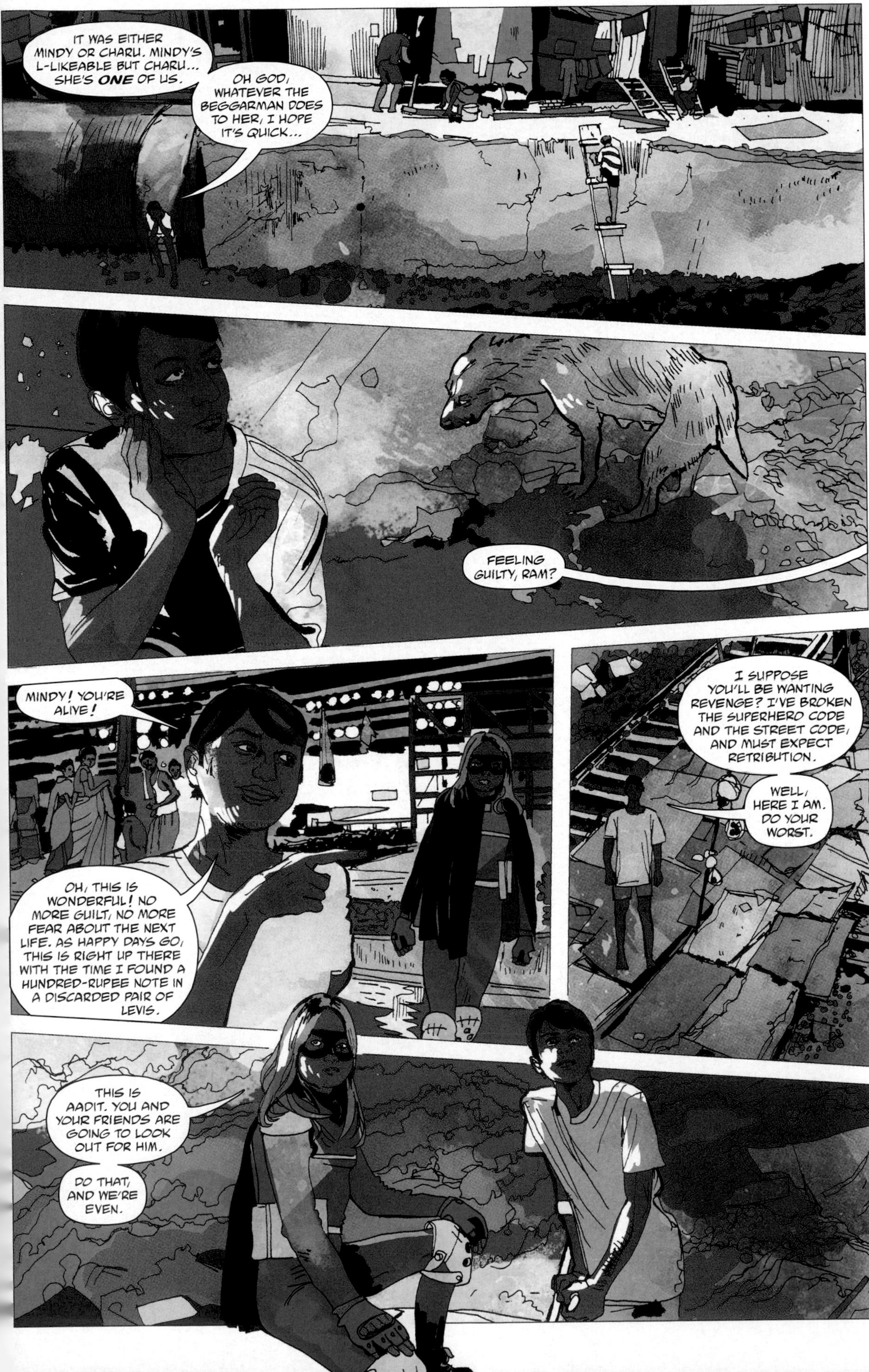
IT WAS EITHER MINDY OR CHARU. MINDY'S L-LIKEABLE BUT CHARU... SHE'S ONE OF US.
OH GOD, WHATEVER THE BEGGARMAN DOES TO HER, I HOPE IT'S QUICK...
FEELING GUILTY, RAM?
MINDY! YOU'RE ALIVE!
OH, THIS IS WONDERFUL! NO MORE GUILT, NO MORE FEAR ABOUT THE NEXT LIFE. AS HAPPY DAYS GO, THIS IS RIGHT UP THERE WITH THE TIME I FOUND A HUNDRED-RUPEE NOTE IN A DISCARDED PAIR OF LEVIS.
I SUPPOSE YOU'LL BE WANTING REVENGE? I'VE BROKEN THE SUPERHERO CODE AND THE STREET CODE, AND MUST EXPECT RETRIBUTION.
WELL, HERE I AM. DO YOUR WORST.
THIS IS AADIT. YOU AND YOUR FRIENDS ARE GOING TO LOOK OUT FOR HIM.
DO THAT, AND WE'RE EVEN.

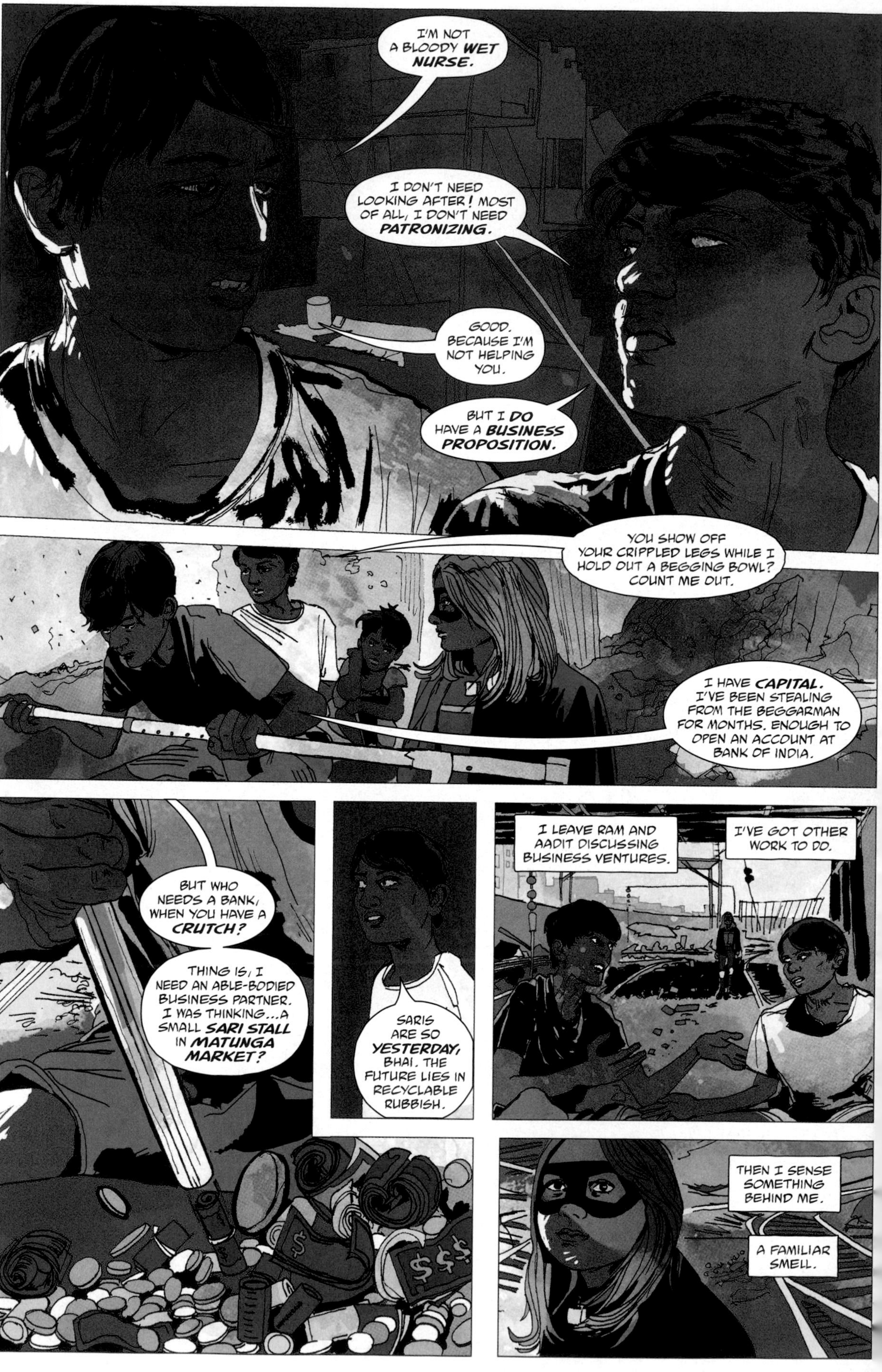
I'M NOT A BLOODY WET NURSE.
I DON'T NEED LOOKING AFTER! MOST OF ALL, I DON'T NEED PATRONIZING.
GOOD. BECAUSE I'M NOT HELPING YOU.
BUT I DO HAVE A BUSINESS PROPOSITION.
YOU SHOW OFF YOUR CRIPPLED LEGS WHILE I HOLD OUT A BEGGING BOWL? COUNT ME OUT.
I HAVE CAPITAL. I'VE BEEN STEALING FROM THE BEGGARMAN FOR MONTHS. ENOUGH TO OPEN AN ACCOUNT AT BANK OF INDIA.
BUT WHO NEEDS A BANK, WHEN YOU HAVE A CRUTCH?
THING IS, I NEED AN ABLE-BODIED BUSINESS PARTNER. I WAS THINKING...A SMALL SARI STALL IN MATUNGA MARKET?
SARIS ARE SO YESTERDAY, BHAI. THE FUTURE LIES IN RECYCLABLE RUBBISH.
I LEAVE RAM AND AADIT DISCUSSING BUSINESS VENTURES.
I'VE GOT OTHER WORK TO DO.
THEN I SENSE SOMETHING BEHIND ME.
A FAMILIAR SMELL.

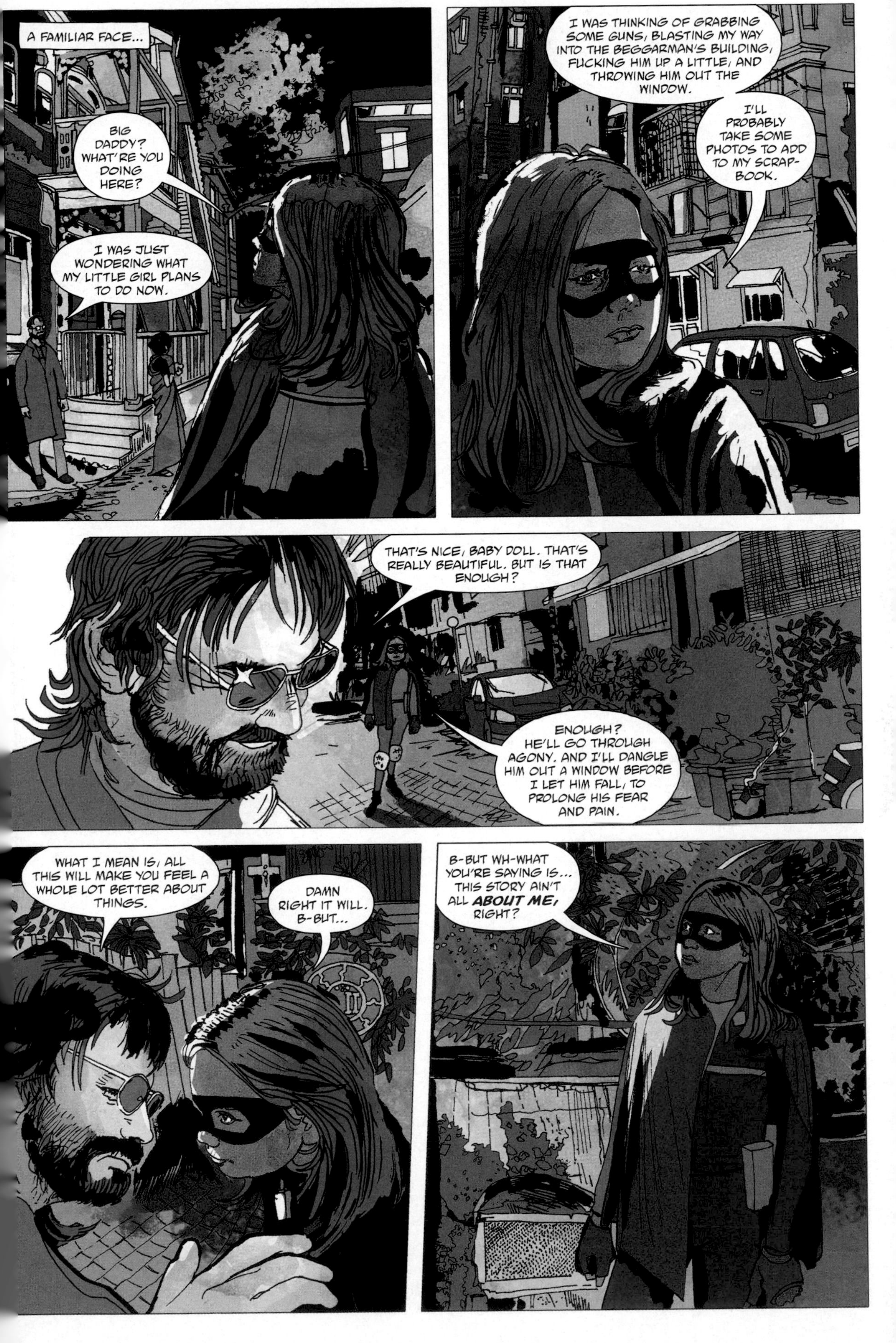
A FAMILIAR FACE...
BIG DADDY? WHAT'RE YOU DOING HERE?
I WAS JUST WONDERING WHAT MY LITTLE GIRL PLANS TO DO NOW.
I WAS THINKING OF GRABBING SOME GUNS, BLASTING MY WAY INTO THE BEGGARMAN'S BUILDING, FUCKING HIM UP A LITTLE, AND THROWING HIM OUT THE WINDOW.
I'LL PROBABLY TAKE SOME PHOTOS TO ADD TO MY SCRAPBOOK.
THAT'S NICE, BABY DOLL. THAT'S REALLY BEAUTIFUL. BUT IS THAT ENOUGH?
ENOUGH? HE'LL GO THROUGH AGONY. AND I'LL DANGLE HIM OUT A WINDOW BEFORE I LET HIM FALL, TO PROLONG HIS FEAR AND PAIN.
WHAT I MEAN IS, ALL THIS WILL MAKE YOU FEEL A WHOLE LOT BETTER ABOUT THINGS.
DAMN RIGHT IT WILL. B-BUT...
B-BUT WH-WHAT YOU'RE SAYING IS... THIS STORY AIN'T ALL **ABOUT ME**, RIGHT?

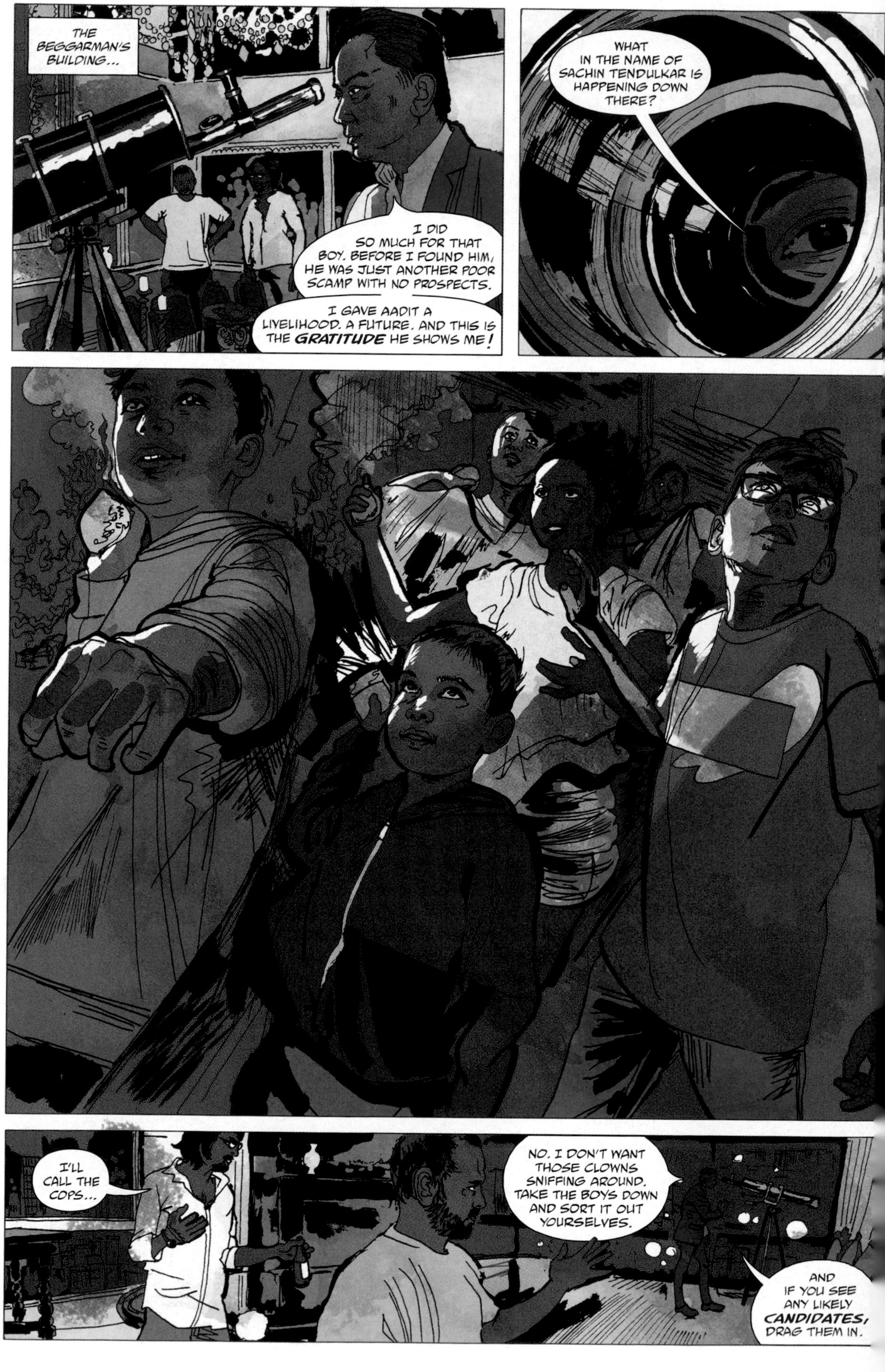

THE BEGGARMAN'S BUILDING...
I DID SO MUCH FOR THAT BOY. BEFORE I FOUND HIM, HE WAS JUST ANOTHER POOR SCAMP WITH NO PROSPECTS.
I GAVE AADIT A LIVELIHOOD. A FUTURE. AND THIS IS THE **GRATITUDE** HE SHOWS ME!
WHAT IN THE NAME OF SACHIN TENDULKAR IS HAPPENING DOWN THERE?
I'LL CALL THE COPS...
NO. I DON'T WANT THOSE CLOWNS SNIFFING AROUND. TAKE THE BOYS DOWN AND SORT IT OUT YOURSELVES.
AND IF YOU SEE ANY LIKELY **CANDIDATES,** DRAG THEM IN.

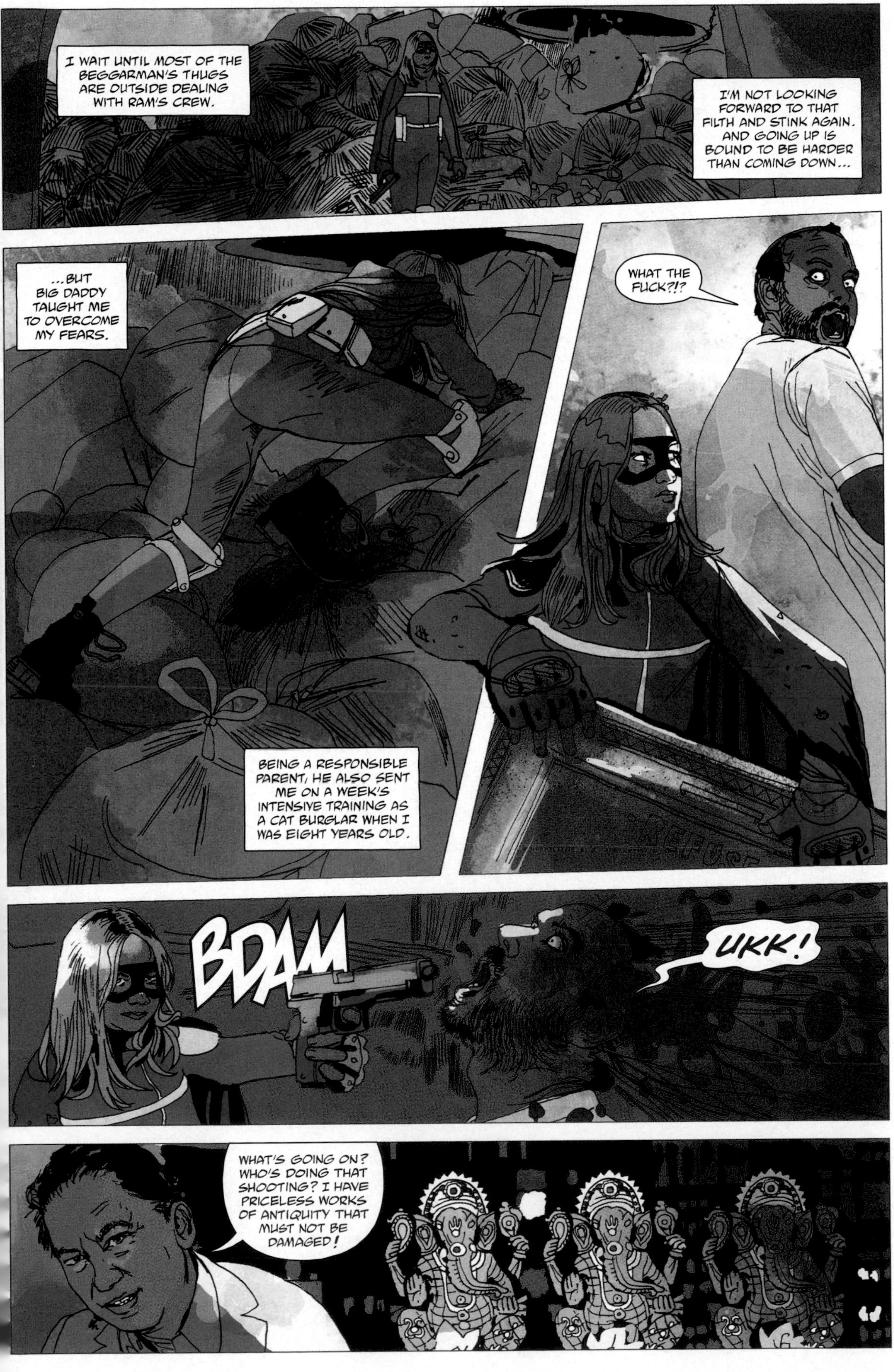
I WAIT UNTIL MOST OF THE BEGGARMAN'S THUGS ARE OUTSIDE DEALING WITH RAM'S CREW.
I'M NOT LOOKING FORWARD TO THAT FILTH AND STINK AGAIN. AND GOING UP IS BOUND TO BE HARDER THAN COMING DOWN...
...BUT BIG DADDY TAUGHT ME TO OVERCOME MY FEARS.
BEING A RESPONSIBLE PARENT, HE ALSO SENT ME ON A WEEK'S INTENSIVE TRAINING AS A CAT BURGLAR WHEN I WAS EIGHT YEARS OLD.
WHAT THE FUCK?!?
BDAM
UKK!
WHAT'S GOING ON? WHO'S DOING THAT SHOOTING? I HAVE PRICELESS WORKS OF ANTIQUITY THAT MUST NOT BE DAMAGED!

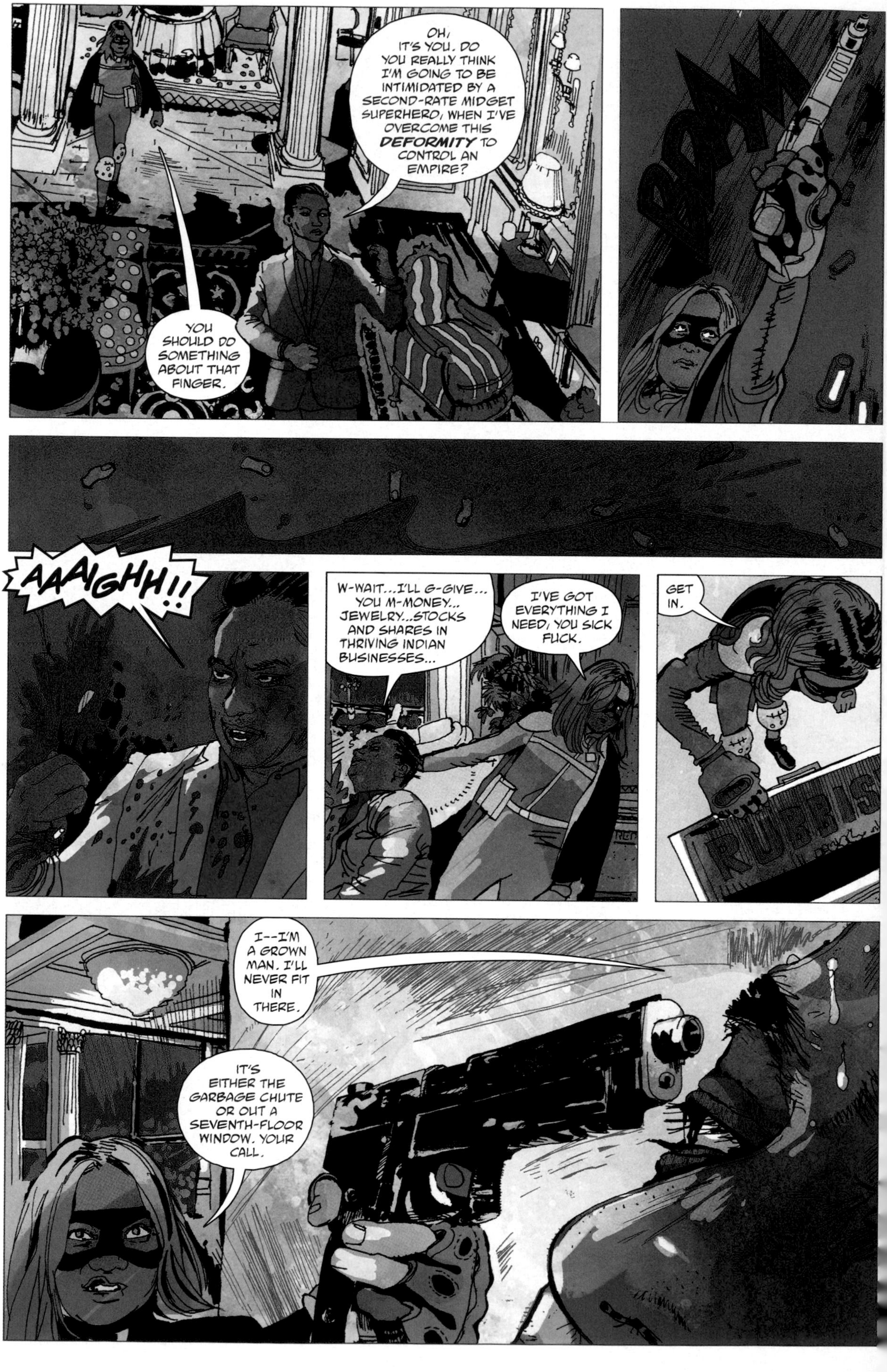
OH, IT'S YOU. DO YOU REALLY THINK I'M GOING TO BE INTIMIDATED BY A SECOND-RATE MIDGET SUPERHERO, WHEN I'VE OVERCOME THIS **DEFORMITY** TO CONTROL AN EMPIRE?
YOU SHOULD DO SOMETHING ABOUT THAT FINGER.
AAAIGHH!!
W-WAIT...I'LL G-GIVE... YOU M-MONEY... JEWELRY...STOCKS AND SHARES IN THRIVING INDIAN BUSINESSES...
I'VE GOT EVERYTHING I NEED, YOU SICK FUCK.
GET IN.
I--I'M A GROWN MAN. I'LL NEVER FIT IN THERE.
IT'S EITHER THE GARBAGE CHUTE OR OUT A SEVENTH-FLOOR WINDOW. YOUR CALL.

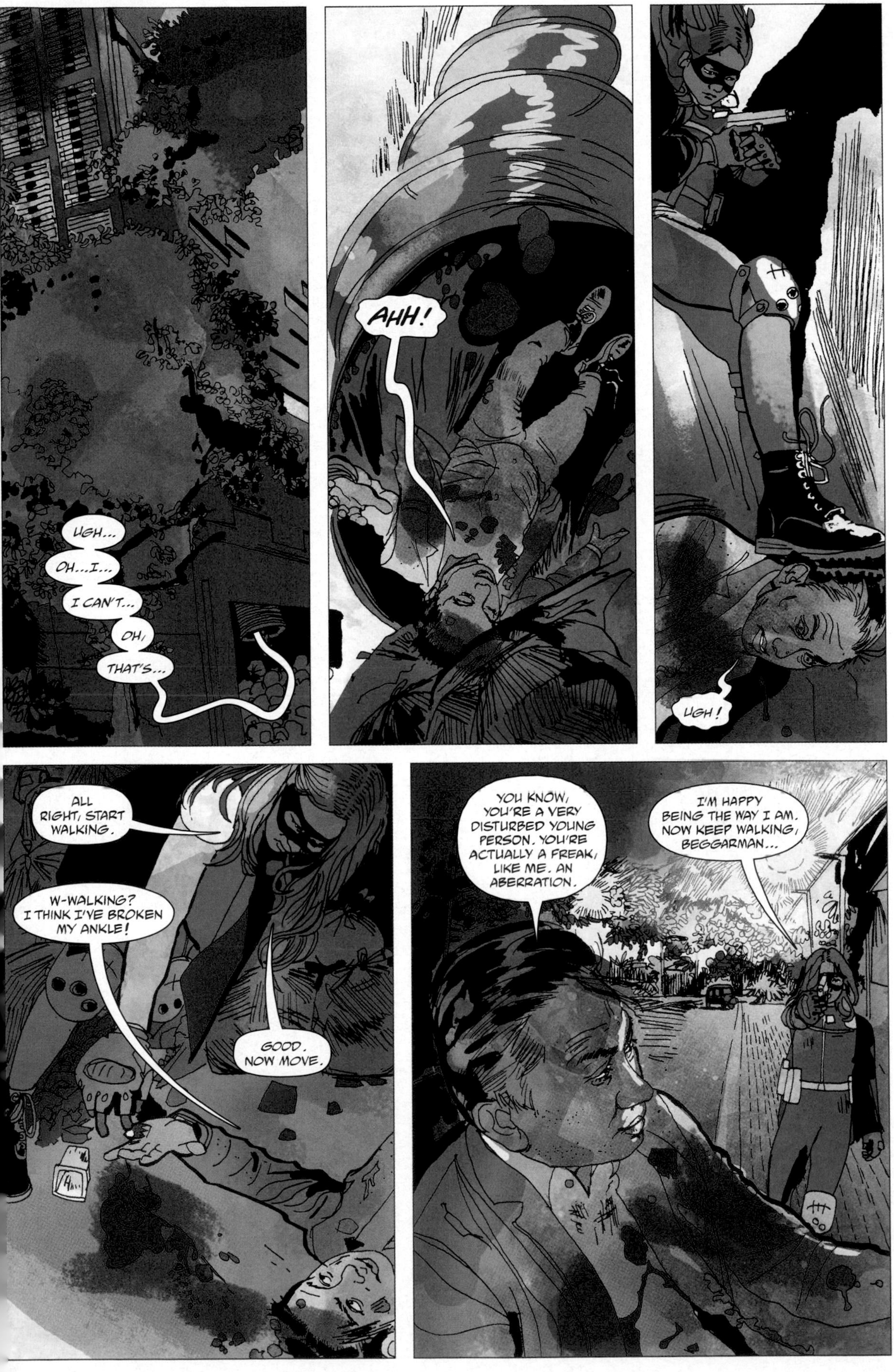
UGH...
OH...I...
I CAN'T...
OH,
THAT'S...
AHH!
UGH!
ALL RIGHT, START WALKING.
W-WALKING? I THINK I'VE BROKEN MY ANKLE!
GOOD. NOW MOVE.
YOU KNOW, YOU'RE A VERY DISTURBED YOUNG PERSON. YOU'RE ACTUALLY A FREAK, LIKE ME. AN ABERRATION.
I'M HAPPY BEING THE WAY I AM. NOW KEEP WALKING, BEGGARMAN...

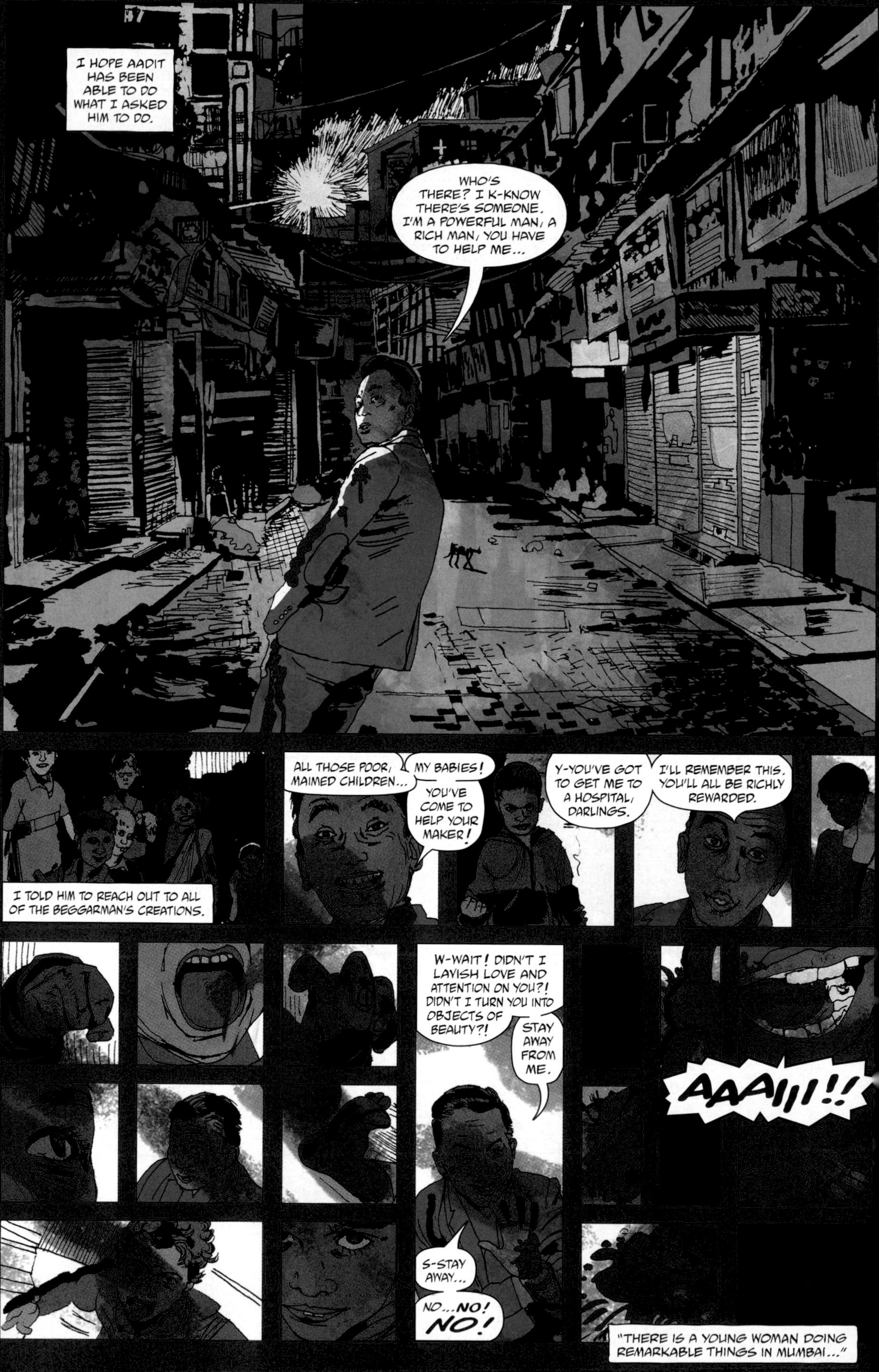

I HOPE AADIT HAS BEEN ABLE TO DO WHAT I ASKED HIM TO DO.
WHO'S THERE? I K-KNOW THERE'S SOMEONE. I'M A POWERFUL MAN, A RICH MAN, YOU HAVE TO HELP ME...
I TOLD HIM TO REACH OUT TO ALL OF THE BEGGARMAN'S CREATIONS.
ALL THOSE POOR, MAIMED CHILDREN...
MY BABIES!
YOU'VE COME TO HELP YOUR MAKER!
Y-YOU'VE GOT TO GET ME TO A HOSPITAL, DARLINGS.
I'LL REMEMBER THIS. YOU'LL ALL BE RICHLY REWARDED.
W-WAIT! DIDN'T I LAVISH LOVE AND ATTENTION ON YOU?! DIDN'T I TURN YOU INTO OBJECTS OF BEAUTY?!
STAY AWAY FROM ME.
S-STAY AWAY...
NO...NO! NO!
AAAIII!!
"THERE IS A YOUNG WOMAN DOING REMARKABLE THINGS IN MUMBAI..."

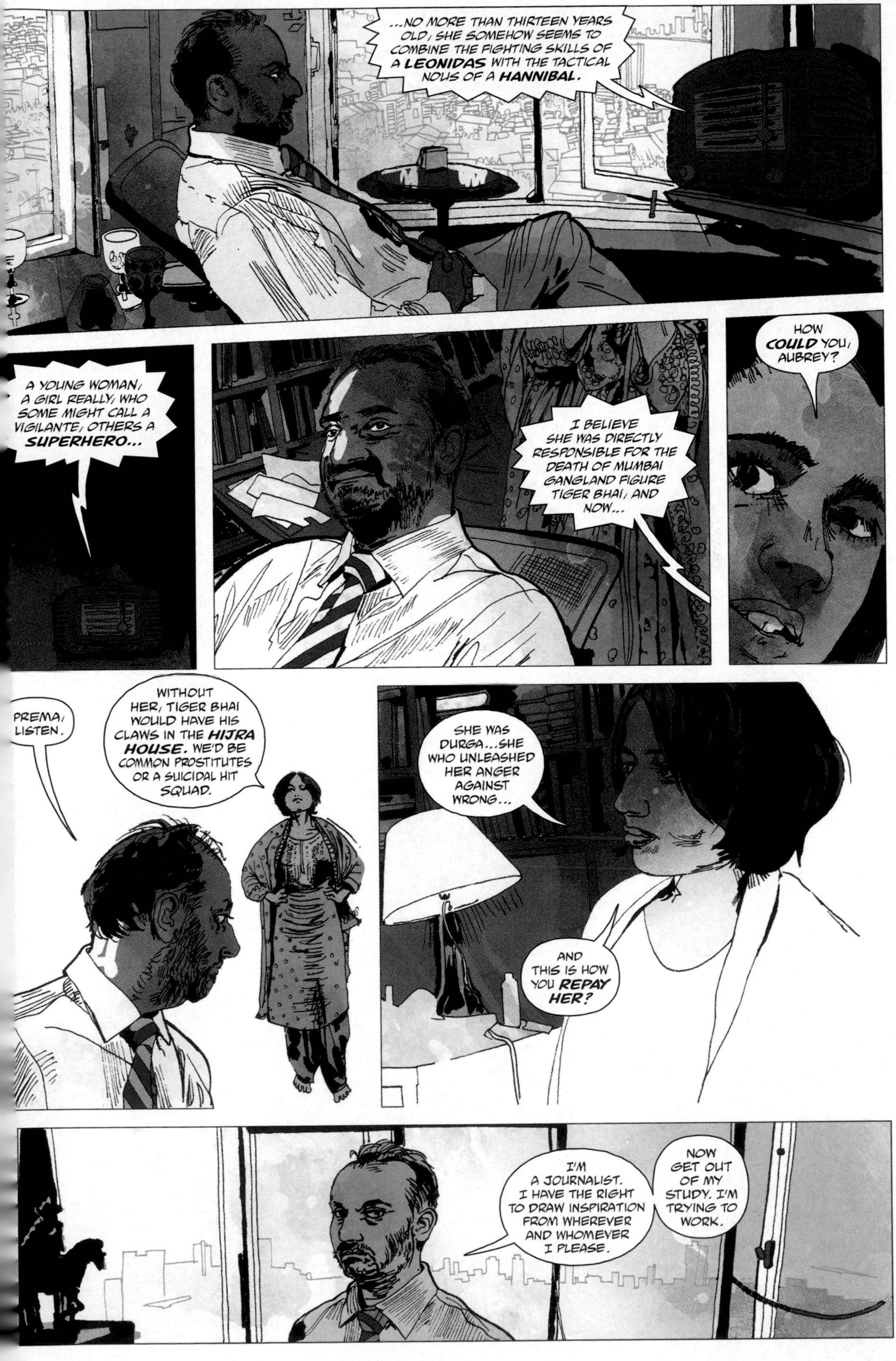
...NO MORE THAN THIRTEEN YEARS OLD, SHE SOMEHOW SEEMS TO COMBINE THE FIGHTING SKILLS OF A LEONIDAS WITH THE TACTICAL NOUS OF A HANNIBAL.
A YOUNG WOMAN, A GIRL REALLY, WHO SOME MIGHT CALL A VIGILANTE, OTHERS A SUPERHERO...
I BELIEVE SHE WAS DIRECTLY RESPONSIBLE FOR THE DEATH OF MUMBAI GANGLAND FIGURE TIGER BHAI, AND NOW...
HOW COULD YOU, AUBREY?
PREMA, LISTEN.
WITHOUT HER, TIGER BHAI WOULD HAVE HIS CLAWS IN THE HIJRA HOUSE. WE'D BE COMMON PROSTITUTES OR A SUICIDAL HIT SQUAD.
SHE WAS DURGA...SHE WHO UNLEASHED HER ANGER AGAINST WRONG...
AND THIS IS HOW YOU REPAY HER?
I'M A JOURNALIST. I HAVE THE RIGHT TO DRAW INSPIRATION FROM WHEREVER AND WHOMEVER I PLEASE.
NOW GET OUT OF MY STUDY. I'M TRYING TO WORK.

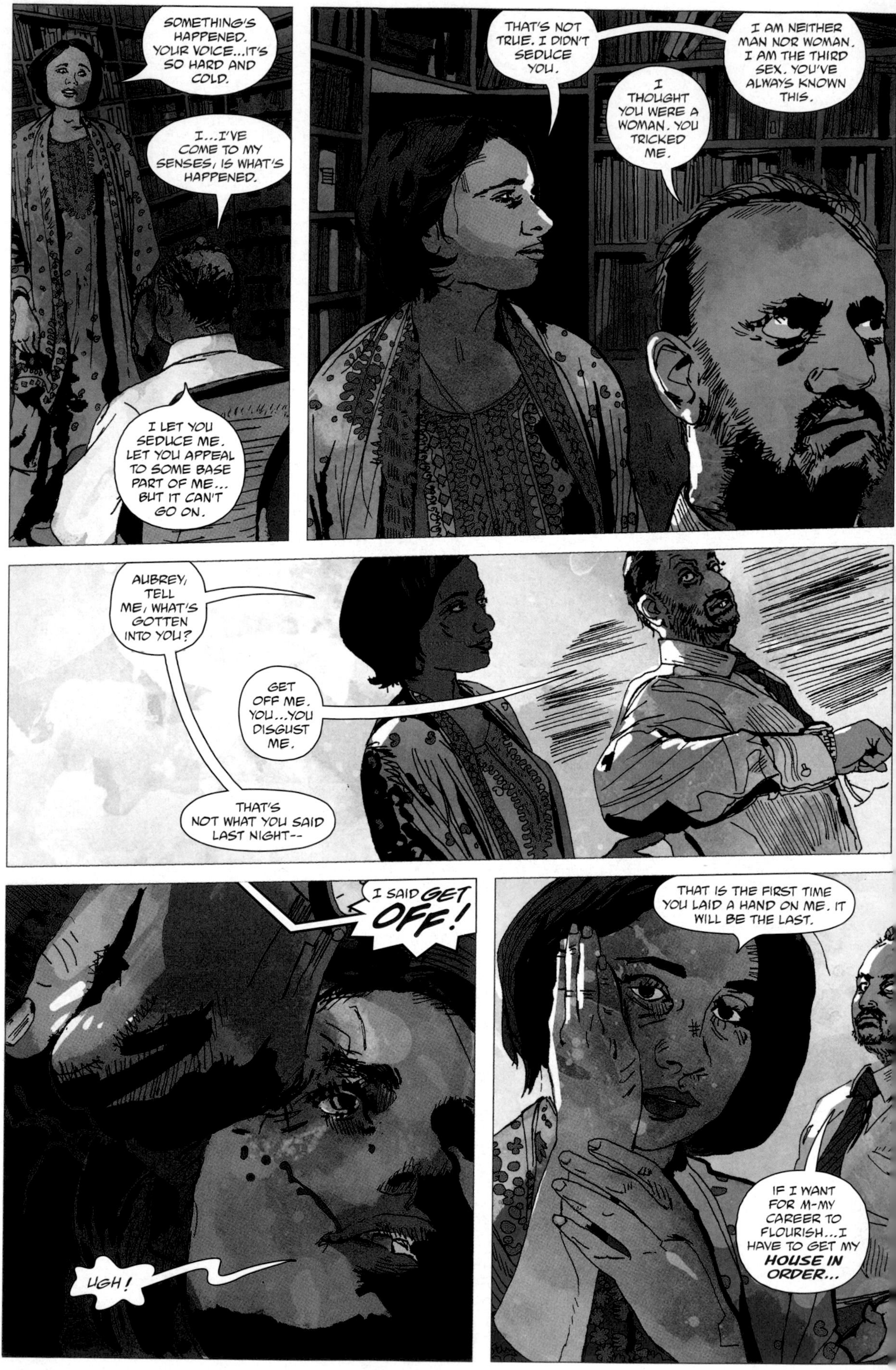
SOMETHING'S HAPPENED. YOUR VOICE...IT'S SO HARD AND COLD.
I...I'VE COME TO MY SENSES, IS WHAT'S HAPPENED.
I LET YOU SEDUCE ME. LET YOU APPEAL TO SOME BASE PART OF ME... BUT IT CAN'T GO ON.
THAT'S NOT TRUE. I DIDN'T SEDUCE YOU.
I AM NEITHER MAN NOR WOMAN. I AM THE THIRD SEX. YOU'VE ALWAYS KNOWN THIS.
I THOUGHT YOU WERE A WOMAN. YOU TRICKED ME.
AUBREY, TELL ME, WHAT'S GOTTEN INTO YOU?
GET OFF ME. YOU...YOU DISGUST ME.
THAT'S NOT WHAT YOU SAID LAST NIGHT--
I SAID GET OFF!
UGH!
THAT IS THE FIRST TIME YOU LAID A HAND ON ME. IT WILL BE THE LAST.
IF I WANT FOR M-MY CAREER TO FLOURISH...I HAVE TO GET MY HOUSE IN ORDER...

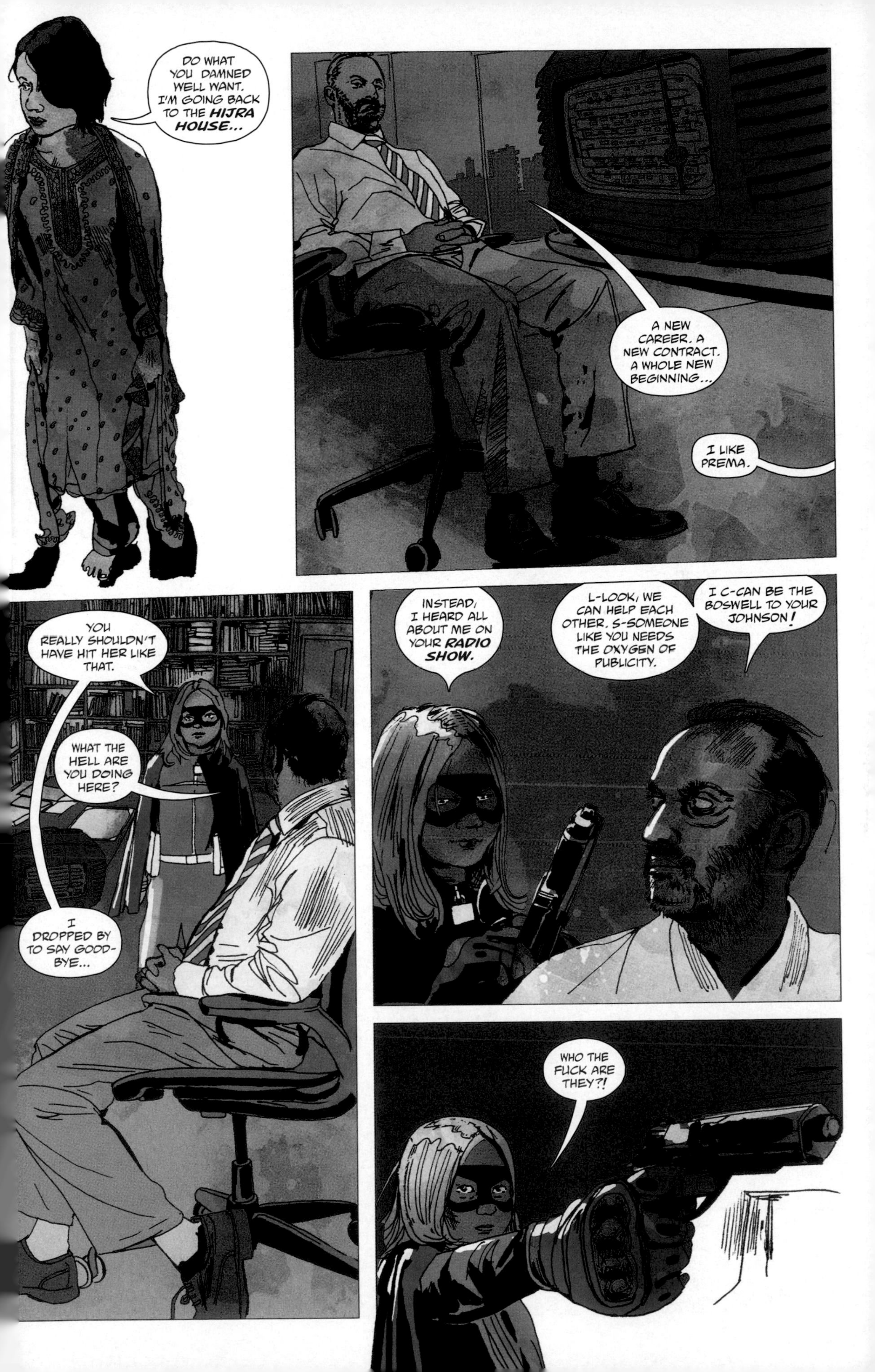
DO WHAT YOU DAMNED WELL WANT. I'M GOING BACK TO THE HIJRA HOUSE...
A NEW CAREER. A NEW CONTRACT. A WHOLE NEW BEGINNING...
I LIKE PREMA.
YOU REALLY SHOULDN'T HAVE HIT HER LIKE THAT.
WHAT THE HELL ARE YOU DOING HERE?
I DROPPED BY TO SAY GOOD-BYE...
INSTEAD, I HEARD ALL ABOUT ME ON YOUR RADIO SHOW.
L-LOOK, WE CAN HELP EACH OTHER. S-SOMEONE LIKE YOU NEEDS THE OXYGEN OF PUBLICITY.
I C-CAN BE THE BOSWELL TO YOUR JOHNSON!
WHO THE FUCK ARE THEY?!

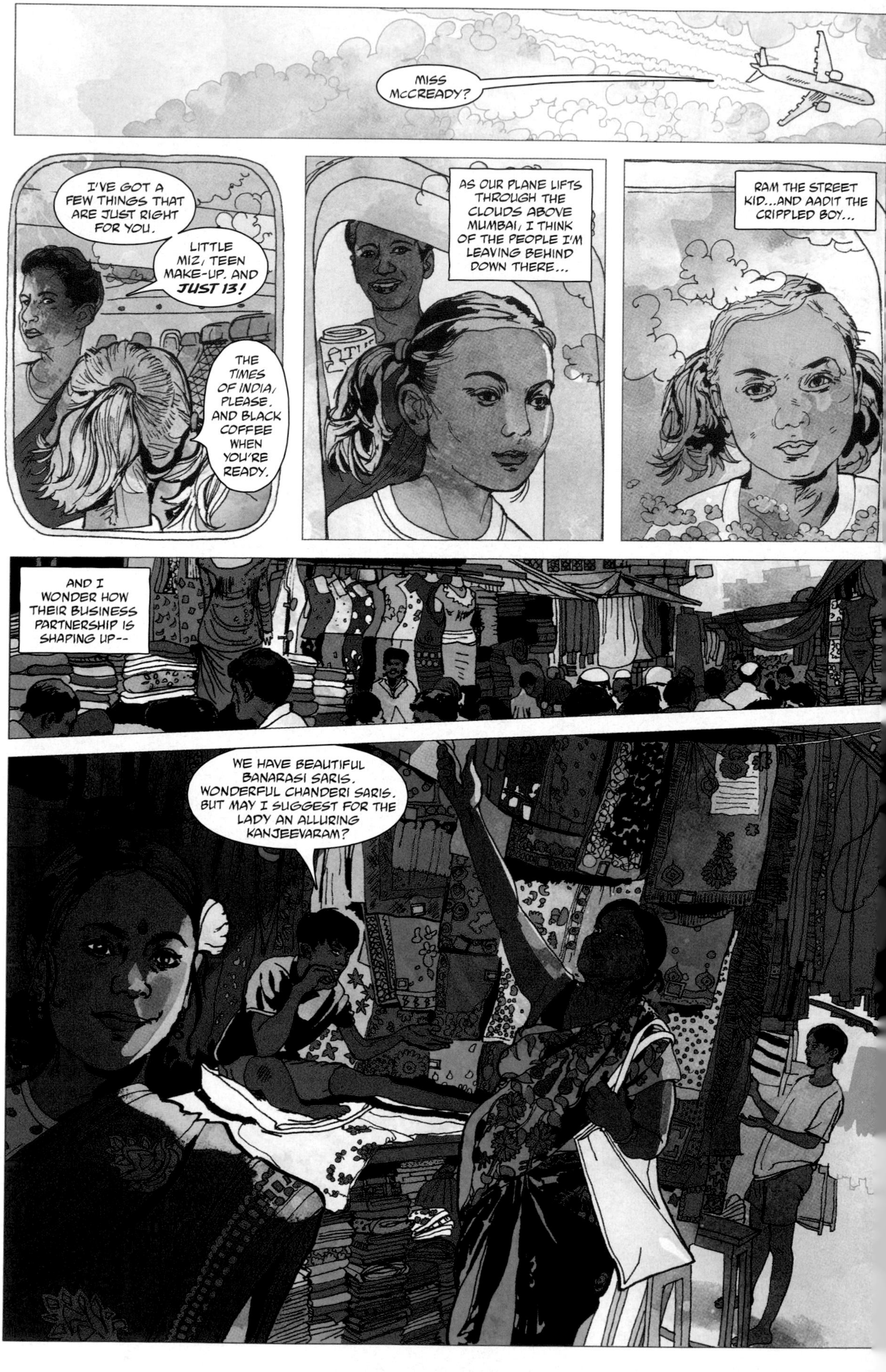
MISS McCREADY?
I'VE GOT A FEW THINGS THAT ARE JUST RIGHT FOR YOU.
LITTLE MIZ, TEEN MAKE-UP. AND JUST 13!
THE TIMES OF INDIA, PLEASE. AND BLACK COFFEE WHEN YOU'RE READY.
AS OUR PLANE LIFTS THROUGH THE CLOUDS ABOVE MUMBAI, I THINK OF THE PEOPLE I'M LEAVING BEHIND DOWN THERE...
RAM THE STREET KID...AND AADIT THE CRIPPLED BOY...
AND I WONDER HOW THEIR BUSINESS PARTNERSHIP IS SHAPING UP--
WE HAVE BEAUTIFUL BANARASI SARIS. WONDERFUL CHANDERI SARIS. BUT MAY I SUGGEST FOR THE LADY AN ALLURING KANJEEVARAM?

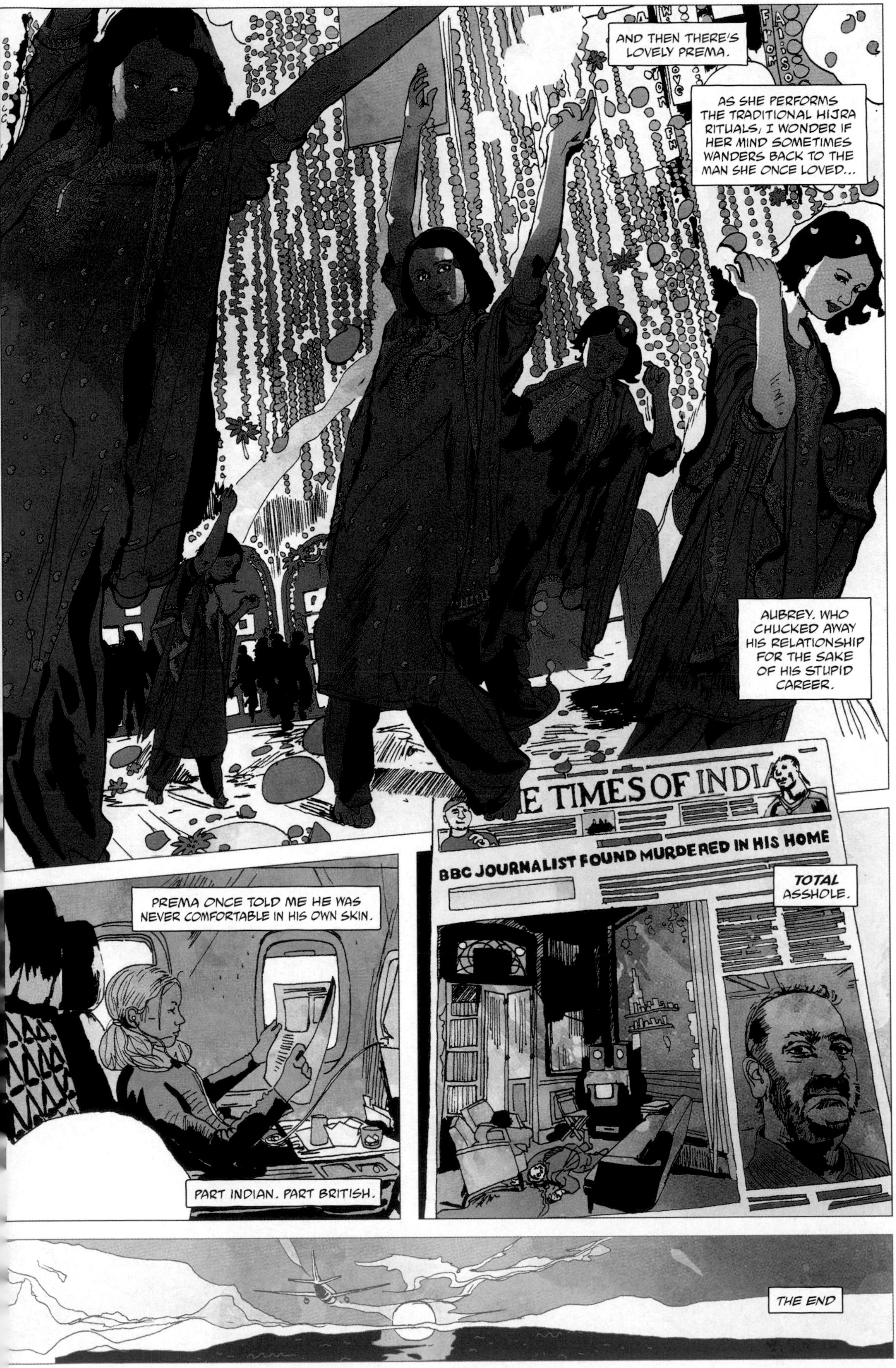
AND THEN THERE'S LOVELY PREMA.
AS SHE PERFORMS THE TRADITIONAL HIJRA RITUALS, I WONDER IF HER MIND SOMETIMES WANDERS BACK TO THE MAN SHE ONCE LOVED...
AUBREY. WHO CHUCKED AWAY HIS RELATIONSHIP FOR THE SAKE OF HIS STUPID CAREER.
PREMA ONCE TOLD ME HE WAS NEVER COMFORTABLE IN HIS OWN SKIN.
PART INDIAN. PART BRITISH.
E TIMES OF INDIA
BBC JOURNALIST FOUND MURDERED IN HIS HOME
TOTAL ASSHOLE.
THE END

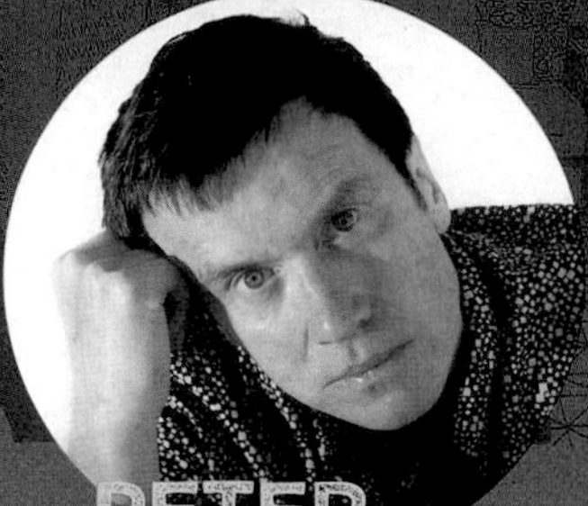

PETER MILLIGAN

One-time Entertainment Weekly's "Man of the Year" Peter Milligan was at the forefront of the revolution in comics which were created for a more sophisticated, adult audience. **SHADE, THE CHANGING MAN** for Vertigo offered a skewed look at American culture, while **ENIGMA**, **FACE**, and **ROGAN GOSH** pushed the boundaries of what comic books could do. The hugely popular **X-STATIX** was a radical reworking of the **X-MAN** paradigm, that led to controversy when Milligan tried to recruit the late Diana Prince of Wales into his celebrity-obsessed bunch of heroes.

Milligan was the longest-running writer of the cult horror comic **HELLBLAZER**, and his take on **HUMAN TARGET** inspired the TV series. More recent work includes the critical hit **BRITANNIA**, a retelling of **THE MUMMY** for Hammer/ Titan, as well as the surreal **KID LOBOTOMY** for IDW.

Milligan has written several screenplays, two of which have been made. **PILGRIM** starring Ray Liotta and the prize-winning **AN ANGEL FOR MAY**, starring Tom Wilkinson.

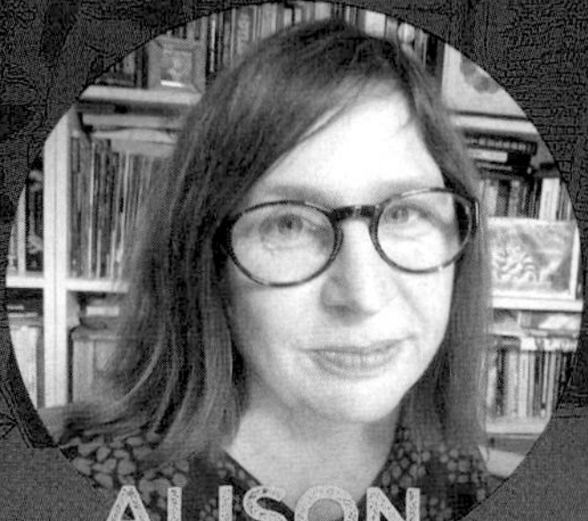

ALISON SAMPSON

is an award-winning artist and architect. She drew the **HIT GIRL: INDIA** comic, written by Peter Milligan, for Image Comics (from October 2019), and is working on the adaption of Stephen and Owen King's **SLEEPING BEAUTIES** book for IDW, for 2020. Amongst other projects, she previously co-created **WINNEBAGO GRAVEYARD** (with Steve Niles) and **GENESIS** for Image, worked on **THE WICKED + THE DIVINE** for the same, drew **JESSICA JONES** for Marvel's **CIVIL WAR 2** event, and made work for DC/ Vertigo, Dark Horse, and BOOM! Studios, and various Eisner-nominated anthologies, including **OUTLAW TERRITORY** (also for Image) and **IN THE DARK** and **FEMME MAGNIFIQUE** for IDW.

London-based, she has never stopped designing, and also makes art (and sometimes architecture) for commercial clients, including the BBC, Netflix, The Guardian newspaper and the Hayward Gallery.

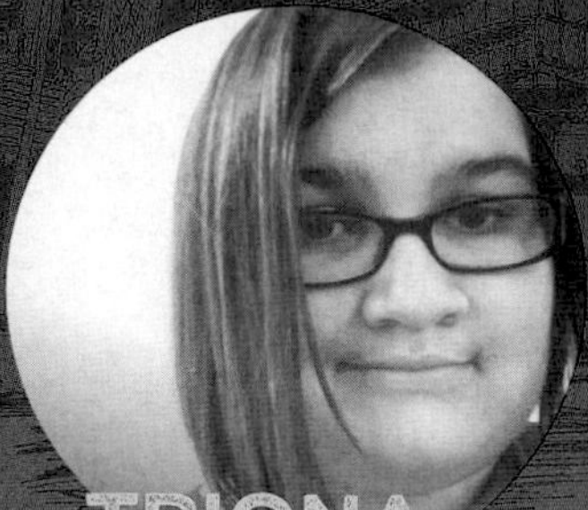

TRIONA FARRELL

is a colorist living in Dublin, Ireland. She's worked on many books across different publishers, such as Marvel, Dark Horse, Image, BOOM! and IDW, and multiple books have been nominated for Eisners. She enjoys all nerdy things and her cat, Leeroy.

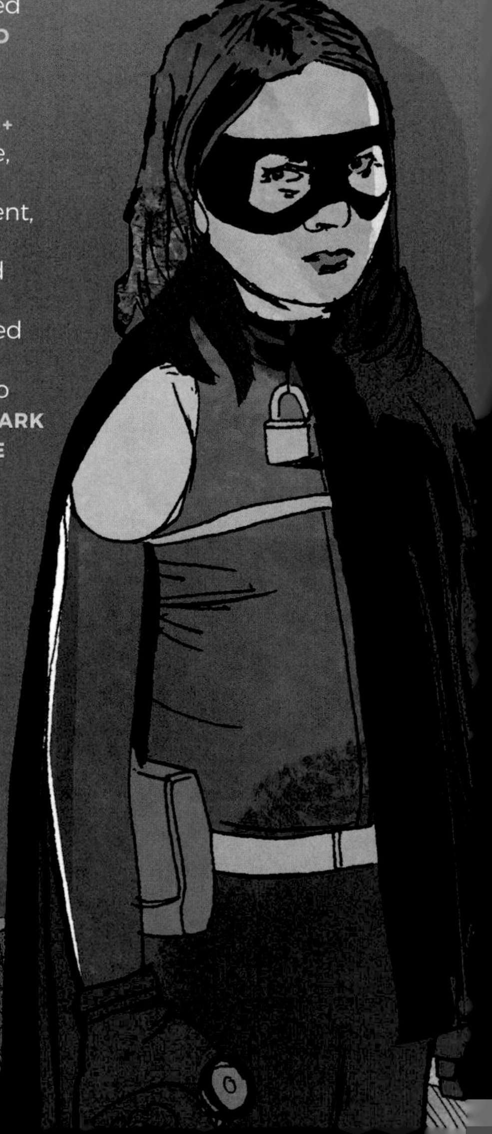

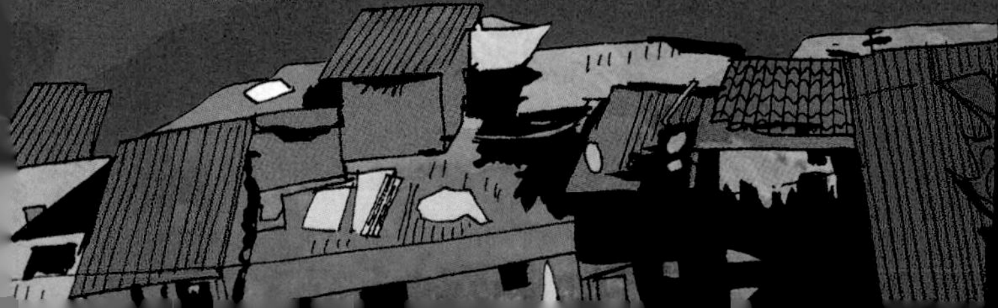

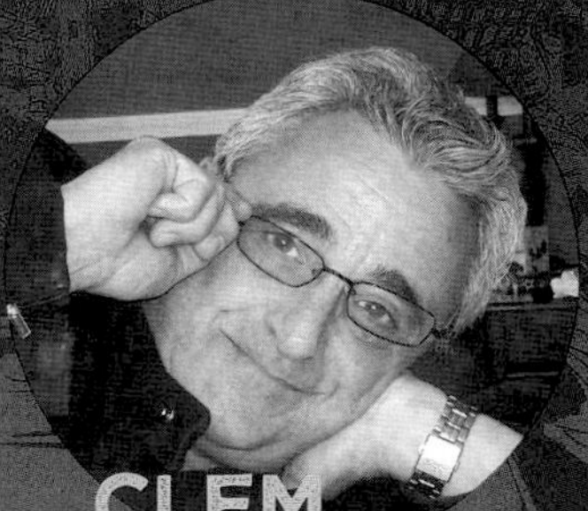

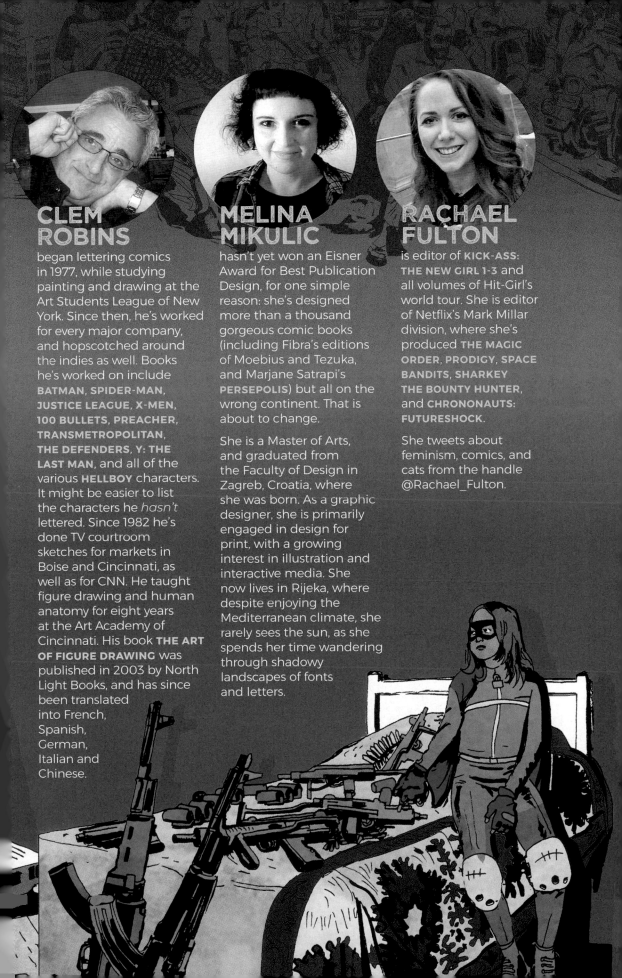

CLEM ROBINS

began lettering comics in 1977, while studying painting and drawing at the Art Students League of New York. Since then, he's worked for every major company, and hopscotched around the indies as well. Books he's worked on include **BATMAN**, **SPIDER-MAN**, **JUSTICE LEAGUE**, **X-MEN**, **100 BULLETS**, **PREACHER**, **TRANSMETROPOLITAN**, **THE DEFENDERS**, **Y: THE LAST MAN**, and all of the various **HELLBOY** characters. It might be easier to list the characters he *hasn't* lettered. Since 1982 he's done TV courtroom sketches for markets in Boise and Cincinnati, as well as for CNN. He taught figure drawing and human anatomy for eight years at the Art Academy of Cincinnati. His book **THE ART OF FIGURE DRAWING** was published in 2003 by North Light Books, and has since been translated into French, Spanish, German, Italian and Chinese.

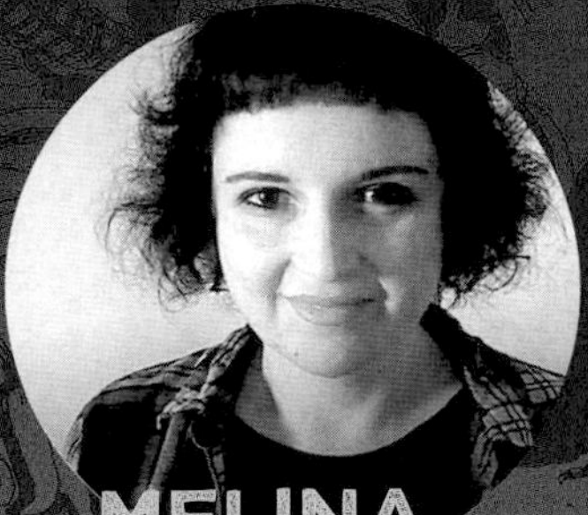

MELINA MIKULIC

hasn't yet won an Eisner Award for Best Publication Design, for one simple reason: she's designed more than a thousand gorgeous comic books (including Fibra's editions of Moebius and Tezuka, and Marjane Satrapi's **PERSEPOLIS**) but all on the wrong continent. That is about to change.

She is a Master of Arts, and graduated from the Faculty of Design in Zagreb, Croatia, where she was born. As a graphic designer, she is primarily engaged in design for print, with a growing interest in illustration and interactive media. She now lives in Rijeka, where despite enjoying the Mediterranean climate, she rarely sees the sun, as she spends her time wandering through shadowy landscapes of fonts and letters.

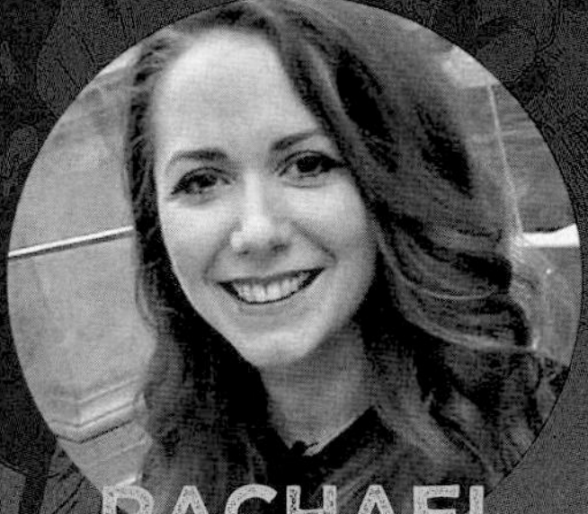

RACHAEL FULTON

is editor of **KICK-ASS: THE NEW GIRL 1-3** and all volumes of Hit-Girl's world tour. She is editor of Netflix's Mark Millar division, where she's produced **THE MAGIC ORDER**, **PRODIGY**, **SPACE BANDITS**, **SHARKEY THE BOUNTY HUNTER**, and **CHRONONAUTS: FUTURESHOCK**.

She tweets about feminism, comics, and cats from the handle @Rachael_Fulton.

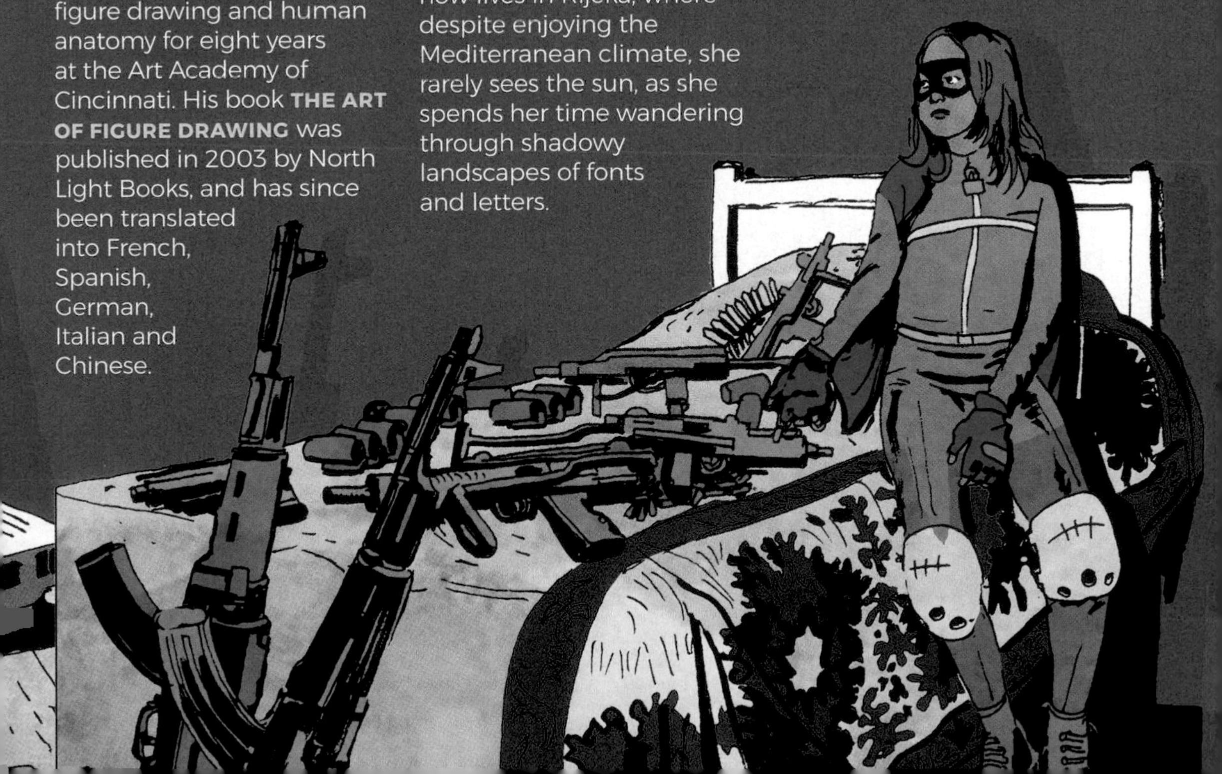

VARIANT COVER

ALISON SAMPSON

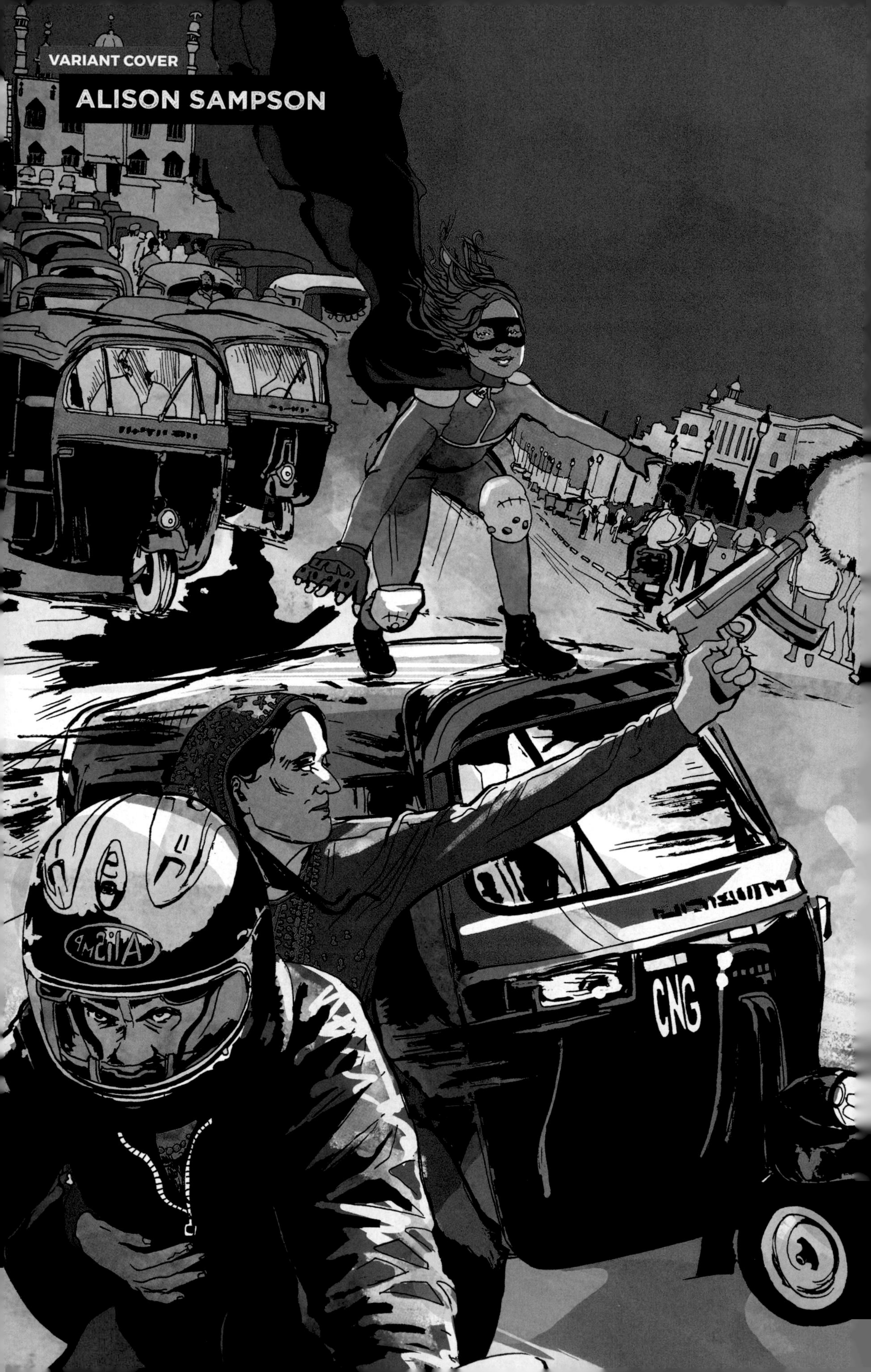
CNG

VARIANT COVER

OZGUR YILDIRIM

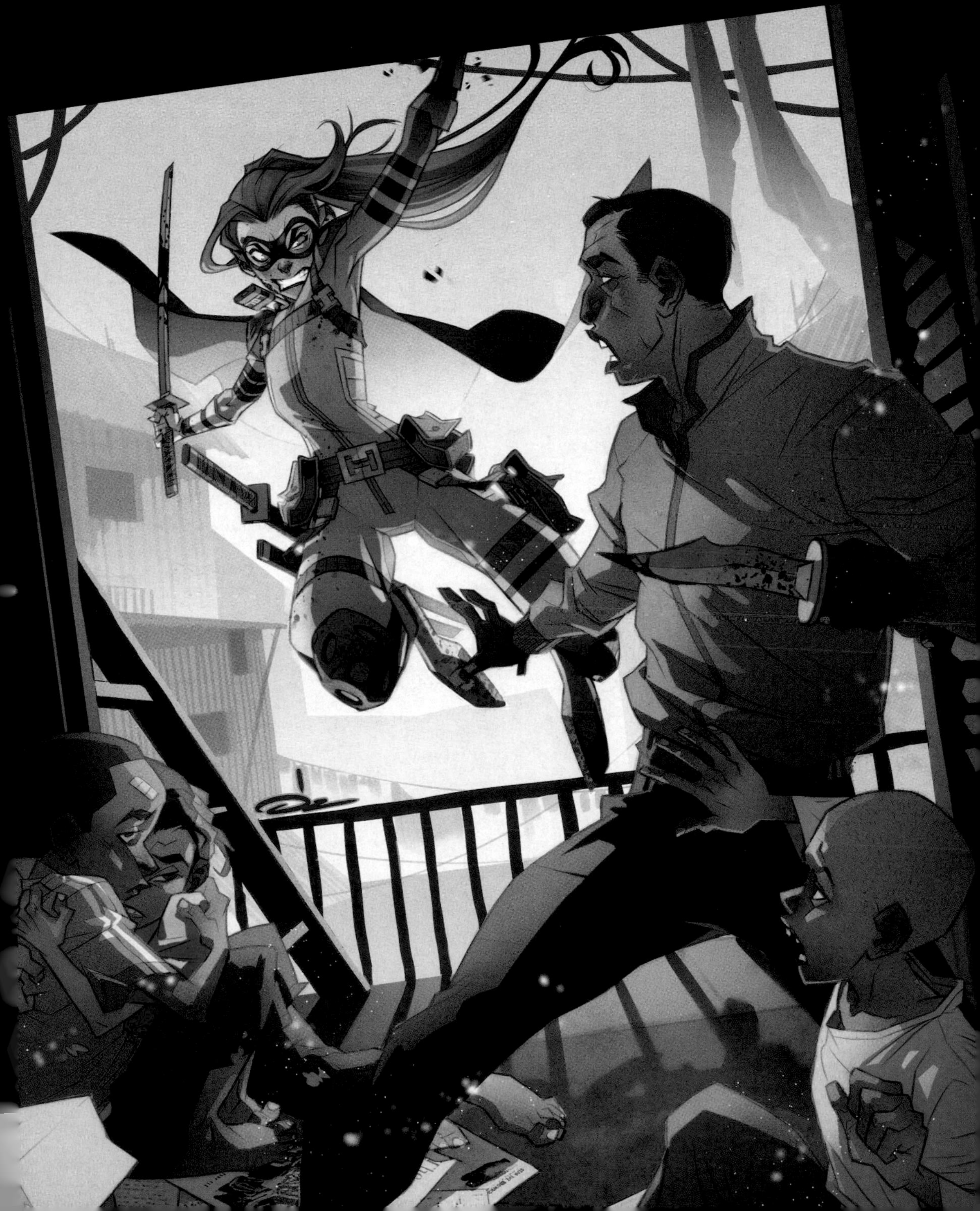

The CO

KICK-ASS

SER

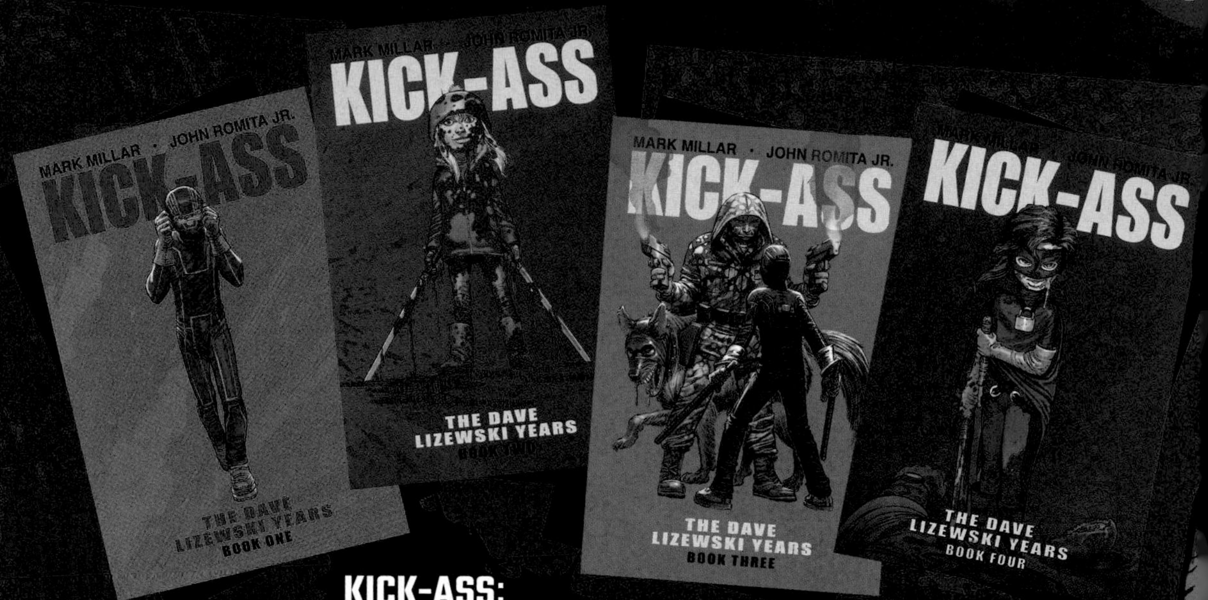
MARK MILLAR • JOHN ROMITA JR.
KICK-ASS
THE DAVE LIZEWSKI YEARS
BOOK ONE
MARK MILLAR • JOHN ROMITA JR.
KICK-ASS
THE DAVE LIZEWSKI YEARS
MARK MILLAR • JOHN ROMITA JR.
KICK-ASS
THE DAVE LIZEWSKI YEARS
BOOK THREE
KICK-ASS
THE DAVE LIZEWSKI YEARS
BOOK FOUR

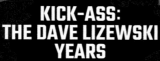

KICK-ASS: THE DAVE LIZEWSKI YEARS

Vol 1-4

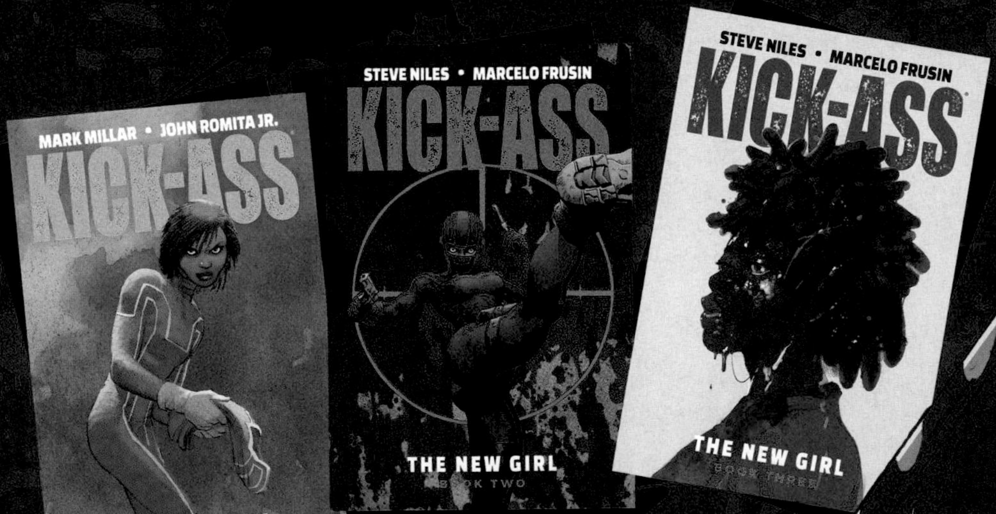
MARK MILLAR • JOHN ROMITA JR.
KICK-ASS
THE NEW GIRL
BOOK ONE
STEVE NILES • MARCELO FRUSIN
KICK-ASS
THE NEW GIRL
BOOK TWO
STEVE NILES • MARCELO FRUSIN
KICK-ASS
THE NEW GIRL
BOOK THREE

KICK-ASS: THE NEW GIRL

Vol 1-3

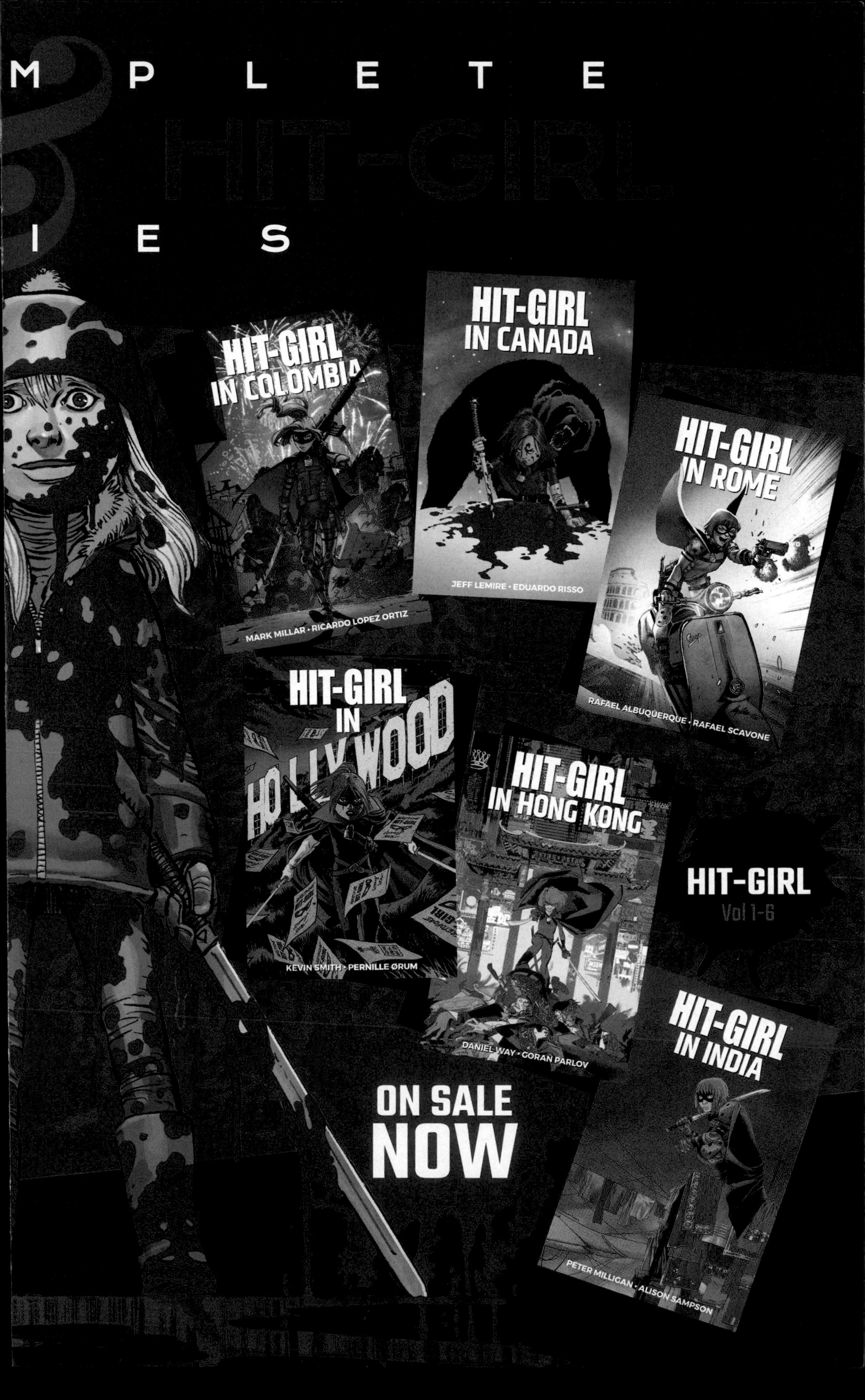
MPLETE
HIT-GIRL
IES
HIT-GIRL IN COLOMBIA
MARK MILLAR • RICARDO LOPEZ ORTIZ
HIT-GIRL IN CANADA
JEFF LEMIRE • EDUARDO RISSO
HIT-GIRL IN ROME
RAFAEL ALBUQUERQUE • RAFAEL SCAVONE
HIT-GIRL IN HOLLYWOOD
KEVIN SMITH • PERNILLE ØRUM
HIT-GIRL IN HONG KONG
DANIEL WAY • GORAN PARLOV
HIT-GIRL
Vol 1-6
HIT-GIRL IN INDIA
PETER MILLIGAN • ALISON SAMPSON
ON SALE NOW

NET

FROM THE MIND OF

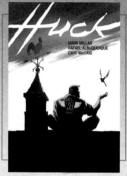

Huck
MARK MILLAR
RAFAEL ALBUQUERQUE
DAVE McCAIG
ART BY RAFAEL ALBUQUERQUE

THE MAGIC ORDER
MARK MILLAR
OLIVIER COIPEL
ART BY OLIVIER COIPEL

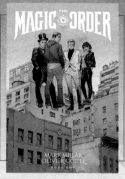

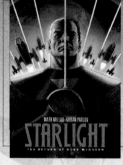

MARK MILLAR · GORAN PARLOV
STARLIGHT
ART BY GORAN PARLOV

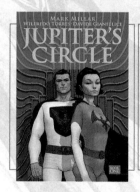

MARK MILLAR
WILFREDO TORRES · DAVIDE GIANFELICE
JUPITER'S CIRCLE
BOOK ONE
ART BY WILFREDO TORRES

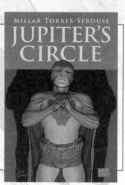

MILLAR · TORRES · SPROUSE
JUPITER'S CIRCLE
BOOK TWO
ART BY WILFREDO TORRES & CHRIS SPROUSE

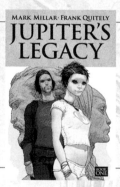

MARK MILLAR · FRANK QUITELY
JUPITER'S LEGACY
BOOK ONE
ART BY FRANK QUITELY

MARK MILLAR · FRANK QUITELY
JUPITER'S LEGACY
BOOK TWO
ART BY FRANK QUITELY

REBORN
BOOK ONE
MARK MILLAR GREG CAPULLO
ART BY GREG CAPULLO

Prodigy.
Mark Millar
Rafael Albuquerque
THE EVIL EARTH
ART BY RAFAEL ALBUQUERQUE

MARK MILLAR & LEINIL YU
SUPERIOR
FROM THE
WRITER OF
ART BY LEINIL YU

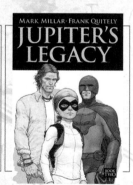

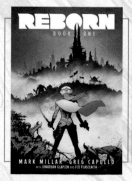

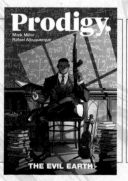

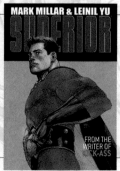

FLIX

MARK MILLAR

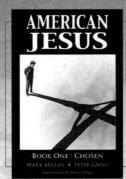

AMERICAN JESUS
BOOK ONE : CHOSEN
MARK MILLAR ✦ PETER GROSS

ART BY PETER GROSS

SPACE BANDITS

ART BY MATTEO SCALERA

MARK MILLAR · SIMONE BIANCHI
SHARKEY

ART BY SIMONE BIANCHI

EMPRESS
BOOK ONE
MARK MILLAR
STUART IMMONEN

ART BY STUART IMMONEN

MARK MILLAR LEINIL YU
SUPER CROOKS
THE HEIST

ART BY LEINIL YU

MILLAR & McNIVEN'S
NEMESIS

ART BY STEVE MCNIVEN

WANTED
MARK MILLAR · JG JONES · PAUL MOUNTS

ART BY JG JONES & PAUL MOUNTS

MILLAR MURPHY
CHRONONAUTS

ART BY SEAN MURPHY

MILLAR · CANETE
CHRONONAUTS
FUTURESHOCK

ART BY ERIC CANETE

MARK MILLAR DUNCAN FEGREDO
MPH

ART BY DUNCAN FEGREDO

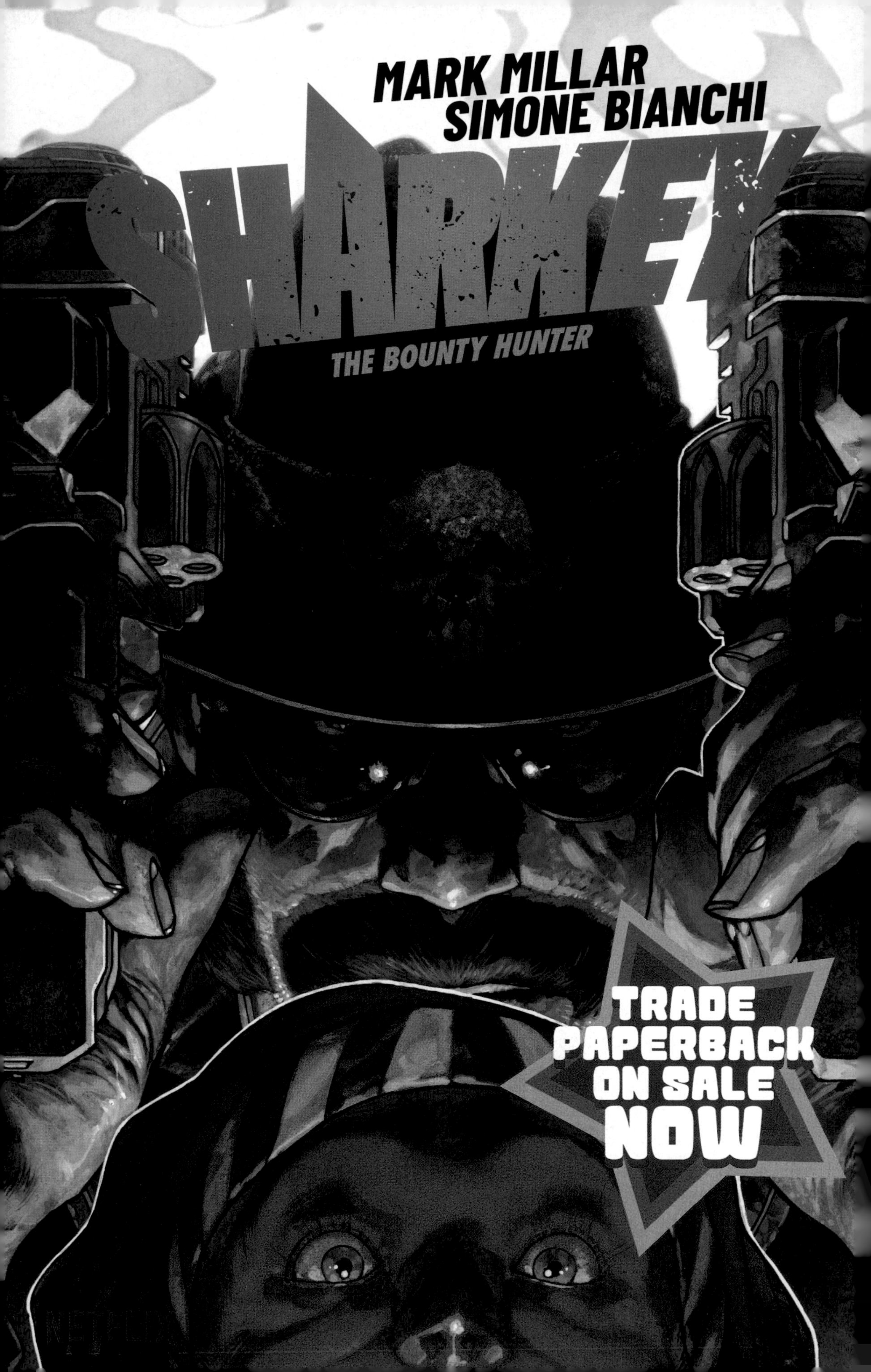
MARK MILLAR
SIMONE BIANCHI
SHARKEY
THE BOUNTY HUNTER
TRADE PAPERBACK ON SALE NOW

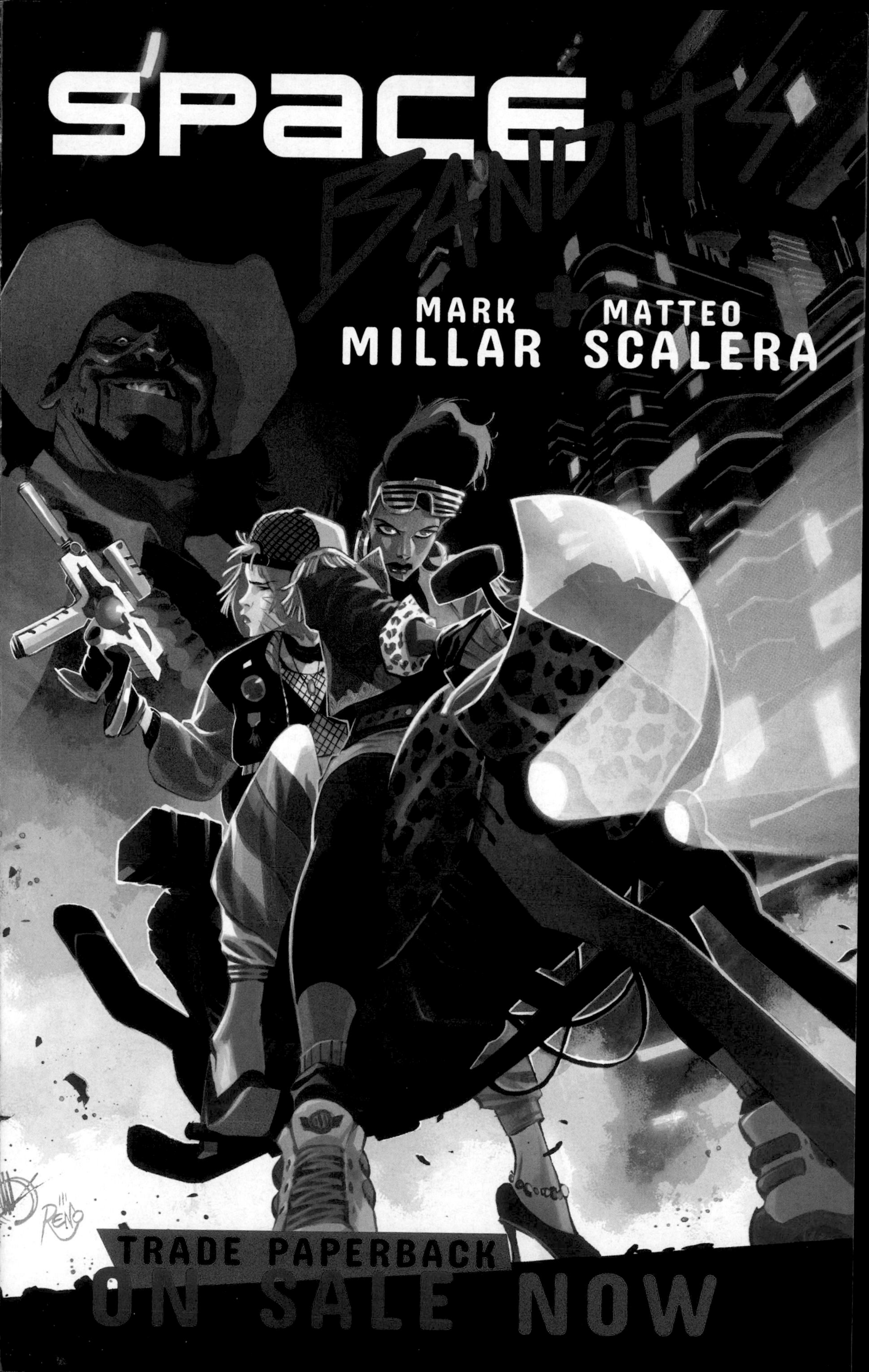
SPACE BANDITS
MARK MILLAR + MATTEO SCALERA
TRADE PAPERBACK
ON SALE NOW

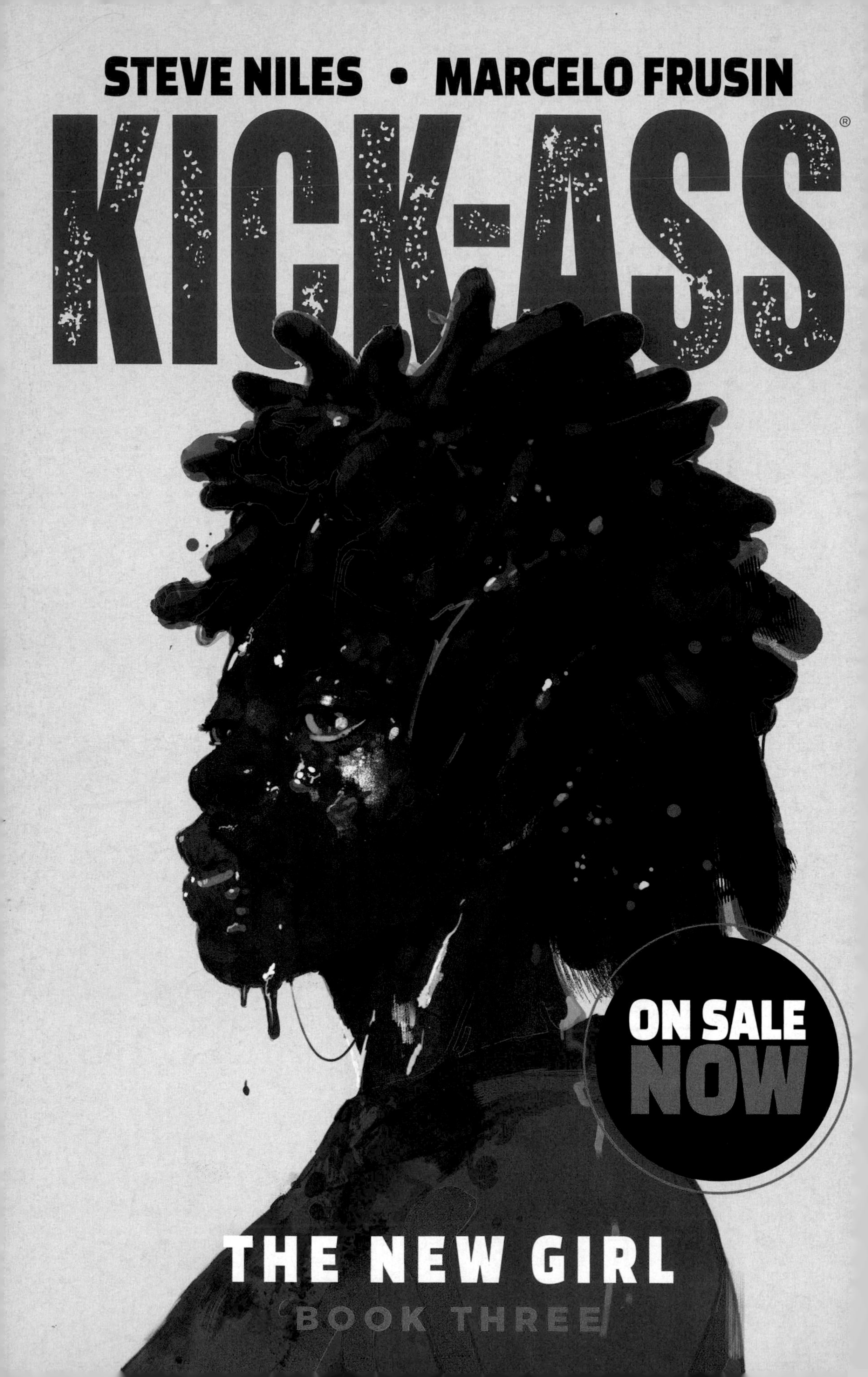
STEVE NILES • MARCELO FRUSIN
KICK-ASS®
ON SALE NOW
THE NEW GIRL
BOOK THREE